WHILE
THE
TOWN
SLEPT

LOOK FOR THESE EXCITING WESTERN SERIES FROM BESTSELLING AUTHORS WILLIAM W. JOHNSTONE AND J.A. JOHNSTONE

The Mountain Man
Luke Jensen: Bounty Hunter
Brannigan's Land
The Jensen Brand
Smoke Jensen: The Early Years
Preacher and MacCallister
Fort Misery
The Fighting O'Neils
Perley Gates
MacCoole and Boone
Guns of the Vigilantes
Shotgun Johnny
The Chuckwagon Trail
The Jackals
The Slash and Pecos Westerns
The Texas Moonshiners
Stoneface Finnegan Westerns
Ben Savage: Saloon Ranger
The Buck Trammel Westerns
The Death and Texas Westerns
The Hunter Buchanon Westerns
Will Tanner, Deputy US Marshal
Old Cowboys Never Die
Go West, Young Man

Published by Kensington Publishing Corp.

WHILE THE TOWN SLEPT

WILLIAM W. JOHNSTONE

AND J.A. JOHNSTONE

PINNACLE BOOKS
Kensington Publishing Corp.
www.kensingtonbooks.com

PINNACLE BOOKS are published by

Kensington Publishing Corp.
900 Third Avenue
New York, NY 10022

All Kensington titles, imprints, and distributed lines are available at special quantity discounts for bulk purchases for sales promotion, premiums, fundraising, and educational or institutional use.

Special book excerpts or customized printings can also be created to fit specific needs. For details, write or phone the office of the Kensington Sales Manager: Kensington Publishing Corp., 900 Third Avenue, New York, NY 10022. Attn. Sales Department. Phone: 1-800-221-2647.

PINNACLE BOOKS, the Pinnacle logo, and the WWJ steer head logo Reg. U.S. Pat. & TM Off.

First Kensington Books hardcover printing: July 2024
First Pinnacle Books mass market printing: October 2024

ISBN-13: 978-0-7860-5083-3
ISBN-13: 978-0-7860-5084-0 (eBook)

10 9 8 7 6 5 4 3 2 1

Printed in the United States of America

Chapter 1

Tim Colter was dressed for spring.

A woolen muffler flattened the brim of his hat against both ears, looped underneath his chin, and then wrapped around his throat and neck. The plaid bandanna covered his mouth and nose, and while it didn't keep his teeth from chattering, the heavy cotton likely fought off frostbite for a while. He couldn't feel his fingers, but the thick gloves still moved when he tightened his grip on the black gelding's reins one way or the other, while the bearskin coat blocked most of the wind he rode into, though he knew he should have patched that bullet hole a few inches below the left collarbone years ago. The Wyoming wind found a way to whistle through the tiny opening, but at least his vest and flannel shirt blocked some of that frigid air.

Woolen pants and sheepskin woolly chaps did a good job of keeping his legs from breaking into icy shards. He wasn't sure if those duds helped keep the horse warmer, or if the black's pumping blood stopped his legs from freezing. His socks and boots? He wasn't sure they helped anything. He kept wiggling his toes to make sure they hadn't frozen solid, but whether or not his toes actually moved, Colter couldn't tell for certain.

Most likely, he'd find out when he dismounted.

He lifted his gaze toward the sky as he rode north, watching gray clouds darken, feeling the wind's icy breath find openings to his body—also protected by his long-handle winter unmentionables—caused by his movement.

I could take this miserable cold, he lied to himself, *if only it would snow.*

To his right, his tracker, pardner, best friend, second father—whatever you wanted to call him—hacked up something nasty but didn't spit it out. That would have frozen his bandanna to his lips. Jed Reno swallowed and said, "January. Forty-nine. You shoulda been here for that. Now, that winter was colder than a witch's . . ."

Tim Colter's muffled curse shut the old mountain man up. For a bit. For a moment, Colter regretted even speaking. His lips cracked. But at least they felt warm for a few seconds.

This was not January. This, by his calendar, was April. It was true that Tim Colter had lived in the American West for pushing thirty years now, in Wyoming Territory for five years, back when it was still parts of Utah, Idaho, and Dakota territories. Before that, he had called Oregon home. He had buried a wife, a daughter, and two sons near the Pacific Ocean. And it was true that, from what he remembered of Danville, Pennsylvania, it could get cold back there, too, even in spring. He and his folks had set out west in '44. A boy grew up quickly in the wilds of the frontier. Especially after a wagon-train massacre left him an orphan. And becoming a lawman kept a man on the move. And moving, he remembered his father telling him, kept a man warm.

Well, he was moving now. Bundled up so that he resembled a grizzly bear more than a human being.

And he was still freezing.

The wind died down just long enough for Colter to hear Reno's chuckling. Jed Reno had been a mentor to Colter, who had survived that wagon-train massacre when he was nothing more than a button kid. Reno had shown Colter how to survive in the wilderness of the 1840s. When Colter returned from Oregon years later, widowed and a lawman, Reno had saved his bacon again. Tim Colter owed that mountain man, who had to be in his seventies by now—he had seemed older than dirt back when Colter was just a kid—more than he could ever repay.

But sometimes . . . *oftentimes* . . . Jed Reno could be just as irritating as the mule the old-timer rode.

Colter made another mistake. As Reno's laughter grew louder, Colter, feeling prickled and cold, drew in a deep breath, and that wasn't the thing to do on a day like this. His lungs felt frozen. His chest ached. He wanted to scream.

Reno laughed again.

"Reckon that's what happens when a feller gets a job

where he spends most of his days in a comfy office, looking at papers, readin', writin' letters, telegraphin' Washington City and Denver and checkin' with the warden over at that prison in Laramie City. Forgettin' ever'thin' this ol' hoss learnt you."

Riding into the wind sure didn't help, so Colter brought his gloved hand to the coverings over his nose, which he pinched and sniffed. He leaned back, stretching the muscles and hearing his back crack.

"See what I'm tellin' you." Reno went right on talking, as though he were gossiping with the old ladies at church—as if Jed Reno had ever set foot in a church—or waiting for his turn to get his hair and beard shorn by one of those tonsorial artists at Barrett's place—as if Jed Reno had ever stepped inside a barbershop. "You ain't been in a saddle in a dog's age. Stretchin' your legs underneath some desk in that fancy guvment buildin'. No, sir. You's done forgots ever'thin' I taught you back when you wasn't so fat."

Fat? Jed Reno was showing the paunch of an old man who couldn't eat panther meat in the mountains anymore and work like a dog trapping, scouting, fishing, and hunting. Hunting wild game. Hunting wilder men.

Colter reined in the black.

Reno stopped a few yards ahead, turned in the saddle, and grinned.

"I hurt yer feelin's?"

Colter's head shook slowly.

The old man chuckled. "You sore from ridin' so much? We ain't hardly covered five miles yet."

The eyes did not focus on the bear of a man, but stared off toward the rocks.

"Them train robbers be puttin' some miles ahead of us."

Still, Colter did not look Reno in the mountain man's right eye. A black patch covered where the six-foot-four behemoth's left eye used to be.

"You want to ride," he said, "go ahead. But you'll be breaking one of the rules you taught me almost thirty years ago."

The old man's expression changed, but he kept his good eye on Colter. Reno asked no question, just waited for Colter to say what was on his mind.

"Never ride into another man's gunsights."

Slowly, Reno's head turned back and stared.

The wind blew harder, but the ground was so frozen and the trees so scarce, no dust blew. In fact, it was a clear day. Would have been pretty to some. Probably was, in fact. Might have been right pleasant if it weren't so brutally cold.

Colter smiled as Reno slowly moved his Hawken rifle across his thighs.

"See it?" Colter asked.

Reno's "Yeah" came out as a grunt.

Sunlight had peeked just enough between clouds to reflect off the metal in the rocks off to their left.

"What do you think?" Colter asked.

"Tough shot, uphill, with the wind blowin' like it is. And we might be out of range, dependin' on what kind of rifle that be."

"If it is a rifle," Colter said.

The mountain man's head nodded again, just once. His rifle did not move. Reno's mule snorted, stamped its forefeet, just to keep warmer.

Colter reached behind him, pulled open the flap of his saddlebag, and found the binoculars. Clouds swallowed the sun again, which was behind him, so there was not much of a chance that the lenses would give them away. Besides, if that was a rifle and it was trained on Colter and Reno, the ambusher already knew they were up here. He brought the spyglasses to his face, but only after thumbing off the front lenses with his gloved thumbs.

It took a while to find the spot, and he adjusted the focus, holding his breath to keep a fog from covering the lenses. Finally, he lowered the glasses and relaxed.

"Well?" Reno tried not to sound impatient.

"Looks like a long gun," Colter said. "But there's no one holding it."

"Man don't leave no rifle lyin' round in this country," Reno said.

A truer statement Colter hadn't heard in a long spell.

"Unless he's dead," Colter agreed, and kicked his horse back into a walk.

"Or . . ." Reno let his mule follow Colter's black. "It's an ambush."

Colter nodded. "Thought about that."

"Yeah."

"Figured you being bigger than me, you'd get shot first. I could dive off my horse."

"You'd be afoot."

"But I'd know where those ambushers were. And I'd still be alive."

Reno chuckled.

Colter and Reno had been doing this for a long time now. Colter kept his eyes to the left and straight ahead, while Reno focused on straight ahead and to the right. Years of practice. Years of staying alive. They did not look behind them. They didn't have to. They had scanned those places when they rode past, and, sure, there was a chance they might have missed something, someone. There was a possibility they had run into owlhoots who were better at this kind of game than they were.

But they hadn't yet.

"I don't think those dunderheads that held up the UP even slowed down," Reno said after they had covered roughly one hundred yards.

Colter kept his focus on the rocks and the general area of the lone rifle. But he wasn't about to second-guess his mentor.

Four men, wearing linen dusters and wheat sacks over their faces, had held up the 109 train at Simpson's Well, about ten miles west of Cheyenne. It was an express run, no passengers, not much freight, and they had cold-cocked the man at the station, and one of them had brought out a red lantern and used that to stop the train. Otherwise, the 109 would not have stopped until reaching Laramie City.

So those owlhoots had some knowledge about trains. And they had made off with about $800 in bonds, cash, and coin. Not a bad haul. Almost like something the Reno Gang might have pulled off back east in Indiana. But this wasn't the work of the Reno boys. Those outlaws had met their end at the end of handy ropes back in '68.

And these Wyoming ruffians hadn't been as smart as the Renos. They had gotten a good bit of money, but the express agent had fooled them, and they had missed the $65,000 in freshly minted coin.

Now Colter reined up. The high rocks blocked most of the wind, but they also blocked out most of the sunlight that crept through the clouds, so it felt colder.

He had not been mistaken. That was a rifle on the rocks. A Winchester Yellow Boy, which was why it had been so easy to spot; the bright gunmetal receiver gave the .44 repeating rifle its nickname, and the bronze-brass alloy sure came in handy at reflecting sunlight.

Reno's mule snorted, and Colter heard him twist in the saddle.

Seeing the gloved hand and arm lying in a crevasse between one slab of rock and the flatter rock on which the Yellow Boy rested, the old trapper sighed, then cursed.

"I don't think them owlhoots done this dirty deed," Reno said, nodding at the horse tracks they had been following since Simpson's Well.

Colter dismounted and walked toward his mentor, handing him the reins.

"Them hombres never even slowed down from a lope."

That guess would get no argument from Tim Colter, who moved into the rocks. He saw the boot prints, and followed them easy enough, twisting toward the west and the higher slabs, then angling southeast, where he saw the man, face planted in a dip in the rocks, right arm reaching toward the rifle atop the rocks, left arm hanging down, knees in the dirt.

He wore a heavy mackinaw, worn boots, heavy woolen pants, and well-worn cavalry boots. No sign of a horse. And he wasn't wearing spurs. But a man did not walk through this country.

The bullet hole was easy enough to spot. He had been shot in the back, down low, and blood had frozen against the checkered woolen coat.

Colter moved his right hand away from his powerful pistol. This hombre wasn't a threat, so the lawman looked around. No, the train robbers had not shot him. They couldn't have even seen him from where he was. And they had been riding so hard they had not seen any sunlight reflecting off the Yellow Boy—if the sun was shining.

He heard Reno dismounting. Colter moved toward the man, put his hand on the left shoulder, and turned him around.

The man's groan took about two years off Colter's life.

"Jed!" he yelled. "He isn't dead."

How a man could survive a bullet in his back and in this freezing wilderness would be one unsolved mystery, though the rocks would have blocked most of the wind, and Reno had heard of hot springs in this part of the country sometimes heating the ground.

Colter caught him, eased him onto the ground, letting the man's big black hat serve as a pillow. He pulled back the man's coat, which was unbuttoned, and saw no sign of an exit wound. The bullet was still in him.

Using his teeth to pull off the right-hand glove, Colter then pressed his finger and thumb against the man's throat. The face was pale. The pulse was slow. Too slow.

Reno's big feet pounded and the old man wheezed as he came behind Colter. He had brought his bedroll with him and used that to cover the man.

"Ever seen him?" Reno asked, and reached for the Winchester .44.

"No." Colter looked at the man's duds, but they held no significance. He studied the face again. Mustache. Beard stubble. The outfit like what he had seen countless times.

"Me neither." Reno coughed slightly, turned, and spat. "Don't see no sign of a horse. Looks like he just dropped here."

No, he didn't just drop here. Colter figured he was hiding here. Reno was right about the lack of boot prints, and that frontiersman might have been long in tooth and gray in hair, however, his right eye was still sharp enough to have found even a moccasin track or signs where the tracks had been brushed away. But Colter had an idea.

"He was hiding."

"To ambush someone maybe?"

"I don't think so," Colter said. "But my guess is . . ." He pointed toward the rocks on the northwest side. "The man who gunned him down came up on the rocks. This guy was keeping an eye that-away." He pointed toward the trail, not the way to Cheyenne, but off to the north. "They sent someone ahead, on the other side of this ridge."

"He had to be a quiet hombre."

"Yeah."

Reno coughed. "We got to get him to a doctor."

"No."

Both men turned toward the stranger.

His eyes had opened. They couldn't quite focus. A bit of blood spilled out of the corner of his mouth. He coughed, groaned, and breathed in deeply, but that was a ragged, ghastly sound, and Colter figured the bullet was in one of his lungs.

"I'm . . . done . . . for. . . ."

Suddenly, the man's left hand reached out and grabbed Colter's coat. He jerked, but he didn't have enough strength, and Tim Colter was too strong. The hand slipped away and fell onto the dirt.

"You . . ." the man whispered. "Stop them. . . ." He coughed again, and this time spat out bloody phlegm.

"My name is Tim Colter." He unbuttoned the coat, pulled it back to reveal the tin badge pinned to his vest. "I'm a deputy US marshal out of Cheyenne."

The man's face brightened for just a second.

"*Gooooood.*"

"Who shot you? Who are you? What happened?"

"Secret," the man said. "Service."

Colter thought he must have heard wrong. He leaned closer, and now he felt dread, cold, and fear. The light was leaving the man's eyes.

"President Grant . . . assassination . . . Dugan . . . trust nobody."

The last breath came short and permanent. The eyes stilled.

Colter's heart pounded. He kept hoping, praying, that the man would revive. He needed a Lazarus. He wanted a miracle. But the man just stared into another world.

And Tim Colter felt much colder than he had since he had ridden out of Cheyenne into this freezing country.

Chapter 2

"Reckon we can cover'm with some sand and rocks. Keep the wolves off'm." Jed Reno nodded in approval of his suggestion. "That'll keep'm, maybe, till we catch up with 'em owlhoots."

Tim Colter was not aware that he was shaking his head and didn't even hear him say, "No."

"Well, I ain't partial to leavin' any man to the buzzards. Even the most rottenest scoundrel deserves that, I reckon."

Colter faced Reno. "We'll bury him." He squatted by the body and began going through the pockets, searching for some identification: a letter, maybe; a watch inscribed with his name; initials on his belt; a money purse . . . anything.

"Ground's froze perty good," Reno said. "Even a shallow grave will take considerable time and effort. And those train robbers is putting some distance betwixt us as we palaver over this."

"Let them go," Colter said and pulled out a few dollars from the corpse's shirt pocket.

"Let 'em go?" Reno thundered. "Ain't like you to let train robbers get off scot-free."

"Shut up, Jed," Colter said, "and scout around. See if you can find any sign, anything this man might have left, hidden, dropped. Anything."

He didn't recollect that rebuke until much later, and when he heard the mountain man's soft footsteps as he gathered the reins to their mounts, tethering them to a good-size stone in a grassy spot, he said, "I need your best work here. Look hard. I don't know exactly what you ought to look for. But if you see something that doesn't fit in this country, get it and bring it to me. On the double."

The hat held nothing. No name written on the sweatband inside the crown and nothing tucked behind the band, but it was a cheap hat, well-used, ancient, the kind a man could buy in a mercantile for ten bits. Colter unfolded his knife and cut away the linings in the coat he removed from the dead man to unearth the same results. Nothing. The shirt was pocketless, and the man wore no locket, nothing like that, and the heavy flannel undershirt revealed only blood from the fatal bullet.

He didn't think the assassin, or assassins, had searched the body as he had. If they thought he had something of value, something they did not want anyone else to happen by, they wouldn't have left the man alive. He was surprised they hadn't made sure he was dead.

Sloppy work for killers. And lucky for Tim Colter.

The boots were harder to pull off, and the worn

socks came off with them, and still Colter found nothing. He sighed. He even felt flushed with heat, though the temperature had to be dropping as the sun continued its ongoing descent behind the high hills and mountains.

His horse whinnied, and Colter found the LeMat he still favored, even though it was pushing eighteen years old and more modern sidearms were available these days. Even Jed Reno packed a .45-caliber Colt, though he preferred his Hawken rifle. But a revolver, good as it was, held only six rounds in the cylinder, and most practical gunmen kept only five beans in the wheel, as the saying went. The LeMat's cylinder held nine .42-caliber cartridges, and just in case Colter needed something extra, there was a smoothbore secondary barrel of .63 caliber that could send a blast of grapeshot into a bad man's face or belly.

He didn't slip that monster from the leather because Jed Reno eased his dark mule into view. He dismounted with a grunt, and Colter went back to work on the dead man's boots.

Which stopped Reno cold when he made it through the path.

Colter glanced up, saw the look on his old mentor's face, and realized just how ridiculous he looked, holding the boots of a dead man that had been stripped to his undergarments.

"Taken an Injun's scalp in my day," Reno said. "Taken pelts, maybe a chaw of baccy, a pistol. Don't recall ever doin' nothin' like that, especially considerin' how worn-out his duds are. And them boots ain't gonna fit you or me."

Colter focused on the boots, running his left hand inside the first one he had removed.

"You find anything?" he asked.

"Tracks. Four horses . . ."

He worked on the heel, hoping to find some secret compartment, and when that failed he moved to the other boot, but he listened as Reno gave his report.

"My guess is they rid ahead. Waited for him. The way I read the sign, what sign there was, 'pears to me that one of 'em scoundrels climbed up the rocks. Found hisself a perch. And waited. Two riders rode back thataway. The fourth one waited with the hosses, smoked hisself some baccy."

There was nothing in this boot either. Colter tried the heel.

Reno pointed north. "There's a cut in the hills about two–three miles up yonder way. I would suspect that the two riders went back there, and I would guess that they had left another rider, maybe more, to make sure that dead man didn't take a detour through that place, though it ain't no easy squeeze for even a sliver of a fellow like this one to get through. But there's a good elk trail that leads to the top, and on the other side, if you been in this country as long as I have, you know how you can get down this side of it."

Colter gave up on the boot and stifled a curse.

Reno stared and Colter met his gaze.

"So they waited for him to pass. Then rode after him."

The big man's head bobbed.

"This feller, he hears the hoofbeats behind him. Gots to hide, he figgers. So finds hisself a hidin' place.

Waited. But didn't know there was a man with a big rifle aimin' to kill him from behind."

Colter considered that. "Lot of trouble. Why not just ride him down if he was afoot?"

"I don't reckon he was always afoot. Not out here."

Quickly grabbing the closest boot, Colter saw the marks of spurs.

Reno read his mind. "Shucked the spurs when he lost his horse. Spurs make noise. He wanted to be quiet. And spurs ain't good fer runnin' afoot."

Colter dropped the boot. "So when he heard the horses coming after him, he ran into these rocks. Hid. Hoping for the best."

"And these be the best rocks for hidin' in this here patch of paradise," Reno said. "A man with a bit of savvy can hide hisself good and hide hisself for a long time." He nodded at the dead man. "He was savvy. Give him that. Just got hisself outsavvied."

Turning back toward the dead man, Colter shook his head and sighed. "He outsavvied me."

"Mebbe so. But now do you mind tellin' me just what in the Sam Hill is goin' on? What that man told you, 'bout Grant and Dugan and asinine—"

"Assassination," Colter corrected.

"Right. Grant I know. Fella paid me a dollar and a bottle of real rye whiskey to vote for him in that election last year. Voted for him twice."

"So you voted for him in '68, too?" Colter would not have guessed Jed Reno had voted in any election, local, territorial, or national.

"Nah. Last year. Man said, no, this country wouldn't last on no Greeley-Brown ticket. He blamed Greeley for foulin' up the Western country, gettin' all these Eastern folks, and foreigners now, claimin' homesteads and the like. I thought he had somethin' there, and then he showed me that dollar coin and that bottle of rye whiskey. So after me and some other gents he had found eager to vote, we went to vote in Cheyenne. Then he paid our way to Laramie City and we voted there, too. Free train rides there—though he tricked us because we had to sneak aboard an eastbound to get back home. But I reckon it paid off for him. Grant got voted into office. Figured my vote might have been the one that won it all for him."

"Your two votes." Colter had wasted enough time. He looked at the body, sighed, and whispered, "Who are you?"

Reno walked closer. "You ain't tol' me what this deal is, sonny. Man like me might come to think that you don't trust me a whole lot."

"That's not it, Jed," Colter said, shaking his head. "It's just . . ."

Colter let out a sigh. Jed Reno just stared, but then his surviving eye shifted, that bearded countenance changing suddenly. Looking at the dead man, the old trapper raised his hand and pointed.

"What," he said, "in tarnation is on the bottom of that feller's foot?"

Chapter 3

Kip Jansen didn't like Wyoming Territory, which was absolutely nothing like the rolling green hills, fine fields for growing food crops—not tobacco, not cotton—but crops that didn't need slaves or share-croppers but were small enough to feed a family, and the lush, fine forests of Alabama. He didn't want to be here. He hated the cold weather. Sure, it got cold sometimes in Morgan County, but he never had felt anything like this. That brutal wind just never wanted to let up, and he had always liked the pretty white snow on those few winter days when it would snow back home. But this snow wasn't pretty and, like the wind, it kept coming and coming and coming. Relentless.

He missed the forests. Longed to be back on that small farm. Yearned for the bustle of carriages and farm wagons and friendly girls and boys of Decatur. Or the scream of a railroad locomotive's whistle. He pined for the Tennessee River and the steamboats that traveled up and down it. He hadn't seen anything resembling a river in Wyoming Territory, or practically any-where in the West since the muddy Missouri. What a Westerner called a river in Wyoming would have been laughed at back home in Alabama and called, maybe, a creek.

Being here was his stepfather's doing. Kip hated that trashy-mouthed man more than he despised Wyoming. Lige Kerns was lazy, mean, and ignorant. What his mother saw in him boggled Kip's fourteen-year-old brain.

But mostly, Kip Jansen despised his stepfather because Lige Kerns fought for the Confederacy during the late War Between the States. Well, most of the menfolk in Alabama had worn the gray. But not so much in Morgan County, and a few other spots in northern Alabama. Plenty of men in Morgan County despised the idea of secession, of fighting a war. There were slaves in Decatur, and in Morgan County—more than a few—but war, Kip remembered his father saying, was a drastic, desperate, and despicable measure when negotiations and compromise could be used peacefully.

When the war heated up, Kip's father put on a Yankee uniform. And because of the Tennessee River, because of those railroads, and because of Union sympathizers, the city of Decatur and its roughly 800 citizens, the Confederate and the Union armies took and lost, lost and took, Decatur what seemed like more times than Kip could count.

For all Kip knew, Lige Kerns had killed Kip's pa in one of those engagements. That's what he made himself believe, no matter how many times his mother kept telling him that the letter she got from some captain said that Kip Senior died of dysentery—whatever that was—in a Union camp across the border in Tennessee. On the other hand, Kip's mother had also said that Lige was good for the family. That's why she had married him. He was a hard worker, and Kip needed a father.

Hard worker—Lige Kerns? All he worked hard at doing was getting his mother's eight dollars she got each month from the US Government as the widow of a Union soldier. But then, Lige started attending meetings that he wouldn't let anyone know about unless the whiskey he drank loosened his tongue, and it didn't take a lot of whiskey to get that scoundrel talking, and Lige Kerns worked real hard at drinking whiskey. That was one thing he was good at.

Before Kip knew what was happening, though, that lazy sack of rotten potatoes had sold the farm and announced that they were bound for Wyoming Territory to start a new life, and a new country. They had made that long, roundabout journey—up the Tennessee to Paducah, Kentucky, and then on another barely riverworthy packet on the Ohio to Cairo, Illinois. Down that river, where Kip wound up working on the decks to help pay passage, to St. Louis. Stagecoaches west, two stolen mules north, and footing it, usually at night, and by the mercy of some friendly farmers with room in their wagons, they made it to Omaha, Nebraska.

That was where Lige Kerns asked his mother to do unspeakable things, and Kip learned that to survive he had to steal—apples, flour, tea bags—and beg—stale bread, rancid bacon, tin cans he could sneak into the pockets of his britches—and sometimes find honest work swamping a saloon or a grocery store. Lige Kerns spent most of his time loafing around Camp Sherman, a military post near the bustling railroad and Missouri River town that some folks in town called Sherman Barracks. The joke Kip often heard was that General William T. Sherman, Yankee hero who helped squash the rebellion, complained that such a small and worthless post was named after him. Finally, they had enough money to board a Union Pacific bound for Laramie City, Wyoming Territory. Finally, Lige Kerns had a massive crate that looked big enough and certainly was heavy enough to hold a cannon.

"It ain't no cannon, boys," he told the men who had to load the canvas-wrapped freight box, "but the latest in agricultural enterprise."

"You a farmer?" one black man asked.

"The best you ever saw," Lige said, and Kip had to stifle the sarcastic laugh.

"Won't do you no good where you're goin'," the black man said. "That's cattle country, Wyoming is."

"Not when I get there."

And here they were—far from Cheyenne and Laramie City, far from humanity—and all but freezing to death.

In the back of a decrepit wagon, where the canvas tarp was ripped with holes, letting the freezing wind through, Kip knelt. Only one mule remained alive to pull the small wagon. And his mother, skin clammy and pale, eyes bloodshot, sweating like the temperature outside was in triple digits instead of below zero, slept fitfully in the back of the wagon. They were almost out of food. About all they had left now was the crate that took up most of the wagon bed. The crate Lige Kerns babied like a new foal or kitten birthed by a good mouser.

The wagon stopped, and Lige Kerns cursed the poor mule and turned to peek through the opening.

"We're here, Sadie." He snorted, then pulled down his bandanna, put a gloved finger over one nostril, and blew his nose. "Dugan's Den."

Kip's mother had no reaction. She stared at her son, but Kip didn't think she saw him.

"I think," Lige added.

You think? Kip felt his face burning with flushed anger, and he slid away from his mother to the back of the wagon, wrapped a worn, dirty woolen muffler over his face and ears, leaving just enough room for his nose to breathe in air yet not freeze and fall off, and slipped outside.

The snow, to his surprise, didn't come past the tops of his brogans, and it no longer fell from the sky. Squinting, hoping his eyelids didn't freeze shut, he tried to make out the surroundings. The trail, which couldn't have been made for wagons, was narrow, passing through a chasm in the towering boulders and hilltops and saw more antelope pass than rickety wagons. But then Kip spotted something wonderful.

A ray of sunlight passed through an opening in the gray clouds. It had stopped snowing. It had to be his imagination, but he thought he could feel that sliver of a ray from the sun thawing his eyebrows, and his eyelids, and he managed to flex his fingers without any pain.

But he also understood that that small ray of warmth,

of hope, was in the western horizon, just inches above the top of that imposing range of brownish-reddish rocks. The sun would sink behind those hills and darkness, and a deepening, deadly cold, would come quick.

"We need to build a fire," Kip said.

No one answered. Lige Kerns probably couldn't hear him over the wind. Kip moved back to the wagon, trying to loosen the stiffened—or maybe frozen—muscles in his legs. Riding in the back of the wagon for all of the day, staying under the canvas whenever Lige, who wasn't completely stupid, stopped to rest the mule.

After looking back inside the wagon, seeing his mother's head turning left and right, Kip waited for orders from that louse. None came. His stepfather had found his jug, figuring the last of the corn liquor might warm him up, Kip figured, and that was fine with the teen. He moved to the mule and started to unharness the beast.

"Leave 'm be." Lige lowered the jug and glared.

"He has pulled us all day, into the wind," Kip started, but the razor-thin fool reached for the revolver he had stuck in his waistband.

"Don't sass me. They'll be comin' this way to get us to Dugan's Den."

"I thought you said *this* was Dugan's Den," Kip fired back, then thought to add: "And what in blazes is Dugan's Den supposed to be?"

It wasn't a town. Nothing resembled a den of anything as far as Kip could see.

"Stop yer sassin' or I'll plant you under." He didn't

reach again for the revolver but raised the jug to his lips.

Kip thought about unharnessing the worn-out mule anyway, but decided against it. His mother was too weak to protect him. Instead, he went back to the wagon, found a bucket, and filled it with water from the barrel next to the big crate of whatever it was they were hauling. It had been Kip's idea to move the water barrel inside the wagon. That might keep the liquid from freezing, and he had been right.

But Lordie was that water cold. He dried his hands on the canvas that covered the big crate, so his fingers wouldn't freeze and rot off, looked again at his mother, left the slight comfort one could find inside, and brought the bucket to the mule, which lowered its head and drank.

The sun was slipping now. His stepfather was still drinking, and Kip wondered what there was to fix for supper.

He waited till the mule finished, then returned to the wagon and found a handful of grain. It wasn't enough to keep the beast alive for long, but maybe they didn't have far to go to this place called Dugan's Den. Perhaps there was a log cabin there. Maybe a doctor. And some good folks, the kind Kip had known back in Alabama.

The mule ate the grain, Lige Kerns kept drinking, and Kip climbed back into the wagon. He crawled over to his mother, who was looking at him, smiling.

"Good evenin', Ma," he whispered and put his right hand on her left one. The coldness of it shocked him.

"We're here," he told her. "Near Dugan's Den." He didn't know what that meant, or where it even was. He couldn't be certain it was even true.

His mother just stared. Still smiling.

"Do you want something to eat?" He wasn't sure what he'd be able to find or fix. The bacon was gone by now. There was no noon meal. Breakfast had been water and a handful of salt, though Kip had made some kind of tea that his mother had managed to swallow. It didn't taste half bad either, Kip thought after he drank what his mother couldn't finish.

He hadn't offered any to Lige.

The man hadn't been drinking anything but the liquor in his jug for the past two or three days.

His mother smiled. Stared.

And then Kip felt colder than he ever had in his entire life. And the night before, Lige had said, the temperature dropped to twenty below, something unimaginable back in Morgan County.

"Ma?"

He shook her shoulder and saw no reaction. The smile did not cease and the eyes did not blink.

"Ma!" he screamed.

"Shut up, boy," came his stepfather's voice, followed by a slew of profanity.

"Ma!"

She was dead. He buried his head against her nearest shoulder and bawled, pulling her tight, praying for God to let her live just a few moments longer. The only answer he got was the moaning wind.

Chapter 4

Tim Colter looked down at the dead man's foot. Jed Reno was right. There was something black on the bottom of the man's left foot, partially hidden by the sock that had not completely pulled itself off when Colter removed the boot. It was not a bruise. Colter could tell that much.

After pulling off the filthy sock and tossing it to the ground, Colter raised the left leg and studied the bottom of the foot. Reno ambled over, grunted, and said, "Them ain't words."

"No."

"Looks like he stuck hisself with a pin. Polka dots and small lines. Why would he do somethin' like that?"

"Morse code," Colter said.

"Huh?"

"Something a professor named Samuel Morse, with help of some other gent, came up with to use on the telegraph lines." He sighed. "A telegraphic coding.

They were working on it for a while after the end of the rebellion."

"Explains why I ain't never heard of it. Don't have much use for no perfessers."

Ignoring Reno's remark, Colter glanced at the dead man's still face, and nodded in approval. "He was a smart man. If he had written anything, if his killers were smart, they would . . ." He shook off the thought but figured he was right. Those vermin would have chopped off his foot. But his killers were sloppy, unprofessional, and stupid.

Colter looked up at his partner, sighed, and rose. He walked to his horse, opened a saddlebag, and pulled out a folded sheet of paper, which he unfolded as he returned to Reno and the corpse. "Now I know why the attorney general mailed this to me." He knelt over the corpse, raised the leg, and leaned the foot against a rock. Glancing at the sheet in his hand, he studied the markings on the foot, then found the same dots and dashes on the paper.

"Dot-dash-dash-dot. That's a 'P,'" he said.

"Don't look like no 'P.'"

Colter grinned. "Like you'd know."

"Same thing right next to it," the big man said.

"Yep." He followed the scratches, finding out what each meant on the sheet of paper. .— .—.. — . .—..

"A-L-M-E-R."

Colter frowned. Jed Reno tugged on his beard, trying to make some semblance of the letters he had never learned.

"'P. Palmer,'" Colter whispered.

The big man chuckled. "I recollect a Patsy Palmer."

The chuckle morphed into an outright laugh. "That wild-cat you tangled with last year, year-and-a-half ago."

Tim Colter, though, was already remembering.

He was in the bank, depositing his monthly pay while taking out enough money to pay his landlord and the owner of the livery stable where he kept his two horses, and keep him from starving till the next check arrived.

The teller, a bald man whose name Colter never could remember, was counting out paper money and coins, when the front door slammed open and Skeet Hatzell stumbled inside and yelled, "Marshal! Marshal! You gotta help me, Marshal!"

Turning, Colter watched the saloonkeeper fall to his knees, tearing his woolen britches and look up pitifully.

The teller mumbled a curse. "Lost my count," he whispered and started over.

"Some tomcat is wreckin' my place. Tearin' it to pieces."

"Skeet," Colter said, trying to smile, "I've told you a dozen times that my jurisdiction is federal, not local. You need to fetch Cheyenne Marshal Russell or one of his deputies."

"But that wildcat," Hatzell said as he rose, though he still appeared unsteady. "She done tossed Russell hisself through the window and cut Deputy Cyrus's left arm plenty deep with a bowie knife."

"She?" the teller called out, then cursed. "Dagnabbit. Lost my count again."

"She!" Hatzell nodded. "But not just any she-cat. It's Patsy Palmer, as I live and breathe."

That sank in. Colter found the LeMat and slowly pulled it out of his holster. Without looking back at the teller, without looking at anyone else in the bank, not even Hatzell, Colter said hoarsely, "I'll be back," and headed toward the door.

He stepped onto the street and angled his way to the intersection, then walked south, where a crowd had gathered on the east side. A chair smashed through one of the windows in Hatzell's saloon, and what sounded like a rabid wolf howled. Two men, one holding a bloody left ear, ran through the batwing doors.

"Marshal!" someone shouted. "God save us all."

Now a table went through what remained of the large window.

Doc Small, new to Cheyenne, was tending to the town marshal's carved-up arm, while two deputies, holding shotguns, stood out of pistol range, not knowing what to do. Glass smashed somewhere inside the saloon, followed by another wild howl.

Tim Colter thought about asking the deputies if they wanted to assist him, but, guessing their answer, he kept walking. He entered the saloon with the LeMat level and let his eyes grow accustomed to the dim light.

Patsy Palmer turned around, a massive knife in her right hand and a bottle of whiskey in her left. She laughed at Colter's big handgun, then raised the bottle to her lips and drank.

"You the only man with sand in these parts, I reckon," she said after lowering the bottle and wiping her lips with a buckskin sleeve.

"I reckon," Colter said. "You're under arrest."

"Nope," she said, "I'm Patsy Palmer. What handle do you go by?"

"My name," he said. "Tim Colter."

She let out a wail. "Tim Colter. As I live and breathe, I been hearin' 'bout you for fifteen coons' ages. Some fool even tol' me that I couldn't best you. I told him he was full of flapdoodle. And here I am."

Colter made himself smile. "And here I am."

She charged, yelling like a catamount, slashing the gleaming blade as she dodged her way around broken glass, overturned tables, and busted chairs. Colter let her come. He even lowered the LeMat and beckoned her with his left arm. "Can't you run faster than that?"

That prompted a bevy of curses, and then she was in front of him, slashing with the big bowie.

He parried the lethal Damascus blade with the barrel of the LeMat, twisting out of her way and letting her crash into the table behind him. Turning quickly, he saw her bounce off the floor like one of those monkeys at the circus that came through Cheyenne two years back. She didn't even have to catch her breath as she charged again, this time pointing the blade like a Sioux war lance.

The LeMat roared, belching flame and smoke, and he leaped out of the way as she thundered past and smashed into a chair that had, miraculously, survived the preceding carnage.

He hadn't fired at her but between her legs, and the smoke had distracted her enough that he could ease out of her way.

"Cain't ya shoots no better than that?" she shouted,

somehow maintaining her balance, twisting around and slashing blindly. She came right back at him, and this time he landed the hot barrel of the giant handgun on her wrist. Bone snapped. The big knife dropped and she yelped like a stepped-on kitten, her eyes now raging with fury and her right hand dangling by her greasy buckskin britches.

"Let's go, Patsy," he told her. "The fun's over."

Her face changed again. He thought her hair was blonde beneath all the grime and sweat and dust. He thought her eyes were blue. She would be right pretty, he imagined, if she weren't so wretchedly despicable and dressed in duds that would make Jed Reno look like a genteel lad from Boston, Massachusetts. And if she didn't look to be just an inch or two shorter and ten pounds heavier than Reno.

"I reckon you're right, lawdog," she said and held out both hands, the broken one dangling like a dead squirrel shot for supper.

When he stepped toward her, her right moccasin kicked him between the legs.

He almost avoided the blow and certainly would have been hurt a lot worse had he not moved just a few inches, but it still hurt. And he felt his breakfast coming up his throat and his breath whooshing out. As he staggered back to get out of this maniac's way and save himself from a horrible fate, she used her good hand to smash his lips. Blood spurted. He fell against a table, then over the table and to the floor. He managed to climb to his knees and, through blurred vision, saw her swinging a bottle she had picked up off the floor at his head.

Colter turned and ducked just enough that the bottle thudded across the top of his head, and Patsy Palmer was swinging so hard she lost her grip of the neck, and the rye tore a gash in the top of his head before it went sailing and shattering somewhere in the devastation.

Then he felt her good hand on his throat and he went down to the floor, but then flipped her over his head.

He heard her crash, swear, and laugh. Colter rolled over and could not believe that this wildcat had already recovered. He dived out of the way of the rising moccasin that would have cost him several teeth, hit the floor, and rolled over shards of glass that tore through his new coat and favorite shirt. He got halfway up on his knees, fighting for breath and vision, when a shoulder caught him full in his sternum and he hit the floor again, with more glass cutting him, and slid several feet until his head met the brass railing for cowboy boots against the mahogany bar.

Her good hand latched on his throat.

His right cracked her jaw.

She howled. He cursed. She tried again, but Colter twisted and tossed her off.

He came to his feet in seconds, though it felt like hours. She blinked away sweat and blood, giggled like a schoolgirl who had a secret, and gave him a slight nod.

"You're good," she said.

"You're awful," he told her.

"Yeah." He saw the pewter beer stein she had found on the floor. It was sailing right at him, but he ducked just enough that it only cut his ear.

"Part," she said, between breaths. ". . . of . . . my . . . charm."

And she came at him again.

He tried to cock her hard with the LeMat. Only he didn't hold the big pistol anymore and had no idea where it was. His fingers rapped the side of her head. He thought a couple of them might be broken but later was pleased to hear from the sawbones that they were just dislocated.

The next thing he knew, he was holding her head against the bar. He couldn't even recall how he had gotten to his feet. Grabbing a fistful of hair, he jerked her head up and slammed it against the bar. Something crunched, and he realized from the pain that it was her big foot smashing his toes. Then she must have found a tumbler or a shot glass on the bar because whiskey flew into his eyes and he found himself swaying.

A fist smashed into his jaw. He backpedaled, cursed, swung, and hit something, but he wasn't certain if he had struck her head, her shoulder, or a two-by-four column that helped keep the roof up. Then she charged again, caught him in just above his gun belt, and they went through the window—the window that wasn't there anymore.

They landed on the boardwalk, and with Colter somehow on top. He rose, punched her right between the eyes, then managed to pull himself up, and her with him, and he shoved her into the water trough. He held her head down as long as he dared, lifted her out, heard her suck in a deep breath, then rammed her head underneath the brackish water.

He held her underneath longer now. Finally pulling her up, he somehow managed to speak.

"Enough?"

"Go to—"

She went under again. He wasn't sure how long he kept her down this time, but when he jerked her out, she gasped and choked out, "Enough. Enough."

And he threw her to the ground and leaned against a wooden column that held the awning above the saloon's entrance.

Or had held up the awning.

Because right then the column collapsed and the awning came down atop Tim Colter.

It felt like a nice woolen blanket. Perfect to curl up in and get a long, long, long rest.

But someone was dragging him from underneath the thatch, shingles and needles.

He was ready, though, for the second round.

Only when he opened his eyes, he didn't see ugly Patsy Palmer. It looked like Jed Reno.

"Right good show, pardner," Reno said. "But I reckon I'd have to judge this'n a draw."

Chapter 5

"Patsy Palmer," Jed Reno repeated.

Colter looked at the sinking sun. "Yeah." He lowered the corpse's foot and nodded to the west. "We better make camp here. It's going to be one mean night."

"It won't last," Reno said, and Colter had known the mountain man long enough not to doubt any of his predictions. "It's springtime in Wyoming. This is just winter's last breath till she comes a-roarin' back ag'in."

"But it'll be cold enough tonight."

Reno's big head bobbed, and he said, "I'll picket the hosses and get us a fire goin'. Don't reckon nobody's gonna be botherin' us tonight, but I'll pick us a good spot where we can defend ourselves and get ourselves out of any pickle—just in case some owlhoots come a-vistin' without any invitations."

"All right. And I'll see about burying him as best I can."

"Sounds like a fair dividin' up of our chores." Reno walked away. "And then, pardner, you and me needs to have a nice long chat . . . about what in the Sam Hill this is all about and why you ain't told me nothin'."

The coffee was awful, but at least it was strong and hot, and Jed Reno had picked a fine place, out of the wind but easy to defend, and easier to escape. The coffee and fire were the only things hot, though, for supper was stale corn dodgers and elk jerky.

"I could go fer some buffler tongue right now," Reno said as he washed down an oversalted ball of fried cornmeal. "And Taos Lightnin'."

Reno sipped his coffee and lowered the cup.

"President Grant is supposed to come to Cheyenne this month."

The big man looked over the small but warm fire and nodded. "Folks in town been talkin' 'bout that for some time. What brings him to Wyomin'?"

"It's what politicians do," Colter said.

"Even presidents?"

"I guess so."

Reno drank more coffee. "Don't reckon I never seen no president before. Exceptin' pictures and the like. George Washin'ton mostly. An' ol' Abe."

Colter nodded.

"The attorney general wrote me a while back," he said. "The Pinkerton Agency, he said, uncovered enough evidence to believe there's a plot to kill President Grant."

Reno set his coffee cup on the ground. "Who'd want to do that? Folks don't go 'round killin' presidents."

"They killed Mr. Lincoln."

A curse slipped out with Reno's breath. "Yes sir, they surely did, didn't they?" He cursed again.

"Ol' Abe saved the Union," Reno whispered. "And, yes sir, so did Gen'ral Grant, if what I hear tale is correct."

Colter nodded. "Grant surely had a major part in the Union victory."

Reno glanced at his coffee cup but did not pick it up. Instead, he looked over the boulders toward where Colter had buried the dead man with Morse code written on the bottom of his left foot.

Closing his good eye, Reno whispered, "President Grant . . . assassination . . . Dugan . . . trust nobody."

When Reno's eye opened, Colter was still staring in surprise.

"You remembered that verbatim," he whispered.

"Didn't need no bait to remember it," Reno said with indignant pride. "I still got both ears to hear with, and even if I didn't, my right eye sees just fine and I bet I could hear good enough if I only had one ear, too."

Colter didn't respond. He was thinking.

"Dugan," he said after a minute.

"That," Reno said, "could mean just one person—if anyone thought Jake Dugan was people. People's got souls. Dugan don't. Not from all I hear tell about that cutthroat."

Again, the old man was right.

Jake Dugan was a Rebel bushwhacker during the late war. No, he had started his own war against the Union long before those South Carolina secessionists opened fire on Fort Sumter. He had ridden in the Kansas–Missouri border wars in the 1850s, killing men, women, and children. And when the war began in earnest, his mayhem increased. How many towns had he burned? Some said he had been worse than William Quantrill, the butcher, the man who had, with his killers, sacked Lawrence, Kansas, in 1863. Blood flowed like water during those years in Kansas and Missouri, and the Southern cause had plenty of men like Quantrill. Bloody Bill Anderson. George Todd. Names Colter couldn't recall. Those men were dead, killed before the war's end. But Jake Dugan had not been captured. He had not surrendered. He had not given his oath of allegiance to the Union.

Jake Dugan had taken what remained of his army—an army of butchers, of thieves, of looters—and left Missouri, left Kansas, and headed west.

To Wyoming Territory. But Dugan had disappeared. Then he would come out of hiding, rob a Union Pacific now and then, or raid a community. Disappear into that country north of the Powder River. Take refuge in Dugan's Den, a place that—if it actually existed—had been impossible to find, other than that mysterious band of raiders. At least nobody had found it yet; nobody wearing a badge anyway, and certainly not Tim Colter, who had worn out some good horses trying to find where a gang of twenty former Rebels could disappear into that rugged country.

Folks figured Indians would kill them. That was about all you could find that close to Montana. But Indians hadn't killed Jake Dugan yet.

"You don't reckon them train robbers was part of Dugan's owlhoots, do you?" Reno asked.

Colter's head shook. "Not his style. Dugan's raiders

have never hit anything that close to Laramie City or
Cheyenne. Trains are too big for him, I think. And the
UP tracks are too far south from his hideout."

Dugan's method was to rob a train, which was a
long way from his northern hideout, and strip down
the telegraph wires and bend enough iron rails so that
when the crime was reported, he and/or his men would
be a long way from any heavily armed, searching posse.
Sometimes, however, he would waylay a wagon train
hauling military supplies to Fort Fetterman or Fort
Laramie. But usually the raiders hit a civilian outfit
heading up the Bozeman Trail to the Montana Territory
gold camps.

Hit. Run. Disappear.

A few people said the Sioux and the Cheyenne were
helping him, but Colter didn't believe that either. The
Sioux and the Cheyenne up north—well, they did not
care for any white man. And that hatred was getting
stronger with each pale face that traipsed through what
had been promised to those Indians years ago.

"Trust nobody," Reno said.

The coffee and supper did not feel so good in
Colter's stomach now.

"That why you ain't told me nothin' much, pardner?"

He couldn't deny that. And Jed Reno was a loyal
man, but he was also prone to drink, and sometimes his
mouth moved faster than his brain.

"The attorney general told me this was top secret,
Jed." And that was not a lie. In fact, the letters—they

had not dared risk sending those messages by telegraph and had used special couriers from the army—
had been explicit.

"That why he writ you . . . and not your boss?"

Colter stared at his friend. Clyde Tobin was a recent
appointment as the district's marshal. But Colter thought
the letter came to him instead of his superior because,
well, Tim Colter had a reputation that stretched far beyond the territorial line. And the attorney general
trusted Colter.

But things were changing. And Colter wasn't sure if
even bluecoat officers who had served under Grant
during the rebellion could be trusted. Trust no one.
Nobody. That was about as explicit as one could get.
And when a dying man—a man who worked for the
Secret Service—used that among his last words, it carried a heavy weight.

Colter's eyes met Reno's one.

"I'm telling you now," he said.

The big man's grin appeared beneath the thick
beard. "I figgered you'd come 'round, pardner."

They finished their coffee.

"What's that tomcat Paula Parker got to do with
this?"

"Patsy," Colter corrected. "Patsy Palmer. And I
don't know."

"She might could know where that Dugan's Den is,"
the one-eyed man offered.

Colter was thinking the same thing. "She gets around."

Reno laughed. "Not since you whupped her good
and got her sent to the big house."

"The Big House across the River" was what most folks called the Wyoming Territorial Prison, which, though it had opened in Laramie City during the summer of '69, the federal government had taken over just a year or so ago. Patsy Palmer was the first woman to be incarcerated there, getting a two-year sentence. She hadn't been tried, at first, for assaulting a federal officer or wrecking a privately owned business in the territorial capital, but for stealing arms from Fort Fetterman and selling liquor to a Crow scout. The more serious charge, theft of rifles—no, it had been one rifle and several crates of ammunition—hadn't stuck. Not enough evidence for the prosecutor to risk taking it to court, but the Indian had identified Palmer as the woman who gave him a jug of rotgut. At least, that was what Colter had read in the Cheyenne newspaper. He had been delivering a prisoner to the Laramie pen when that decision was reached. Then the federal attorney had decided to add the charge of assaulting a deputy US marshal.

Colter, still in Laramie City during the quick trial, hadn't even had to testify. He wasn't even sure if they had read his statement into the record, but several witnesses had testified, and a traveling photographer had taken enough photos of the wrecked saloon and a blurry one of a bloodied, handcuffed Patsy Palmer being escorted by Colter and two deputized civilians away from the carnage, had been shown to the jury, at least according to the newspaper article.

Anyway, the jury reached a verdict quickly and the judge gave Patsy Palmer two years at hard labor.

Actually, she was one of the first men or women to be sent to that foreboding compound along the Laramie River. She had roughly a year and a half more to go, unless she got some time off for good behavior.

Good behavior? Patsy Palmer? That wasn't likely

"Well, I guess . . . when's President Grant 'sposed to get to Wyomin'?"

"End of this month . . . if he comes."

Reno spit into the fire. "That don't give us much time."

"It doesn't."

The wind blew, but they were warm for the time being.

"One of us gots to see what that gal in the Big House knows."

"That'll have to be me."

Reno nodded his agreement. "Then maybe I ought to head north. Anybody can find a way into that Dugan's Den, I'm guessin' I'd be the one. One white man, I mean."

"No." Colter shook his head. "My gut tells me that Patsy likely knows the way to Dugan's Den. If I can get the warden to loan her to me, she can get me there."

Reno came to his knees, moving quickly like a wild animal ready to defend his ground. "You ain't thinkin' 'bout tryin' to take that gang by your lonesome, pard?"

"No, Jed. I'm thinking about saving our president— the president of our United States and territories— from getting killed if and when he comes to town. I'm also thinking that we have to split up. I go north. You stay around Cheyenne. You—"

What could Jed Reno do?

"You . . ." Colter sighed. "You snoop around Cheyenne. See what you can find out."

Reno cursed but sat back down. "You mean I hang out in the saloons and liveries and places like that. Because folks in 'em parts won't pay no attention to a white-haired, one-eyed, fat old man who don't talk 'bout nothin' 'ceptin' 'em old days when I was fightin' cutthroats and trappin' prime beaver back when this country was wild and tame and free."

No argument came from Colter.

"I don't like that plan at all," Reno grumbled.

"I'm not partial to either plan myself," Colter whispered.

"Then why don't we sleep on it and discuss it over breakfast?"

"Because the situation won't change. I have to get Patsy out of the Big House, unless that dead Secret Service agent mentioned her for another reason. And even if Patsy means nothing, one of us has to try to find Dugan's Den and get there to save President Grant's life. And one of us needs to be—must be—in Cheyenne when President Grant arrives. Because . . . because . . ."

Reno cursed and leaned against a boulder.

"Because there's a fairer'n middlin' chance that the fool who tries to sneak into Dugan's Den won't be alive to save the president."

Neither spoke for several seconds.

"Maybe he won't come iffen he knows his life's in danger," Reno whispered.

"He'll come," Colter said softly.

"How come?"

"Because he's Ulysses S. Grant." Colter sighed. "No one's going to call him a coward."

Chapter 6

She blamed it on the warden. Nah, now that Patsy Palmer thought about her situation, it was that hardheaded, harder-hitting, and impossible-to-put-down-permanentlike deputy marshal from Cheyenne. He was to blame for her freezing in the morning wind in the yard of the Wyoming Territorial pen, wearing itching wool of black-and-white stripes as she left her cell for the wash tubs, where her chore for the rest of her sentence was to wash the garments of prisoners and guards.

Patsy knew she should have killed that lawdog when she had the chance.

Then she corrected herself: *What chance?*

He had whipped her fair and square.

"Move." The guard behind her jabbed his narrow but hard club into the small of her back.

"Watch it, Mick," she said, "or I'll put fleas in yer unmentionables."

"Just move," Mick told her.

She saw the roaring fires and steam rising from the tubs of bubbling water. The male inmates made brooms. But Patsy got laundry duty. She glanced at the sky, saw the dark clouds moving southeast, and figured that would be the last of the cold weather. But a body never could be sure that winter actually ever ended in Wyoming. It was still cold to her, but that fire would warm her considerably. She'd be sweating before noon chuck.

Patsy stopped and straightened.

Mick swore at her and poked her back again.

"C'mon, Palmer, I want to get back to my coffee."

"You mean whiskey."

"Just move, gal. You know what you gotta do."

"I know what I been doin'." She pointed. "By myself." Now she turned her head and stared at the potbellied man with a thick gray mustache. "Who's the fresh meat?"

Mick stepped back. Smart man. Patsy smiled and gave him credit for brains she didn't think he had. He shuffled off to her right so that she couldn't jump him, take that club, and bash his face in before one of the guards on the towers filled her with lead.

The guard took one quick look at the clothes-washing and let out a breath of relief.

"Oh. Yeah. That's Ginger something-another. Foreigner."

"Ginger ain't no foreign name."

"Maybe so. But her husband was. Late husband, I mean. She p'isned'm. Arsenic."

"That so?"

He shrugged. "What the warden said."

"Couldn't beat him to death?"

"We all ain't got your muscles." He pointed to the club. "Move. Else I'll have to put you on report."

She let the wind carry her spit a few rods and looked back at the new female inmate in what had been her washing kingdom. She had drowned Deputy Marshal Colter many times in those vats, had wrung his neck till his eyeballs popped out of their sockets while drying some two-bit warden's long johns.

"She looks even punier than you, Mick." Patsy walked forward, and Mick followed her, still holding that club at the ready.

Black-headed, dark-skinned—might even be a half-breed, Patsy guessed as she covered the distance. Puny. Pathetic. Worthless.

She pulled out big trousers that had to belong to the guard the inmates called Lard Gut and pinned them to the sagging rope that served as a clothesline. The rope that, Patsy had already figured, wasn't long enough to reach the high walls and get her out of this miserable place.

"Ummm." Mick stepped away so he could keep a cautious distance and see both women inmates. "Patsy Palmer, Number Eighteen, this here be . . . ummm . . . Ginger . . . ummm . . ."

"Number Twenty-Eight," the runt said.

The surname came to the slow-thinking, if he ever thought at all, guard.

"Burricchia."

"That was the name of my late husband, the swine," Number Twenty-Eight said, her black eyes as cold as a prairie rattlesnake's. "You just call me—"

"Burro Chicka." Patsy laughed.

"Don't mock me, sister," the little witch said.

Patsy tried another name, keeping the Burro but amusing herself with a rhyming play on a fouler barnyard phrase.

And before Patsy could take a step back, Lard Gut's britches had been ripped from the short-rope clothesline and flung into Patsy's face. Wet trousers that size hurt like blazes when they struck her and wrapped around her head. She hadn't even seen them coming until it was too late, which served her right for underestimating a scrawny little witch she didn't know at all.

"Hey, now," Mick sang out, "them pants was washed!"

Patsy found a dangling leg, pulled, coughed. The little tigress had not done a good job of rinsing because soap half blinded Patsy. She tasted it on her tongue, pulled the pants leg the wrong way.

A whistle shrieked. She heard something else, corrected her movement, and got the leaden weight of Lard Gut's soapy britches off just in time to see a snake coming right at her.

No, that wasn't a snake. That was . . .

Ginger Burricchia lowered her left shoulder, which caught Patsy right in the stomach. Lard Gut's pants fell into the dirt.

Patsy crashed to the ground and felt a vice on her throat.

That whistle screeched again.

When her eyes opened again, she saw the fury and intensity in the little wench's eyes as those bony fingers dug deeper into Patsy's throat.

But Patsy had a good fifty pounds on that poisoner,

and she just twisted to the right, hard and fast, and tossed the little black-headed killer onto the ground.

"Stop!" Mick bellowed.

"Let'm at it!" another guard yelled.

"Yeah. Let'm fight."

"Catfight!"

"Fifty bucks on Patsy."

"You gotta give odds."

Prisoners joined the guards. They cheered. They hooted. They laughed, cursed, and groaned when, somehow, Ginger Burricchia managed to get her left arm free and planted a tiny fist in the center of Patsy's big nose. Blood spurted, and Patsy lost her hold on the little gal.

"She busted her nose!" a prisoner or a guard yelled and laughed.

"Ain't the first time, from the looks of that snout," a guard or a prisoner fired back.

Patsy coughed, shifted, and realized that Ginger had managed to slide out and away from being crushed by Patsy's weight.

Then a fist that felt like a sledgehammer caught Patsy right in the temple and she fell onto the soggy pillow that was Lard Gut's pants.

She rolled from instinct. Patsy had been in too many fights to rest, no matter how much she was hurting and bleeding. She even managed to get a blurry look at a brogan that was coming up high and moved before Ginger tried to stove in Patsy's head with the sole of the heavy footwear.

Then Patsy came back to her knees. And when Ginger swung at her, she parried the blow with her left forearm. The little wench screamed in pain and backed up. That gave Patsy time to scramble to her feet.

"Get her."

"Kill her."

"Drown her."

"Stomp her."

"Pull off her clothes!"

"All of 'em!"

More whistles screeched. More guards joined the circle.

"I thought this was a riot," Patsy heard someone say.

"Better'n that," came a reply.

Then came Ginger's fist. That caught Patsy in the ear, and she roared like a tiger and followed with a sweeping right that connected with something.

"Ooof."

But that sounded like a man's voice.

"She put Duncan on the ground!"

Laughter followed from everyone except Patsy . . . and Ginger Burricchia . . . and, most likely, the guard named Duncan.

Patsy definitely wasn't bemused, and the look on Ginger's face revealed an intensity that had Patsy thinking she had made a serious mistake in picking on this new woman to the Big House across the River. Puny little thing was too quick to catch and throttle. She was tougher than nails, reminding Patsy of that won't-stay-down lawman with the federal badge that had put her in this prison to begin with. Didn't look a thing like him, but Ginger Burricchia—Patsy wasn't going to make a joke out of that last name anymore—had the same fierce temperament. One of the few who didn't know the meaning of quitting. Like Patsy Palmer herself.

"Palmer," someone called from the back of the circle of men that formed a ring around the washing grounds. "If you cain't beat a scrawny little thing like that, the warden's gonna pardon you and send you off to a nunnery."

"Hey, you ignorant, yellow-livered pickpocket," Ginger Burricchia said, though the feisty little wench did not take her cold, hard eyes off Patsy. "She's got more grit than you. And after I've planted her, I'll be whuppin' you till you cry for your mammy."

Guards and prisoners laughed.

Patsy almost smiled. She probably would have. But right then, the tigress charged.

And Patsy realized the hellion had made her first major mistake. Patsy let her come, then let her shoulder plant itself into her midsection. But while she was doing that, Patsy was inching backwards, moving toward the big cauldron of water. Not the boiling water for the hot wash. That would've been bad for both fighters. She let herself be carried to the dirty cold water of rinsing. Patsy also twisted so that they hit the giant tub sideways, then fell into the water side by side. Only Patsy knew what was coming, and when they hit the bottom of the tub, Ginger Burricchia was resting against dungarees and longhandles and shirts and woolen pants and shirts, and Patsy was on top.

And Patsy Palmer could squash this feisty little husband killer easily.

All she had to do was stay there, under the water. Patsy had a mighty big pair of lungs and could hold her breath for a long time. But once she managed to hear the bubbling of water from that poor little critter, Patsy rose, pulling the tomcat up till she felt the coolness of the morning, and heard the cheers of men surrounding them.

She held the coughing, gagging, and exhausted Ginger in both hands, while Patsy breathed in and out deeply, already cold now.

The sawbones who stitched up the wounds of prisoners and guards came out of the circle of men and Patsy let him take the weakened newcomer to the Big House.

"You hurtin', Palmer?" the doc asked.

All over, Patsy thought, but she said, "I'm finer'n crystal."

Someone tossed her a towel; damp, but it was good enough to wipe off her face, though she felt a loose molar on her upper right jaw. Her tongue pushed it down a bit, and it might not fall out if she was careful not to eat a hard potato on that side of her mouth for a few days.

She looked at Ginger Burricchia, who was sitting on the rim of the tub, letting the doc hold her upright as she managed to cough out the last of the water from her innards.

Then a part of the circle of men parted, and the fat, bald, bellicose warden stepped through, surrounded by his two best men—the only good men, inmate or guard, in the whole place—next to the old sawbones, at least when the doc was sober.

"What's going on here, Mick?" Warden G. Breck Glenn demanded.

"Fight between the inmates, sir."

The warden's dark eyes showed no mercy.

"I told you to take Number Eighteen to work the laundry, Mick, not ruin it."

"Yes sir. But she and Number Twenty-Eight had words, and them words turned into blows."

The warden moved in closer, his narrow gray eyes getting smaller as he glared. "A week in the hole didn't seem to teach you a thing, did it, Number Eighteen?"

His breath stank of tobacco and coffee and his teeth were about the color of the dirt on which Patsy Palmer stood.

"I didn't forget nothin'," she said, "that's certain."

"Let's see if two weeks will teach you manners and rules." The warden turned toward Ginger Burricchia. "With her."

"Together?" Mick's voice trembled. "In the hole?"

"That's what I said," the warden bellowed.

The doc cleared his throat. "They might kill each other in two hours, let alone two weeks."

"And that. . . ." The warden turned away and walked through the path in the crowd. "That would be justice served."

Chapter 7

Tim Colter threw off the blanket and sat up, feeling the chill of the morning but not the brutal bite of winter. Nobody would call it summer, but at least the misery had passed. That was Wyoming Territory for you. That weather—well, it wasn't of a predictable nature.

"I dreamed," Jed Reno said from underneath his blanket, "that you brought Taos Lightnin'."

"Well." Colter made himself stand, feeling his muscles fighting the movement, but moving got the blood flowing, and he stamped his feet on the ground to help that process. "If you want whiskey, you best go back to sleep."

The big man grumbled and sat up, then started scratching his hair like a dog trying to find fleas. "You come up with a better plan this mornin'?"

Colter shook his head. "You?"

"I ain't never been one for plannin'. That was your department."

"My plan hasn't changed." He moved toward the horses.

"Well, it ain't a good one. I ain't keen on you headin' north with that fire cat." His bones creaked and popped and he farted long and hard as he rose and began shaking his blanket. "She ain't to be trusted."

"Never said I'd trust her."

"Ain't rightly sure how you plan on gettin' her out of the Big House, neither."

"I'll talk to the warden."

"That warden don't listen much."

"I'll figure something out."

"Yeah. And I got a notion you already is schemin'. No sir." He began folding the blanket.

Colter found enough grain to placate the two horses. He stared southeast and Reno looked down the trail and started chuckling.

"I reckon that posse the town law was formin' is slow at pursuin' train robbers, bank robbers, pickpockets. . . ."

"Did you expect anything different?" Colter grabbed his canteen and took a pull.

Reno found his pipe and began tapping that Indian mixture into the bowl. He didn't answer the question. It didn't need an answer.

"I still don't like your plan."

Well, Colter still wasn't finding much comfort with the idea of Jed Reno, big, bellicose, and bold as brass, snooping around Cheyenne, trying to find men conspiring to murder the president of their United States. But he couldn't think of another idea.

Trust nobody.

"Jed." He brought the canteen over and offered it to his mentor, and the one-eyed man nodded and set his pipe on the boulder. He took a pull, leaned his head back, gargled, and spat out the brackish liquid into the dirt, then returned the container to the federal deputy.

"I know you ain't gonna insult me by tellin' me to be careful, and to watch that I don't tell nobody nothin' 'bout what I knows."

Colter shook the canteen and jabbed in the stopper tighter.

"Wouldn't think of it," Colter lied. He breathed in, exhaled, and felt his face harden.

"You need to ride hard and fast to Cheyenne. Tell my bosses that we split up, with the understanding that if the trail was lost, one or both of us would return to Cheyenne. You lost the trail. The storm blew away the signs and you didn't have any choice but to return. Those were my orders, after all."

"I *lost* the trail?"

Colter grinned. "You've lost trails before. And that storm likely did wipe out any sign by now."

"*Me*. I *lost* the trail. I might've lost a trail left by a Sioux or Cheyenne, even an Arapaho, but I ain't one to lose no trail left by some dern fool robbers runnin' fer their lives."

"Which would explain why you are hanging out in liveries with a jug or in saloons drinking what you can buy or steal, just wandering aimlessly, checking out the trains when they come in, asking passengers if they can spare a couple of bits for a one-eyed, old mountain man."

"Beggin'?"

"Acting. Spying. Looking for people who don't fit in. Men, maybe even a woman or two, who you find suspicious. Southern accents might be the key—that sounds just about right if Jake Dugan is involved in this. But I've been employed by the federal government long enough to know that there could be some Union men in this, too."

Reno's one eye blinked.

"You ain't serious?"

"I am dead serious, Jed. We don't know who is behind this. And like the Secret Service man said, *Trust nobody.*"

"*Trust nobody.*" Reno tested the words. Then that unmistakable grin cracked through his thick beard. "'Ceptin' you."

Colter extended his hand. "And you, pard. Always."

Laramie City was closer than Cheyenne. Colter knew he couldn't push his horse too hard, not after riding hard after those train robbers, with him all weighed down against the cold, but he could still get there sometime late morning. Jed Reno most likely would not reach Cheyenne until sometime that afternoon.

He'd need a new horse; a fresh one, and one that had a lot of stamina, a horse that a rider in for a long journey could depend on. For a federal lawman that would be easy enough. A deputy marshal who drew a salary from the federal government had pretty good credit wherever he was, and Tim Colter was well-known in Laramie City. Besides, the town had always been a trail town, and had always catered to travelers.

The town, the river—actually, two rivers, the Big and the Little—the county and the fort well off to the northeast, and even a mountain peak took their name from a mountain man named Jacques La Ramée, who had arrived in this part of the world so long ago even Jed Reno never met him. Other bold men like La Ramée seeking to trap for fur pelts made their way west to the mountains, including Reno, through the region. Men who worked for General Ashley. Men like Jim Bridger. And soldiers and explorers like John Frémont. Tim Colter, on the other hand, had not seen this part of the country when he traveled west with his family all those years ago. The Oregon Trail went north of here, and it wasn't until Cherokee Indians came through on their way to California in 1849 that the route become popular with westering wayfarers.

After the Civil War, more men and women moved west, and the army had set up a fort, called John Buford to begin with, but that was quickly renamed after some other Union general named Sanders— another general, the joke went, that no one had ever heard of. The fort wasn't as big as Forts Fetterman or Laramie, but if Colter couldn't find a good enough horse at one of the city's livery stables, he figured the army would loan him one.

Fort Sanders was manned to keep the Union Pacific Railway workers from getting killed by Indians, but the way Colter remembered it, the army could have done a better job by trying to keep the soldiers from getting killed in the Hell on Wheels town that sprung up on the line. The railroaders named the town—what else?— Laramie.

That had been five years ago come next month, when the first train reached the rough-hewn city of mostly tents. Laramie City was no different from other Hell on Wheels, rawhide towns formed to entertain the railroad workers with crooked games of chance, loose women, and stomach-eating rotgut whiskeys. At best, the men were cheated. Sometimes they were murdered. The law here was the bullet or the garrot. Until the braver citizens, those who saw something in Laramie other than a Sodom, formed a vigilance committee and the town toughs realized that men who wanted to build something permanent were men who would fight hard for it. Telegraph poles were turned into gallows, and Laramie changed into a place that wasn't so wicked.

Most Hell on Wheels towns faded into bad memories once the tracks and crews pushed west, but the Union Pacific brass decided to make this town—if one wanted to call it that—its western headquarters. That didn't last long. The UP and the Central Pacific finally met up at Promontory Summit in Utah back in '69, and the headquarters moved out of the city.

But the town kept growing, maybe numbering a thousand, or close to it. The tents, for the most part, were gone, replaced by buildings made of wood brought in by the railroad from the forests all over the country, and later of stone. That included the prison, and its sandstone blocks, two-feet thick, which looked like an impenetrable fortress.

When Tim Colter rode into town, he knew he could eat some of the finest foods between here and Sacramento, and he could stay in a fancy boardinghouse where he could sip English tea or fine coffee. The county courthouse was made of brick—bricks made in the city—and so were a few stores. He had delivered enough prisoners to the warden to know the prison fairly well. Three tiers, each holding a couple of rows of seven cells. A few prisoners had tried to escape, and their bodies were found downstream in the Big Laramie.

He stopped and dismounted at the telegraph office at the depot, tied up his horse at the hitch rail, and walked inside, removing his hat and nodding at the bald man wearing a visor.

"Marshal." Colter never could remember the man's name. "Did you catch those robbers?"

He shook his head, found a pencil and a pad, and began scratching words down for the telegrapher to send to the Cheyenne office.

LOST TRAIL OF ROBBERS

That was partially true. Colter and Reno just hadn't looked for any trail that morning.

IN LARAMIE CITY PLAN TO GET REMOUNTS SUPPLIES AND RIDE NORTH

He thought, and wrote some more.

SENT RENO BACK TO CHEYENNE

And concluded:

WILL RETURN AS SOON AS POSSIBLE

He printed and signed his name and gave the slip to the bald man. "Send that as fast as you can. I have another to go after this one."

Back at the desk, while the telegrapher tapped out his message, Colter tried to listen for the keys, wondering if he could make out the letters without his folded paper. That, he knew, would be impossible. He began writing but stopped, tore the slip into pieces, and returned to the counter as the little man finished and waited.

The machine clicked again, and Fraser—that was the little man's name—looked up from his seat and said, "They got the message, Marshal. Where do you want the next one to go?" Then he realized Colter had no slip of paper.

"Changed my mind."

"Oh." The man seemed disappointed.

"What's the charge?"

He paid Fraser and walked to the door, then stopped and looked back at the man.

"What livery has the best horses in town?"

"I wouldn't know, sir. I walk to work."

"It's all right. I'll figure it out. Thanks again."

"If there is a reply from Cheyenne, where do I bring it?"

"I won't be here long enough," he said, though he knew that was a lie. He had to go to the prison. He had to find horses and supplies. He would be lucky to be back on the trail by morning. But the last thing he needed was his boss, the district marshal, to order him not to ride out alone or to return to Cheyenne; that this was a job for local, not federal lawmen.

He opened the door, and stepped out into the crisp, clear morning.

"You sure you don't want to send that other telegram?" Fraser asked.

"I'm sure." Colter closed the door behind him and studied the town.

He whispered to himself, "*Trust nobody*."

Chapter 8

Kip Jansen woke to a strange noise.

Angels, he thought. Angels singing. But the sleepiness and the bits of pieces of remembered dreams faded away, and he realized no angels sang. But a bird sang. He didn't know what kind of bird, and then the chill hit him and he sat up.

It wasn't a bird. It might be an Indian.

His heart pounded and then he looked down into his mother's face. She was dead. Still dead. And he felt the tears well in his eyes and roll down his dirty face. The Indian kept singing. The mule grunted, and another feeling struck the fourteen-year-old.

He wasn't cold.

Well, he wasn't freezing, and he could see rays of sunlight. He scrambled through the back of the wagon and stared into the sky. It was so blue, so beautiful. Why, Kip had never seen skies this blue, not even in Alabama, and certainly he had never seen any sky this big. It stretched across the landscape forever. And the rays of the sun, rising over the peaks to the east, warmed him.

Maybe he was dead, too. Maybe he was in heaven.

Another sound reached him and he saw his step-father, that louse, curled up under a buffalo robe next to the front wheel, snoring away.

No, this couldn't be heaven. Not if Lige Kerns was here.

He found neither an Indian nor an angel, but the song continued. Not a song but a whistle. Over and over again. *Fee-fee-fee-fee. Fee-fee-fee-fee.*

Indians, he reminded himself, could mimic any bird. That was how they talked to one another, especially when they were coming in for the kill. At least that was what he had heard from peddlers at the forts and the riffraff that Lige Kerns associated with in saloons and livery stables. But he had also read that in at least two of the half-dime novels Mr. Stricklyn had given him for sweeping out the general store he ran in Decatur. Surely a writer would not lie about such things.

Now the tune changed to something he had heard before.

Chic-a-dee-dee-dee-dee-dee-dee.
Chic-a-dee-dee-dee-dee-dee-dee.
Chic-a-dee-dee-dee-dee-dee-dee.

The song came to his right, and he turned, backed up, and saw the small bird—grayish, it seemed, with a head of black and white—fluttering atop, singing a pretty song. A tiny bird. With a big voice.

It sang again, then flew away.

Kip shook his head. He must still be dreaming. This was wretched winter, and birds flew south for the winter. Everybody knew that. But that song . . . what a wonderful way to wake up! The bird was flying into the big sky, the big blue sky, up . . . up . . . up . . . up. And he thought of his mother. And he decided that the bird, this tiny chickadee or whatever it might be, was carrying his mother's soul to heaven.

He also knew that while no one would call this morning summer, it sure felt more like April than the past few days had. What little snow the wind had not blown into the shade already glistened with waterdrops. He didn't think the temperature could be much above freezing, but the sun was so big and bright, it was melting the snow. Sunshine warmed him, much as had the little bird's song, and now, thinking of his mother in heaven, he felt a warmth he had not felt since Alabama.

Kip stomped the ground with his right foot. Well, the ground wasn't ready to be tilled. It was frozen hard. But there were rocks all about, and Kip set out to make a grave for his mother. He would remember this place. He would come back when he could and return his mother to her people in Morgan County. Someday. But right now, he knew, he had to bury her. Maybe, he thought, he could do it before that louse he had for a stepfather awakened.

To his surprise, he managed to do that, for Lige Kerns slept into the afternoon. By then, Kip was putting larger stones on the grave. His hands were scraped and bleeding and he was sweating. For the past few days he thought he would never sweat again, but he was. Hot. Stinking. Working. He stopped every now and then to cry, remembering something about his mother—sometimes even about his dead, Civil War hero father.

But the chickadee's song stayed with him. Now and then he would look again into that never-ending sky and try to find the bird, but she—or he—had gone away. But the song stayed with him.

A bird like that, just hours after a wind-howling snowstorm. Maybe the bird flew in behind the storm. Perhaps it was a sign that spring had finally arrived in this horrible, unpredictable country. But Kip wanted to think something else. It was a miracle. A gift from God. A sign.

He found no wood to make a cross, but he took a dull knife from the crate that carried their dinnerware and carved his mother's name into a rock. That practically wore him out. He could not remember the year she said she was born, and Lige Kerns had traded the family Bible for food in one of the towns they had traveled through before reaching Omaha.

So he just scratched into the rock:

D. 1873

RIP

It was, he knew, pathetic, but it was something. Kip's intentions were good. And he promised his mother again that he would return to take her home. Take her to the place she—*they*—never should have left.

Lige Kerns muttered something, and Kip feared the worthless cur was waking up, but he rolled over and grumbled something Kip couldn't make out and started snoring again.

Now Kip knew he had to hurry. He blew his mother

a kiss and hurried back to the wagon. What did he need? How many days had they been traveling since the last town? That was . . . Laramie City? He sighed. There wasn't enough food, and even as much as he despised Lige Kerns, Kip wasn't going to leave the lazy bum with nothing to eat. He found his coat and his blanket—the one his mother had quilted for him for his tenth birthday. One canteen, which he filled with water, and then his mother's.

He would have to live off the land. Wasn't that what he had heard many a wayfarer say on the arduous journey from Alabama? A frown hardened his face. Well, he had not seen a whole lot of living land since that cattle ranch they had crossed north of Laramie City.

Don't think about such things.

Kip felt his stomach rumbling. Some cowboy had ridden up to them, said they were welcome to camp for a couple of nights on the Diamond Bar C while they traveled to their destination, but they weren't to butcher any cattle. That would be frowned upon, and while this particular cowboy said that he, personally, had never hanged a woman or a kid, the owner of the ranch would have no reservations. Nor would most of those who rode for the Diamond Bar C.

Lige started to curse the man, but then Kip's mother told him to keep his mouth shut because, she whispered, she had seen the running iron hidden under a calfskin in the back of the wagon—and if that cowboy found it, she would finger Lige Kerns as the owner.

The cowboy had tipped his hat, then eased his horse closer to the wagon, where he pulled out a greasy sack of jerky and handed it to Kip.

"Compliments," the young man had said, "of the Diamond Bar C. Safe travels to y'all."

He saw the calfskin and he had looked at the running iron, which had made no sense to him, but the blanket would be enough. He didn't think he wanted to chew on calfskin, and while Lige Kerns said a good chaw of tobacco would curb a man's appetite, Kip thought it would more than likely just make a teenage boy sicker than a poisoned dog. There was a small sack of nuts—mostly pecans. He tried not to think of those wonderful pecan pies his mother used to bake.

The nuts would not last long, but he helped himself to a few pieces of jerky and a stale piece of corn bread. There was still enough jerky, cornmeal, and bacon grease that could keep Lige Kerns's belly from holding nothing but rotgut corn whiskey. The piece of scum was muttering in his sleep now, and Kip didn't want to waste what little time he had. He needed to start walking south. Now.

But first he brought a bowl of water to the mule. It wasn't much. He could have taken the mule with him. He would treat it better than Lige Kerns did, but then he had heard what these Westerners did to horse thieves, and he didn't think they'd go easy on him because he was a boy and he had stolen a mule, not a horse.

He pulled down his cap and climbed out of the wagon and started walking. The urge to stop at his mother's grave pulled strong, but he refused to look at the rocks. He had already said his goodbyes. And he would see his mother—and his father, his true father—after the Rapture.

Kip walked. He watched where he put his feet because he had been warned about prairie dog holes. Some old men had told him that rattlesnakes were especially aggressive when they came out of that hard winter's sleep. Kip didn't know if it was still too cold for a rattlesnake, but he had no desire to get bitten by one. At least rattlesnakes gave a fellow a warning. Not like the copperheads and water moccasins in Morgan County.

How far had he traveled? Kip stopped and tried to find the sun, but when he did, his brain could not remember what he was supposed to do next. How does one tell time by the sun?

He ground his teeth. What an idiot he was. Not paying attention. Well, it wasn't that far to his right. It had a ways to go before it slipped behind the mountains to the west. But his feet hurt. The muscles in his calves and thighs ached. His mouth felt dry. His gut begged for something more than half a pecan.

Tugging on one of his canteens, he shook it gently and heard the water splashing around inside. He smacked his cracked lips and said, "Ahh. That'll do. That was mighty fine water. Mighty fine."

Talking hurt. He shouldn't have done that. It only made his throat and mouth feel rawer. He thought he might have convinced himself that he actually had a glassful of clear spring water and that would keep him going.

It didn't.

But what he heard next did.

"Boy! Boy, I'll whup the tar plumb outta you oncet I finds ya!"

Lige Kerns. The words echoed off the rocks. Kip had never imagined the louse would come after him.

"Thief! Runaway!"

The echoes haunted him.

Thief-thief-thief-thief . . .

. . . *a-way-a-way-a-way-away* . . .

He ran to the small bend in the trail, slipped behind a large chunk of rock, and tried to catch his breath. Now his throat truly ached, and his lungs worked hard. His chest burned, too. He thought he was sweating. His heart felt like it was about to break through his rib cage.

He slid down the rock and grabbed his knees.

Lige Kerns would track him down, cut his throat, and not bother to bury him. Kip wondered if he could find a good hiding place. Looking again at the sun, he almost started to cry but stopped. He might as well become a man now. He had to. He had no mother, no father, nobody to depend on anymore but himself. So he found a rock that fit nicely in his right hand. And if Lige Kerns was fool enough to try to throttle him, Kip Jansen would give that man a headache that was worse than any he had ever suffered through.

For the longest while Kip heard nothing except his own breathing and his pounding heart.

He tried to figure out how much time had passed, but he couldn't be sure. When he found the sun, he couldn't even recall where it had been when he checked earlier.

He waited. Waited longer. Finally he made himself

stand and inch his way along the hard-rocked wall to the edge. He twisted around and let his left eye take in the trail.

Kip blinked. After wetting his lips, he slid further until he stood in the canyon. Lige could gun him down now, he knew, except that Lige wasn't any hand with a long gun. The wind felt refreshing. He cleared his throat.

Maybe Lige had climbed up to the rim's top. Maybe he had sneaked on ahead and planned to waylay Kip as he walked into some kind of ambush.

Or maybe . . .

Kip's lips turned upward in a cracked smile. Reason returned to the brain beneath that thick skull. Lige Kerns was the laziest human being Kip had ever met or even heard of. That man wasn't going to come chasing him down over a few nuts and things. He had his big crate and he had reached the spot where he wanted to be. That was all Lige Kerns wanted.

Feeling free at last, Kip pulled down the brim and began walking south. He had nuts and stale bread to fill his stomach. He had meat for supper because jerky was meat, and he could pretend it was Mama's roast beef or a thick steak fried up just the way he and his daddy always liked it, with a touch of pink. He also had water to wash that food down. He had a blanket to keep him warm at nights, especially now that that winter storm had passed.

He stopped when the sun felt too hot, and he recalled his mother always warning Lige Kerns not to push that mule when the sun was blazing. Lige never was one to listen to anybody, but Kip began to see, and feel, the sense in what his smart mother had said.

So he found a shady spot and rested. He even napped, but woke with a jump, thinking he had dreamed that Lige Kerns was after him, with a big knife and the whip he used on animals.

Once he was sure he had only been dreaming, he moved with the shade and waited till the sun finally dipped below the hills. There would be enough light for a few more hours, so he started walking again, after taking a couple of small swallows of water.

He tried to think of any water holes he had passed, but none came to mind, though in the deepest part of the canyon he found some icy snow. Which looked fairly white and his throat felt mighty dry, so he clawed out a chunk that was more ice than snow and treated himself to a cold refreshment.

The snow, he knew, would not last long. That storm had been hard, but it had moved through fast, and the wind had blown the snow all over creation. But he had two canteens. His mother's remained full, but he realized he had consumed more from his own than he'd thought.

Kip clawed the snow and dropped it into his canteen, then licked his fingers, not minding the dirt that came with the icy refreshment. When there was nothing left of that bit of snow but rapidly drying mud, he moved to another shady spot and kept adding snow and ice to his canteen till he couldn't pack anymore in. Then he ate what snow he could find, or let it melt in his mouth and cool his throat. He felt like a glutton when he rubbed the cold water over his face and neck, then even stuck a piece of snow inside his hat and let it wash his hair and freeze his brain.

Of the few times he could remember snow back home in Alabama, he didn't recall any snowball fights. No one in Morgan County that he knew had a sled, and he had only seen pictures of sleighs in storybooks and some of those illustrated newspapers Mr. Stricklyn sold in his store.

He remembered how excited he and his mother were when the first snow fell, and he could not forget how Lige Kerns cursed them both as fools, warning them that snow was not a game and was a long ways from fun in this country. They hadn't believed him, but now Kip knew Lige wasn't wrong about everything. That storm had been fast and furious and brutal. But they had survived it. And now, he knew, because of that snow, Kip had more water in his canteens and in his stomach than he would have had.

The Lord works in mysterious ways.

That's what his mother had told him. His father said the same thing many a time.

Kip lifted his head and gave a slight nod. "Thank you, God," he whispered. "Thank you for everything."

For the first time in a long, long while, Kip felt refreshed. No, maybe he felt revived. That wasn't the right word either. He recalled his father telling him that finding the right word came hard for many men and women.

But now Kip knew the word that described his feelings.

He was alive. Wonderfully alive. All he had to do was be smart, stay alert and ready, and keep his eyes open. In one of those illustrated newspapers Mr. Stricklyn had let him read, he recalled the tale of a man who had survived six days without water, but the writer of the tale said the survivor was the toughest man alive in the territories, that most folks would have died after two days, or three. Six days without water. The writer had never heard of anyone going that long without water. The most he could recall was three days. Six days. Almost a week! That was something. And Kip Jansen had food. Not much. But that story also said that a strong man can make it three weeks without food, providing he has water. Three weeks without food. Three days without water.

Kip had water and food. And he was certain they had not been out of Laramie City for more than a week.

After that, feeling like he was a mountain man like Colter and Bridger and those other names he had heard in Laramie and such places, he began walking down the trail.

Ma would be proud of him.

So would Pa.

Chapter 9

The pocket watch told Tim Colter that the time was ten minutes till six o'clock. He let the silver-plated, open-faced watch drop back into his vest pocket and he swung off the horse he had bought for forty-five dollars at Dolan's Livery Stable. Fifteen hands, gray in color, freshly shod and groomed. Hector Dolan said he had some Arabian in him, and Colter figured Dolan wasn't just making that up to drive up the price. To Colter, the gray's arching neck and high tail made Arabian blood possible, and Dolan said even if there wasn't an ounce of Arab blood in the horse—Joe was the name Dolan had given the stallion—he would carry a man a long, long way.

"He'll have to," Colter said as he handed the livery-man three gold pieces.

The bay gelding Colter pulled behind him Dolan had let go for fifteen bucks. That was about five dollars more than it was worth, but the liveryman had tossed in a well-used McClellan saddle, those favored by the United States Cavalry, or at least by the government contractors who bought saddles and tack for the army. Colter had not yet found a horse soldier who liked those saddles.

After tethering the two horses to the rail, Colter nodded at one of the guards at the lookout post and walked to the entry door.

"Marshal." The guard with the mustache looked surprised when he peered through the iron bars.

"Is the warden still here?" Colter asked.

"Well, it's . . ." The man turned and looked inside the compound. "Here he comes now, Marshal. You almost missed him. It's late in the day for visitors."

That's exactly what Warden G. Breck Glenn said when he met Colter inside the prison compound. The guard's key rattled as he locked the iron door after letting the deputy marshal in.

"Warden," Colter said with a nod, noticing that G. Breck Glenn did not extend his hand. The man did not appear happy to see a federal deputy at this time of day. "Hate to bother you, but I need to see a prisoner."

"Can't it wait till tomorrow?"

"Afraid not, Warden."

The warden looked at his watch, which was much fancier, and gold, than Colter's, and probably kept better time, too.

"Who is it?"

"Patsy Palmer."

The warden sent the watch into his vest pocket and glared. "Why on earth would anyone want to see that rough-hewn cutthroat?" He sighed, shook his head, and added, "Impossible, *Deputy*." He made sure Colter caught the emphasis, that he was a mere assistant to the appointed United States marshal, and that G. Breck Glenn was in charge of this prison.

"Inmate Number Eighteen, your Patsy Palmer, is in solitary confinement. Come back in two weeks and you can have that disgrace to her gender for as long as you want. With luck, she'll try to escape and you will do us, and all of Wyoming Territory, a favor by gunning her down."

"I don't have two weeks, Warden." Colter felt the edge in his own voice, and he wasn't acting. "I need to see her now. This evening. And even that might not give me enough time to do what I have to do."

The warden stepped back, studying Colter intensely. He wet his lips, started to look at his fancy gold watch again, but instead hooked his thumbs in the corners of the pockets on his coat. "Give me a good reason."

"You heard about the train robbery this morning at Simpson's Well?"

Glenn nodded. "I presume you did not catch those scoundrels."

"No sir. But we got a reliable tip from an informed source that the robbery was tied in to that stolen gun shipment from Fort Fetterman."

The warden's face slackened. He had to pause to find the words. "Number Eight— . . . Palmer . . . those charges were dropped against her. She had nothing to do with that act of treason."

Colter thought "treason" was a mite strong, but he wasn't going to argue with the only man who could get him to Patsy Palmer—and he had to get Patsy Palmer or President Grant might not live through this month.

"There was not enough evidence to the prosecutor's liking. That charge was dropped without prejudice— that's what the federal solicitor told me." Attorney Gordon Auburn had told Colter no such thing, but it sounded good, legal and weighty to Tim Colter at that particular moment. Auburn hadn't said anything to Colter about the trial other than, "It's a good thing that brute of a wench tried to put you six feet under, Colter, or we might not have been able to convict her of kicking a kitten."

The warden's eyes hardened. He pursed his lips and unhooked his thumbs from his fine coat.

"Who told you that?"

"I didn't talk to the source. Gordon Auburn told me that right after we got the telegram about the robbery."

All the federal lawyer had told Colter that morning was that he was taking the eastbound to Council Bluffs, Iowa, to meet a beautiful blonde from Alton, Illinois, who had agreed to marry him after a six-month courtship through one of those mail-order-bride outfits. They planned to honeymoon in Omaha for a whole month.

The warden's face paled. He must have decided that Colter's lies carried some merit.

"It's important that I see Patsy Palmer as soon as I can, Warden," Colter said.

"I imagine it is." Glenn wiped his mouth and nodded at the guard at the gate. "Leech," he said, "take Deputy Marshal Colter to the hole. Let him talk to Number Eighteen." He paused, thinking. "What's the name of the other inmate in that sweatbox with Palmer?"

"Number Twenty-Eight is Ginger something another.

A regular fire cat. Some Eye-tallen handle that nobody can recollect."

Glenn nodded. "All right." He frowned. "Wait. We put another prisoner in solitary two days ago, didn't we?"

"Yes sir, Warden . . . we sure did. And not just any inmate. It's Mad Ben Gore."

The warden's frown deepened. Colter found himself biting his bottom lip.

"There are two cells used for discipline, Deputy," Glenn let him know. "Our two female inmates, Numbers Eighteen and Twenty-Eight, are bunking together. Ben Gore has a cell all his own. And iffen it was up to me, I'd let him finish his life sentence, though how he did not get a hangman's rope for all that he has done is beyond me. But I wish I could keep him in that dark hole for the rest of his days."

"I don't blame you," Colter managed to say.

"This is highly irregular," Glenn said and withdrew his watch to check the time again.

"You are free to sit with me during the interview with Palmer," Colter said. "With as many guards as you would advise."

If Glenn accepted that offer, Colter didn't know what he would wind up doing, but he figured he had to say something like that.

"No." The warden let the watch fall back into his pocket and he nodded at the sentry at the gate. "No, Deputy, I have an important meeting myself." He faced the guard. "Get Mick. Let him accompany Deputy Colter. I will see you in the morning." He faced Colter again. "I wish you all the best, Deputy. Happy hunting. Happy hunting."

Then he started for the gate. "Let me out, Leech. Then take Colter with you. Get Mick to help you." He looked back at the peace officer and smiled. "I figure you would not mind extra guards, Marshal. . . ." Colter cocked his head and smiled when the warden didn't make him a mere deputy. "Especially after your last tangle with that rabid witch."

He let Leech open the iron gate, then slipped outside. "Don't forget to lock up, Leech," the warden said and laughed at his own joke.

Colter let his breath out as the guard walked to him and heard Leech ask, "Ready?"

Jutting his jaw toward the gate, Colter inquired, "You going to leave that unattended?"

"Ain't nobody comin' this time of evenin'," Leech said and started whistling as he walked toward the cellblocks.

"I wasn't thinking about them coming," Colter said, but he followed the guard to a structure away from the cellblock. It didn't look like a jail cell, at least not any Tim Colter had ever seen, and on the Western frontier he had visited many a cell.

"Inmates dug them holes a few years back," Leech said. "Glad it was them and not me." He looked over his shoulder and grinned. "On account this dirt is hard, mighty hard. Took ten prisoners better'n a month to get the pit deep enough."

The guard went on with his explanation. Once the hole was deep enough, the prisoners brought in logs to cover most of it, leaving one section free. Tarps were then laid over the logs, and over the tarps, buffalo hides, and over the hides, most of the dirt that had been shoveled out of the pit. For a while the mound had re-sembled a hill, but over time it flattened out till there was just a gentle rise.

They stopped at the path between the two rises, and Leech pointed at two trapdoors, both made of rusted iron—something that might have come off an old iron-clad from the late war, Colter thought. "This one goes to the first hole." His jaw jutted toward the other iron door. "That one's where Mad Ben Gore is contemplat-ing what landed him in this patch o' purgatory."

"How do they breathe?" Colter asked.

"They's shafts dug in," the guard answered. "Only sunlight they gets comes from 'em air holes, too. Ain't a place I'd care to be for an hour, let alone a coupla weeks. But that's why I walked the straight and nar-row." He shook his head and turned toward the cell-block and yelled, "Mick! Mick! Shake the lard out and come a-help me and the marshal."

Mick did not come and Leech cursed again, then gave Colter a pleading look. "Marshal? You mind helpin' me get this door opened? Weighs nigh a ton, and my back ain't what it was thirty years ago."

The guard wasn't exaggerating. One of the chains had been unlocked and dragged away, and both men had to squeeze their fingers underneath the hot iron and grunted and swore as they lifted up the door, the muscles in their calves and thighs straining and their arms burning as they pushed and rose, then let the door drop onto the ground with a thunderous bang.

Both men wheezed, and Colter shook his hands to get the blood circulating in his fingers again.

The noise, however, got the attention of Mick, who

came out of the shadows and hurried over to the punishment pits.

"What's goin' on?"

"Official business. And thanks," Leech said as he tried to catch his breath. "For nothin'," Colter heard movement in the dark pit. Leech waited a minute before he straightened and walked to the open doorway. "Palmer. Show yourself."

"It ain't been no two weeks," she said.

Another voice screamed from the other side of the pits, "What are you guards doin'? Gonna have a dance with 'em two concubines?"

Leech shook his head and swore softly. Facing Colter again, he shrugged. "They ain't supposed to talk, but it ain't like we can keep 'em from that. And prisoners have a way of learnin' things."

"I know." Colter gave the old man a reassuring smile.

By then, Number Eighteen, Patsy Palmer—Colter had no trouble remembering that savage and shrill voice—was cursing Mad Ben Gore with every bit of profanity Colter had heard and then some; he could only guess at their meanings.

Mad Ben Gore laughed.

"What about me?" That must have been the Italian inmate.

"You want twenty minutes of the evening air, Number Eighteen? Or do you want to go back in the hole and read a book in the dark?" Leech looked again at Colter and grinned before whispering, "Take as long as you want. That twenty minutes was just a ruse."

Patsy Palmer fired back, "At least I can read, you dumb mule."

Leech's face reddened in embarrassment. "I can read better'n you."

Mick cackled. "You can't read to write your own name when you get paid."

"I—"

"Boys," Colter said calmly, "I really don't have much time. This is urgent federal business."

The quietness did not last long.

"You ain't gonna shoot me when I come out into the hallway?" Patsy Palmer asked.

"Shoot her. Shoot her down like the dirty dog she is," the other female prisoner shouted.

"Then shoot that other one, too," Mad Ben Gore shouted, "so I can get a decent night's sleep for once."

"Iffen either of y'all opens your mouth again, I'll tell the warden to add another month to your time in the hole," Leech said.

For a moment, Colter heard just the wind and his own breath, still heavy after struggling with the iron bars. Finally what looked like a shadow came from a tunnel, and Colter wondered if this hole, this miserable, hot dungeon of depravity, had any place in a federal prison. How could men think women, even women as raucous as Patsy Palmer, could be reformed this way?

Mad Ben Gore? Well, Colter knew there was no reforming a man like that. But he didn't have a say in what a prisoner got after being convicted by a jury. That was up to the territorial statutes and the judge who presided over that particular case.

Patsy Palmer crawled out and came up on her knees. She looked at Leech first, then at the guard named Mick, and started to look toward Colter when Mad Ben Gore unleased a stream of profanities.

"That's enough out of you!" Mick bellowed. "Keep that up and you'll be getting bread without any water for another day. Keep that up and you'll be left with nothin' to drink but what's in yer slop bucket."

"It'd be better than the stinking water you give us!" yelled the female Italian prisoner.

"Shut up!" Leech roared and slammed his night stick on the iron door, which rang loud and angrily.

Finally the noise quieted, and Patsy Palmer pulled herself up. Now she was reaching up through the opening in the ground, staring at Leech for help before her eyes turned to the man who had come to see her.

The hands dropped to her side and the anger flashed in her eyes as she saw Tim Colter.

"Oh," she said. "It's you, you . . ." And Patsy Palmer proceeded to spit out every insult and every curse at the deputy marshal.

Chapter 10

Dusk was coming in at a hard lope when Jed Reno reached Cheyenne. His mule was worn to a frazzle and the old mountain man had worked up one powerful thirst. Sometimes he wondered how he ever wound up in Cheyenne. It was a right far piece from those shining mountains to the northwest, and even that country wasn't the same anymore, but what fine memories he had of those rendezvous days when he could outdrink that kid Jim Bridger and that wild demon with a horse, Hatchet, or Hawken—Liver-Eatin' . . . What was that fellow's last name?

Reno reined up. The mule snorted. "Don't get old, pardner," he whispered and rubbed the animal's neck before he swung out of the saddle and planted his moccasins on the sandy streets with a grunt.

He led the mule to the livery stable on the far side of town. Walker Chester ran this one, and he sure treated Reno and Reno's mule right. That might have been on account that Jed Reno shared any jug with the white-haired old stable man, not to mention any story or any profit. Well, this evening Jed Reno would see how far that long friendship with Walker Chester went.

"Halloooo!" he hailed from the corral gate and began removing the saddle from the gelding's back. "Your long-lost bunkie has returned home, Pa!" He laughed and grunted as he swung saddle and blanket onto the top rail of the corral. "Chester! Walker Chester!" No answer, but that wasn't out of the ordinary.

This time of evening, a man might be grabbing some chuck for supper. Or . . . maybe . . .

Reno glanced at the saloon across the street. He wet his own lips. Then he shook his head, muttering a few unkind words, and opened the gate, led his mule in, slipped off the bridle, and slapped the animal's backside.

"Get reacquainted with your pards, but don't get to fightin'." The mule trotted toward a buckskin mare. "And don't drink till you've cooled off a mite."

After closing and latching the gate, he hurled the bridle atop the saddle and walked toward the barn.

Walker Chester wasn't there either, which made that saloon, the Deuce of Diamonds, mighty tempting.

Instead, he saw the dipper and the water barrel and helped himself.

And then he thought about Tim Colter. And recalled their talk.

The water tasted as bitter as gall.

"I *lost* the trail. *Wind* blowed away any sign. Tim Colter sent *me* back." He spat out water.

Well, the courthouse would be closed by now, so there was nothing to be done till . . .

He swore softly and hung the ladle on the hook and wiped his wet beard.

But, he told himself, *there's always some pup or hoss put out to pasture in the federal marshal's office.*

So that's where, reluctantly, Jed Reno walked.

He was passing the Texas Saloon when the batwing doors banged open and out stumbled Walker Chester, drunker than a skunk but not too drunk that he couldn't see straight.

"Reno, ol' hoss, you's back?"

Things might be looking up. Jed Reno nodded, his eye fixed on the jug the old stableman held in his gnarly right hand.

"I ain't no illusion." He held out his right hand, still staring at the jug, but Chester shoved it into his left and grandly shook hands.

"Where'd you catch 'em bank robbers, hoss?" Chester asked.

"Didn't," Reno whispered.

"Ah. Shot 'em all dead, then. Good work. How many did you kill yerself?"

"They . . . ummm . . . they robbed a train, Walker, not a bank."

"Bosh." He waved the hand that did not hold the jug. "Don't matter. How many did ya kill yerself?"

"None," Reno barked. "They . . . they got away. Fer the time bein' anyhow."

The man's strong, broad shoulders slumped.

"Got away. How?"

"Lost . . ." The lie tasted bitter. It also felt embarrassing. "I lost the trail."

Walker Chester blinked. He held out the jug. "Here, hoss. You need this more'n me."

Reno felt his fingers balling into fists, but not in anger and not to punch Walker Chester in his big mouth. That was to keep him from knocking that liveryman back into the Texas Saloon.

"Cain't," he said. "Not yet nohow. I need to make . . ." He thought. "Report." Yeah, Tim Colter spent half his time in that office that was too hot in the summer and too cold in the winter. Making reports. Filing reports. Giving reports.

Fur trappers, back when beaver was prime, didn't have to make, file, or give nothing. They were their own bosses, lived their own lives, did what they wanted to do when they wanted to do it and answered to no man, except the company man who told them how much money their haul fetched them and what all they could get for that in trade.

"I'll see you back when I'm done, hoss." Reno walked down the boardwalk, feeling his ears redden with embarrassment.

He heard Chester's whining voice again. "Don't let it get you down, Jed. Happens to the best of 'em. I bet Jim Bridger even lost a trail oncet."

Two federal deputies were sipping coffee in the office when Reno pushed through the door. The smell of strong coffee reminded Reno that all he had put in his belly was jerky and water. He knew the young deputy with the corn-silk hair and peach fuzz for a mustache. That one was called Collins. Jack Collins. The older one was new to Cheyenne, but he looked tougher than some of them railroaders Reno had tangled with back when he was a young man in his midsixties.

He nodded, wiped his mouth, and went into his lie. Of course Jed Reno had been telling lies all his life, but never a lie that might get him fired from his part-time job as a tracker for the federal lawmen, and not telling a lie that might get his pard, and only real friend left around these days, in a heap of trouble.

The yellow-haired deputy set down his mug and pushed the bangs out of his eyes. "You and Tim lost the trail?"

Jed's head felt as heavy as a ship's anchor when he nodded, or what he figured a ship's anchor would feel like.

"That wind was fierce," he said. "And the snow and sleet come down somethin' awful."

Both deputies rose and walked to the big map that hung on the north wall of the office.

"Where'd you lose the trail?" the older one asked.

Reno looked at the parchment with its words and lines and arrows. He blinked and shook his head.

"Well, c'mon, old man," the new deputy barked, but Jack Collins understood. He moved closer to the map and traced his finger over a line.

"This is Cheyenne," he said, "and I'm following the Union Pacific to Laramie." He tapped where his finger stopped. "Here."

That was all the prompting Reno needed. He made

his way to the map, took a broom, and used that as a pointer.

"Went up on this side of the Laramies. They was raisin' dust—or woulda been, had that storm not come in—movin' at a fast lope northwest."

"Toward old Fort Caspar?" the new lawman asked.

"I don't think so," Reno said. "Colter and me didn't think they'd go that far east. Platte River could be troublesome, 'specially after that dumpin' of snow and sleet we got oncet it melts."

He pointed west, and then moved in a northwesterly angle.

"I'd guess they'd be makin' for the South Fork of the Powder. Lose their trail in the Bighorns."

"But you lost their trail a long way from those mountains," the older lawman said.

"It could happen to anyone, Frank," good old Jack Collins said.

Reno frowned. Now it was getting so that young pups were coming to this old hoss's defense.

Then the young lawman drew in a deep breath. He pointed at the map.

"Isn't that Dugan's Den?" he asked.

Reno nodded. "Well, it's supposed to be in that rough country. Somewhere."

The more experienced lawman laughed. "That another trail you lost, old man?"

Reno managed to laugh. "Cain't say I ever recollect lookin' for it, pardner."

He liked the smile that spread across young Collins's face.

"Where's Marshal Colter?" the lawman named Frank asked.

"He went on ahead. Planned to anyhow." Jed nodded at the map. "I taught Tim Colter enough to know that if anybody could pick up that trail that I lost, it would be that young whippersnapper."

"He's not that young," Collins said with a chuckle.

"Well, compared to me," Reno said, "Methuselah is a young whippersnapper." He turned toward the older deputy. "Ain't that right, Frank?"

The lawman had no chance to answer because at that moment the door slammed open and a timid man in a plaid suit stepped inside. "Marshals." His mouth opened, but the words stopped when he spotted Reno.

"What is it?" young Collins asked.

The man's face paled and he glanced at the yellow piece of paper—telegraph paper, Reno knew that much—and then shoved it into his pants pocket.

"There's . . . there's something . . . something has happened. I need . . ." He studied Jack Collins and then looked at Frank.

"Marshal Smith, can you come with me? It's a . . . it's . . . urgent."

Frank Smith. Now that was a made-up handle if Jed Reno had ever heard of one. Deputy US Marshal Frank Smith. Why not just call hisself Marshal John Jones? Man probably had to light out of one of those civilized states in the East. South Hampshire or Old Jersey or one of those places. Changed his name to Frank Smith to stay one jump ahead of the law by posing hisself as a federal deputy. Reno glanced at the wanted posters on the south wall. He'd study those and see if any bore a resemblance to this Deputy Marshal Frank Smith.

"All right," the deputy said and grabbed his hat off the rack. "Don't let this relic sell you a lame horse, Jack. I'll be back in a jiffy."

He grabbed his gun belt off a hook and let the telegraph man lead him outside.

Reno figured he might as well leave, too. He had done his part. But Deputy US Marshal Jack Collins had manners and said those magic words before Reno could head back to find Walker Chester. Maybe that ol' hoss hadn't emptied that jug he was carrying.

"How about some coffee, Mr. Reno?" the deputy offered. "It's not as strong as I like mine, but it'll do in a pinch."

"It's coffee," Reno said with a smile, smacked his lips, and sat down.

The young deputy smiled, and they sipped strong brew in silence. But the door opened before Reno had slurped down half a cup and Deputy Marshal Frank Smith came inside, his eyes burning, and slammed the door. The telegraph clerk wasn't with him.

"So you lost the trail." The sarcasm was unmistakable.

"What is it, Frank?" Jack Collins cried out.

"So Deputy Marshal Tim Colter rode on off after those train robbers? Rode northwest toward that hard country in the Powder River territory?"

"That's what I said, ain't it?" Reno decided not to lose his temper. Frank Smith would be busted up and out of service for six or seven months if Reno wasn't careful.

"Yeah."

"Frank?" the young deputy said, his voice nervous.

"Then tell me this, you old fool." Smith leaned forward, placing both hands on the table. "If Tim Colter was busy chasing after those train robbers, why did he just break some prisoners out of the pen over in Laramie?" He pulled the yellow telegraph paper out of a vest pocket and waved it in front of Reno's face.

"Twenty minutes ago!" Smith bellowed.

Chapter 11

There were no steps for Patsy Palmer to climb out of the pit, and certainly no ladder, for a ladder could be used, Tim Colter reasoned, as a way to get over the wall. The way Palmer glared up at him, Colter wasn't about to extend his hand to help pull her up. But this must not have been Palmer's first time in the hole, for she looked at Mick and said, "I'm ready."

Mick didn't seem that ready, but he unbuckled his belt and lowered the end—not the buckle, for a buckle could be used with the same effect as brass knuckles—and wrapped the other end over his beefy palm.

"You try what you tried last time," Mick warned, "and you ain't never gettin' out of this dungeon till Judgment Day. It'll be your grave, darlin'."

Palmer laughed, then spat in the dirt. The belt hung down and she wrapped the leather over her right fist, then clasped the part just above that fist with her left.

"Whenever you're ready, sugar dumplin'," she said, mocking a Southern accent.

"Give me a hand," Mick said. "Not you!" he barked when Colter took a step toward him, and Leech stepped up, then knelt at the edge of the opening.

"Step back, Marshal," Leech told Colter, who obeyed. These guards knew what they were doing.

They groaned, for Patsy Palmer had a lot of fat and plenty of muscle on her, but the simple method of muscle and leather got her up high enough, and Leech released his hold on the belt and grabbed her arms. Mick came in, too, and they dragged her out of the pit.

"Stay on the ground," Leech told her as he rose, catching his breath. "Watch over her, Marshal," he said.

"If she moves," Mick added, "blow her head off."

Then both men went back to work to close the heavy iron door. That seemed like a waste of muscle because Colter thought his interview with Patsy Palmer, in all likelihood, would be fruitless, and she would be returning to the hole after a few minutes and he would be out of luck and would have to think of another plan. She wasn't going to tell him a thing if she knew anything about President Grant's visit. And he didn't think he could beat any information out of her even if Leech and Mick pitched in to help. He felt certain Mick, at least, would enjoy a chance to torture that evil woman.

With the iron chains back in place and the heavy door closed tightly, Leech kicked the soles of Palmer's big shoes. She rolled over and waited.

"On your feet," Leech told her, and she grunted as she stood, then brushed the sand and dirt off her filthy striped uniform.

For the first time it hit Colter that she was wearing

britches and a shirt, not a dress or a skirt. Such attire on a woman was unheard of in this day and age. That was what most of the good citizens of Cheyenne had been talking about after Palmer's brawl in the saloon. Oh, certainly they spoke about the damage she had done, but from cafés to church socials to barbershops to saloons, folks had been astir that that woman was dressed like a man.

Leech must have read Colter's mind. "We never expected to get no female inmates, Marshal. All we had was men's duds."

"Be hard to find a seamstress who could sew up something for that gal, too," Mick added.

Patsy Palmer spat in the dirt.

"All right if I have a private talk with her?" Colter asked Leech. "Just out of earshot." He smiled. "I don't want to be left alone with her—not after that ruction she caused in Cheyenne."

That got chuckles out of both guards, and they walked toward the cellblock and leaned against it, then began rolling cigarettes. Colter looked back into Palmer's hard eyes.

"You want to sit down?" Colter began. "Make yourself comfortable?"

"Don't see no pews or chairs," she told him, which was true. There wasn't even a shade tree inside the prison. "And 'bout all I do in that pit is sit down."

Colter nodded. "All right. Tell you the truth, after all the riding I've been doing the past couple of days, standing feels pretty good to me, too."

"What do you want from me, lawdog?" She grinned. "If it's an apology, you rode hard for nothin'."

"No apology. I want to know what you can tell me about President Grant."

He saw a flash in her eyes. It didn't last long. There at the mention of the name, then covered up in an instant. But he had not imagined it.

She chuckled. "Sweetheart, while it's true that women gots the right to vote in this here territory, I ain't got no interest in who's governor or who's congressman or senator or president of the United States of America."

The first territorial legislature had allowed women the right to vote in the territory, and the governor had signed that in December of 1869. Since then, not only had women voted in elections but a woman had been appointed justice of the peace way up in South Pass City and Colter himself had testified in a trial in Laramie City that had a woman sitting on the jury. The verdict, guilty, had pleased Colter immensely.

"Now, if there was an election for a federal marshal or who gets to be one of his deputies, I might wander into that tent and vote as often as I could—a'g'in you."

"How's Jake Dugan doing?" Colter asked.

"Who?" She beamed, then looked over at the smoking guards. "Hey, boys, how 'bout rollin' a smoke for me?"

They both suggested that she'd be smoking herself in the fiery pits for eternity—and not soon enough for their liking.

Colter walked closer to her, then knelt and pushed back his hat. "Jake Dugan has plans to murder our president."

She snorted. "Jake ain't got no idea of how to get to

Washington, sonny. He fights his own Civil War here in this territory. He knows to avoid cities and towns, and while I ain't never been east of the Missouri, I hear tell that Washington City is chock-full of people."

Colter nodded and grinned. "So you know Jake Dugan."

Her grin vanished. "I hear stories. That feller in the hole with me, Mad Ben Gore? He tells many a story about that outlaw."

"Did he tell you about the crates he wanted you to steal at Fort Fetterman?"

Her face froze.

"You got that Crow scout drunk."

"I . . ." She paused.

"So drunk he couldn't recall what happened to those crates of carbines."

"Weren't carbines!" She gasped, covered her mouth, and then spat. "I don't know," she said, her voice trying to sound calm, "what you're gabbi' about."

Colter grinned. "The newspapers said the stolen crates were filled with cartridges for those new trap-door Springfield carbines."

"I didn't read no newspapers."

"No. But you knew the crates weren't filled with .50-70-450 cartridges but .45 caliber. For a Gatling gun."

She forced a laugh. "I don't know what the blazes you's talkin' 'bout, but since the sun's goin' down, you keep right on jawin' and I'll hear what you gots to say."

"All right." Colter glanced at the guards, then looked down at the big woman. "Ever heard of Mary Surratt?"

"Nah." Then the name must have registered. "No. I take that back. She was . . . she was one of 'em . . . had somethin' to do with ol' Lincoln."

"She was hanged as one of the conspirators who led to President Lincoln's assassination."

Palmer's head shook as she clucked her tongue. "For shame. For shame. For shame."

"She was the first woman hanged by the US Government." He sighed. "I guess you'll be the second."

That got her attention. "Now, wait a minute, buster. I ain't done nothin' and I ain't never been East and I wasn't nowhere near Washington when Abe got kilt. Besides, I was for the Union all the way."

"I'm not talking about Lincoln. I'm talking about President Grant. And I know—because a Secret Service agent told me as much with his last breath—that Dugan plans to kill President Grant."

She had recovered by then and laughed. "Well, sweetheart, believe all you want, but trust me, Jake Dugan ain't goin' all the way to Washington to kill nobody. He ain't leavin' Wyoming till he's made his pile, and then we's all goin' to Mexico. Find us a beach on the ocean. Live like we was kings and queens."

"He doesn't have to go to Washington," Colter told her. "President Grant is coming here."

Trust nobody rang through his mind, but, criminy, he certainly didn't trust Patsy Palmer. But he had to get her on his side. And while that seemed practically impossible, he had to at least get her to slip up and tell him something. He was shooting for the latter.

But now he saw something else in her face, something he never expected to see.

"Grant's a'comin' here? To Laramie City?"

Let her think that.

She wet her lips. "Nobody said nothin' 'bout killin' no president."

One of the guards had crushed out his cigarette and was walking to one of the outhouses, maybe two hundred yards away from the hole. The other flicked his into the dirt and started walking toward Colter and Palmer. That one had to be Leech.

"I need to know how to get to Dugan's Den," he told her. "And I need to know everything you can tell me."

"I don't know nothin' 'bout no plans to kill the president," she said, her voice filled with urgency.

"If you cooperate—" There was more than enough urgency in Colter's own voice.

"You gotta take me with you," she said.

He felt as if she had hit him with one of her numbing blows. Later he realized he should have figured she would try to use that as a way out of the federal prison, but right then he could just see that looming guard covering the distance.

"I can't tell you how to get inside that hole in the wall," she said, but this time Colter didn't think she was lying. "Doubt if I can even show you. But I can get inside. That much I can do."

"Marshal." Leech stopped a few yards away. "It's gettin' dark and my shift's 'bout up. I need to get that witch back inside the hole. So I hope you got what you needed."

Colter rose. "I got what I needed."

He saw the anger on Palmer's face.

"But I need something else." He pulled a telegraph

paper from his vest pocket. "This is an order of Palmer's release into my custody. As ordered by Ebenezer Rockwood Hoar, attorney general of our United States."

"Huh?"

Colter held up the telegraph in the fading light. He sure hoped he was right in his suspicions and that Leech was illiterate. He prayed that Leech was also simpleminded and would not tarry, would not wait until Mick finished his business in the outhouse. Mick might be illiterate, too, but with the shift about to change, one of those guards likely knew his letters.

"Didn't Warden Glenn mention that to you, Sergeant Leech?"

The guard stuttered, then straightened, liking his promotion to sergeant. Sergeants, sometimes, could read.

"Well . . ."

"We can go to the telegraph station in town, Sergeant Leech." Colter was spreading it mighty thick. He turned toward the door to the dungeon. "I can help you get Inmate Number Eighteen back inside till you get verification from Eb. Ebenezer, I mean." He chuckled and shook his head. "We're old pals."

Well, they had never met, and the president went through those faster than Jeb Reno went through tall tales. But Tim Colter's name was bandied about in the nation's capital. He had seen his name in Eastern newspapers because, as Cheyenne's newspaper editor told him, Tim Colter made really good copy when he went after some lawbreaker. And folks back East loved reading about gunfights and bank robbers and justice being served.

Colter shook his head. "Hate to go through all that trouble, though. I mean, not the telegraph. But having to open up that cell again. Put her in. Then close it, go send that telegraph, come back . . . wears a man out just thinking about it."

The outhouse door opened and then banged shut. But Mick stopped to roll another cigarette.

Nearby, Patsy Palmer sucked in a long breath and held it.

"All right," Leech said, taking the telegram, looking at it, blinking, then returning it to the marshal. "Looks in order, I reckon. Though it's hard to tell in this light."

"I'll get Palmer back to you as quick as I can, Sergeant."

They started toward the gate.

Chapter 12

He walked toward the gate, keeping Patsy Palmer a respectable distance in front of him, but Colter felt the butt of his giant LeMat in the holster. The fact that neither the guards nor the warden said anything about Colter bringing a loaded revolver into the prison was not that big of a shock, this being the frontier, and Tim Colter having a certain reputation. But the fact that no one suggested he not lock up the revolver when talking to a prisoner was a bit disturbing.

But then, this warden, and this prison, had a certain reputation about not following the book.

Tim Colter had no problems, sometimes, at not following the book. He certainly wasn't on any legal grounds doing what he was doing right now.

Mick saw where they were going and angled his way to meet them at the gate. The sun was now gone, and with it most of the light would leave, but for the time being, Colter could find his new gray horse and the bay gelding once they were out of this place.

"Ain't fair," Mick grumbled when they reached the gate.

"What ain't fair?" Leech said. "He's got an order for this monster's release from the gen'ral attorney hisself."

"Huh." Mick shook his head. "Nah. I mean, Bennett and his bunch. They was supposed to be relievin' us ten minutes ago. I got a powerful thirst."

Leech found the key, then laughed and remembered that he had not locked the gate after the warden left.

The door opened with a moan.

"Don't you need to sign nothin'?" Leech asked.

"You have anything I need to sign?" Colter asked as Patsy Palmer stepped through the gate. "That's far enough," he told her, and his voice did all it needed. She stopped.

"I mean, gettin' her out of prison?"

Colter found the telegraph and held it out. "You want this? To give to the warden?"

Leech wet his lips. Finally he shook his head. "I reckon I read it, so I knows it's good."

He heard footsteps and spotted the shadowy figures of men approaching, leading horses behind them.

"Here comes your relief, boys," he said.

"Thank the Almighty!" Mick sang out.

Colter passed through, thanking the guards before telling Patsy Palmer to turn right and head for the horses.

"What the devil are those fools bringin' horses?" Leech said.

"Maybe they's plannin' a hoss race when they finish for the night," Mick said. "Hey, maybe we can borrow their horses. We'll get to Harold's saloon a lot quicker."

By then, Colter was a few feet behind Palmer.

"The bay's yours," he told her.

"You got supplies?" she asked. "It's a right fer piece to Dugan's Den."

"In both saddlebags."

"No pack mule?"

"We're riding fast," he told her, "and we're riding hard. But you ride too fast and you won't be riding at all."

She laughed. They were at the horses. He drew the LeMat and pulled back the hammer. There was no need to warn the woman. She heard the clicks as the hammer went to full cock. And she had seen the big revolver.

He untied the horse and swung into the saddle. A few of the night guards were milling about, some holding reins to horses, but by now there wasn't enough light for Colter to see what the others were doing, and he was in a hurry to get as far away from Laramie City as he could.

"Mount up," he ordered but did not lower the LeMat's hammer.

"Is you boys comin' in or ain't ya?" Leech's voice rang out in the thickening dark.

"What's with all that hoss flesh?" Mick asked.

Patsy Palmer was in the saddle.

"A slow walk," he said. "You kick that horse into just a trot before I tell you to, I blow you out of the saddle."

Most of the new guards were heading to the gate.

Mick started to say something but stopped.

Tim Colter followed Patsy Palmer, their horses' hooves clopping softly on the ground. He took one quick look back at the prison. Most of the men had gone into the entry port, but two remained with the horses.

Something's not right about any of this, he thought.

But he also knew that nothing he was doing at the moment was right in a legal sense either.

When they were far enough from the prison's entrance for their voices to be heard, Colter let the gray get closer. "We ride through town. To the Brakeman's Saloon. Then turn north."

"I know the way," Palmer said.

"I know you do. But don't try to beat me there."

She laughed. "I know a thing or two about hosses, pardner, and I know this one wouldn't outrun yours in a month of Sundays. And you give me one of 'em buttocks-bouncin' army saddles fer a reason."

"Remember that. And remember this: I'm not your partner. Call me that again and you'll rue the day."

"I'm already ruin'," she said, paused a few seconds, and chucked out a "pardner."

Colter let them trot the rest of the way till they reached the outskirts of town, then they had to slow to a walk. Men were lighting the streetlamps—there was talk they'd go to gas lamps in five or ten years, maybe sooner—and it must have been payday because the saloons were already packed.

Like Cheyenne, Laramie City kept growing. The railroad could be thanked, or blamed, for that. And people had been flocking West since the end of the war. The West, they were promised, was a land of opportunity—and it could be, had been, for Tim Colter. But then, it also attracted people like Mad Ben Gore and Patsy Palmer.

Patsy Palmer was getting all the attention right now.

For even in a wild town like Laramie, which was a Hell on Wheels when it was founded, some sights were new. Like a big woman wearing the black-and-white-striped shirt and pants of an inmate from the territorial pen down near the Big Laramie River. Who was being followed by a tall, tough-looking man wearing the badge of a deputy US marshal and carrying a hogleg on his right hip that looked to be about the size of a small cannon.

Two cowhands stopped fighting in front of Slick Jim's Gambling House and watched the two riders pass. A priest mouthed a silent prayer and made the sign of the cross as they passed.

"Hey, Marshal!" called out a toothless drunk from the batwing doors of the Whiskey Galore saloon. "Ya's headin' the wrong way, pardnuh. The prison—" And here he doubled over in a wheezing laugh before he stood up and leaned against a post and pointed in the opposite direction. "It's yonder away."

He noticed the eyes of other men move from him to Patsy Palmer. But the railroad tracks were ahead, and some seemed to think that he must be escorting the inmate to the train station, to take her to some other territory or a state to be tried for whatever nefarious crime she—it was a she, wasn't it?—had committed there.

"Good riddance!" a scantily clad woman called out from a balcony.

He saw the Brakeman's Saloon ahead.

"That's where we turn," he told Palmer.

"Want me to tear it down like I did that bucket o' blood in Cheyenne?" She laughed, snorted, spat at a gawking teenage boy, and wiped her nose. "Don't worry, pardner, I ain't forgot yer strict orders."

They had to pass a giant wagon, a relic from the Oregon Trail days that had been converted to haul railroad supplies. The oxen ignored Palmer and Colter, and they reined up to let a mother and three children cross the intersection.

Then came muffled explosions far behind them.

Colter stood in his stirrups and looked down the street. Men were pointing. The ground shook, and he spotted an orange flame shooting toward the clouds.

Men swore. A woman screamed. The mother, now on the boardwalk, wrapped her arms around her children, her mouth moving in silent prayer. The ground rocked again, and this time a lantern fell from the Brakeman's Saloon and erupted in fire. That startled a cowboy's horse, which started bucking. Colter and Palmer had to pull hard on their reins.

"That's comin' from the prison!" someone yelled.

A lawman ran down the street but did not look at anyone.

"It must be a prison break!" someone yelled.

And to Tim Colter every eye seemed to be locking on Patsy Palmer.

He had two choices. Ride back and help stop a prison

break. Or ride like the wind and get out of town—and save President Grant from possible assassination.

Ride away and, barring a miracle that Colter couldn't see happening, his career as a lawman would end. He'd become a wanted man.

"Spur him hard, Palmer!" Colter drew the LeMat, aimed over his head, and let the grapeshot barrel explode. That scattered the crowd, and Colter raked the gray's sides with his spurs. Palmer was already galloping hard. She had a good lead, but Colter caught up with her before they reached the tracks of the UP.

The crowd lessened once they were north of the tracks, but they did not slow down. Then there were no more lighted streetlamps. A short while later and there was no more Laramie City. They rode hard, moving north, and Colter saw no more flames in the sky—nothing—toward the prison.

He had no idea what had happened back there and he wasn't riding back to find out. Now he had committed to this plan—if one could even call it a plan.

They rode in and out of a gulley, and Palmer reined up at the top. Colter let the gray stop, too. Palmer was panting and Colter slid the LeMat into his holster.

"What in tarnation was that about?" Palmer asked once she had caught her breath. "At the prison?"

"I don't know. But we're not going to have as big a gap between us and any posse as I was hoping for." He nodded. "So let's see how much ground we can put behind us."

"It's gettin' darker every minute, pardner. You ride

like we been a-doin', you gonna risk bustin' one or both of our horses' legs. Not to mention our necks."

Colter shook his head. "Horses have better eyesight than we do. Let them pick their own paths. You just sit tight and enjoy the ride."

He wiped his mouth. His throat felt dry, but he wasn't about to waste time taking a sip from his canteen. He could drink later.

"Ride," he said.

And they rode.

All through that night. Loping hard for a bit, then slowing down to a walk. Sometimes they even dismounted and walked their horses for ten minutes or so. Then they were back in the saddle, riding hard, covering some miles. When the moon rose they felt better, and that's when Colter finally took a pull from his canteen. So did Palmer.

They walked their horses up a rise, then turned and looked behind them. A cloud was heading toward the moon, but for the moment they had a pretty good view of the country behind them.

"I don't see nobody," Palmer said. "Can't even see the lights of that dung heap of a town no more."

She shook her head. "What do you think happened back yonder? At the prison?" Then she laughed. "By golly, I sure hope that they kilt Ginger Burro Chicka. Nah, I don't really. But if they kilt the warden and Mad Ben Gore, I wouldn't shed no tears."

"Let's ride." Colter nodded north. "At a walk for a few miles."

"All right, since you're bossin' this show. But we's gonna need to find me some passable duds. Not only does this dirty uniform itch like tarnation, it's gonna cause quite a bit of gossipin', as you've already seen, iffen we runs across wayfarers and lost forty-niners, pardner."

"Just ride," Colter said. "And keep your mouth shut till daybreak."

Chapter 13

Jack Collins and Frank Smith questioned Jed Reno for twenty-seven minutes. Reno knew that for certain because he looked at the clock on the wall. At the twenty-eighth minute the door opened, and a tired-looking, thick-bearded man walked in. For a moment Reno thought it was General—no, President—Ulysses S. Grant, and he almost knocked his chair over when he stood up. But, nah, it wasn't Grant. Not from the pictures Reno had seen—like the one hanging on the wall behind the US Marshal's desk. But it was the US Marshal, and he didn't look happy.

His coat he carried over his left shoulder. He looked around, shook his head, and turned to Deputy Collins.

"I've been at the telegraph office for the last half hour. I didn't get to finish my supper. And no one thought to put a fresh pot of coffee on the stove?"

"Sorry, Marshal Tobin." Collins sprang from his seat and moved toward the potbellied stove. "I'll fix up a batch for all of us."

"You might sweeten it with the rye Deputy Smith keeps in his drawer."

Frank Smith's face turned white.

Now US Marshal Clyde Tobin hung his coat on a hook and moved until he stood directly in front of Reno, who was sitting on a bench in front of one of the iron cells. The head lawman of the territory looked directly into Reno's eye, but his question was for the deputies.

"What has he told you?"

"A pack of lies, if you ask me," Smith said. "They lost the trail of the bank robbers."

"Train robbers," Reno corrected.

Smith glared at the mountain man and looked up at his boss. "Reno was sent back by Colter, and Colter said he was going after them."

"That's what I said and I told the truth, by thunder, like I always do," Reno lied.

That, at least, got a cough and a smile from Marshal Tobin. His tie was crooked, his collar unbuttoned, his sleeves rolled up on his forearms, and he ran his fingers through that thick beard.

"Jed," he said softly. "Tim was identified by several men in Laramie City. Men who know Tim Colter quite well. The warden telegraphed that he asked to interview Patsy Palmer. You remember her, I warrant."

Reno thought to grin. "Ain't likely to forget her. Nor is Tim."

"He didn't. He asked to interview her. Do you know why?"

"No, your honor."

"Marshal," Tobin corrected.

"Yes sir. No sir. Tim didn't say nothin' 'bout that tom-cat. I mean, tammy cat. Well, no, she's more man than she-male."

Frank Smith slammed his hand against his desk. Jack Collins threw some kindling into the stove.

"What happened at the prison?" Collins asked.

"I was hoping Jed Reno might tell us." The marshal put his hands on his hips.

Reno shook his head. "I ain't been through Laramie City since me an' Tim was on the trail after 'em owl-hoots robbed that train at Simpson's Well."

"Well, you certainly weren't with Colter." He sighed and glanced at the stove, as if that might get his coffee hot and ready sooner. Then he turned around, found a chair, and dragged it over. He sat down with the back of the chair in front, resting his arms on the top, and let those blue eyes burn into Jed Reno's.

Tobin pulled a telegraph paper out of his shirt pocket.

"Colter interviewed Palmer. About Jake Dugan. Warden Glenn had left for the evening; Colter didn't get to the prison to just before six in the evening, right before the warden usually leaves for the day, and before the night shift arrives for duty. Somehow, Colter managed to get the guards to release Patsy Palmer into his custody." He looked back at his deputies. "That, I assure you, was not authorized by me or anyone in the department."

Facing Reno again, he said, "He walked out with the prisoner about the time some of Dugan's men, it appears, came into the prison posing as the guards for the night shift. They forced two guards to the punishment cell where Mad Ben Gore was being kept and got him out. Other guards, ready to end their workday, came out. A gunfight erupted. Dugan's men, or whoever they were, had at least two sticks of dynamite, and that was enough to drive the guards back. By then the two guards who had been hoodwinked first were tossed into the cell from which Gore was broken out. Those fiends then, covered by their cohorts, escaped. The other outlaws threw one more dynamite stick and got out, too."

After dropping the first yellow paper on the floor he found another telegram from his pocket and continued.

"So Mad Ben Gore is out of prison. The guards claimed they wounded several of the jailbreakers, but I think that was wishful thinking, bragging, lying, whatever you want to call it. In the confusion, and the fear of the dynamite, the outlaws got away."

That paper fell near the other one at the marshal's city shoes. His laces, Reno noticed, were untied.

"And Marshal Colter got away with Patsy Palmer."

"Nobody got killed?" Collins asked.

Tobin's head shook. "By nothing short of a miracle. Two superficial gunshot wounds to two guards. The two guards who were forced to release Gore were roughed up a bit, and both suffered concussions when they were coldcocked with pistols and thrown into the cell, or whatever they call it, where Gore was being held."

"I don't know what got into Tim's head," Reno said, "but I can guarantee you it was for the good of Wyoming and our United States."

Frank Smith cursed, but the marshal nodded calmly at Reno.

"I'd like to believe that, Jed. Tim Colter is one of the best lawmen I've ever known. Or *was*. But he had no authority to get Patsy Palmer out of prison. I really need you, Jed, to tell me everything you know. Everything Tim told you. You two have been partners for many a year, and you've saved his hide and he has saved yours more times than either of you can count. But if you want to save his hide now, you really need to tell me everything you know."

Reno wet his lips. That coffee had to be warm enough by now. He thought for a minute. He really wasn't sure what Colter was planning and he knew he could trust the marshal. Tobin had been mighty good to both Colter and Reno since his appointment.

His mouth opened.

And then he heard in his mind Tim Colter's voice: *Trust nobody.*

Reno's head shook. "Boss, iffen I could help Tim and I could help you, you know I would. I'd do anything for that boy. He's been like a son to me. But . . ." He sighed. "I just don't know what in the Sam Hill's goin' on. We lost the trail." His pride took over.

"Well, even Kit Carson lost a trail. And I bet had we looked long and hard, we might coulda found it ag'in. Plumb sure I could. But Tim figgered it best for me to come back. We hadn't outfitted for no long trackin' job and that weather was fiercesome." He held up his right hand. "Honest as that Piegan lass I knowed at the Bear Lake rendezvous back in '28."

Tobin stared at Reno for a good thirty seconds, then sighed, and turned toward Collins. "That coffee warm enough, Deputy?"

The coffee was warm enough, and Reno felt relief that Jack Collins was doing the pouring because he was pretty certain Frank Smith would not have given him a cup.

"At least," Collins said as the four men drank, "only one prisoner escaped."

Marshal Tobin shook his head and moved his cup away from him while his left pulled out another telegram.

"No," he said. "Not just one." He glanced at the paper. "Another female inmate." He shook his head. "What is this country coming to when women can wind up in federal penitentiaries? Burricchia. Ginger Burricchia. She got out, too, though it is unclear if she just took advantage of the situation or if Dugan's men meant to free her as well."

"Well," Smith said, "a woman ain't much of a threat."

"Patsy Palmer certainly has been," Tobin said and looked at the telegram once more before letting it fall to the floor. "And this Burricchia was serving twenty-five years for murder."

He was surprised they let him go. Frank Smith suggested they throw him in a cell and starve him for a week. Then he might tell them what they wanted to hear. But Marshal Tobin said they had no reason to hold him. Smith was about to argue some more, but Tobin told him that two prisoners had escaped from the territorial prison and he needed Smith to form a posse as quickly as possible—hiring good men at two dollars a day, the men had to supply their own horses and saddles, a dozen men, no more. They were to meet here to be sworn in. They'd need a tracker, but not Jed Reno.

Reno acted hurt, but he was mighty relieved. It would be hard for him to snoop around Cheyenne and find out what he could about this plan to kill the president if he had to lead some posse, though tracking sure sounded a lot more exciting than any snooping.

He wished the boys luck and stepped into the crisp, dark evening.

The saloon across the street looked promising, but, no, he felt plumb worn out. At his age, most men were rocking on porches at this time of night, more likely in bed sleeping under the covers. Actually, most men at Jed Reno's age were dead.

He laughed at his joke and moseyed his way back to Walker Chester's livery stable. A good night's sleep. That's what Jed Reno needed, and he would get that tonight. Then start all this snooping and detecting and such, help Tim Colter.

He looked at the clouds coming in and shook his head. "Colter, ol' boy, I sure hope you knows what's you're doin'."

When he reached the livery Walker Chester still wasn't around, and it had to be pushing midnight by then. Those federal lawmen sure kept him there for a long time when they could have been getting that posse formed and going after them prison breakers. He paused. Well, maybe that was a good thing. Maybe Marshal Tobin was protecting Colter, letting him get a head start, though Reno had been to Laramie City enough to know that the county sheriff would have formed his own posse and lit out after young Tim.

Still, there was nothing he could do about that. He had his own job to do and he had told Tim Colter he would do it. He lay down in his stall, pulled up a blanket, and closed his eyes. He hadn't even had time to start dreaming—wasn't even sure he had fallen asleep—when he was awakened with something sharp against his throat.

He started to swallow, but that sharp, cold thing pricked his skin. Blood trickled.

"Do anything sudden and I cut off your head, *imbecille*."

I must be dreamin' was Reno's first thought, *'cause that voice sounds like a woman's.*

Chapter 14

Kip Jansen was dead.

Well, not yet, he thought, but it wouldn't be long now. He saw the sun creeping above the eastern bluffs and he looked at his canteens. *Not yet*, he told himself. *I gotta save water*. He stared at his swollen left ankle and fought back tears of pain, fear, and even shame.

How had he been so utterly stupid? He could hear Lige Kerns mocking him, berating him, cursing him as a fool city boy who had no business coming West.

Well, coming West hadn't been Kip's idea.

But here he was.

As good as dead.

Walking at night had its advantages, he had thought, because Lige Kerns had told him that Indians never attacked at night, and now that that cold Wyoming spring storm had passed, the night was cooler. Sometimes cold, but it sure beat feeling that sun on a body when the only water around is what a man's got in the two canteens he's carrying. For a boy afoot even the April sun in Wyoming makes a kid feel like he's crawling across the Sahara desert. Or from what he had read in some of those half-dime novels about the Sahara desert, or the Mojave. He should have waited for the moon to rise, but he thought he might fall asleep and his legs weren't aching too much. He could just walk some in the dark, then rest a bit, maybe have a bite of something and a few swallows, walk some more till he got too tired, and then find a good place to rest and sleep. Walk again in the morning till the sun came up too high and too warm, find a shady spot.

He would live to see Laramie. Or Cheyenne. At least he would live.

But then he stepped into that hole and fell hard, hearing the twist and pop of the ankle and feeling the heat of pain sear all the way from his toenails to his hip bone. He had stepped in a hole. Prairie dog hole maybe. After crawling a ways Kip had tried to stand but couldn't, so he dragged and pulled himself to the rocks alongside the canyon wall. And there he had managed to pull off the shoe on his left foot. There he had wrapped the ankle tightly after ripping off his left shirtsleeve. If he didn't move the ankle, the pain was somewhat tolerable. He wanted to curse himself, but instead he had prayed. And eventually, somehow, he had drifted into a fitful sleep, which never lasted too long—at least it never felt like he had slept more than a few winks—but he remembered looking at the stars one moment and then the next his eyes woke to a blue sky and a crisp Wyoming wind.

So here he was, leaning against a boulder, and he

would never live to see his sixteenth birthday. No marble tombstone would ever grace his mother's grave, and for Kip? Well, no one would ever find his bones. That was the way he saw it. He cringed at the thought of coyotes or wolves ripping apart his dead flesh and carrying off his bones for their pups to gnaw on.

He wasn't hungry, and now he worried that the busted ankle would make him sick if he put anything in his belly, but he fingered a few bits of pecan out of the sack and into his mouth, washed those down with water, and after that decided to take a bite of jerky. The latter proved tougher and harder, but the juice the jerky produced in his mouth tasted wonderful. He had eaten beef jerky before. When a family has Lige Kerns for a provider, beef jerky was like a roast beef supper. And now the dried meat lifted his spirits just a tad.

Might as well, Kip thought, *die with a full belly.*

His teeth latched onto a larger chunk of jerky and he pulled until he ripped it off and started chewing, swishing the juice around his mouth like he had seen Lige Kerns do with whiskey.

Then Kip saw the stick. It had not been there when his foot found that hole, but he could see it plain as day now. It wasn't driftwood or anything like that, for the wind caused some feathers to dance, and there was no sign of a bird's nest around.

After corking the canteen and swallowing the jerky, he looked up and down path, then cringed as he started to crawl toward that stick. It seemed long enough to serve as a crutch. He hoped it was strong enough. He stopped suddenly, not from the pain that still ran from his left foot and up his leg but the track on his left. No . . . tracks. It was a horse's hoof, but this horse was not shod.

The sudden breath Kip drew hurt his chest.

Indians.

Again, he looked up and down the trail. Yes, now he saw the hoofprints, how some horse—maybe it was a wild mustang—had walked over to check on him. Maybe it had nuzzled him and Kip had slept right through it. Kip wasn't much at reading signs, but it looked like the horse had backed up toward the trail.

So he waited, perhaps as long as five minutes, looking for something to the south and north, on the ridgeline and in the rocks. Nothing. Nothing but a horse's tracks and some fancy stick.

He dragged himself toward it, then saw and smelled the relatively fresh droppings of a horse, or horses. Those had not been there yesterday either, and he knew now that a party of Indians had found him.

But they left me alive!

Why would they have done that? He couldn't guess. Maybe there was no honor for an Indian in killing a sleeping boy with a busted ankle. Maybe they figured it was a good joke, to let this puny white kid die a long, agonizing death. He spat, then regretted that action because every drop of moisture had become precious. But he could not get one thought out of his mind.

I would have been better off had they killed me in my sleep and taken my scalp.

But there was that stick, the feathers beckoning him, and suddenly he was glad to be alive. There wasn't much of a chance for him to live out the day, let alone a week or so, but there now was at least that chance.

Kip crawled, biting back the pain, until he reached the center of the trail. There had been more horses—maybe a dozen—and there was that wonderful, gorgeous, fancy crutch.

The top was bent into a circle and wrapped with hide of some kind, with sinew-wrapped sticks stretched to divide the hole into quarters, and some kind of shell in the center of the circle, painted and with a feather hanging from its center. The shaft was much thicker, and wrapped in the furry hide of some animal. Silk ribbons hung about a third of the way down, one red, one blue, one green. The shaft was about four feet long, and when Kip sat up and pulled the fancy piece of Indian—it had to be from an Indian—equipment across his thighs, he pushed hard on the shaft. It did not budge. The circle part wasn't near as solid as the shaft, but it might be strong enough to support his weight if he leaned on it.

He prayed for a full minute before he tried to rise up on his knees. That caused him to throw up the jerky, pecans, and water, but he merely wiped his mouth and then began to stand, resting his armpit around the circle and gripping the shaft with his left hand.

Dizziness almost sent him back to the ground, and Kip figured if he fell, he wouldn't be getting up again. He would just lie there and die.

That was what kept him standing three or four minutes until the world stopped spinning and he saw his sack and those precious canteens back near the canyon wall.

He moved his crutch—lifting his busted ankle just enough—and brought his right foot forward. After the fear and nausea passed, he took another step. Then another.

Once he reached his campsite, after again studying the unshod prints of an Indian pony, he sat down to rest, hoping he could summon the stamina to get back on his feet. He studied the fancy stick he held. Was it a Sioux crutch? Cheyenne? Why had an Indian left it? Or had he dropped it in the darkness? He turned the fancy stick over in his hands. Kip didn't know much about Indians, but he had to figure this was special. Maybe even holy. And an Indian, he had to think, would not have lost it.

Fear made him jump and look hard toward the south. The owner of this stick might be loping back to find it. Kip's first reaction was to throw it away, then find a good hiding place. But he gathered his wits. Throw away the stick? That stick might keep him alive. At least for a day or two.

If the Indian owner came back . . . well, he would put Kip out of his misery.

He made himself drink another swallow of water, then gathered his belongings and screamed in pain as he made himself stand.

Deciding to stay as close to the canyon wall, he began stepping—Kip figured that to call what he was doing walking was a stretch of even one of those half-dime novelists' imagination—slowly toward the south. At some point he knew the canyon side would become too rough, quite dangerous, and he would have to move onto the easy path that had been cut by buffalo and elk, by Indians and cavalry troopers, by single wagons like the one that had carried him and his mother as far as they could go.

He was moving, heading south, about four to six inches for each painful step.

For the first excruciating eternity he could walk only five or six steps before he had to rest, and he became smart enough after three passes to rest while standing in the shade instead of sitting or lying down.

After a long rest that felt too short he tightened the wrappings on his ankle, found that beautiful Indian stick, and struggled to get back to his feet. This time he made himself walk—gingerly, but he pushed himself.

He wasn't sure how far he had come when he stopped to rest again, and this time he rested only for a few minutes before he struggled to his feet and began moving south once more. By the time he knew he couldn't go farther, he found a shade tree that sprouted up and stretched toward the heavens from a mound of fallen boulders. That gave him enough shade, he figured, and the position of the sun told him he would have to wait out the rest of the day here. But it was a good spot. The tree's roots must have found water down below, but that was too deep for Kip to dig.

After a long pull—*too long*, he told himself after capping the canteen—he checked his bum ankle, sighed, and found a spot that seemed a bit shadier, a bit more hidden from the trail, and about as comfortable as could be found in this savage frontier.

He would wait out the day here, till it was darker,

cooler, and then he would move about some till what his mother used to call "the gloaming" turned into pitch black. Then he would find another good hiding place and wait till the moon rose.

He held the Indian stick close to him. The Indian stick gave him confidence.

Kip told himself that he was going to live.

And, completely exhausted, he fell asleep, gripping the fine stick in his right hand.

Chapter 15

Walker Chester entered his livery stable late in the morning, limping worse than usual. That right leg always gave him fits. In fact, by Jed Reno's clock, called his stomach, it had to be pushing noon.

"Where you been?" Reno demanded from the hay bale he sat on inside the wind-leaking wooden structure.

"Why you need to know?" the crotchety old-timer shot back.

Old-timer? Reno shook his head. By his figuring, Reno probably was ten or twelve years ahead of the livery owner. "I built this place. I own this place. Reckon I can come in whenever I feel like comin' in. And I see you ain't done a lick of work this mornin'."

Reno shut his mouth.

Keeping his hands on his hips, Walker Chester glared, then, seeing Reno had gone mute, shifted the mountain of tobacco around in his mouth and walked to the coffeepot.

"I . . ." Reno hung his head. "I ain't gotten 'round to makin' no fresh pot this morn, either."

"Don't matter." The old man found a cup and filled it about half full of yesterday's brew, which might be, Reno figured, even older than that. "I been drinkin' cold coffee most of my life." That man could drink coffee, or beer, or whiskey, without removing the tobacco from his mouth. Most men would get sick if they swallowed just a bit of tobacco juice, but Walker Chester had to have a stomach made of cast iron.

Once the cup was empty, Walker Chester wiped his silver beard and stared at his boarder.

On his fattest and tallest day, Chester was half the size of Jed Reno. Everything about him was small, except his arms. Muscles bulged everywhere on those two limbs, and that man could handle a forge or a hammer better than any of those Union Pacific workers. His teeth were almost chocolate from chewing all that tobacco and the beard had been darkened from the juice at the corners of his mouth.

He wore a muslin shirt and thick denim britches, tall work boots, and a yellow-and-white-striped bandanna. A railroaders cap topped his head. Chester said he hailed from Missouri, before the war drove him west. He said he had moved to Lawrence, Kansas, until he was burned out by Quantrill's Raiders back in '63, and then he had kept moving west to Denver, hoping to find a fortune in gold. When that didn't happen he decided to head up to Laramie, where a Hell on Wheels was starting up. He had not regretted that decision at all. Fact was, he was always saying, he figured in all his life he had made only one mistake: He had invited

Jed Reno to bunk in a stall, corral, or hayrick anytime, whenever Reno felt the need or lacked the coins to get a cleaner, more comfortable place to sleep.

With cold coffee in his belly, Chester found the heavy work apron and pulled it on, spat a stream of juice onto the dirt floor, and limped toward the stables, mumbling something at Reno as he passed, then stopped and spun around—quick for a man his age, especially with that bad right leg he had gotten, he said, in Lawrence, taking a bushwhacker's lead ball as he ran to hide in a corn-field. His eyes sharpened and Reno felt his Adam's apple bob.

"What the devil did you do to your throat?"

Reno reached up and gently touched the scabbed-over cut across his throat.

He cringed at the touch of his big, gnarly, old mountain-man finger. It felt almost like that big, sharp, deadly knife was right there again.

"And the top of your forehead, too!" Walker Chester leaned closer and sniffed, as if he could smell blood—or maybe the scent of that wildcat who had gotten the jump on Reno last night and, for a moment, had come close to taking his scalp and cutting off his head.

"Awww." Jed started thinking up a lie. "You know how I get, pardner. A bit of whiskey—"

"You ain't never had a bit of whiskey, you fat, one-eyed ol' codger." Then he grinned that browned grin of his.

"But I'd hate to see the drunk railroad fool who thought you was too old and too fat to give 'm much of a fight."

Reno's heartbeat slowed down a tick or two and he

made himself grin. The lie came to him quickly. "Well, ol' hoss, I reckon I had too much forty-rod to recollect actually who wound up the better in that bare-knuckle wrasslin' match."

The livery owner laughed, turned, and again started for his chores.

"Some feller come in earlier this mornin'," Reno said, trying to make his voice sound natural. "Said somethin' 'bout a prison break down in Laramie City."

Walker Chester turned around and stared long and hard at Reno. Finally his head bobbed.

"Did that hombre mention your ol' pal the marshal?"

Reno made his head bob.

"Reckon you want to know iffen it's true." Chester spat again. "Well, I guess it is. Ol' Tim Colter has gone bad."

Reno's head shook and he made himself swear underneath his breath. "I just don't know how that could be."

"Ever'body can go bad, Reno. That's somethin' you might oughta remember."

Reno frowned as Walker Chester made his way toward the stalls. Finally he stood and followed the limping man.

They worked for a few hours, mucking stalls, feeding and watering horses and mules, inside the stalls, and then shoeing a couple of mustangs in the corral. Reno had never thought he would be a liveryman's helper, but jobs were scarce for old men his age, especially those with just one eye. Even if his pay was just a stall to sleep in, if one was available. But the goodness, the adventures, and the fights with railroaders and cowboys and those mule skinners—even the fight with that boxer whose boss man said if anybody could stay upright for three rounds, he would win fifty dollars. The boxer had only stayed up for two rounds against Jed Reno.

When the boss man said he only had thirty-seven dollars on him, the crowd let Reno and Chester take the money while they rode the two rapscallions out of Cheyenne on a rail.

They finished after three or four hours, and after that Walker Chester said he had done enough work and that he might as well find a saloon to cut the dust. Reno said he would join him later, but Chester shook his head.

"No, you ain't." Before the mountain man could object, the liveryman spat juice between Reno's moccasins. "You's aimin' to figger out some way to help that young whippersnapper of a marshal you tried to bring up to live the straight and narrow."

Reno thought about an answer but shrugged, shook his head, and muttered, "Well, I reckon I ain't the one to bring nobody up to live the straight and narrow."

"You tried, pard. You tried. He just turned out no good. Breaking a crazy killer like Mad Ben Gore out of that pen, and that renegade witch who trashed a mighty good saloon here in town. And that fool temptress. I reckon he busted her out, too. You get drunk if you wanna. There's a few stalls available and I ain't seen too many riders comin' into town today. Get drunk. Drunker than you ever got. And get some sleep. Do you some good."

He pulled off the apron, hung it on the nail, turned around, and stared long and hard at Reno.

"See you in the morn, unless you get some wild hair and go after that deputy pal of yourn."

Walker Chester was gone for maybe five minutes before Reno walked to the entrance. He really hadn't looked at the street all day. Usually Cheyenne was bustling. Trains stopped here every day on the UP and Denver Pacific lines, but the town seemed quieter, tamer. Reno thought about getting a horse and riding after Tim Colter, but he kept remembering what he had been told. *Stay here. Find out what was going on.*

Well, Walker Chester was out of sight and it sure looked like the owner of this place had been right. Nobody was coming to this stable, at least not until after sundown. Maybe some cowboys would ride in from one of the ranches, but usually cowboys just left their mounts at the nearest hitching rail or in an alley. Cowboys didn't make enough money to board a horse at a livery.

Reno moved back to the mound of hay. He kicked it and mumbled, "You can crawl out now."

Ginger Burricchia muttered something Reno couldn't understand, then pushed through the hay that had kept her hidden all morning and now into the afternoon. He could see her better now. Last night he thought she was the spitting image of Lucifer, but now he understood that she was a handsome woman, and a woman with a fine figure. Those dark eyes remained intimidating, but if she put on some clothes other than a dress Reno managed to swipe off a laundry line that was too big for her anyway, and she was wearing a pair of boots a drunken cowboy had left behind . . . That puncher had earned or saved or stolen enough money to pay for a stall, but then he'd swallowed far too much whiskey and had left his boots when he staggered out the next afternoon. He left his horse, too, because it wasn't his horse, and he told Reno and Chester that a feller named Holden would be by at some point with a bill of sale for the roan. "Just goes to show you," Reno recollected the young waddy saying, "that a jack high flush ain't that good of a hand when some other trickster has a full house, aces over queens."

Ginger Burricchia asked for a rag of wet water so she could get some of the dust and grime off her. Reno obliged her and waited. She looked even handsomer with her dark skin glistening with water.

She still held the big knife in her left hand, but now her face softened when she looked up into Reno's face.

"I am sorry," she whispered. "Do you believe me now?"

"No." He shook his head and pushed back his hat. "That's one thing I ain't never gonna believe."

"Mad Ben Gore is free. So is that big, evil woman. She was even identified as riding alongside your famous and brave and loyal and upright deputy marshal."

Reno shook his head again. "Tim Colter is as honest as I am a crotchety old fur trapper."

"You sure?"

His one eye locked on her and that hard Italian face softened.

To his surprise, Ginger Burricchia smiled at him. She didn't look so tough and hard when she smiled.

"You want to know something, old man?"

Reno did not answer.

"I don't think your partner knows what he's doing."

Reno couldn't remember the last time he had been unable to talk so little.

"I don't think he knows what he's getting into either," the pretty woman said. "What did he tell you before you two split up?"

The first words Reno recalled, but he did not say, were about trusting no one—and that would have included Ginger Burricchia. He kept his mouth shut.

"That's what I figured." Ginger Burricchia approached him, leaned close to him, and whispered, "I wouldn't trust anyone either. But I'm here to keep President Grant from becoming the second president to be assassinated by rotten Johnny Reb sympathizers. We have a mighty strong country, and a good country, but I'm not sure it can withstand two presidents being murdered in less than ten years. So we—you and me—are going to have to do something hard, something neither one of us will like, but it's the only chance we have."

"Who the devil—and what the devil—is you?" Reno asked, thinking to add: "Exactly."

"It's just like I told you last night when I deduced that you're too stupid and too dang loyal to this country to be involved in an attempt to murder President Grant. I work for Allan Pinkerton and it's my job—and now yours—to stop this conspiracy. And maybe we can figure out a way to keep your pal, the deputy marshal, alive, too."

Chapter 16

When Patsy Palmer reined the bay to a stop, Tim Colter stopped his gray and drew his LeMat. He had his thumb on the hammer and was ready to cock the revolver when he realized why the half-crazed woman had reined in. Colter didn't pull the hammer back, but he did not holster it either. Clucking his tongue and tapping the gray's sides, he eased up alongside the inmate he had sneaked out of the territorial prison. He was smart enough to keep the bay and its big rider a respectful distance from him.

"Reckon you see that," Patsy Palmer said.

Tim Colter wasn't blind.

"Them ain't pigeons, boss man."

Buzzards circled high in the cloudless afternoon sky. He tried to judge the distance, wet his lips, and let out a long sigh, for he was hoping, though the thought sickened him, that some wolves or coyotes had found the remains of the Secret Service man.

But if Colter's calculations were right, the Secret Service man had to be five or six miles farther north.

He eased out of the saddle and, holding the reins, walked ahead of Palmer and the bay a few feet, trying to estimate the distance again.

"Get down," he told Palmer without looking back at her. "We'll walk these horses a ways."

"I ain't much fond of walkin'," Palmer told him.

"Are you fonder of dying?"

"Well, lawdog, I talked you into gettin' me out of that stinkhole. Me a-sobbin' and carryin' on like I wanted that red-handed butcher Grant to live fer ever. Fooled ya."

She laughed. "I don't reckon Mad Ben Gore or my ol' pal Dugan gots no plans of killin' me. You gots me out of prison, Colter, but you didn't know what you was gettin' out."

Colter stared at her. "I wanted you out of prison. You're taking me to Dugan's Den."

She studied him long and hard, then shrugged and dismounted.

"Them there birds could be just eyein' a injured wolf or coyot'."

"Could be. And it could be that bunch that raided the prison last night."

She snorted. "I don't recollect no hosses passin' us last night."

"Because they took Jenkins Cutoff. The short way. And they rode their horses way too hard." He smiled at her. "Dugan's boys aren't as smart as we are."

They walked their horses a ways.

"Well, you might need a fast hoss, but I'll give you

fair warnin' that Ben Gore ain't no slouch when it comes to shootin' a man down with a long gun. I've seen him drop a feller seven-tenths of a mile away, and that feller was ridin' at a full gallop and Mad Ben was shootin' downhill to boot, with a strong southerly wind."

"What makes you so sure those birds aren't waiting to pick the bones of Mad Ben Gore and the boys who busted him out of prison?" Now Colter looked at the big woman. "Cheyenne haven't been overly fond of white folks of late. And the Sioux haven't been happy with us for longer than that."

Patsy Palmer wiped her mouth and then she looked at the buzzards. Then, without a word, she began walking north again.

Colter walked alongside her, looking at the ridgeline for any sign, studying the rocks for the reflection of a rifle or the ruffling of feathers on a Cheyenne or Sioux headdress. And then he would look at those buzzards.

And when the bay started getting closer to Colter's gray, he put his hand on the holstered LeMat's butt and said, without even glancing in Palmer's direction, "The path here's mighty wide. No sense in crowding my horse or me—unless you want to die suddenly."

Again Palmer laughed and moved off to the western side. She pulled the quid of tobacco from her back pants pocket and shoved it all in her mouth.

"Reckon you ain't got no tobaccy on ye?"

"You reckon right."

She shrugged. "Might be some unlucky traveler has one on'm a coupla miles up the trail that won't be needin' his'n no more."

Colter nodded. "Might be." He stopped long enough

to draw the Winchester from the scabbard before continuing north.

"Or it might be that prison ain't dulled Mad Ben Gore's senses of stayin' alive and he's got hisself an ambush planned and you'll be dead soon." She laughed and spat in the dirt.

"Might be," Colter said. "Might be that you'll be dead, too, just a second before I am."

They had climbed back into the saddles probably just less than a mile back when they discovered what had attracted the buzzards. By then some of the carrion had swooped down to live off the dead, but they all took flight when Colter and Palmer came into view.

Colter grimaced when he saw the corpses. They managed to get about forty yards from the dead men and horses before the gray and the bay began fighting bit and spurs, and Colter reined in and swung down, ordering Palmer to do the same.

"I don't plan on a-gettin' caught afoot and let 'em Injuns do to me what they done to my pards."

Colter had found the hobbles in one of his saddlebags and bent down to put those on the gray's forefeet. Without looking up, he said, "You don't get off that horse, he's gonna buck you into the rocks. With luck, you'll break your neck."

She dismounted and spat in his direction.

"We get caught afoot—"

He barked louder than she did. "We get caught on horseback we're as good as dead in this country. I haven't met a white man alive who can outrun a band of Cheyenne in their own country. Now I don't have hobbles for your horse, so if he gets away, I'll leave you afoot and you can see if your fat legs and fat head can outrun or outthink a Cheyenne war party."

He had to hear her cursing and complaining, but she did a good job of tying up the bay so he wouldn't be able to pull loose and get away from the dead, which were already beginning to stink in the high sun.

"You gonna give me a gun?" Palmer asked as they began walking slowly to the grisly scene ahead of them.

Colter did not have to answer. He pulled up his bandanna over his nose and his prisoner did the same.

The pony tracks—unshod—only came as far as the last dead man, whose back was filled with arrows and whose scalp had been taken.

Lucky for us, Colter thought, for he knew that had he and Palmer ridden into those Cheyenne, he and Palmer would be just like these dead men. Scalped, as was the custom of the warrior, with bodies filled with so many arrows they resembled porcupines.

He had to lift his bandanna over his mouth to spit out the awful taste as he looked into the terrible face of the last man, most likely, who was killed. His horse was killed, and he must have been wounded as he dragged himself toward the rocks. But there was no escape. There couldn't have been. There must have been at least twenty Indians on horseback, against maybe half a dozen men who weren't expecting to run into a Cheyenne war party.

But these men had not learned from Jed Reno, whose words ran through Colter's head.

You don't rides into nothin' till you knows what's

*you're ridin' into. And don't you never think you're safe
when you're in this country, cause Safe is about a thousand miles east of here.*

"Tarnation."

Kneeling over the dead man, hardly more than a boy
who was wearing Johnny Reb britches and what had
been a white-and-red-print cotton shirt, Colter looked
up as Patsy Palmer squatted by the bloated corpse of
another man in gray woolen britches.

"It's Rascal Griggs." Palmer turned and shook her
head at Colter. "I was married to him for 'bout six weeks
three years back." She shook her head, then something
caught her eye and she let out a Rebel cry and reached
down and brought up a brown square that had to be
chewing tobacco.

She blew him a kiss as she stood, her joints popping,
and nodded down at the dead man.

"I always knowed you really loved me," she told
Rascal Griggs and kissed the tobacco before shoving it
into a pocket.

"Looks like they rode right into 'em," she said as
she moved to another dead man.

Colter left the dead kid and the dead horse and joined
Palmer.

"They saw them coming," he said and pointed. "Half
of them rode to hide behind where half that ridge fell
down." Next, he nodded at the eastern side. "Most of
the others took their horses into that arroyo." He gave
the Cheyenne a nod of respect. "Whoever led the bunch
knew what he was doing. I think some of them took
their horses into the rocks, probably laid them on their

sides, and once Mad Ben Gore and his boys got past them, they came up on their horses to cut off any chance of escape."

After chewing on the tobacco in her mouth for half a minute, the big woman shook her head. "You make that chief sound like Stonewall hisself, or Robert E. Lee."

"No," Colter said deliberately, "because the Cheyenne head man didn't lose."

Her eyes hardened and she spat onto the top of his right boot.

"I don't like you, Colter."

He answered, "I don't like you either."

She laughed. "Yet you're gamblin' that I can get you close enough to Dugan's Den so that you can be a hero like Kit Carson or Dan'l Boone."

"I'm just doing my job."

"And not too good at it neither." She laughed, spat tobacco juice again, and put her hands on both hips. "That Cheyenne brave, chief, sergeant at arms, or whatever, he ain't quite won this war yet. Because ain't you noticed somethin' amongst all these dead pards of mine?"

Colter took a few steps back. He didn't trust Patsy Palmer—figured he never would—and he didn't want to give her even an inkling of a chance to surprise him. The big woman leaned against a boulder, then folded her arms across her chest and grinned a tobacco-clouded smile.

"Let's see how long it takes you, Per-fesser." She laughed.

Colter looked at a dead man, the blackened blood

thick around where he had been carved up with knives, lances, and tomahawks, and then he found another dead man.

Suddenly he turned, looking down the trail, then up. The Cheyenne had ridden north maybe thirty yards before turning west, and he saw another one of those holes in the canyon wall where they could have easily ridden through.

With the blessings of the Lord, that meant the Cheyenne probably weren't around these parts now. He didn't have to worry about them taking Patsy Palmer and himself by surprise and leaving them scalped and rotting in the dirt. But he had to worry about something else.

He walked to another dead man in gray trousers and used his boot to turn him face up.

Gray woolen pants. Gray Johnny Reb pants. That was what he saw, but what he didn't see was the black-and-white-striped uniform of a man who had been busted out of the prison down in Laramie.

"Mad Ben Gore," Colter whispered. "Where the devil is Mad Ben Gore?"

Chapter 17

"**D**on't rcckon he rode off with 'em Cheyenne, does ye?" Patsy Palmer let out a belly laugh and slapped her thigh.

Not a chance. Colter knew that much.

He took in the site of the fight, paying closer attention now. Three dead horses. Six dead men. If any Cheyenne had been killed, their companions would have carried them off. They would definitely have taken the three horses with them. But could Gore have escaped on horseback? Colter had to find out.

So he turned back toward Patsy Palmer and this time he aimed the Winchester at her.

That quickly removed that smart-aleck smile from her face, and he tilted his head to his right. "See that boulder?" he said.

Slowly, the big woman turned and did not look back. "Yeah," she answered in a heavy sigh, as though she knew what was coming.

"Climb up there—it's not that big or tall for a woman like you—and sit there."

She did not look back at him, but she worked up enough saliva to spit on the ground.

"Sit there and don't make a sound, and don't move, and sit there until I'm done."

"Done what?" Palmer spat out those words.

Colter answered by earing back the Winchester's hammer slowly. "Climb," he said, and Palmer did.

When she was settled atop the warm rock, Colter went to work, inching slowly across the battleground, reading the signs, remembering everything Jed Reno had taught him all those years ago—and what Colter had learned on his own through trial and error and surviving the wild and dangerous Western frontier for nigh thirty years.

Even Jed Reno, he knew, would have some difficulty in sorting out this scene. Somewhere between fifteen and two dozen Indian ponies. The surprised outlaws had not had much of a chance, but Mad Ben Gore was known for his luck.

After a half hour of studying the tracks of shod and unshod horses, moccasins, and boots, he walked to where they had tethered the horses. Colter returned the Winchester to his scabbard, removed his mount's hobbles, and gathered the reins to the bay and the gray. Leading the animals, he walked down the trail. By now the stink was thick and sickening and the horses wanted no part of it, but he used all his muscles, grinding his teeth, urging them to keep walking.

The Indians had cleared a path for their own mounts and Colter had bought two smart horses in Laramie.

They saw the way past the blood, the gore, and the dead, and Colter went into a jog and the horses readily followed him until they were past the carnage. Colter's luck not only held, it improved. The wind was blowing southeasterly, so once they had passed the dead men the stink wasn't as heavy.

"Where you goin'?" Patsy Palmer cried from her perch on the boulder.

Colter did not answer as he again hobbled his horse and tightly tethered the bay in a shady crack in the rocks.

He was sweating now, but he wiped his face with a shirtsleeve and looked back at his prisoner. She hadn't moved off that rock.

"Just keep right on doing what you're doing," he called out to her.

Again Colter studied the broken ground made by up to two dozen Cheyenne Dog Soldiers who were leading . . . how many horses?

An hour later he had figured it out. Four horses. That fit. Six outlaws were killed by the Indians. Could one of them—Mad Ben Gore—have been captured?

That wasn't likely, but for all Jed Reno had taught Colter, he couldn't tell if any of the shod horses had been carrying a rider.

After moving up and down the canyon for two hundred yards, south to north, north to south, even east to west and west to east, he found nothing else to help him figure out Gore's fate. Colter checked the sun's position and walked back to where he had left the horses. He had to think a posse would be after him, but once the posse reached this battlefield many of the deputized citizens would be resigning their temporary commissions and returning to Laramie City. He had to hope so anyway.

He brought a cupped hand to his face and called out to Palmer, "All right. Climb down and walk over here. We're riding on."

His voice echoed across the canyon, but that didn't worry him much. The ambush happened last night or early this morning. The dead couldn't hear. The Cheyenne were practically home by now. And Mad Ben Gore?

That was the one thing that concerned Colter.

Patsy Palmer started walking, stopped, bent, came up with her bandanna now pulled back up over her nose and mouth, and picked her path between the carnage. When she was out of the battle scene she stopped to catch her breath, shook her head, and pulled down the bandanna.

Slowly she walked, and by the time she reached Colter and the horses she was sweating and panting like an overheated dog.

"You tryin' to kill me, Colter?" she demanded. "I ain't built for walkin'. I'm built for lovin'." She laughed.

Colter did not smile. Instead he nodded at the bay.

"Mount up. We're riding north."

"Good." And when she turned back to her horse Colter drew the LeMat and cocked it.

Patsy Palmer froze.

"Before you get into the saddle why don't you pull that busted knife out of your boot top and pitch it into the rocks?"

She turned slowly, her face trying to register confusion.

"What knife?"

"The broken one—that's why the Cheyenne didn't take it—that was next to one of Dugan's cutthroats who got his own throat cut."

Palmer blinked, shook her head, and said, "I don't know what you're talkin' 'bout, buster."

"Maybe a bullet in your foot will remind you."

She read his face, then laughed and knelt. The knife blade came up slowly. It wasn't a bowie, but it would do the job even with the point broken about halfway up its ten-inch blade.

"I was thinkin' you was blind not to've seen it." She flipped it in the air and caught it by the handle. When she started to flip the knife again Colter brought up the revolver and shook his head.

"That's a poor pot to bet your life on, Patsy," he told her.

She froze, blinked, and tried to grin. "What you mean, buster?"

"That you can catch and throw that knife at me before I gun you down."

The face hardened and then she sidearmed the knife into the rocks. When she looked at him again she said, "I knowed I shoulda waited till it was dark and then just jammed that busted blade into you good and hard and twisted it whilst you begged for your mammy."

Colter pointed the barrel at the bay.

"And I thought you weren't stupid enough to think that I wouldn't have seen that knife in the dirt. Or missed you dropping out of sight when you stopped to pick it up."

She moved to the bay and a minute or two later was in the saddle.

"I'll kill you yet."

"I don't think so." Colter had already removed the hobbles from the gray. He pulled himself into the saddle and turned the horse north.

"After you," he said.

She let the bay carry her a few yards north.

When Colter reined up behind her, he said, "Ride slow."

"Don't worry," she said and laughed that awful-sounding howl again. "I ain't in no hurry to catch up with no Indian butchers."

They had ridden just a few miles when Colter began to figure out what had happened. Prints of a galloping shod horse showed up on the western side of the trail. One of the Cheyenne Dog Soldiers was following that trail, but the Indian was smart enough to keep his horse at a walk or a trot. From the signs Colter could read, Mad Ben Gore was running his horse into the ground.

"What a fool," he whispered and looked up the trail.

Patsy Palmer made no comment. She just spat tobacco juice at a beetle.

The main party of Cheyenne had ridden on the eastern edge, trotting and walking, confident.

When the canyon and trail bent west Colter saw the buzzards again.

That, he realized, could have been the dead Secret

Service man, but Colter again drew the Winchester from the scabbard and rode with caution. Once they neared the site he whispered to Palmer to rein up and keep quiet.

He remembered every detail about this part of the canyon. He knew where a man could hide and he knew how the ambushers had shot down the government official. The trail of the main body of Cheyenne and those horses, their trophies of battle, continued on. But that one rider had kept following the horse, which now lay dead and was providing an early supper for the carrion.

"I see a dead hoss," Palmer whispered, "but I don't see no dead Gore."

Colter did not respond until his eyes studied every crevasse, every boulder, every elk trail and path and the ridgelines.

"One of them must have been greedy for a scalp," he whispered. "The others were satisfied with what they had."

She hooked the well-chewed shreds of tobacco out of her mouth, spat, and pitched the remnants of her chaw against a rock.

"Young buck, I'd reckon," she said. "Wantin' to count his first coup."

Colter nodded.

"My money's on Mad Ben." She almost laughed too loud. "Five'll get you ten."

"Not my kind of bet," he said. He looked at a few buzzards, barely visible, perched on a high sphere, then at the circling birds.

Her horse whinnied and Colter tensed.

The seconds felt like hours, but finally the answer came.

Palmer heard it, too. Both looked to the west, and at that moment two big, black, ugly birds rose from the rocky fortress where Reno and Colter had found the dying man who set them off on this journey. Flapping winds sounded ominous as they rose toward the ridge top.

"That hoss ain't dead, pardner," Patsy Palmer said and chuckled softly.

"No," Colter whispered. "But those turkey buzzards were eating something in those rocks."

She stood in her stirrups and studied the terrain as best she could. Colter had the advantage over her. He knew where the Secret Service man was killed and he and Jed Reno had spent much time looking over the area. No one could say that Colter knew this part of Wyoming Territory like the back of his hand, but he had a good idea of where a man would set up an ambush.

"So who be you bettin' on, pardner?" Palmer bit off another chew. "An Injun or a tried-and-true Johnny Reb who ain't decided his cause is lost."

He wasn't about to answer that question. He already knew the answer. A Cheyenne would not have waited around. Young as he had to be, he would have taken his first scalp and loped off to join his comrades so they might sing songs about his bravery and let him regale them with stories about how he had killed his first enemy.

No, that had to be Mad Ben Gore.

But why had Gore stayed in those rocks? To ambush the posse that was in pursuit? If that were the case, the murdering swine had more confidence in Laramie City's posse than Tim Colter did. He deeply believed that once those men saw what had happened to the prison breakers, they would call that justice enough and already be halfway back to the UP town to brag about their bravery and glorious deeds.

"Get off your horse," he said and dismounted his own. He quickly found those hobbles again and began securing them to the gray's forefeet.

When he looked up Patsy Palmer still sat in her saddle, chewing the new tobacco and smiling down at him.

"I told you to get down," he told her.

"I heard ya," she said and then kicked her horse into a run, screaming, "It's Tim Colter, Ben! It's Tim Colter. Kill that son of—"

Chapter 18

The gray gelding reared up and grunted, but just once. He was too smart to try that again with his feet hobbled. Colter already had the stock of the Winchester braced against his shoulder. The bay carried the overweight, rough-hewn woman toward the rocks, and while hating to do it—and despising Patsy Palmer for making him do it—Colter pulled the trigger.

He had already levered another round into the chamber and moved toward the side of the rock wall, hardly watching the bay somersault four times after sending its rider crashing to the ground. Some people don't deserve the luck they are blessed with and Patsy Palmer was one of those. She could have been crushed by the dead horse, but she had been thrown clear. She could have smashed her brains and rib cage against the hard rocks, but she had landed on the ground churned up by Indian ponies and stolen horses. And when she came up on all fours she could immediately have been sent to the fiery pit by four bullets fired from a Winchester repeater.

Instead, Tim Colter let the bullets kick up dirt all around her. She backed her way until she had nowhere to go. Blood poured from her nose and mouth and her eyes were wide. The muzzle of the rifle probably looked like a cannon on an ironclad to her. Then a bullet ricocheted off the top of the boulder just over her head.

She flinched, cursed, and looked to the southwest.

"Ben!" she yelled. "Ya dern fool, it's—"

Another bullet left a white mark on the grayish-brown rock over her head after it shattered and whined.

Patsy sank down as low as she could.

For a moment Colter thought he had been mistaken, that it was a Cheyenne brave with a rifle on the high ground. And that Mad Ben Gore was dead.

The murdering cutthroat let him know the truth once the echoes of the gunshot and the ricochet drew their last hurrahs.

"Patsy?"

The name echoed almost as loud as the gunshots.

Pat-see . . . Pat-see . . . seeee . . . seeee . . . seeee . . . seeee . . . seeee . . .

"Is that you?"

You . . . you . . . you . . . youuuuuuu . . .

"Ben," she yelled when the echoes subsided, "Tim Colter's with me." She grinned. "But he's alone."

A-lone . . . lone . . . lone . . . lone . . . lone . . .

Silence came again, but Mad Ben Gore did not let it linger.

"Good."

Good . . . good . . . good . . . good . . .

"I'll finish him off . . ."

Off . . . off . . . off . . . off . . .

"And we can get our business done."

Done . . . done . . . done . . . done . . .

When he could only hear the wind, Colter breathed in and out. He fished out cartridges for the Winchester first, feeding them into the gate until it was loaded to capacity. Next he filled the LeMat's empty chamber with a cartridge.

"Guess you'll be dead right soon, lawdog," Patsy Palmer told him, speaking softly so her voice would not echo.

Her shriek, however, was loud, and it was still bouncing off the canyon walls after Colter had charged across the open ground, carrying the Winchester in both hands, right hand gripping the lever but his pointer finger not pressing on the trigger and his left hand around the barrel just below the front sight.

The forestock of the weapon connected with Palmer's head, splitting it open and driving her against the rock she had used as a backrest. Colter might have sworn that the sound of walnut meeting flesh and skull echoed, too, but knew that was far from likely.

He came up against the rock next to the big woman and dragged his feet and legs up tight against his stomach and chest.

No shot came. No curse. Nothing from Mad Ben Gore.

A minute eked by. Two. A few buzzards began circling again, waiting to see how many dead things they would have for supper.

After lowering the Winchester Colter put a finger and a thumb against Patsy Palmer's throat. He found a pulse but did not wonder how he would have felt had he not felt a beat. There was no time to shackle her and his handcuffs were in the saddlebags. It didn't matter. Palmer was not going anywhere. He did take time to unknot her bandanna and he even took time to tie it over the split in her forehead, which was already swelling with a massive bruise starting to form. She wouldn't bleed to death, though he had to think she would wish she had when she woke up.

Now Colter studied the ridgeline. He had to think. He found a spot and decided that was where Mad Ben Gore had fired the first shots. But that murderer was too smart to stay in one place, so which way would he go?

Colter remembered everything Jed Reno had told him after scouting around the area. A man that high on the move, well, he would have to watch his step. Trip over a rock or slip on loose stones and if he were too close to the edge, he would have a long, fatal fall into the rocks. And he would have to watch where he stepped anyway. That meant he likely could only keep an eye on what was happening below whenever he stopped.

The question then became nothing more than a guess.

Is Mad Ben Gore looking down into the canyon with a long gun at the ready?

Or is he walking to his next position?

Colter looked until he found the entrance to the natural redoubt where the Secret Service man was killed . . . and where the buzzards had flown away . . . and where a horse had whinnied.

He came to his feet then though still crouching, let his eyes and brain take everything in in a quick scan of the ridgeline, and then he exploded forward, almost feeling his racing heart pounding against his chest. Reaching the rocks, he dropped flat and waited.

Nothing.

He began crawling like a snake, slower than a rattler, and made it to the entry. He could see the hoofprints where the Indian had managed to get his pony through the opening. But Indians were magicians with any horse.

Colter moved cautiously. That was another thing he had learned as a lawman: You don't want to get caught beneath a man with a rifle. Shooting downhill was tricky. So was shooting uphill. But there was a reason military leaders wanted to hold the high ground. And Gore had that advantage.

Hugging the rocks closest to where Gore had been, Colter dragged himself till he saw the Indian.

Dead. The top of his head was blown off. Not old, probably in his early teens. His head was turned toward him, eyes open—at least the one Colter could see. No feathers. Arrows had spilled out of the beaded quiver on his back and the bow was a few feet away. The rawhide hackamore was wrapped around his left wrist and the horse stood over him. A good Indian pony. Real good. The blood did not trouble the horse. It was a pinto, brown and white, the head almost completely white. It stamped its left forefoot and snorted, trying to get his rider to stand again, to climb onto his back and ride like the wind.

Colter felt sorry for the horse—and its dead owner. A kid, really. But it took a miracle for anyone to live to see old age in Wyoming. Jed Reno had taught Colter that a long time ago.

He read the signs again the way Reno had taught him, but this trail was not particularly difficult, especially after all the years Colter had lived and all the trails he had followed.

After riding his horse to death Gore had found his way to the natural redoubt, and more than likely he knew of its existence. Gore had been in the territorial pen for a couple of years now. Maybe he had told Dugan about it.

He shook sense back into his head.

That doesn't matter. Don't play detective unless you want to die.

He heard the horse and looked at it.

The pinto now stared at him, but Colter only looked at the animal for a second. Then he started backing away.

"I'll be back," he whispered. "I'll be back for you, boy."

When he was out of the animal's sight he rolled over and turned around. Now he crawled with urgency. Gore had to have a horse and he wasn't a good enough rider to get this horse out of this carnival. The horse the outlaw would be going for would be the gray.

The question for Colter to figure out was which way Gore would come down. Colter had to guess he'd come down from the southern side. Slip around the back way. He wasn't betting any money on that, though, because Mad Ben Gore hadn't survived that long on the frontier. It was a guess. Nothing more.

When Colter came out of the rocky fortress he still hugged the rocky wall as he hurried back to the main trail. He stopped quickly, rolling onto his back and staring up to the northwest. That was where Reno and he had figured the assassin had put that bullet into the Secret Service man.

His racing heart hurt.

No, he decided, if Gore was in that position, Tim Colter would be having a palaver with Saint Peter. He had to be coming down the ridge from the other side. Coming to get Colter's gray.

Turning around, Colter moved as fast as he could.

He stopped when he came to the dead bay. The bravest of the turkey buzzards sat on the rocky wall on the eastern side of the pass. They all waited with grim patience, like all buzzards and vultures. There was a fine horse to eat. And there might be dessert, too.

A quick look at Patsy Palmer told Colter that she was still alive. He might have hit her too hard. She might never wake up. But that was her own fault. And Colter had more pressing concerns. He moved slowly to the corner and saw the buzzards studying him with some interest, but they did not consider him a threat. A few others kept circling overhead. Colter tried to look at the top of the ridgeline, but from here he didn't have a good angle or much of a view.

He drew in a deep breath, held it for a few seconds before exhaling and inhaling deeply but quietly. Then he raced across the trail till he was at another rocky wall. He slid into a tight crevasse and thought about how good a tumbler of good rye would taste right about then.

The urge to rise and look up proved powerful, but he fought it down and wiped his palms on his trousers. But this place was no good. He couldn't see much of anything and he needed to get a beeline on the gray. Because that was what Mad Ben Gore wanted.

His mouth felt like desert sand. The canteen was secured to the horn of his saddle.

He started to move when one of those buzzards saved his bacon. It launched itself into noisy flight and joined those circling overhead. Two or three others, though, remained perched on the rocks to Colter's right.

He listened, but the flapping wings drowned out every noise, even Colter's hard breaths. Realizing how hard he was breathing, he stopped that, too.

Colter waited. His ears strained for any noise.

"Ohhhhhhhhhhh."

He frowned. Patsy Palmer was coming to.

But then came another noise, and Colter put his hand on the LeMat. He lowered the Winchester to the ground, and when Patsy Palmer groaned again, he thumbed back the hammer to full cock.

Colter froze, tense, and listened.

The gray snorted as it walked. The clopping came closer.

Patsy Palmer groaned and cursed Colter softly, cursed her own stupidity, then called Tim Colter every vile word she likely knew.

The horse was getting closer.

And no horse, not even that gray, could get out of hobbles on its own.

The footfalls stopped. Patsy Palmer groaned, cursed, and groaned again.

"Psssssst."

Colter held his breath when he heard the whisper.

"Patsy?"

He waited, daring not to move, trying to make even his breathing as quiet as possible. But his heart beat so hard, he thought it sounded like one of those UP locomotives while pulling away from a depot.

"Ohhhhh, my head."

"Patsy."

"Somebody shoot me."

"Pssssst."

"Or give me a whiskey."

"*Where is he?*"

"Oh, God, just strike me . . . dead."

The whisper turned into a long curse and the steps came closer.

Colter closed his eyes, remembered something Jed Reno had told him.

Don't just see the land . . . feel it. Know it. Remember ever'thin' about it.

He had ridden through this country many times.

And he and Reno had just been here. He could see it clearly with his eyes closed. Where Patsy was. The width of the trail. The rocks, where the tallest part was. The turn that led to the redoubt. He knew this land. It was part of him. He heard the steps of a murderer and a fine gray horse.

The eyes came open. He breathed in and out and then he stood, bringing up the cocked LeMat and yelling, "Gore!"

Chapter 19

"**B**en!" Patsy Palmer screamed.

Tim Colter only heard her voice. He didn't see her.

"Look out!"

The verbal warning was not necessary. Men like Mad Ben Gore didn't live long in their line of work unless they had those proverbial eyes in the back of their heads or that sixth sense. The man who was dropping the reins of the gray gelding, spinning around, and bringing up his revolver. He must have shoved his long gun in Colter's saddle scabbard, preferring the short gun for this kind of work.

Colter felt the same way. Though he had made sure the LeMat's hammer was set to fire one of the .42-caliber rounds—not the massive grapeshot barrel, which would likely have peppered and perhaps even killed the gray.

He remembered a whooshing sound, something odd,

and there was one brief moment when he wondered what that wonderful noise was.

Bedlam soon replaced that sound.

Two shots sounded like one and Colter felt a blinding, searing pain across the right side of his neck. Somehow he managed to block out that pain and keep his muscles working. He staggered to the left. Ben Gore must have expected him to move to the right because Colter heard another gunshot but felt no impact of a bullet, no burning heat of a miss. The LeMat roared again. Colter felt the big gun buck in his hand, though he could not even recall cocking the single-action revolver.

Wind roared to his right. How he heard that over the blasting of firearms he wasn't sure. He stopped moving to his left, pushed himself to the right, and those instincts kept him alive, for another bullet whistled past him on the left. Colter's vision cleared. His nerves steadied. He felt like he was watching a dream he was in. A dream in which he was invincible, Achilles without the bad heel.

He saw Gore clearly, saw him staggering back, trying to bring up a Colt revolver. Blood covered his prison shirt. More of it spilled out of his mouth to be trapped in his thick beard. He saw the gray gelding—Colter's horse—loping away, not north or south but down the turn that led to the redoubt. He saw the gun in Gore's hand coming up to the killer's hip and then he heard his own revolver roar.

He stepped aside, out of the white smoke that almost burned his eyes, and aimed the LeMat again. It was already cocked. He aimed at . . . nothing.

His left hand caught the rocky wall. Colter didn't even remember starting to fall. His tongue tasted gunpowder and his nostrils burned from the scent. His ears rang and he remembered that strange noise that drew his attention before chaos broke loose.

Colter looked into the blue sky and knew what the noise was. Those buzzards had taken flight, and now most of them circled the blue sky over his head.

Looking up made him feel dizzy. He shoved the LeMat into the holster, missing completely. The heavy revolver dropped into the dirt, but Colter did not pick it up. That kind of thinking—or laziness, he realized later—could have gotten him killed. He had to lean against the rocky wall for support and inched his way out of the crevasse.

His left hand clasped against his neck, feeling the stickiness, the thickness, and the warmth of his life's blood.

When he cleared his hiding place he leaned against the warm rocks. With his right hand he wiped sweat off his forehead. Swallowing hurt. He shook the cobwebs out of his head—or tried to—but that just caused more pain in his neck that almost dropped him to his knees.

When he saw the body lying face up in the dirt, he reached for the LeMat that no longer was there. He forgot where he had put his rifle.

He blinked again, wiped his forehead, too, and looked at the bloody corpse.

Colter had only seen Mad Ben Gore's likeness on the Wanted dodgers posted in the offices of lawmen across the territory. Never in the flesh. He had read the descriptions in newspapers—as though those were accurate—and had heard stories of two women, one stagecoach driver, and three deputy sheriffs who said they had run across him, been waylaid by him, come this close to capturing him. But some other lucky dog had caught that piece of man-killing trash and collected that big reward.

Movement grabbed his attention and he spun, reaching once again for a weapon that he didn't have.

Patsy Palmer was on her knees, sliding across the dirt toward the man Colter had just killed. She stopped when she knelt over him and sighed. Finally she turned and stared up at Colter.

"You done it. You kilt him."

"Wasn't . . ." He cringed at the pain just saying those two syllables caused. His lips parted, but he decided not to speak. There wasn't much he could say anyway. Not that that would pacify a woman as hard and as heartless as Patsy Palmer.

"Well," Palmer said, "what now?"

Colter was standing. He had been anyway. Now he knew he was on the ground, his back against boulders, his legs stretching out toward the man he had killed and the woman who was probably waiting to kill him.

Not that he had any way to stop her. His LeMat lay in the dirt somewhere, along with the Winchester. He might have a chance to get his pocketknife out of his pants pocket, but by the time he had one of the two blades open his brains would be spilling onto the sand to mingle with Mad Ben Gore's blood after Palmer bashed his head open with a rock.

He saw nothing but sweat-filled blurs for a few seconds, then a not-too-clear Patsy Palmer came back into focus.

Why doesn't she finish me off?

She wasn't even looking at him, at least not in the eye. He didn't want to turn his head because the pain would likely send him into unconsciousness, but his eyes moved, over then down, and he saw what had fallen right next to his right hip.

Mad Ben Gore's long-barreled Colt Peacemaker.

How many shots had the outlaw fired? Three? More than that?

Maybe not six, and a desperate man like Gore wouldn't likely keep one chamber empty for safety measures. Colter's right hand went down, and the walnut grip gave him strength.

He heard Palmer swear, then spit, as he brought the revolver up and braced the revolver on his thigh. To him, it seemed like it took a month of Sundays just to pull back the hammer to full cock.

"You . . ." Pain silenced him, but he had to speak. ". . . want to live?"

Palmer spat, but she wasn't chewing tobacco.

"All I got to do is wait you out, pilgrim." She grinned, then howled like a wolf. "You'll either bleed out or pass out. Then I'll be on my merry way. After I spit in your dead or dyin' face."

He didn't hear a word she said.

"Get a fire going," he told her. "Take that dagger out of Gore's boot top." He turned just enough that the pain didn't knock him out but that she could see the gash the bullet had torn. "You're going to cauterize this."

She laughed and spat saliva toward his boots.

"Give me a knife that close to your throat, pardner, and I'll do more than cauterize that li'l ol' scratch you got cuttin' yerself a-shavin'."

"Get a fire started now," he said. "Cauterize the wound."

"No." She shook her head, which hurt, and she almost bent over. Gasping, she straightened, and he saw the tears of pain running down her dirty cheeks.

"Cauterize the wound," he said when she seemed to have recovered.

She did not laugh this time, but she did smile.

"I wouldn't trust me with no knife right now, pardner. Thanks to you."

He waited. She laughed and tried to find her chaw of tobacco but gave up and leaned toward him. "I'm gonna watch you die."

The barrel of the .45 took her attention.

"You'll be dead before I am," he whispered hoarsely.

Now her face changed.

"You're bluffin'," she said softly, then made herself laugh to convince her of the truth of what she had just verbalized. "You're a lawman. You can't just . . ." She paused, reconsidering, as she stared at his cold eyes.

"If that knife slips to a place I don't like . . ." He wasn't sure how much longer he could keep talking. If he passed out, he was dead. Well, he figured he was pretty much dead now anyway.

"If I . . ." The dizziness almost capsized him.

The gray snorted and stamped one of its feet.

". . . If I don't like anything about you, you're dead."

She tried to smile, but he aimed the pistol at her big chest.

"If you don't do . . ." He stopped just long enough to swallow and to steady the heavy Colt. "If you aren't getting a fire going in the next five seconds, I'll kill you where you sit."

For a big woman, Patsy Palmer moved fast. That surprised him. She gathered buffalo chips, dried grass, horse droppings. She dumped the makings from a sack she pulled out of Mad Ben Gore's vest pocket and found some matches in another pocket.

In a moment she had a fire going, which she kept going and growing as she added twigs and more buffalo chips.

Colter kept the revolver on her the whole time.

She lay Gore's dagger into the flame and he watched the shining blade turn over. He could almost feel the heat. When she lifted the knife from the fire and came on her knees toward him, he lifted the blade toward his bloody neck, then stopped.

Their eyes met.

"This is gonna burn worser than the devil's bad likker," she whispered. "And I don't want you to accidental-like pull that trigger when I stop that bleedin'. So do you mind puttin' that hogleg down a bit whilst I save your worthless hide?"

"You better try your best," he said and knew he couldn't hold up the heavy Colt for much longer, "and be as gentle as you can."

Their eyes held for two seconds.

She swore under her breath. "I'm a-bettin' that we both die right about now."

The fiery blade landed on his neck.

Colter thought he heard himself scream. And then he felt, and saw, absolutely nothing.

Chapter 20

Storm clouds had blown up way over to the west and Kip Jansen studied the horizon for a long time. The way it looked to him, admittedly no expert when it came to reading or predicting weather, those thunderheads weren't coming his way. He could barely hear the thunder and he had seen lightning flashes that looked a lot deadlier back in Alabama. What those clouds were doing right then, though, was blocking the sun.

There was plenty of daylight and he could put a few miles behind him, so he tightened the wrappings around his ankle, grimacing at the pain, and grabbed all his plunder before he used that fancy stick to get back to a standing position.

He drew in a deep breath, held it, and took a tentative step toward the trail, then another. Either he was getting tougher or his ankle was turning number—maybe a bit of both—but he could go a bit farther now before having to stop to let the pain subside or for him to catch his breath.

Kip had no idea how long he had rested. He had been so worn out, he just sat down and fell asleep. Now he certainly felt awake. He could see where he was going and the wind in the canyon was cooler, thanks to those dark clouds miles and miles to the west.

This time he wanted to get as far as he could. That meant he had to ignore the fiery pain in his left ankle and leg. He didn't want to stop to drink water because he wanted to preserve as much as he could. He remembered that story from one of those half-dime novels in which the thirsty hero would stick a pebble in his mouth to work up saliva. He tried that but couldn't tell for certain if it worked.

What worked, he thought, was moving. Going south. When the pain in his lower left leg became too intense he focused on the pain his newfound crutch was causing. Sometimes that stick felt like it would dislocate his shoulder. When the blisters on the palms of his hands became too painful he stopped just long enough to tear a strip off the bottom of his shirt and use that as a bandage. He took a small swallow of water and tested his hand on his crutch.

The pain lessened by a mere fraction as he began moving again, but that reprieve did not last long. This time he tried to block out everything. He just wanted to move. Move. Keep going. Get closer to . . . people . . . a town . . . Morgan County, Alabama.

How long he walked he had no idea, but now he had been sweating for some time and the wrapping around his mangled palm had fallen into the dirt a long time ago. Kip bit back pain as he pulled his blistered, blood-ied hand from the fancy stick. Somehow he managed to lean the stick against the boulder that kept him up-right. Sweat poured down his head, burning his eyes, and he had to fight the urge to open a canteen and bathe his face.

His lungs burned for oxygen, but the more he breathed in and out the worse he felt. When his vision finally cleared he turned west and saw that those thunderheads had moved on, well down the canyon now, and in a bit he wouldn't even be able to see them.

The sun? Well, that he could see, but he figured luck was on his side just a wee bit because that orange ball would be below the ridgeline in . . . ?

An hour? Two?

He realized that he had pushed himself too hard. That kind of mistake could get him in serious trouble. It could get him killed. It hurt to reach across his chest to find the strap of one of his canteens, but he managed to bring it around and he removed the stopper, then struggled to bring it to his lips.

Not too much, he told himself.

He almost did not listen, but a coughing fit stopped him from drinking more and he managed not to spill but a few precious drops when he up-ended the con-tainer. The strap bit into his neck and the canteen banged against his side. The hat dropped to the ground and he wondered if he would have the energy to bend over to pick it up.

Kip's eyes closed, and when they opened he was staring across the trail. His legs stretched out in front of him and his back was braced against a rock. He must have been sitting on his hat, but at least the canteens were upright and capped. Sighing heavily, he leaned his head back and—

He said something again that would have had his mama threatening to wash out his mouth with soap. His head hurt. He had leaned back and felt the granite or sandstone or just a big chunk of earth connect hard against the back of his poor skull. Gently he brought up his right hand behind his head, cringing when he felt a knot that was already starting to form. At least he didn't feel any blood.

Sighing, he wondered for just a moment if he should just sit right here and die.

His muscles ached. His feet hurt. The make-do crutch had rubbed his left underarm raw and his left hand was badly blistered. He breathed in deeply and tried to soften his exhale so his ribs and chest would not hurt so much.

He also stank to high heaven.

But . . . He thought he heard his mother's voice. *You are alive.*

He told himself that he would not fall asleep again. He would just close his eyes for a moment. Just rest a bit. He could get up and cover another mile or two at the least. Then he would need to stop and sleep for a few hours. Till the moon rose. That was what he needed to . . .

A horse snorted and he knew he was dreaming. But when some unintelligible words followed, and then laughter, Kip's eyes jerked open. He gasped at the sight before him. This had to be a dream—a nightmare.

He was still sitting in that canyon, his back against the boulder, and while it was darker than it had been when he must have drifted off to sleep, he could still see.

Kip looked to his left and right, finding more riders. He had nowhere to go, no place to run. He looked north to east to south, counting as quickly as he could. Ten. Ten? No. There were more than ten riders. He could make out some behind those who had corralled him.

The laughter stopped and one of the riders slipped off the back of his dark-colored pony. He was an Indian. They were all Indians. Kip knew that much. This one was dressed in nothing but a breechcloth and moccasins and some white- and yellow-boned breastplate that was decorated with black feathers and brass beads. He carried a lance, long and lethal, with a blade Kip could already feel ripping into his flesh.

But the Indian just used that as a pointer and he was pointing it at Kip's crutch.

He barked something in guttural words.

Kip looked at his crutch, then back at the Indian, who pulled away the lance and spoke to the rider in the middle.

That was who Kip decided to focus on. He seemed not much older than Kip, and he wore fine moccasins decorated with fringe and red, yellow, and green beads, soft leggings that were also fringed and beaded, and a smooth leather shirt. Around his throat was a colorful necklace and his hair hung in long braids. The face was oval, dark, the nose Roman, the eyes black like his hair. He carried a rifle, one of those Winchester repeaters Kip had heard called a Yellow Boy because of the brass-like part where the bullets went in.

This time the one with the lance pointed his finger at Kip's crutch. The one with those dark eyes just looked at Kip. He said nothing.

The one with the lance grunted something, shifted the lance, and reached suddenly for the fancy stick.

He was going to take it. Leave Kip crippled and without a way to walk. He'd have to crawl all the way to Laramie City. He would . . .

Another thought struck him. *If they don't kill me.*

And what were the chances of that?

But when the Indian's hand grabbed the crutch, Kip lunged, managing to knock it down, and then he fell on top of it, covering the crutch with his body.

The noise from the Indians surprised him. They laughed. Those deep, throaty words came flying out between hoots, but then something kicked Kip in his side and he cried out in pain. The second kick managed to turn him over and he saw the one with the lance glaring at him. He tossed the lance to another rider, who caught it like an expert.

Kip tried to move on his back, but his left ankle stopped that. He yelled, and when the Indian on foot kicked his thigh he screamed again. The Indian came toward him and grabbed the stick, started to jerk it out of his hands. But Kip pulled back and the Indian's fingers must have been slick with sweat or something because he lost his hold on Kip's crutch and fell onto his hindquarters.

That caused even more laughter from the rest of the Indians, who backed their horses away a foot or more. And Kip tried to push himself back against his rock.

The Indian on the ground roared, and this time he pulled a long, dark knife from a beaded and fringed sheath. He said something in that hard language, and this time when he came toward Kip, he wasn't after the crutch. He was coming in for the kill.

But the leader, the young one, said something that caused the warrior with the knife to stop. He turned, spoke again, and spun around. Kip tried to pull up his legs to make himself into a ball, but he could only get the right leg to move. The Indian came closer, but this time when he stopped his eyes fell onto Kip's left leg. Suddenly the copper-skinned man grinned. His teeth were crooked and yellow.

He turned and spoke to one of his comrades and then faced Kip again and took another step. His right foot fell onto Kip's left ankle.

Kip screamed. The back of his head struck the rock again and the Indian lifted his foot and pressed down on it again. The pain almost caused Kip to vomit. Tears practically blinded him. The Indian's foot came off, but that did not lessen the pain, and now the Indian was raising his right leg high and Kip knew what was coming. The Indian was going to smash his foot down on the ankle. Kip could already feel the agony.

"*Éneoestse!*"

Kip's eyes remained tightly closed. He felt as though time had frozen, but the eyelids lifted and he saw the brave still standing, but his right leg lowered and he turned to face the young leader. *Is he a chief?* Kip wondered. Mighty young to get that rank.

"*Éneoestse*," the young man said, but softer this time, and now he handed the braided hackamore to the rider on his left and slipped off his fine horse.

The one who was primed to smash Kip's ankle barked something and again pointed at the fancy stick, but the young one uttered more strange syllables and the vicious Indian backed away toward his own horse.

Now Kip stared up at the young leader, who pointed at the fancy stick.

Kip looked at it and then stared into the young brave's impenetrable eyes.

"I need it," Kip told him and motioned at his bad ankle.

The words meant as much to the Indian as the Indian's had meant to Kip.

So the Indian brought up his hands, and they move rapidly, fingers doing this and palms that, and Kip was lost after just a few seconds. He had heard about sign language, but it was as foreign to Kip as French, Spanish, or Russian.

He shook his head when the Indian stopped speaking with his hands.

"I . . . I don't . . . I don't understand."

The Indian frowned. He pointed at the stick and spoke again.

"I don't . . . I . . . don't understand," Kip repeated.

So the Indian bent down and grabbed the staff of what had become Kip's crutch. He lifted it, but Kip pulled it back. The Indian just stared long and hard, and when he lifted the stick again Kip released his fingers and saw his one chance of saving his own life go away.

Maybe, he thought, *they'll kill me quick.*

The young Indian rose to his full height and looked down at Kip. He said something, longer sentences this time, then turned to some of his riders and spoke to them. They all nodded—except for the mean one, but when that one started to talk he stopped, drew in a deep breath, and exhaled. The young one waited, but the mean one said no more.

So the Indian squatted again, and this time he handed the fancy stick back to Kip.

This had to be a trick, Kip thought, but he swallowed and slowly felt the hide of the shaft and saw the feather in the center move with the breeze. He pulled the stick closer.

The Indian knelt before him and motioned with his hands, as if he were begging for food.

Kip opened his mouth, but the only words he could say were those he had been saying. "I don't understand."

The Indian pointed at Kip, then at the stick, then pointed at Kip again, and then at himself. He said something.

Kip studied him, and a thought struck him.

"You want to . . . trade?"

The Indian's head cocked sideways. He said the same word he had spoken moments ago.

"Trade?" Kip asked.

The Indian sighed. He might be getting impatient. So Kip twisted. What did he have to trade for a crutch that might save his life? What did he have of value? No gun. Two canteens, but he couldn't give those away. He needed them. A crutch would help him walk, but water meant life.

He saw the sack, though, and his stomach almost turned over. That would be a really bad trade, but what else did he have?

So he pulled the sack toward him, then held it out toward the young Cheyenne—if he were Cheyenne. Shoshone? Arapaho? Crow? Sioux?

Tentatively the Indian took the bag and brought it closer. He shook it, hearing the slight rattle.

Kip motioned with his hands. "Eat," he said and pretended to reach into an invisible sack, pull out a pecan, and eat it. Then he grinned and rubbed his belly.

All of the Indians laughed at that—except, of course, the mean one. Well, the young one didn't laugh exactly, but his eyes beamed with delight and his lips turned upward in a smile.

Kip held his breath as the young brave worked the drawstrings and dipped his hand hesitantly into the sack. He pulled out half a pecan and smelled it.

Again Kip made the motion of eating it.

The Indian stared.

Kip had another horrible thought. Stuart Benjamin didn't like pecans. Back in Decatur, he told Kip that he was allergic to those nuts. One bite, he said, would send him to the doctor or the boneyard.

Kip froze as the Indian put the nut in his mouth. He chewed. Kip waited.

Then the Indian's lip turned upward and he nodded with delight. He tightened the drawstring and moved toward his horse. One of the riders reached down for the sack, but the leader barked roughly at him and then slapped away the greedy hand.

A moment later he was on the back of his horse.

Kip watched the mean Indian glaring at him, but then he moved to his horse, leaped onto its back, and reached out for his lance. That one rode away first and Kip was glad not to see him anymore.

The others began backing their horses, turning them north.

The sun was gone now. The young leader let his horse walk closer to Kip. He nodded at the stick, then held up the sack of nuts and shook it, smiling at the rattling, before turning his horse to follow the others.

Before he kicked the pony's sides he looked down on Kip one time.

His head bobbed once. Kip nodded back.

Then the Indian said, "Trade" and galloped after the others.

Chapter 21

Jed Reno knew why he didn't care a whit for Cheyenne—or any city. There were far and away too many people, and the problem as Jed saw it was that all those men and women—and even kids now, by thunder—weren't far enough away.

He had heard someone say that the city had more than three thousand permanent residents—permanent breathing residents, not counting any of those planted in cemeteries. Six UP trains arrived and left every single day, and now that the Denver Pacific Railroad came here, too, there were two other trains coming in and pulling out each day. Then there were the stage-coaches, just coming and a-going, some bringing mail, some just passengers.

Jed never had spent much time observing the goings-on in Cheyenne. He just did a few menial chores at Walker Chester's livery when he had a mind to, or had himself a rip-roaring drunk at one of the saloons. But now he studied the signs. Not that his reading amounted to much, but the big wooden gun over the awning told him that that place was a gun shop. And he could peek inside a window or through an open door to figure out a grocer's or a place to buy clothes and other duds. Hat stores and crockeries and even a place that sold heating and cooking stoves. He heard a man with sleeve garters tell a middle-aged woman that he was a wholesaler and retailer with more tin, copper sheet iron, and holloware than you could shake a stick at. There were two coffin-makers, though one of those also made cabinets, and he remembered the days when men—there were few women here in those days, except for squaws—got planted with what they were wearing when they died, though if the dearly departed had a bedroll, they might wrap him up in that for his eternal sleep.

There was a place with nothing but books—*books!*— on the shelves and newspapers on the tops of countertops. Doctors and tooth-pullers. Bakers and druggists. And if you didn't have a place with a roof over your head, you could be like that feller across from the land agent who was selling a patented post-hole auger, guaranteed to dig through soil, roots, or bedrock—and he was the only licensed agent in the entire Wyoming Territory.

Well, he had walked up and down every street in town as near as he could tell. Been into six livery stables and somehow managed to stay out of the dozens of saloons that peppered Cheyenne like bird shot. And he didn't think he had learned one blessed thing about anyone wanting to kill the president of the United States.

His feet hurt. There had been a time about a thou-

sand years ago when Jed Reno could walk up and
down peaks fourteen thousand feet high, ford raging
streams afoot in the spring, fish beavers out of traps
and drag those sopping wet carcasses back to camp,
and fight two or two dozen angry Blackfoot Indians on
the trail back to his camp. Smoke a pipe, eat some
supper, crawl under his bearskin, and then wake up
before dawn and start another day.

Now he wanted to find a place where he could soak
his aching feet—if he could get those blasted moccasins off.

He stopped at the next street corner, watched a
buggy go by, saw the men lighting the streetlamps again.
That got him thinking that he had not seen Ginger
Burra-something-another since they had separated. He
had asked her where they would meet again and she
had said she would find him. He had asked her what
time they would meet and she had told him that he'd
know when she found him.

Women. They weren't any funner than those Black-
feet and Crow he had known in his younger, wilder,
more mobile years.

Well, he might as well go back to Walker Chester's
livery stable. If Ginger needed him, she could look for
him there. Reno turned down the street to the pie shop,
then cut down the alley. That, he knew, was the quick-
est way to get to the livery—and sometimes that pie
man made the mistake of leaving a huckleberry one on
the back bench for cooling.

No luck this time, but Reno decided his feet hurt too
much to eat anything sweet anyhow. Whiskey was what
he needed.

He saw the end of the alley and quickened his pace, but suddenly slowed when two men stepped into the alleyway and walked toward him. They wore linen dusters and black slouch hats, but it was their boots he noticed. Cavalry boots, poorly made and patched, but the tops had three letters stitched in a rough buckstitch.

Jed Reno couldn't read a lick, but he wasn't stupid. He had figured out in this very alley that "P-I-E" spelled "pie." He knew from Tim Colter's badge that "US" spelled "United States," and he had seen the letters on the uppers of those boots to know that those meant trouble:

CSA

They stopped, smiled underneath their thick mustaches, and the one on the left pushed up the brim of his hat, while the one on the right tossed the tail of his duster behind his gun belt. He did not reach for the revolver but hooked his thumbs in the belt.

"Howdy," the one on the left said.

"Evenin'," Jed said when he stopped a few feet in front of them. They did not move to let him pass, and the alley was small.

"Where you been, old-timer?" the one on the right said before explaining, "We been looking for you practically all day."

"You found me." Experience told him this was not going to end well—for two punks who had fought to destroy these United States and her territories.

The one on the left now pushed the tail of his duster to make his silver-plated pistol easier to reach.

"Where's that raven-haired gal you were cozin' up to

at Chester Walker's livery stable this mornin'?" he asked.

"Walker," Reno corrected, "Chester. That's his name. Not the other way around."

"Well, we're new to Cheyenne, ya hear?" said the one on his right. "Come over from Missouruh by way of Georgia. The woman?" There was no friendliness in his eyes or voice now.

Reno shrugged. "Ain't seen her since this mornin'. Now I'm tired and want to hit the hay."

"Well," said the one on his left, "it's you who's a-gonna be sleepin' if you don't start tellin' us what we want to know. Ya hear?"

Reno studied the two men without moving a muscle and barely moving his eye. It was like that time in '41 when the two Shoshone caught him alone at South Pass. 'Course he was a lot older and heavier now than then, but those two Shoshone had been spry and much more dangersome than these two punks from Missouri by way of Georgia.

He breathed in and out, sighed, and shrugged. "I hear," and he turned to point, then swung around and slammed his forearm against the side of the one on his right's head.

That knocked him, as he was starting to draw his revolver, into the one on the left, and they both toppled into the dirt.

Back in his younger days he would have let the two men start to get up and then his right leg would have flown up and caught one of them in the chin, and when that leg touched down his left would have smashed the other one's nose. But he couldn't do that kind of dance anymore, so he did the next best thing. He leaped off his feet and crashed down on the nearest one.

That, Reno realized, might not have been the right way to attack this situation. Oh, his bulk and his hard head, which had smashed into the gunman's nose, mashing flesh and cartilage and snot, would send that fellow to a painful sleep for a while. But it had also come close to knocking the wind out of him and Reno was hurting in places he had long ago forgotten about.

There was another CSA man with a gun, too, and Reno couldn't just lie there trying to get up. He had to get up. Quickly.

He managed to get to his knees despite his rapid breathing and pounding heart and hurting head and saw the other man coming up with his own revolver.

Reno faked his left, which almost took his shoulder out of its socket, but the ruse worked and the man flinched just long enough for the one-eyed man's other hand to take hold of the wrist of the arm that held the six-shooter. He squeezed and twisted and the man cried out as the bones snapped, and the gun—which the slow-as-molasses Confederate raider had not even cocked—toppled onto the rat dung and brown sod that ruled Wyoming Territory.

The gunman cried out in pain and Reno gave him a hard shove. When the man went down Reno lunged forward and fell on top of him. He heard the whoof of breath rush from the man's lungs. He saw the man's tanned face turn white. He felt the vomit as the man threw up all his whiskey and breakfast and steak for supper.

When the gunman's eyelids opened Reno let his forehead crack against the Johnny Reb right between the eyes. The man broke wind, wet his pants, moaned, and fell into an ugly unconsciousness that would hurt even more when he woke up.

Jed Reno lay there for a long, long while. He thought he might just sleep there, but then he remembered Ginger. These owlhoots were looking for her. He needed to find her to warn her, and he made himself stand.

Well, not stand, but he was on his knees. He peered up the alley. The street was maybe fifteen yards ahead and people kept walking right on by, north-south or south-north, and no one even took a peek down the alley. Perhaps they were in a hurry to get home because it was getting dark now.

Somehow Reno found a way to stand and then he leaned against the big trash barrel next to a side door of some Cheyenne business. What outfit this was he had no inkling, except he was certain it didn't belong to the post-hole auger peddler.

Those two Reb ruffians wouldn't be troubling anyone for a long time, so he found an overturned crate and sat on it. When it didn't crash underneath his weight he figured his luck was changing.

Then he felt the cold steel of a revolver's muzzle pressed against his left ear.

"You're good, old man." The Southern voice had the same effect of a thousand tons of ice. "But not good enough."

Jed Reno sighed and raised his hands as high as his arms would take them.

"Yeah?"

"Where is . . . ?"

"Mister," he told the man who held the gun at his head, "I ain't seen hide nor hair of that petticoat since I walked out of Walker Chester's livery this morn. Like I tried to tell 'em two hardheads. All I want to do is get back to my stall so I can sleep—and maybe when I wake up I'll figger out that this was just a real bad dream."

"When you go to sleep," the man said, "when you wake up you'll find yerself in hell."

That, to Jed Reno, sounded like a sixty-day furlough—if "furlough" meant what he thought it meant.

Chest heaving, sweat swimming out of pores he didn't know existed, he tried to catch his breath before he looked down the muzzle of a .44-caliber Remington revolver.

The wiry man whispered in a tobacco-tarnished breath, "I'll give you ten seconds to start tellin' me where that lady spy has got herself hid."

"Mis-ter," he breathed.

"Jed Reno!" a shrill voice cried out, and the man fell back, a professional, keeping his eyes on both Reno and the slim, gray-bearded feller in stinking buckskins and mismatched boots.

"As I live and breathe." He clapped both hands hard on Reno's shoulder, and Reno tried to remember which rendezvous he had seen this old cuss.

"Mister." The Confederate traitor waved his gun at the person Reno couldn't quite place. Harry Flint at Henry's Fork in '25? Nah, Harry froze to death six years later. Little Adorno at the mouth of the Popo Agie in '38?

"Don't ye remember me, hoss?"

The runt turned, not even noticing the cocked Remington in that cur's right hand and laughed. "Ain't that like this ol' reeperbate?" He howled like a coyote.

"Mister," the Reb said, "you can have your beaver-trappin' pard after I'm done—"

He didn't finish the sentence because that little runt was wearing something on his fingers, something shiny that went crunch when the little fellow's fist slammed into the man's forehead.

The Remington slipped perfectly out of the falling man's right hand into the little one's left. Then the little stranger rose and somehow managed to pull Reno to his feet.

"Let's get out of here," the runt said. "I've got a place where we can talk in peace."

Reno wasn't that out of sorts. "No," he insisted. "No. Ginger's in trouble. These bushwhackers are after her. We gots to find her before somethin' bad happens."

"You bloody idiot." That voice Jed Reno recognized. "I'm Ginger Burricchia!"

Chapter 22

Reno followed the little runt who said he was Ginger the Pinkerton man . . . woman. At least he tried to keep up with her as she jerked off her hair and mustache and beard and slammed them into a waste bucket in the stinking alley before she took off running again. Jed Reno was heaving and hurting for breath when he found her stopped between two water barrels on the side of the café that attracted only the cowboys and the soldiers and the drunks and the women of the tenderloin.

She was pulling off her trousers now, and Reno gawked.

"What? Don't you—" He ran past her and opened up his jacket as a curtain just in case someone turned down the alley and saw this woman in her unmentionables.

He heard Ginger's laugh, but that quickly died.

"Did you recognize those men?" she asked.

He shook his head. The street was just ten yards ahead of them, but so far no one had crossed from the café to the saloon. "Did you?" he managed to ask.

"I wasn't looking too hard at those curs. I was trying to save your hide. I told you that I'd meet you at the livery when I could."

He nodded, then remembered that she probably wasn't looking at him. And he definitely wasn't looking at her until he was sure she was presentable. "But I tol' Tim that I'd try to find out what I could about this plot to kill the gen'ral, I mean, our president."

Ginger Burricchia had managed to get her breathing under control. "You trust Tim Colter?"

Now he turned to face her. "I'd trust Tim with . . ." The words trailed off and he blinked to make sure this was the Italian woman who had not slit his throat when she had the chance.

Her hair was red and she had painted her face just like a tramp. And that wasn't exactly what Jed Reno would call a dress she wore. Why, it wasn't much more than a camisole. No, camisoles only came down to the waist if he recalled correctly, and this one was yellow and a bit longer than that, and she was wearing black stockings and little shoes she had slipped on. The yellow thing, well, she might have been wearing that over the duds she had on when she was a cantankerous old man. Same with the black stockings, but at least she wasn't posing as some old rapscallion. Maybe she had stashed those little shoes in the water barrel.

Thinking of the water barrel made him lower his arms and cup his big hands before he splashed them into the barrel and came up to wash his bearded face. He was feeling mighty warm right about then, his heart pounding.

He blinked away the water and looked at her again. Her arms were bare—all the way to her shoulders— and that little yellow garment went over her left shoulder and around her neck to the back to connect with the rest of this whatever-a-body-was-supposed-to-call-it. But that left a lot of pretty skin about the same color as a deer hide, all the way from her throat to . . .

Reno swallowed and made himself splash more water over his face. Why, this Ginger gal had no shame. He could see enough of her cleavage to know that she wasn't nothing like Harry Flint or Little Adorno. She was, by all that was holy, a woman sure enough.

She smiled at him, then squatted and pushed the garments she had been wearing into an opening at the bottom of the saloon for the rats and other critters that had taken a home underneath the floorboards.

"Come on," she said once she was standing again, and she took him by the arm and began giggling and patting his hand as they emerged from the alley just as two railroaders staggered by and gawked at her. The burly men were headed toward the café.

"How come that ol' man gets a woman like that?" one of them asked.

"'Cause he's got more money than we gots right now," the other said. "He can afford more than Potato King's coffee."

They disappeared into the café while Ginger turned Reno in the opposite direction and they stepped onto the boardwalk, and she began rubbing his left arm and singing softly to him. The tune reminded him of "Aura Lee," but she sang it differently.

> *When the blackbird in the spring,*
> *Warbling o'er the lea,*
> *Sat and rocked I heard him sing,*
> *Singing: Jed Reno,*
> *Jed Reno, Jed Reno,*
> *Man of silver hair,*
> *Sunshine come alon' with my hero,*
> *And swallows in the air.*

The Sledgehammer Saloon was crowded, but there was a table in a dark corner and Reno felt himself being steered there as Ginger kept singing. Releasing her grip, she stood, still smiling, and Reno recalled what little manners he had ever had and dragged out a stool so she could sit on it. Then he sat in the rickety stool opposite her.

She sang the chorus:

> *Jed Reno, Jed Reno,*
> *Man of silver hair,*
> *Sunshine come alon' with my hero,*
> *And swallows in the air.*

Then another woman showed up, and she was fatter and meaner, with a hard face that rouge and such could not make look any better. Her dark eyes did not hide the hatred and jealousy she had for pretty Ginger, but she managed to look away from the young woman and barked at Reno.

"What'll it be, buster?"

Reno blinked. "Uh . . ." He glanced hopefully at Ginger.

"A glass of your best red wine, deary?" she suggested to the ugly woman.

"Our best tastes like dung. But if that's what you want, it's fine with me. And you?" She glared at Reno.

"Rye . . . uh, no. Let's make it the same as hers."

"Two red wines." She stretched her arm across the table and turned her hand palm up. "That'll be a dollar . . . in advance."

"Oh." Reno had never been in a saloon like that, but this wasn't exactly the trusting part of Cheyenne. He started fishing through his pockets while Ginger reached up and into her bosom and withdrew a rolled dollar bill.

"Here you go, sweetheart." When the rude lady snatched the bill away and stormed up toward the crowded bar, Ginger turned to Reno and batted her eyes. "Isn't this lovely?"

"Uhhh."

Reno couldn't think of what to say, so Ginger spoke.

"It's loud here," she said. "And nobody pays mind to anyone as long as they're drinking. And paying in advance. But don't drink the red wine. That old hag is tougher than my great-grandmother, but she speaks the truth. Take a sip, turn your head, and spit it onto the floor. It does taste like dung."

"Oh."

She leaned closer. "And I don't want you drunk."

"Oh," he said again.

The wine arrived. The mean woman slammed both glasses—tumblers, not stemmed wineglasses—on the table, splashing a bit of wine over the rim and onto the table. She did not wipe it off.

"I'll be back," she said. "Just don't walk out with our glassware."

Ginger took one of the glasses and raised it. Reno stared.

"Toast?" she said after ten or twelve seconds.

"Oh." Reno found his glass and let it tap the side of Ginger's, then he brought it to his nose and sniffed.

"Smells like grapes," he said.

"Tastes like arsenic," she said but took a sip, then turned her head discreetly and spat it onto the floor. When she looked back at Reno she found a handkerchief from some hidden place and wiped her lips. Reno took a bigger sip and forgot to spit it out. But he smacked his lips and grinned at her like a schoolboy.

"I ain't never tasted wine before," he said with excitement. "It ain't bad."

She laughed and shook her head. "You need to come to Italy sometime, Jed. Or California."

He took another sip, nodded, and looked at her.

"Which is closer?" he asked.

"Let's get back to what I asked you earlier. Do you trust Tim Colter?"

He put the glass back on the table.

"There ain't a dishonest bone in his body, ma'am. He's true. Gives his word, he means it."

"How did he find out about the plot against President Grant?"

Reno looked at his wineglass and when his right hand reached for it his left hand pulled it back. His eye found Ginger again and he rubbed his beard.

"Trust nobody," he told her.

"How's that?"

"Trust nobody. No one. Somethin' like that. The meanin' was clear. And I do what Tim Colter tells me. Mostly."

She nodded. "I see." She picked up the wine but held it over Reno's glass and refilled it to the brim. "You don't trust me."

"No, it ain't that." He shook his head and found the wine, drank about half of it down, and set the glass back on the warped tabletop. "You saved my bacon back yonder. And you didn't kill me when you coulda. I figger you is exactly what you say you is. A . . . a . . . operator for that Pinkerton feller."

She smiled and refilled his glass with hers. "Operative," she said. "Copper. Detective. Spy. Whatever you want to call it. Do you know who Pinkerton is?"

"Never met him. I know that much. But it don't matter who he is. I believe you and Tim is out for the same thing—and that's to keep Gen'ral Grant alive." He drank more wine and she emptied her glass into his. He picked it up, smiled, and tapped the tumbler she still held.

"It ain't gonna do you no good, Miss Ginger," he said.

"Drop the 'Miss,' Jed. Just call me Ginger."

"Ginger." He liked the way the word sounded when he said it. He finished his glass and they returned both to the table. "It still ain't gonna do you no good."

The mean waitress came by and grabbed the two empty glasses. "I'll bring you two more rounds," she said, but Reno grunted something and she stopped and turned.

"No more for me," he said. "I promised my ma years ago that I'd have only one glass—to help me sleep—and nothin' more." His eyes darted to Ginger and he added, "But bring another round for my gal here."

Ginger's face was unreadable, but the waitress was holding out her hand and the Pinkerton woman found another rolled dollar between her bosoms and let the ugly hag snatch it and bull her way back to the bar.

She put her elbows on the tabletop, brought her hands together, and rested her chin on her two thumbs, leaned forward, and pinched the tip of her pretty nose with her two forefingers.

"Grant is," she said, "taking the Kansas Pacific to Denver. No politics. No meetings with the Colorado legislature. Nothing but pleasure. Just the president, his wife, and his personal secretary and his wife. Cheyenne is an option. He doesn't have to travel here. We urged him not to come to Cheyenne . . . unless we knew for certain his life was not in danger. But . . ." She sighed. "He's still a general at heart and fear isn't something he knows."

"The DP," Reno whispered when he realized that was all she was going to tell him.

"Right. It's an easy ride on the Denver Pacific from Denver to Cheyenne. Then he takes the UP east to Omaha, where nobody wants to assassinate him."

She returned with the red wine. Licking his lips, Reno thanked her when she handed him the glass, held it up as a toast to both women, and emptied about half of the wine into his mouth.

"Right." Ginger raised her head and let her arms rest on the table. "We know about Jake Dugan. Now if we could be certain Dugan would stay up in his den, Grant might bless the people of Cheyenne and the Territory of Wyoming with a trip. He's going to be the first president to ever visit Colorado. Wyoming Territory wants some of that action, too, and the administration likes the idea. It would be good for the country. Good for the Western territories and states. But that robbery at Fort Fetterman gives the Secret Service concern."

She stopped, and waited.

"You haven't swallowed your wine," she whispered.

He nodded, turned, and spat it onto the floor. The liquid would disappear quickly between the cracks in the floorboard. He wiped his mouth with the back of his hand and slid the glass in front of Ginger.

She shook her head.

"Well, I ain't much at detectin', but it struck me that that ugly woman . . . she could be a Pinkerton gal, too." He focused unintentionally on Ginger's cleavage and then sat up straight, embarrassed, and looked back toward the bar. "Then ag'in, seein' you in all your disguises, that ugly gal . . . well . . . she might be a Pinkerton man. And I mean a real man."

Ginger Burricchia's shoulders slouched. Her head shook, her arms came up, and she dropped her face into her hands.

"She's not." Reno could barely hear her whisper. "You're not helping the president, the territory, your country."

Slowly her face rose and she sighed again, shook her head, and said, "Trust no one?"

Jed's face remained like granite.

"But you trust Walker Chester."

Reno cocked his head. They stared at each other.

Finally Ginger picked up the glass of wine and finished it, then set it on the table. "I think that wine turned years ago," she said.

He didn't know what she meant by that but kept quiet.

"All right." She stood. "I thought we might be able to work together. But that's not happening. You work your side of town. I'll work mine. Good luck."

She walked out of the saloon.

Jed Reno caught up with her in the alley.

Chapter 23

When Tim Colter came to he kept his eyes closed while trying to clear his head. The right side of his neck burned, but he didn't want to move his arm to touch it. He wanted—he had to—*think*. The sun was up. Even with his eyes closed he could tell that much. His head was propped up on a pillow. No, most likely it was his bedroll. He flexed his fingers, then his toes, and opened his mouth and let his tongue wet his lips. Slowly his right hand moved off his stomach and to the holster—but he felt no leather, no belt buckle, and certainly not the grip of the big LeMat.

He let his ears see for him. The wind moaned through the rocks. A horse began to urinate. Somewhere a raven began to *kaw, kaw, kaw*. And someone spat juice that splattered against the sole of his left boot.

Opening his eyes, Tim Colter found Patsy Palmer squatting a few feet away. He had to blink a few times to clear his vision, and when he focused again he saw her wiping her mouth gently. Her bottom lip was busted and there was a cut across her forehead stretching from the corner of her left eyebrow all the way to her hairline. Those were new wounds. She was also rubbing her left hand and he could see the bruises and the two splints she had fashioned on her pinky and ring fingers.

Colter wet his lips.

"Welcome to the world of the livin'," Palmer said and then turned to find the sun. "Or the dyin'." And then she turned to the body at her feet. "And the dead."

Colter's eyes moved to that direction and saw the corpse of Mad Ben Gore.

The dying. And the dead. That was what troubled Colter.

He opened his mouth and tried to talk, but pain burned his neck into his throat and mouth so much that his teeth hurt.

The big woman grumbled and her knees popped as she rose. Colter watched her come to him, dragging her left leg, then gently knelt beside him, and water sloshed around in a nearby canteen that she had picked up.

One of her big hands slipped under his head and she lifted it gently, then brought the canteen to his mouth. The water was tepid, but it tasted wonderful, cooling his throat, lessening the burning in his neck, and reducing the size of his tongue. She withdrew the canteen and let his head fall onto the bedroll, then took a short pull from the canteen herself.

Their eyes met and held.

"Why didn't you kill me?" he asked. "You could've been miles away by now."

That was about a dozen words too many for the way his neck and throat hurt. He hardly recognized his voice.

Palmer turned and spat tobacco juice against a rock, then shrugged.

"My plan was to leave you fer the buzzards. Ride north as fast as I could."

Colter waited.

She pointed at the scab on her forehead, then held up her hand with the busted fingers.

Colter's lips parted, but he decided not to talk anymore—at least for now.

"I decided I needed you alive if I was to get out of this patch o' purgatory." Palmer hooked her thumb at Colter's gray. "That monster you ride bucked me off five times." With her good hand she spread her thumb and forefinger half an inch apart. "Come this close to killin' me three times. That's when I give up."

Her head then turned and nodded toward the redoubt.

"And that Injun pony . . . well, sir, I tried. I surely tried. But I just couldn't figure out a way to get that hoss out of that pen." She sighed and took another pull from the canteen. "That's when I figgered that if I want to live, you gots to live."

She held the canteen toward him, but he shook his head.

She spat brown juice on his shirtfront.

When he glared at her she said, "You need water,

bucko, since I ain't got no hankerin' to die right now. You needs water so you can get back on yer feet and we can get out of here." She looked over at the dead outlaw. "And he's gonna turn ripe right soon. Already stinks to high heaven." She looked up and Colter followed suit.

Buzzards were circling again.

"Ever'body's gotta eat." She knelt again and this time did not ease his head up but jerked it. He cursed, then clenched his jaw at the pain in his throat.

The canteen was coming to his lips.

"Now drink," she told him.

He slept for another two hours. Then rested for one more. By then the sun was moving to the west and Colter had Palmer sit him up so he could rest his back against the rock. She gave him a slice of jerky and told him to just let that sit in his mouth and swallow the juice.

"Don't think your stomach wants to hold no beefsteak right now, but the juice will get you through. 'Sides, we ain't got no beefsteak, though I reckon I could cook us up some hoss meat."

His hand gently touched the bandage around his throat.

"It was a deep cut and you bled like a stuck pig. But my hot knife fixed that. Don't worry, Colter, it'll leave a real fine scar you can tell big windies 'bout when you're an old man. I reckon even a perty lady will find it interestin'." She spat again. "Don't worry, sonny, you ain't never gonna be as ugly as me."

Colter turned and smiled at her. "You saved my life. You're lookin' beautiful to me right now."

She cackled and nodded at the dead outlaw who had come inches from killing Tim Colter. "Better'n him."

Holding his right hand out toward her, he said, "Help me up."

"You ain't ready to stand, darlin'."

"Help me up."

He had to lean on her shoulder for support, but once they reached the dead man Colter could stand on his own.

"Can you look in his pockets for any papers?" he asked.

"Done that whilst you was snoozin'," she told him. "Nothin'. Nothin' on him but malice. Which was always the case."

Colter eyed her with doubt.

"Sonny," she said, "he was just busted out of that territorial pen. He's still in his prison duds. He ain't gonna have no map to Dugan's Den, if that's what yer thinkin'. And he sure ain't got no plans written down about killin' no traitorous president." She laughed, spat juice again, and stared at the dead outlaw.

Tim Colter couldn't argue with her logic. He wasn't thinking straight.

The big woman grunted and whispered something too soft for Colter to understand. When he turned his head she was staring at him, then she looked down at the dead murderer, and then back at Colter.

"Well, I swan," she said and wiped her mouth.

"What?" Colter asked.

"Never noticed the resemblance between you and ol' Benji-buttons."

Colter took another glance at the killer and then stared at Palmer. He knew her mental faculties weren't that strong, but he never thought she could be that daft.

"He doesn't look a blessed thing like me," he told her and studied the dead man again just to be sure.

The hair color was about the same, though Gore's was filthier, but the man's thick mustache hid most of his features and his beard was more than just stubble. It resembled black bristles on a brush meant for scraping bricks.

Colter's second shot had caught the man in the center of his forehead and the blood had dried black, so he couldn't tell much else. The first had hit him right below the rib cage and that blood had dried black, too. His eyes were open and they looked exactly like Colter's—same color, eyebrows the same shape, and there was even a scar over the left eyebrow that was shaped like a waning moon, but Colter's was a bit larger, and his was shaped like a waxing moon.

No, there was no true resemblance.

Colter touched his neck, flinching at the pain. Mad Ben Gore didn't have a long trench on the right side of his neck either and Colter knew he would have one for the rest of his life. Another scar to his trophies for being a peace officer.

"You didn't never seen ol' Ben when he was clean-shaved," Palmer told him. "And he had that mustache for years. Right proud of it. It growed real fast."

"There's no—"

"But put a mustache and beard on ya or take his off'n his face and you'd pass, maybe not for twins but for brothers."

"Patsy," Colter said and started to move back to the bed she had made for him. He was getting dizzy. "You're full of . . ." But he stopped and looked down at the face that stared up at him.

Without looking back at his prisoner, his guide, he whispered, "There's a razor in my saddlebags. Fetch it for me."

Someone once old him that undertakers shaved dead men before their funerals. Colter didn't know if that was true, and even if it were, it didn't help the nausea that kept making Colter turn and spit into the dirt as he scraped off Mad Ben Gore's facial hair. Patsy was right about the thick beard. Twice Colter had to stop and sharpen the blade on the strop he carried in his saddlebags, too.

His prisoner wasn't much help. She just squatted at the dead man's boots, watching the barber shave the customer.

"Keep nickin' his cheeks like that," she said with a snort, "and you ain't gonna get no tip."

"Shut up," he muttered. He knew, however, that when he quit lawing he wouldn't try barbering as a profession.

She howled like a coyote.

Finally he folded the blade into the handle and tossed it on the saddlebags Palmer had brought over.

"What'd I tell you?" she said with another snort.

The razor had done a good job of cutting the face, but now that the massive mustache and the rough beard were gone, Colter could see the resemblance.

"Huh."

Palmer turned and looked at Colter, then back at the corpse. "I musta plumb forgots 'bout that cleft in his chin." Again she studied Colter's face. "Yer beard stubble's growed too much. Funny how that works. You get thick chin whiskers and over that poutin' upper lip of yourn, but not nigh as much on the cheek." She laughed. "Yer cheeks look just like a baby's."

"Shut up," he told her again, but he rubbed his chin and felt the growth.

"You got that hole in your chin, bucko?" she asked.

Colter looked at the body again. "I might not need one," he whispered.

"How's that?"

He didn't answer. His beard would cover the cleft in one day, maybe two.

"Well." She turned to spit and then wiped her mouth. "Ya might look like ol' Mad Ben, but you don't sound nothin' like'm."

Colter gently touched the bandaged neck and then he looked hard at Patsy Palmer.

"I might not have to."

Patsy fell back onto her hindquarters and let out a hard, raucous laugh. "Pardner!" She slapped her thigh. "You is loco. They called him—" She nodded at the dead man and stopped to catch her breath. "Called him 'Mad' and he was hard crazy, killin' crazy, he was a feller nobody dared to cross. But he wasn't stupid crazy."

She leaned forward. "You think you can pass for Mad Ben Gore?"

"Maybe," he whispered.

She howled with delight. "Well, sonny, what would keep me from lettin' Dugan hisself, or any one of his Rebel pards, know the truth?"

"What's to keep me from killing you?" he told her.

She laughed again. "Well, for one thing . . . you ain't got no idea of how to get there . . . without my help, which you still ain't gonna get none of."

"We'll see about that." He needed more rest. "Take off his shirt and pants," he ordered.

"I ain't doin' no such thing. 'Sides, there's blood on that shirt."

Colter opened his mouth, then closed it. He exhaled so hard he cringed at the pain that shot across his neck.

"You're right," he whispered, and thought to add, "I'm sorry."

She looked at him as if he had completely lost his mind.

The first thing he did was pray. For forgiveness. He even prayed for Mad Ben Gore's soul, not that Colter thought Gore had any chance of redemption at this part in the game but perhaps because he was going to need all the help he could get. In fact, he would need a miracle. Then he went to work.

He used his thumbs to close Mad Ben Gore's eyes and then he unbuttoned the shirt and pulled it away, the dried blood cracking and ripping skin and cloth. He left the shirt on for the time being and then moved on his hands and knees to the feet.

The boots were heavy, and he held a bottom against the soles of his boots. They would fit. He left on the socks. Colter wasn't going to go that far. Then he unbuttoned the pants and pulled them off, pitching them over the shoes after he had gone through the pockets, which carried only a rough, handmade die. For prison gambling, Colter figured. Dice were easier to hide than poker cards. He had to rest for a few minutes after he rolled over the body, but then he managed to get off the dead man's shirt.

"Yessiree," Palmer said, "you is crazier than Mad Ben, that's fer shore."

Colter took a long swallow from the nearest canteen, then tossed it to Palmer. "You feel like covering your pal with some dirt and stones?" He looked up at the still-circling buzzards.

"Ain't that a man's job?" Her eyes beamed as she sat on a small stone, legs outstretched.

"Usually." Colter's head went up and down twice. "But I thought maybe I'd get that Indian pony out of that rock prison. And then you and I could get out of this place."

She came to her feet quickly.

"Now that, hoss, is a plan to my likin'. Sure, I'd be right proud to play Ben's undertaker. And prouder to light a shuck out of this place. It just stinks of death."

He grabbed a handful of oats from a sack in his saddlebags before he went to the rocky fortress and weaved his way through the path until he saw the pinto. The horse's eyes were wild, nervous, but he waited until he was certain he had his scent. Then he began humming and walked easily toward him. The humming hurt his neck, but he kept at it.

It was a small horse even by Indian standards but a good one. Colter could see that much in him. The hackamore had fallen off and the saddle—Cheyenne from its looks—needed straightening. Colter realized why Patsy Palmer had never gotten the animal out of this rock pen.

"What an idiot," he whispered, then resumed his melody.

She had tried to ride the horse out. She had not tried to remove the Indian saddle and put on the McClellan. And a woman that size on a horse like this—Colter couldn't figure out how she had lived through the whole show.

"Here you go, White Face," he said soothingly to the frightened animal and held out his offering of oats.

The horse backed up. Colter nodded and smiled. "I know. That's all right. It's good to be cautious. Take your time, boy, I'm not going to hurt you." He tilted his head toward the way in and out. "But I can get you out of here."

Five minutes passed. The pinto's nostrils flared often. Colter found a good spot to rest and just kept on humming, holding out the hand that held the oats. There wasn't much grass to forage in this den and the rocks were hard on a pony's feet. He waited longer, patiently.

How long he stayed there he couldn't guess. But the pinto's hunger got the better of him and he stepped closer, pulled back, then sniffed the air. A minute or two later and that coarse tongue slapped Colter's hand.

He had to stifle the laugh because he knew that would torment that gash across his neck something fierce.

After that Colter rubbed the pinto's neck gently. He refastened the hackamore and straightened the Cheyenne saddle.

"Let's see about getting you out of here, boy," Colter said and took a couple of dallies of the hackamore around his right hand. Then he started walking, still humming, and the pinto followed him. He had to pick the right path, but the tracks remained so he knew how that Indian boy had gotten the horse in here.

The narrow path was the toughest. That took a good forty-five minutes to maneuver through, and had the pony been much bigger he never would have fit. But Colter's humming, his steady hand, his patience—and the horse's good eyesight and instinct—got both of them to the side trail.

"By golly!" Patsy Palmer said from her perch on the rock. "You done it."

Colter walked toward her and handed her the hackamore. "Better get acquainted. Then we'll get your saddle on him and start riding."

She motioned to the sun.

"Gettin' late, lawdog. Don'ts ya think we oughts to camp here one more night. And not to hurt yer feelings, but that neck of yours ain't gonna like no hard gallop for a day or two."

"We're riding out. I don't plan on galloping anywhere today. But I want to be shed of this place. It reeks of death."

Palmer slid to the ground.

"Won't get no argument no more from me."

Chapter 24

"What makes you so darn tootin' shore that that miserable cur of a butcher of a bluebelly is comin' to Cheyenne anyway?" Patsy Palmer sang out when they had cleared the canyon and moved onto the windblown hills. "Let alone that Jake Dugan plans to give the mad-dog killer what he deserves?"

Colter nodded ahead. "There's another canyon we'll have to go through two, three miles ahead. Let's put these horses into a lope to make up some of the time we lost."

"I ain't much good at lopin'," Palmer said. "And you didn't answer my question."

"Spur him," Colter ordered, "or I'll slap his rump with my reins."

She cursed, pulled down her hat tight, and kicked the pinto into a fast walk, positioning herself, and then a trot. She couldn't post a trot worth two bits and quickly realized that a lope was much easier on one's backside than a trot. Colter let her get a good-sized lead before he let the gray run—and the gray wanted to run. But Colter didn't let the gelding go all out in case Palmer lost her seat or the Indian pony stumbled.

It was good to feel the wind in his face, though his neck still throbbed. The hills weren't all that high and the ground was made for a good, hard lope. After a while Colter moved to Palmer's left and they slowed to another trot, then finally, as they crested a rise and saw the next rocky canyon, reined their mounts back into a walk.

He remembered when he first saw this part of the territory. Jed Reno had called it "Lonesome Territory," and that name certainly fit, though the Cheyenne likely had a better name for it. He would have to ask Reno about that when he got back to Cheyenne. Ten minutes later they reached the entrance of the canyon. This one was tighter than the canyons to the south but still easily passable for horses or . . .

"Hold up," he ordered and waited for Palmer to rein in the pinto.

Then he slipped off the gray and with his left hand holding the reins, squatted and looked at the tracks.

"Same Injuns who left Mad Ben afoot," Palmer said with a snort. "I can read that trail even from up here, pardner."

"Not unless that Cheyenne raiding party took to driving a wagon," Colter said.

Palmer spit tobacco juice on the other side of the horse and then climbed out of her saddle and led the pinto toward Colter.

"Huh," she said and moved a few feet ahead of the lawman, where she squatted.

"You got good eyes," she said and traced her finger along the imprint made by one of the left-side wheels. "Pony tracks covered most of this sign." She looked up ahead. "Maybe 'em bucks is gonna get some more scalps." She chuckled, shifted the tobacco to her other cheek, and said, "Dumb emmy-grints."

"How old?" Colter asked.

She looked at him and gave a tobacco-flecked grin. "You mean you cain't read that trail?"

"No," Colter answered honestly and quickly. "Not after an Indian party galloped over the same trail."

After spitting juice and wiping her mouth, she rose and moved slowly into the canyon, keeping her eyes on the tracks in front of her.

"You keep an eye up the road," she said. "I'll study on this mess of sign and see what I can cipher out myself." She laughed. "This'll be a challenge." She looked back. "I mean it, hoss. You keep a look ahead—and behind—this ain't my favorite patch of Wyomin'."

"Mine either," Colter said.

"Then you likely know what white folks and red ones call this place," she said.

Colter nodded. "The Canyon of Sorrows."

Fifteen minutes and one hundred yards later she stopped and Colter, still mounted, reined up.

Palmer spat at a rock and stared at him. "Wagon was movin' up before those Injuns rode south." She turned and stared down the Canyon of Sorrows. "Bet we'll find the burned-out ruins of the outfit up ahead tomorrow or sometime. By my guess the wagon was headin' north a day or two ahead of 'em butchers that come down to kill poor ol' Ben Gore."

"What would a freight wagon be bringing through this country?" Colter asked.

She snorted. "You ain't no tracker, pardner. This ain't no freight wagon."

Colter studied her. "But it was hauling something mighty heavy."

"Yep. With just one mule to pull it." She sighed. "Poor, dumb family of homesteaders."

Colter shook his head. "Homesteaders?" He pointed. "Those tracks weren't made by a Conestoga and this isn't the Oregon Trail. I've been on the Oregon Trail."

She sighed. "I didn't say it was no big ol' Conestoga. Wagon that size would have a mess of oxen pullin' it, and I knows all 'bouts the Oregon and California and all 'em other trails. But it was a family." She pointed to footprints Colter could barely make out leading into the rocks.

"My guess is that the mammy had to answer nature's call." She traced the closest print. "And them tracks was made by a she-male." She pointed to another set of prints Colter had missed. "And that is either a right puny man or a kid in his teens."

"Mother and son?"

Palmer's knees popped as she stood. "Likely the daddy stayed put in the wagon. So mammy, pappy, and sonny comes West to start over."

Colter nodded up the trail. "There's no white settlements ahead."

"Might be bound for Montana," she countered.

"Then they would have taken the Bozeman Trail,"

he told her, pointing northeast and then turning his arm northwest. "Or take the old Oregon Trail. Go the long way. Fort Bridger and—"

She interrupted him. "It's a mystery fer shore." Palmer walked to her pinto. "And one I don't reckon nobody'll ever solve in this here world. Maybe in the hereafter." Taking the reins Colter had been holding, she grunted as she climbed back into the saddle, then let out a loud fart and laughed as Colter swore while she finished swinging her right leg over the pinto's back. "'Cause my bet is that those Cheyenne bucks caught all three of 'em and massacred 'em."

The pinto started walking and Colter looked at the tracks again, frowning, then letting the gray follow the big woman on the small horse.

"Massacred 'em just like that butcher buddy of yourn, Gen'ral You Stink Grant."

Colter managed to snare a jackrabbit around sundown and they made camp at a bend in the canyon. He skinned the animal while Palmer grained and picketed the horses, and they risked a campfire to cook the rabbit on a spit Colter had made from a dead tree. No salt. No pepper. No coffee to wash it down, but they ate greedily, wiping their fingers on their pants legs.

"Can I ask you a question?" Colter asked.

She stared at him long and hard before picking her teeth with a fingernail and finally said, "Yer gettin' soft, pilgrim. Never asked no permission for nothin'."

Colter shrugged. "You did save my life."

She laughed and leaned back against a boulder. "I

done tol' ya that I didn't have much choice in the matter. Saved yer life, shore, but I was savin' my hide, too." She studied him again, then shrugged and folded her hands across her full stomach. "Ask away, pardner. Don't expect me to answer you, though, and iffen I do, don't take what I tell ya as gospel."

"Why do you hate Grant so much?"

The smile and any softness that had materialized because of a plump jackrabbit supper vanished. Her fingers tightened into fists and her eyes turned a deadly cold. But Colter kept his face blank, waiting patiently, and after Palmer took in a long breath and held it for several seconds he knew she would tell him.

Her exhale was long and hard and she crossed her arms across her chest.

"Yer president murdered my fam'ly."

The first sentence was just a whisper, and for a moment Colter thought that would be the entirety of her answer, but he kept quiet, figuring that would be the best way to learn what really drove her.

"You know, lawdog, I wasn't always such a mean, hard, bitter, man-killin' scoundrel." She smiled suddenly. "Didn't have all these extree pounds on me neither. And I could talk real smooth and sweeter than Georgia tea." She affected a thick accent that rang of cotton and the Carolinas.

Then she fell silent, and that stretched until a piece of wood in the fire popped and sent sparks flying into the coming darkness. She jumped at the sound, so caught up in her memories was she, and then stared into the coals for what had to have been more than five minutes.

Still, Tim Colter kept quiet. He had learned that from Jed Reno, and from the many times he had to use his brain and his interrogation skills to figure out a crime, instead of his guns. Most folks would think the opposite, but Colter preferred that way over using his fists or his LeMat.

"Did you know I was born in Galena?"

"Illinois?" Colter asked.

"That's right. 'Course, ol' Ulysses S. Grant wasn't there then, and I was gone afore he got there, right before the War fer Southern Indy-pendence come along." She sighed. "Moved to St. Louis. And did you know that that blackhearted butcher lived there, too?"

Colter shook his head, though he knew Grant had lived in the city before moving to Galena.

"You might could say that Grant, he just took a notion to follerin' me." She laughed and found the last of her chewing tobacco, started to shove it into her mouth, but then sighed and said, "Better let this last till I know I can find myself a new plug. Maybe when we happen upon 'em wayfarers in that big wagon. Injuns don't have the fondness for a chaw like I gots."

She stared into the dying coals.

"Grant wasn't in St. Louis when I was there neither. I don't think so no-how."

She fell silent, and Colter thought he saw tears welling in her eyes, but that might have been caused by the smoke. He wanted to stand, kick the fire out. They were done and it would not be a cold night. He didn't want anyone to give away their position. But Palmer beat him to that.

She leaned forward, scooped sand over the coals, then stared down at the mound and sighed.

"Resembles a grave, don't it?" she said.

Colter did not answer.

Palmer returned to her rock, but her eyes remained on the mound that covered the firepit.

"No, I reckon Grant wasn't follerin' me." She did not look up. "Don't reckon he ever come to New Madrid County." Her eyes lifted and found Colter again. "Ever been there?"

Colter shook his head. "I don't think so."

"No need to go. I ain't goin' back. And Grant . . ." She sighed. "He didn't go there neither. I don't think so. Well, he shore wasn't there after April of '62. Iffen he was, and iffen I'd seen him there, I would have kilt him deader than a dog."

Her eyes found him again.

"Ever heard of Shiloh? Nah, that ain't what you Yanks called it. You dubbed it . . ." She waited for the name to come to her. "Pittsburg Landin'." She breathed in deeply, held it, and clenched her fists so hard they shook. "On the banks of the Tennessee River."

He knew what had happened then, what had embittered her. Living in Oregon, Colter had been spared the horrors of the Civil War, but he had heard the stories of savagery and brutality, of dead soldiers in blue and gray that shocked the American people. Bull Run. Gettysburg. Antietam. Cold Harbor. Fredericksburg. And a battle named after a river landing by the Confederates and after a meeting house—Presbyterian, he thought, but couldn't quite be certain.

In April of 1862, it had been the deadliest battle of a war then hardly a year old—more than 23,000 dead and wounded—a number that exceeded the total casualties of every American war before the conflict between the North and the South.

Colter nodded his head slightly and Palmer again focused on the mound.

"My man died there," Palmer said softly and brushed away a tear. "Place they called the Peach Grove." Her head shook. "That don't sound like a place a man would die in battle. But I guess Shiloh Meetin' House don't sound like that neither. Don't matter. My man died. And your hero, your Gen'ral Grant, stood on my man's grave to get hisself elected president of *your* United States."

She stopped, but something about the way she stared at the ground made Colter believe she had not finished.

"I got the letter from Charley Kramer three months later. Taken me three months to learn that I was a widder. Took me five, ten minutes to write a letter back to Charley to ask about my son." She stopped for another two minutes. "Luke woulda been fifteen then. Wanted to be a soldier like his daddy. They made him a drummer." She pretended to tap sticks in a rhythmic beat on her left leg. "He played our pie-annie real good." Her head shook and she laughed. "Don't know where that boy picked that up. My man and me . . . we never caught that bug to play no music."

And she fell silent again.

"Charley never writ back. Got word in December from his mama that he died at Corinth. That was a set-to in a big town in northern Mississippi. I'd never heard of it. Well, I don't reckon nobody had heard of Shiloh neither till after 'em horrible two days.

"Luke . . . he was like his ol' man. Never learnt his letters. I went to the preachers in town, I had somebody write newspapers, even had Parson Preston writ to General Johnston—but I learnt that he'd got hisself kilt at Shiloh, too. And you might believe it or not, when I learnt that Gen'ral Grant was responsible for that trickery and bloodlettin' on the Tennessee, I had a letter writ to him, too."

She sighed and let her face fall into her hands.

Her body shook as she sobbed and Colter stayed quiet, letting the big, brutal woman cry herself out like a widow . . . and a mother.

"Took me two years before the word got to New Madrid County," she said after she straightened. "Two years. More'n two exactly. Henrietta Maye, her bein' the postmaster's wife, she brung that letter over to me. Said it had been mailed from Chicago, Illinois. Don't know nobody from way up that way and I had her open the letter and read it to me. And she done it, but she read it to herself first, and when I seen 'em tears in her eyes, I knowed. I knowed my Luke was dead."

She stopped crying and did not wipe away any tears. Malevolence filled her eyes as she focused on Colter.

"Ever heard of Camp Douglas?" she asked.

"No," Colter whispered.

"Prison camp," she said. "That's where my boy, my precious little drummer, rotted hisself to death. My li'l' baby boy."

She spat onto the mound and glared at Colter. "So that, Yankee Law Dog, that's why I aim to do my part and see yer precious gen'ral, yer husband- and baby-murderin' butcher, deader'n all 'em soldier boys wearin' blue and gray that he got kilt."

When she rose Colter moved his right hand closer to the LeMat, even though he didn't think she was a threat. He watched her grab her bedroll and walk off into the darkening night. He heard her roll out the bedding, then drop onto it. She was a loud snorer, but she didn't for a long time.

He listened to the sobs she tried to quiet and for the first time felt sorry for her.

Chapter 25

Jed Reno dragged his bedroll to the mound of hay in Walker Chester's livery, picked his teeth with a horseshoe nail, tossed it onto Chester's messy desk, found the jug, and used his teeth to remove the cork. The forty-rod burned his tongue, but it did wonders to get the taste of that wretched red wine out of his mouth. He had gone practically all day spitting and hacking and had to give Ginger Burricchia some credit for warning him about that stuff.

Yes, by Joseph Bijeau, there was not a better cure for anything that ailed a body than bona fide Taos Lightning.

He was still smacking his lips when Walker Chester limped in.

"Where you been all day?" the grumpy skinflint said as he made his way to fetch his bottle.

"Doin' what I do best," Reno said, smacking his lips.

Chester had a sip of his own liquor, lowered the bottle, and wiped his mouth with the other arm. "Which is?"

Reno grinned. "As little as possible."

The liveryman took a longer pull, but after that he corked the bottle and dropped it into the drawer. "That ain't the way I hear it."

Reno's one eye focused tightly on his landlord.

Smiling suddenly, Chester held his hands just under his chest. "What Trent Mayhem tol' me was that wasn't little at all. Trent says they was big and 'bout to bust loose."

Reno took another pull from the jug, but this time the forty-rod tasted just as bad as that nasty wine he had pretended to like.

"I don't reckon she was yer daughter." Chester tilted back his head and laughed like a coyote, slapping his thigh. "You know, the Sledgehammer ain't no place to take some fancy woman." He snorted, took another drink, and leaned closer to the mountain man.

"I sure hope you didn't bring her here, pardner."

Reno corked the jug. "I think Trent Mayhem saw some feller who looks like me."

That caused Chester to laugh and howl and slap his thigh even longer and louder until finally he managed to catch his breath and wipe his eyes. "Jedediah . . . son . . . ain't nobody in all this country and ever' other country in the world could be mistook fer you, hoss." He howled again. "Trent says that when she left the Sledgehammer you run after her like a puppy dog chasin' his master or his mammy. Where'd y'all go?" Again Chester looked around the livery. "Don't want some waddies and UP or KP boys to mistake me lee-gitimate business for some bawdy house of ill repute."

Gene Harriman, who ran the gun shop where Reno

and Colter bought their ammunition and had their firearms repaired, gave Reno a break from the ribbing Chester was giving him when he led a chestnut mare into the livery.

"Walker," he said, "Louise here threw a shoe. I know it's after hours, but I was hoping . . ."

Chester frowned, but Reno knew Harriman was too good a customer—and he fixed Walker Chester's firearms, too, and sent a good bit of business his way—for Chester not to do this favor. He rose from the chair still carrying his bottle, which he handed to the gunsmith, and took the chestnut's reins.

"C'mon to the shed, Gene. They's daylight enough left for me to get that job done."

When they were gone Reno wiped the back of his neck.

"Who is Trent Mayhem?" the voice whispered from the mountain of hay behind Reno.

Reno kept his eye on the entrance to the stables. "A no-account jackass who don't know when he oughta keep his mouth shut. I'll shut it for him next time I see him. Mark my words. I'll shut him up good."

"Was he in the saloon when we were there?" Ginger Burricchia whispered.

Reno thought quickly and shook his head. "Place was so crowded and I wasn't looking at no people."

"I know exactly what you were looking at." Ginger giggled.

Reno felt his face warming.

"Well, I didn't see him. Reckon he was there if Walker Chester says so."

The ringing of a smithy's hammer against a horseshoe sang out at the shed near the corral.

"Tell me about Mayhem," Ginger said.

"Ain't much to tell. Handyman in Cheyenne."

"Does he drink at the Sledgehammer?"

Reno snorted. "He drinks wherever and whenever he can." He paused. "Well, that place serves mostly the UP boys. Not them who works for the KP. You know, railroaders. They's like cowhands. Ride for the brand. Don't mingle unless it's over cards or horses or fightin' over some loose woman."

When Ginger did not respond Reno shrugged. "But I can't say Mayhem don't drink there. Gosh. I think that was the first time I ever set foot in that place—that I recollect anyhow." His laugh became a snort. "Sometimes, Ginger, I don't recollect where I done my drinkin'."

"You're a man after my father's heart," Ginger said.

The ringing of the hammer stopped.

Reno stared out the door, waiting and holding his breath. When the hammer began banging on the shoe again his lungs began working once more and he tried to think back to his short visit to the Sledgehammer Saloon with pretty Ginger, then a redhead, not back to . . . well . . . he wasn't exactly sure what color her hair really was. Even though he had caught a glimpse at what might have been her real hair when she was changing her clothes, and hair, running through those alleys.

"What do you know about Walker Chester?"

"He lets me sleep right here, don't charge me nothin'

more than doin' some work for him, and by work I don't mean shoeing no hoss."

"Where's he from?"

"You don't trust nobody, do you?"

"I trust you," she said. "You're the one who doesn't trust anybody."

"That's just because of what Tim tol' me to do."

"Trust nobody," Ginger said.

"That's right."

"Tell me about Chester."

"Ain't much to tell," Reno said and eyed his jug but discouraged that tempting he was getting to pull the cork again. "Got run out of Missouri when the war started up. Least that's the way I remember his story. Opened his livery in Lawrence. Reckon you knowed what happened there."

"Rebel bushwhackers burned practically the whole town to the ground in '63," she said.

"Makes me glad I was up in these Rocky Mountains. The West was heaven to all that hell."

"Go on," she said.

"That's 'bout it. What Quantrill done sent him all the way to Denver. Then, when he didn't find no pay dirt, he opened a livery in Laramie City when it was just started out and there was hardly a hoss in all the territory except for Injun ponies. He musta see'd the future was in Cheyenne, on account he sold out in Laramie City and opened up this here livery, oh, three, four years back."

"Do you trust him?"

Reno shrugged. The hammering had stopped, but

now it started up again with a different kind of ringing. He was nailing the shoe into place, and that would not take long.

"Well, I reckon I did. Till Tim told me not to trust nobody."

He heard her sigh.

"I trust you, too," he said in a whisper as he turned toward the hay. "But you see, I give my word to Tim."

What he heard sounded like a laugh.

"Jed Reno," she whispered, "you're the most loyal and honest man I've ever met."

He laughed loud and was still shaking his head when Walker Chester limped in with Gene Harriman right behind him.

"What you laughin' at, Reno?" Chester asked, slapping his railroad cap on his thigh. Harriman seemed to be looking around for someone.

"I told you I heard Jed talking to somebody," Harriman told the liveryman.

Chapter 26

Kip Jansen groaned when he awakened. Not because of how sore his left arm and armpit were. Or the burning in his things. Or the intense throbbing of his left ankle. Or even because he was awake again, with another morning to start walking till the sun got too high and he became too tired and he had to find a place to wait out the rest of the day.

And not, he thought, as he shook one of his canteens and heard the sound that told him this one would be empty before nightfall.

No, Kip had been dreaming. And it had been a wonderful dream. His father had come home from the war. All those letters had been wrong. Why, he hadn't been killed at all. The Union Army couldn't get anything right when it came to things like that. No, he hadn't even been wounded. He had saved his regiment from disaster and was now a colonel. In the dream Kip Jansen had never heard of Wyoming Territory and his mother was young and beautiful and baked the best pound cakes in Decatur, and his father had bought Kip a horse and he was riding it all across Morgan County, swimming that fine stallion across the river and back just to say he had done it.

He could smell magnolias and not eat pecans but his mother's pecan pie. Not drink tepid or lukewarm or sometimes hot water from a canteen but fresh milk and lemonade.

And when Mary Elizabeth Sublette asked Kip if he had ever heard of someone named Lige Kerns, Kip could honestly answer, "No, Mary, who is he?"

"Some sidewinder my daddy locked up." Mary Elizabeth's father was a Decatur constable. "They're tarring and feathering him at the courthouse this afternoon. Do you wanna come? We can sneak a peek from the window in Daddy's office."

And now here he was . . . oh, a thousand, fifteen hundred, two thousand, twenty thousand, a million miles from Decatur. And about as far away from Laramie City and the Union Pacific Railroad as one could get.

He had also dreamed that he had been on a train, heading for Sacramento, California, shooting buffalo from the window as the train rocked its way west, and watching that young Indian boy wave his fancy stick—which Kip must have returned to him—and yelling in English that Kip Jansen was the greatest shot any Indian had ever seen.

Such wonderful and beautiful dreams . . . and here he was in a vast, grim patch of nothing. He realized that even when he got out of this canyon he'd have to climb up and down hills, and there would be little shade from the sun in that bit of country. Then there was another canyon he had to pass through. And after that . . . ?

His mind fogged over. He looked at the fancy crutch he had traded for. Why couldn't he have traded for a horse?

Well, that answer came readily and he answered it aloud.

"Because no Indian in his right mind is gonna swap a horse for a sack of pecans and such. And I didn't even have a full sack to offer him."

He wished he had not spoken aloud. It made his throat hurt. And the only way to soothe that was to drink some of his precious water.

He made himself swallow. That hurt, too. But he did not drink. Not yet anyway. He started gathering up what little he had, emptied what little his bladder held, and cleaned his hands with sand and grit.

Cringing when he leaned his shoulder into the fancy stick, he drew in a deep breath, let it out, and began hobbling down the canyon.

Right foot, the good one, out first. Then pray moving the left one didn't send flashes of lightning up his entire leg.

He put his right foot down again, then the left. Right. Left. Right. Left. Right. Left.

Right.

Left.

Over and over again, just as he had been doing for

what seemed like all the months he and his mother had traveled with Lige Kerns.

Right.

Left.

When his bruised and scratched shoulder began to ache he stopped to rest. This time he made himself drink water from the canteen and though he didn't mean to do it, he drank the last of the water from that one. So Kip called himself stupid and a glutton and threw the empty canteen to the dirt.

He started walking again. Right. Left. Right. Left. Then stopped and wondered how he had managed to survive as long as he had already. It hurt like blazes to turn around, but he did and eased back to the canteen that rested in the dirt. That meant bending down to his knees without screaming from the pain in his ankle.

That meant using the crutch as a brace to lean down and grab the canvas strap of the water container and lift it, then drape it over his shoulder next to the almost full canteen. That meant biting back the fire that burned the entire left side as he forced himself back to his feet.

Then he leaned against the rocky wall of the canyon and rested. His heart beat like a drummer boy sounding out the advance. He didn't want to do it, but he opened the other canteen and took a short pull.

His mother made wonderful tea. He thought about drinking glass after glass on hot summer days in Alabama, when they had hauled ice out of the cave to make the sweet drink cold and delicious. He tried to imagine that he was drinking lemonade, cold and sweet and equally delicious, and not brackish water from some dirty pool days and weeks ago.

And then he realized how many days had passed since his mother had died and he had stolen what he could from Lige Kerns and begun his . . . well, since he had run away.

When he realized how long he had been walking, he wanted to cry. He even thought that at the pace he was going he would be better off turning around and walking—or crawling—back to Lige Kerns. He might live longer that way.

Enough!

Kip thought the word. He did not speak it. He didn't even open his mouth. He had to conserve his energy, and the sun was rising and warming.

The fancy Indian stick hurt even more now, and the wrappings around his left hand did little to protect the blisters that had already busted open. He even thought that new blisters had formed over old ones. Maybe he could switch: use the crutch under his right arm. But then he figured he would just fall facedown in the dirt, and if he fell like that he couldn't really see himself getting up again.

Two hours, he told himself. He could make two hours. Then he would have the rest of the morning and all the way till dusk to sleep and rest and dream. Maybe he would dream of trains again. Of Decatur. Of his mother and father. But right now he had one thing to do. One thing he had been doing since he was still in diapers.

He walked. He figured he walked better when he was just learning how to walk than what he was doing right now. But after a few minutes he forgot about everything. The movements became mechanical, like Whitney's cotton gin. Like the paddlewheels on the steamboats that used to roll by so wonderfully and mysteriously on the Tennessee River.

First he began humming, not loud and not very well. The words came maybe fifteen steps later.

He mouthed them at first, but before long he heard his dry, cracked, strained, and wretched voice.

> *Shall we gather at the river,*
> *Where bright angel feet have trod . . .*

He had forgotten the rest of the words to the hymn, but he hummed till he got to the chorus. Then, delirious and, for all he knew, dying, Kip started singing—if one could call it that.

Mary Elizabeth Sublette would have said he was yelling.

And later, when he remembered what he had been doing, he figured he was yelling instead of singing. But he was walking while he did it.

> *Yes, we'll gather at the river,*
> *The beautiful, the beautiful riii-veeer;*
> *Gather with the saints at the river*
> *That flows by the throne of God.*

He thought he was delirious. But Kip stopped singing and walking and blinked his eyes repeatedly, then squeezed the lids over them tightly and slowly opened them.

He could see the end of the canyon. He remembered coming through there not that long ago. First he waited. He had heard and read about those things known as mirages. Where weary souls stuck in desert wastelands saw things that didn't exist. Like an oasis. Whatever an oasis was.

He let his eyes blink repeatedly and then he slowed his breathing and stared down the trail.

That's not an oasis.

Kip almost laughed. That was a bend in the canyon, and he remembered looking at it through the back of the wagon. And at that bend . . . Kip drew in a deep breath. The fog rose from his brain. Someone had told Lige Kerns that there was a hidden spring in that wide bend and there might have been, but it had been hidden too well for Lige or even Kip to have found.

But he could rest there. Wait till the sun was down. Cross the hilly, dry, windblown country in the night, and be in the next canyon by dawn.

Maybe he could find the water hole. He had to.

Right. Left. Right. Left. Right. Left.

He was moving with purpose now, ignoring every part of his body that ached. He blocked out the fire in his ankle. Remembering a verse suddenly, Kip started singing again.

> *Soon we'll reach the shining river;*
> *Soon our pilgrimage will ceea-eese*
> *Soon our happy hearts will quiver*
> *With the melody of—*

"Peace." He stopped singing and whispered the word as he turned into the camping ground and found himself staring down the muzzle of a big rifle held by a man who looked a whole lot tougher than Lige Kerns or any grown-up Kip had known in Morgan County, Alabama.

Chapter 27

"Hold it right there, pardner," Tim Colter told the lousy singer.

Almost immediately he lowered the Winchester's barrel, then pressed the trigger gently and cautiously lowered the hammer.

"Lord have mercy," Patsy Palmer said from a few yards to Colter's left. "He ain't nothin' but a saplin'. No wonder he can't sing worth a hoot."

The boy just stared.

After shifting the Winchester to his left hand Colter started walking toward the kid, though he kept his right hand as close to the butt of the LeMat as he could without spooking the boy, and he didn't stop when he reached him but eased over a few more feet so he had a clear view down the trail.

"You don't trust nobody no time nohow," Palmer called out with a laugh.

"Keep your voice down," Colter told her, speaking evenly and studying everything he could down the trail. He didn't think the boy was being followed and, seeing no signs to change that, he walked back to the kid.

Sunburned, sickly looking, maybe even dirtier than Patsy Palmer, and wearing rags that weren't fit for burning, the boy's Adam's apple bobbed, but he said nothing.

His lips were chapped, his stomach practically against his backbone, maybe fifteen years old. Maybe no more than ten. Colter didn't think he was any younger or older . . . at least not in years civilized people counted by. But looking at that ankle and the determination in the boy's eyes, Colter reevaluated the boy.

He's a keeper, he imagined Jed Reno telling him.

Colter pushed back the brim of his hat. "My name's Colter," he said. "Tim Colter. I'm a federal marshal out of Cheyenne." He pointed southeast. "Pursuing some . . ." He thought for a quick moment and decided to say, "robbers."

His eyes fell to the only thing holding that boy up.

"You want some water?"

The boy stared.

"Food."

Colter saw the boy falter. The Winchester dropped to the sand and Colter caught the boy before he fell. The canteens rattled against each other as Colter turned. The kid felt lighter than the empty canteen. Water sloshed in the other one.

"Is he dead?" Palmer asked.

Not answering, Colter brought the boy to the camp-ground they had made and lay him on his bedroll.

Putting a thumb and a forefinger against the boy's throat, he felt the pulse throbbing away.

"Let's make him comfortable." Colter's left arm disappeared under the skinny boy's back and he lifted him up, bracing his head against his forearm. "Get these canteens off him."

"Maybe one's got filled with Taos Lightnin'," Palmer said, smacking her lips.

"Just do what I tell you!" Colter roared and waited for the canteens to get out of his way. "Get his hat and my Winchester," Colter barked.

She wiped her lips with the back of a hand, sighed, and walked away.

"And I had better not hear that hammer click," Colter told her.

She hacked up a laugh and Colter grabbed the canteen and untied his bandanna. He let some water soak his wild rag—it was water, not Taos Lightning—and laid the cloth over the boy's ugly lips. Next he brushed away the bangs and looked up to make sure Palmer was doing exactly what she was supposed to be doing.

The big woman ambled back, keeping her hand on the forestock of the Winchester and away from the hammer and trigger. She laid that against a boulder and tossed the hat onto the kid's chest.

"Where'd he come from?" she asked.

"I don't know."

"If I was guessin' . . ." She wiped her mouth again. "I'd say straight out of perdition itself."

Colter remembered. "Get that fancy stick the boy was using for a crutch."

He watched her walk away and then he went through
the pockets, but there was nothing to identify the kid.
So Colter went to work, inching toward the small fire
they had started and scooping away some ash. He
jacked a shell from the rifle, found his knife, and pried
the lead bullet from the brass casing and dumped the
gunpowder onto a tin plate he kept in his saddlebags.
From the boy's canteen he splashed some water onto
the plate and scooped up a handful of ashes, now cool,
and dropped those into the mixture, which he began
stirring with his finger.

"What the devil is you doin'?"

Colter looked up at Patsy Palmer, who held the
fancy stick in her left hand.

"There's some salt in my saddlebags," he told her.
"In a sack. Bring it over here. Along with the flask of
whiskey."

"Whiskey." Palmer's face brightened and she tossed
the stick beside the unconscious kid. "Ya been holdin'
out on me, ol' hoss."

"Don't drink it," he ordered. "It's for medicinal use
only."

She faked a cough. "Yeah, but . . . 'pears I'm comin' down with somethin' awful."

"I might have some camphor that's better suited for
you," he said and went back to stirring the mixture. He
did not look up as she walked toward where the horses
were picketed, but he did call out again: "Don't drink
the whiskey."

She was back in a couple of minutes and handed
both sack and flask to Colter. He first added a good bit
of salt to his concoction and then splashed in about two

shot glasses of rye. The sack he dropped by his side, but he screwed on the lid to the flask and pitched it back to a surprised Patsy Palmer.

"One drink," he told her. "One short swallow. That's all." He glanced at the kid. "We might need some more of that for him."

He started stirring again.

"Your mama teach you that?" Palmer asked after taking a small pull from the flask.

"My mother did not drink ardent spirits," he said and looked up. The big woman tossed him the flask, which he caught and set down near his boot.

Nodding at the plate, Palmer said, "That's for his sunburn, right?"

Colter nodded.

"I always used sugar and turpentine with my wood ash. And sassafras or anise when I could get it. Never heard of gunpowder."

"Sulfur," Colter told her and shrugged. "It's the only thing I could think of."

"Never heard of whiskey neither."

"Same as turpentine."

She laughed. "Some of the whiskey I've had tasted worser than turpentine."

Colter laid down the plate, turned to the boy, and sighed. His neck burned.

"Here." The big woman came over on her knees. "I can do that fer ya. This needs a she-male's touch. And you might wanna go check that trail ag'in. Just in case somebody's huntin' this runt of a runaway."

Colter stood nodding, as he had been thinking the exact same thing. He had another thought about why the boy was walking south, though, and Jed Reno had always told him never to count out anything when you're in rough country filled with rougher men.

Grabbing the Winchester, he moved back to the trail. The sun was brighter now, with not a cloud showing on the horizon, and he studied for a good ten minutes before he was satisfied that no one was coming north. He looked south, too, but found no rising dust, and saw nothing that troubled him. After a final look back north, he returned to the boy and the big woman.

Kneeling beside the kid, he shot a glance at Palmer and said, "You did a good job."

She said nothing but pointed at the wrapped ankle.

"That'll need fixin'," she told him.

"That's why I told you to drink only one swallow from the flask."

"Gettin' a li'l boy drunk." She clucked her tongue and shook her head. "What would yer mammy say 'bout that?"

Instead of answering Colter picked up the flask and sat next to the kid. He shook the boy at the shoulder and heard him groan, and then shook him just a little harder.

The eyes fluttered, finally opened, and a few seconds later focused on Patsy Palmer.

"Mama?" the boy asked sleepily.

Spitting, then swallowing, Palmer moved to the boy and rubbed her fingers through her hair. "Sonny," she said, "time for your milk an' cookies afore bedtime."

Colter brought up the opened flask.

"Cookies . . ." He had to be delirious.

A swallow of whiskey had the boy coughing most of

it up and then Colter held his nose with one hand, letting Palmer take the boy's chin and forehead, and between the two of them, they managed to get three or
four swallows down the kid's throat. He coughed but
nothing came back up, and Colter pulled the flask
away and let the boy breathe.

"That's . . . aw-ful," he said.

They made him drink again.

And again.

"That's enough," Colter said and gave the flask to
Palmer. The boy bent over coughing but not throwing
up. Now Colter handed him the canteen.

"Drink," he said. "It's water," he added.

He had to help lift the canteen to the boy's mouth,
and the water chaser helped.

The kid brought his hands to his throat and leaned
his head back against the rock. "My esophagus is on
fire," he said in a husky, delirious voice.

"Yer what?" Palmer said.

"Hold him," Colter told her and he moved away to
the ankle. "I've got to set this."

He just caught a glimpse of the hard woman's face,
noticing something that did not fit. Tough Patsy Palmer
looked different. She looked soft. Her eyes filled with
concern. She resembled a loving mother as she held
the boy close.

He heard her whispering to him, "It's all right, my
little drummer boy. You's gonna be fine, Luke. You's
gonna be just fine. This is gonna hurt just for a moment, son. Just a moment. Don't you worry. You just let
out a good cry and then fall asleep. Your mama's got
you, Luke. Your mama's got you."

Clenching his teeth, Colter made sure of his hold on the boy's foot. Then he jerked.

Patsy Palmer's scream was louder than the boy's—but both were brief.

Later, looking down at the boy's face, Colter told Palmer: "Those tracks with the wagon. The young kid's. This must be that boy." He took a long breath, nodded, and exhaled. "Maybe the Cheyenne attacked the wagon. The kid got away. That's where he got the coupstick."

He looked for Palmer, saw her patting the unconscious boy's face.

"That's what I think," Colter said. "Reckon we'll find out when he wakes up."

"No." Palmer was stroking the boy's hand. She didn't look up at the lawman. "It's God's will. God's will. The Good Lord has give my boy back to me."

Tears streamed down her face and she started humming a hymn Colter vaguely recalled but couldn't name.

Chapter 28

Where the devil had Gene Harriman gone?

Jed Reno looked all around the Crow Creek Saloon but didn't see him. Though after all the whiskey he had been drinking that night, Jed Reno was surprised he could see anything.

He rubbed his eyes and reached for but missed the glass in front of him.

Walker Chester laughed and told Reno that he was "a blind, staggerin' drunk."

"No, I . . . ain't." Reno had trouble speaking. His tongue wasn't keeping up with his lips and his brain was about a mile behind both. He rubbed his eyes and glanced through the batwing doors. Night? Night had ended. It was daylight. Morning. Reno glanced at the big mirror behind the saloon's bar. The bartender was sipping coffee, sitting on a stool in the corner, trying to stay awake. No one else's reflection showed up except the swamper, who was sitting in the one chair he had not picked up and placed upside down on the tables. He was drinking coffee, too.

Coffee. Reno looked at that whiskey. Coffee was what he needed.

He grabbed the glass and filled his mouth with whiskey, but this time, for once, he did not swallow. Instead he swished around the foul concoction in his mouth, which he figured would clean his teeth and purify his breath, then leaned over and spat into the spittoon.

That was when he saw Gene Harriman, lying face up on the floor, snoring away, his fine shirt covered with dried vomit.

So that was one mystery solved. He knew where Harriman had gone. *Man who can't hold his liquor shouldn't drink with them that can*, Reno thought, and he looked around until he found Walker Chester, who was leaning against the bar right next to Reno.

Reno tried to replay the evening through his foggy, aching brain. He had been in Chester's livery . . . with . . . with that Pinkerton gal who had been hiding, as she had been for, well, as long as Reno could recollect, in that mountain of hay in Chester's livery. They had been talking about . . . about the president of the United States, who was thinking about visiting Cheyenne, and those fiends who kept hoping he would so they could kill him deader than Honest Abe Lincoln—which would ruin the country.

And then something came to Reno that was clearer than a Henry's Fork of the Green River in the spring.

* * *

"Jed Reno, you're the most loyal and honest man I've ever met," Ginger Burricchia whispers from beneath all that hay.

Which strikes Reno so absurd, he laughs like it's the funniest thing he has witnessed since the folks at Holly's Hog Ranch ran out that cardsharper all the way to Rawhide Creek over Fort Laramie way.

"What you laughin' at, Reno?" Chester asks.

Reno fiddles with his railroader's cap and Gene Harriman's head turns every which way as though there's somebody hiding in the livery—which Reno knows there is because he has been talking to her for a long time.

"I told you I heard Jed talking to somebody," Harriman says.

He doesn't hear pretty Ginger anymore. And if he doesn't do something right now, the next thing he might hear is her dying scream, because Chester has grabbed a pitchfork.

"Rat!" Chester roars. *"Stinkin' rat."*

And Reno comes up with a windy.

"I ain't been talkin' to no rat, you dern fools. I been talkin' to myself to keep my head from splittin' because of that infernal racket y'all two has been a-makin'." He hurls his railroader's cap at Gene Harriman, but it falls far short.

"You oughts to knows better'n bringin' a hoss to be shod at this time of day. I was thinkin' that I ain't tied on a good and pleasurable drunk in some time, but now my head aches so much from that shoein' your lame hoss got that I don't reckon I can do nothin' more than wait till that poundin' leaves my ears."

Harriman and Chester exchange glances, then both men stare at Reno.

Chester shakes his head and Harriman picks up the cap and brings it back to Reno, handing it to him without a word.

For a long while a quietness fills the livery and Reno makes himself forget the hay—and the woman hiding there.

A grin shows up on Chester's face. "How was you a-plannin' to get drunk, ol' pal o' mine?"

"Well . . ." Reno shrugs. He looks up at the gun shop owner. "Ain't he paid you for that shoein' job you just done for him?"

Chester roars in laughter and the two men pull Reno to his feet and they amble out of the livery and find their way to the closest saloon.

Three saloons later—or was it four?—they found themselves in the Crow Creek.

Chester looked at the bartender, who tried and failed to stifle a yawn. "Any chance of us gettin' a mornin' bracer?"

The young redheaded man with the twisted mustache didn't even look over at the two patrons. He took a deliberate sip of coffee and spoke, still without turning his head. "You can drink all you want, startin' 'round four this afternoon." He drank again and set the cup behind him. "Providin', o' course, that you got some cash money on you."

Chester spat on the floor and wiped his lips. "Ain't my credit good no more?"

The barman still did not look in their direction. "Your credit run out about three hours ago." He made a motion toward the floor. "Your pal's credit run out when he passed out."

And then he looked up at Jed Reno.

"And his credit was used up, I'd say, before this bucket of blood ever got built."

"Fine way to treat upstandin' citizens," Chester muttered and pushed away from the bar and looked at the swamper. "And you ain't gettin' no tip neither." He swayed but somehow kept from falling and nodded at Reno. "Let's go." He staggered toward the doors, and Reno glanced at Harriman before turning to follow the liveryman through into the morning.

"Take your pal with you, boys," the bartender ordered, "unless you want me to fetch the law and have him dragged to the calaboose."

"Fine treatment," Chester said as he walked back to the bar. "Fine treatment indeed." He nodded at Reno, and the two men bent, Reno taking the head and shoulders and Chester the feet, and they backed out of the saloon, with Chester deliberately kicking over the spittoon.

The batwing doors banged as they exited and turned down the boardwalk.

Cheyenne was always busy, but this time of day was quieter. The restaurants filled the air with smells of biscuits and coffee and flapjacks. The streetlamps had already been extinguished till this evening and a few businessmen were opening their doors, though most would remain closed till a more reasonable hour.

Hitching rails were empty now and they saw just two buggies being driven down the streets. The first train, Reno vaguely recalled, had arrived before dawn. He recalled the whistle and how the saloon's walls rattled as the train pulled in toward the Union Pacific depot, and the walls had shook so hard Harriman, Chester, and Reno had to grab their glasses to keep them from sliding off the bar when it pulled out ten or twelve minutes later. The passenger trains—for the UP and DP would not hit town till afternoon, nor would the mixed and other freight loads.

"Where's he live?" Reno asked.

"Above his store," Chester said. "Like most folks."

"Most folks live . . . above his store?" Reno tried to figure out how that was possible.

"No, you blitherin' dunce." Chester turned and spat into the street. "Most businessmen live above where they work. Turn right at the corner. Then left down the alley. We'll go in through Gene's back door."

When they reached the back of the gun shop, they half laid, half dropped Harriman onto the dirt, and Reno braced himself against the frame building while Chester leaned over the passed-out, snoring man and began going through his pockets till he pulled out a key.

"Hope this is it," the liveryman said, and he managed after three attempts to stand up, then stagger, trip, and fall against the door.

"I shoulda gone straight to bed," he moaned but pushed himself back, straightened, then bent and slid the key into the hole.

Reno heard the click and the door pushed inside.

"Thank the Lord," Chester said, and he moved back to Harriman's legs.

The back storeroom smelled of oil and powder. Chester instructed Reno on where to lay the gunsmith down and stuck the key back in the man's vest pocket.

"He'll wake up, I reckon, and figure out where he is, and maybe even thank us for gettin' him home," Chester said, then extended his right hand toward Reno. "Help me up, pardner."

Reno easily pulled Chester to his feet and then looked at the wall. He saw the flag pinned high, but this was not the flag that was waving over the capitol building or hung on the other wall at the US Marshal's office.

"Ain't that . . ." He pointed. "Ain't that the Confederate flag?"

Walker Chester groaned and turned to look across the kegs of gunpowder and various crates of rifles, ammunition, and revolvers.

"Battle jack," he corrected. "One of 'em. Them dumb Rebs never could figure out a flag that worked for 'em." He snorted out a laugh. "Maybe that's why they lost the war. Can't figure out a flag, you probably ain't that good at fightin' neither. Or maybe worryin' 'bout a flag instead of figurin' out how to win a war cost 'em."

He pointed. "That battle jack, that was in the corner of the first national flag of the ol' C S of A. Like ourn flag with the blue cloth and white stars. Then, instead of thirteen stripes, red and white, the Reb flag—the national one—it was all white. And that, the dumb oafs in Richmond later figgered, caused them graybellies all kinds of trouble when the wind weren't a-blowin'. If you couldn't see the red and blue in the corner, it looked like they was surrenderin'."

He spat again, wiped his mouth, and walked to the door, still open, and stepped out into the alley.

When Reno stepped out the liveryman closed the door, then laughed. "Maybe it woulda done 'em Rebs some good had they surrendered then. Just quit and figgered out if they couldn't get a flag right, they probably wasn't gonna win no war." He spat again, and Reno followed him back to the street.

They sure had covered a lot of ground between the saloons, Reno realized, as they walked down the boardwalks back to Chester's livery.

"That don't bother you none?" Reno asked as they walked. His head wasn't hurting so much, but he could sure use a healthy dose of black coffee.

"What don't bother me none?"

"Harriman," Reno answered. "Him with a Johnny Reb flag in his storeroom. I mean, you got wounded at Lawrence when 'em raiders sacked that town. That's how come—"

"How come I limp." Chester spat and Reno felt shamed. But they kept walking.

"Jed, do you know how long ago the war ended?"

Reno shrugged. "Two years, maybe three?"

Laughing, Chester shook his head.

"Right at eight." He stopped, turned back, and looked down the street, then lifted his head and stared at Reno. "This month. Maybe even today. No. Not today. No, it was the ninth of April. That's when Lee, Robert E. Lee, decided he'd had enough. Other generals did the same. Edmund Kirby Smith give up and went back to Richmond to take the oath. That was in May. He was the last, well, except for that ol' Cherokee gen'ral named Watie, who turned in his flag in the Indian Territory in June. And the war was over. No more fightin' to do but over poker hands and perty dance hall gals, don't you know!"

He waited for Jed to say something, but he didn't know what to say.

"Point is, pardner . . ." The liveryman turned around and started walking. "The war is over, Jed. Been over for eight years. I ain't ashamed to be limpin' on account that I earned this limp fightin' fer what I figgered—and still figger—was for the right thing. To preserve the union. Now let's stop all this palaverin'. It ain't good to talk this much over no empty belly. Ain't good to talk when a body's head is rattlin' something awful like as we both is gettin' up in years and can't drink likker like we used to do—glory be those fine years of glorious drinkin' and fightin'."

Reno could see the livery stable now.

"Let's get back to work. I'm sayin' it's yer turn to make the coffee this mornin' and you'd better make it stout enough to float a dozen horseshoes or we ain't never gonna get nothin' done today."

When they entered the barn Chester pointed to the coffeepot and began shoving paper and sawdust and hay from the stash where Ginger, the pretty Pinkerton gal, hid whenever she needed hiding. The old man with the bad leg did not spend much time with the straw and used flint and steel to get the fire started.

"Good and strong, Jed," he ordered and went to feed the animals in the stalls first.

Reno found the sack of coffee and scooped a lot into the big pot, then dunked the pot in the water trough out front. If it was good enough for a horse to drink, he had been saying since he had become a city person, it was good enough for a man.

He shook the water to mix up the grounds with the wet stuff and laid the pot on the stove when Walker Chester limped back with a pitchfork in his hands.

The old man said nothing and Reno sucked in a breath and held it when Chester jammed the sharp tines into the hay. He pulled it out, cursed his clumsiness, and speared the mountain again.

"I musta drunk way too much," Chester said, laughing, then wiping his forehead with his left arm. "Tryin' to get these hosses some breakfast and . . ." He looked over at Reno, who let out his breath and walked over, taking the pitchfork from the old cripple's hands.

"Why don't you get some sleep, hoss?" Reno said, and he turned and looked at the hay. He raised the pitchfork and jammed it hard into the pile, then brought it out with a mound of breakfast for one of the horses.

"Who gets it first, hoss?"

"The sorrel."

Reno walked away, some of the hay falling to the floor, pitched that into the first stall, and returned. Without looking at Chester, he jammed the tines of the pitchfork back into the hay, scooped it up, and took that one to the sorrel, too.

"The buckskin gets two as well," Chester told him. "The rest just one."

Reno went at it, feeding all the horses in the barn, then taking loads to the corral. When he had finished with that he walked back to find the old man looking at the hay.

"We ought to move some of that closer to the door to the corral," he told his landlord. "That pile's all but gone."

Chester's head bobbed. "I was thinkin' the same thing."

So Reno went right on destroying Ginger Burricchia's hiding place, stopping only to mop his sweating forehead when he saw nothing out of the ordinary on the ground where the Pinkerton lady had been hiding. He wasn't sure if Walker Chester would have noticed.

"Want me to find Barrett and see if he can haul in some more hay?" Reno asked the stable owner.

"Aww." Chester stopped to think. "Nah. I'll see him later today and do it myself." He nodded at the pot on the stove. "'Sides, I've worked you plenty hard after our little fun hoorawin' and howlin' night." He grabbed a mitt and used it to lift the well-used pot off the stove.

Reno leaned the pitchfork against the wall and wiped his hands on his trousers. "I have to say," he said, smacking his lips, "that I've worked up a powerful thirst."

"You done a powerful lot of work, too, for a crotchety old fur trapper."

Their mugs clinked together in a toast and they blew on the hot, black, strong brew, then tested the coffee.

"Just as awful as I can take it," Chester said with a grin.

Reno sipped and nodded. "Yours is always worser."

"Yep." The old man laughed. "And I'll try to make mine even nastier tomorrow."

Reno laughed and found a good, comfortable place to sit. Chester joined him, squatting where the secret hiding place once stood.

They drank and stared at each other for the first few drinks.

Reno crossed his legs at the ankles. "That was a mighty good night," he said.

"Good to get stinking drunk," Chester agreed.

They sipped more coffee. It was, Reno had to concede, powerful strong and just plain awful.

"I sure bet ol' Harriman could be using some of this right about now," he said.

They laughed again and Chester started to climb back to his feet. He peered through the cracks and said, "Must be nine o'clock, nine thirty by now, Cheyenne time."

Reno drank more coffee.

"I ought to go check on Harriman. Make sure he ain't throwed up and choked to death on his own vomit."

Trying to rise, Reno gave up and leaned against the picket wall but still managed to make the offer: "Want me to come with you?"

"Nah. You go 'bout your day, pardner. I'll see you later."

Reno watched him go. He stared at the black coffee for two or three minutes and drank some more. Then he looked at the place where the hay had been and shook his head.

"Timmy Colter, ol' hoss, I sure wish you was here to help me figger some things out."

Chapter 29

His eyes shot wide open, then closed tightly because of the blinding sun that, for one fearful moment, he thought was the flames of Hades. His head hurt. He felt the warmth of the sun and heard the sound of a horse—no, horses—stamping their hooves on hard-packed ground.

"Ohhhhhhhhhhh," Kip Jansen moaned. "What . . . ?"

"Easy, sonny," a somewhat feminine voice whispered, and Kip felt rough hands slip behind his neck. "I'm a-gonna lift you up just an itty-bitty bit so you can drink some water."

"Nooooo." His whisper sounded horrible, like his mouth was filled with desert sand and his tongue had quadrupled in size. "I gotta . . ." It hurt to talk, but he had to be clear and adamant about this. ". . . gotta . . . save . . . water."

He felt the wetness of the lip of his canteen against his lips. His head shook. "I can't . . ."

"Yes," the voice told him. "You can and you will."

"No. Gotta save—"

"Boy. You made it this far. There's a spring here. Good water. Nice and cold."

The water was cool. It soothed his lips immediately and then he felt some trickle into his mouth and gloriously fall to the back of his throat and down toward his empty, awful stomach.

When the canteen was pulled away from his lips Kip reached urgently for it. "No." He coughed out that word, and managed a pathetic whisper. "More. . . . Please."

For a long while to him at least, he heard only heavy breathing, but a few seconds later the wet canteen was back at his lips. "One more sip. Jus' one. Ya hear? Your belly ain't ready for too much food or too much water."

He heard. He nodded. He tasted wonderful water again. So beautiful. His tongue moved around the inside of his mouth, no longer caked with windblown and kicked-up sand and grit and wretched dryness. The canteen moved away from him, but this time he did not plead for more. He felt his head against the softness of a blanket that smelled like a well-used saddle.

"Thank you," he thought he whispered but was not sure until he heard the reply.

"You're welcome, Luke."

He wanted to correct that name, let this angel know that he was Kip Jansen of Decatur in Morgan County, Alabama, but the blackness was coming hard for him again. And for all he knew, Kip Jansen had been a dream. Maybe his name was Luke.

Whoever he was, he slept again.

*   *   *

In his dream he rode with the Indians who had given him that fancy crutch that had carried him so far south. Kip's hair hung in braids and he wore a white-boned breastplate decorated with the feathers of hawks. He wore leggings and rode a brown-and-white pinto, carrying a lance. He rode with his friends, the Indian who had given him the stick he no longer needed.

Kip Jansen, better known as White Warrior, rode horses like he had been born to them. They rode over the hill and then down, and now his mother, who had also been adopted into the Cheyenne tribe, led the songs for the hunters.

> *We're tenting to-night on the old camp ground,*
> *Give us a song to cheer*
> *Our weary hearts, a song of home*
> *And friends we love so dear.*

The words, Kip thought, sounded like they were English, but he heard them in Cheyenne.

A great herd of buffalo began running in the valley below and now the Indian men yelled and cheered and sang their own songs.

"There will be meat in our bellies tonight!" Kip yelled, and he realized he was speaking in the dialect of the Northern Cheyenne. He raised his lance and saw a fat, young buffalo bull. Kip charged after him.

When the Mean One, the Cheyenne who had never liked Kip or White Warrior, also turned his pony toward that bull, Kip yelled, "Find your own, Mean One. One that you can handle. This one is too much for you. And he is mine!"

Mean One grunted and gave Kip a look of bitter resentment, but he also knew that Kip was not a warrior to trifle with, so he jerked the hackamore of his pinto and went after a lame cow.

Raising the lance higher in his arm, Kip smiled. The wind blew his braids behind him. It slapped his coppery face. The pony closed the distance and the words of Kip's father—his white father—whispered into his ear.

"This is not Decatur. You can't go back to Decatur. There's nothing for you in Alabama. The Union forever. But the West is where you belong."

The buffalo bull made a sudden turn to the right. Lining his heart perfectly for the point of Kip's lance.

He yelled out a shout of victory and let the lance fly.

Kip woke to a world of no buffalo, no green grass, no Cheyenne warriors. He was dressed in practically nothing and lying on a gray woolen bedroll. Behind him were voices.

"I's surprised you come back fer us."

"How's the kid?"

"Sleepin', which I was a-doin' my ownself till you rid back up. What'd you see?"

"He walked a long way."

"You find the wagon? Or his folks?"

No answer. But Kip could have told them that. The wagon might still be there, and maybe even that poor, abused mule. But not Kip's folks. One was buried up in that lonesome country. The other was buried with a long line of other heroes who wore the blue not far from the Tennessee River—the same river that was responsible for how big and booming Decatur, Alabama, was. Funny, Kip wondered, that he had never thought about the connection between Decatur and Pittsburg Landing.

"Well, I reckon yer trackin' down ol' Gen'ral Dugan ends here. You come a long ways for nothin', Deputy Colter, 'cause you sure cain't bring no li'l boy with you into that nest of cutthroats."

Kip's lips parted. He swallowed what little saliva remained in his mouth. He thought about the dream that was quickly fading from his consciousness and he said, "Who . . . are . . . you?"

The first face seemed familiar. It was a woman's face. Or was it?

She wasn't dressed like a woman and she sure didn't have the face of Kip's mother, but she settled beside him and lifted his head off whatever it had been resting on.

"How you feelin', Luke?"

She brought the canteen to his lips and let him drink as much as he wanted.

He stared into her eyes, licked the moisture off his lips, and whispered, "My name's Kip."

"Kip." The newcomer squatted on Kip's left. The first thing Kip noticed about him was the giant pistol leathered in the holster on the tall, quiet, confident man's right hip. Kip saw the star pinned to his vest.

Deputy

US

Marshal

The man brought his right hand toward Kip's.

"My name's Colter. Tim Colter."

Kip raised his hand weakly and liked the strength in Deputy Marshal Tim Colter's grip.

"You hungry?" the big woman asked.

"I . . ." He wet his lips again. "Yeah. I mean, yes, ma'am."

The big woman started walking away and the deputy turned toward her and said, "Make it broth for right now." He looked back at Kip and grinned. "Just not to send your stomach into shock."

Kip looked at the lawman, who was studying him long and hard until the woman came back with a cup that was steaming hot and smelled like nothing more than wet beef. But it might as well have been fresh buttermilk with sugar cookies to dunk into.

"I'll tend to my horse," the lawman said and left Kip with the big woman, who appeared not to have bathed in quite some time. Then Kip, when he reached for the cup, realized the same could be said for him, too.

The woman hummed some melody Kip could not recognize as he sipped the hot brew till it cooled down enough so he could swallow enough to give him something to live on.

It tasted . . . different.

He looked up at the woman.

"What is this?"

She shrugged. "Just somethin' I fixed fer you."

Kip hoped his stare told him he wanted a better description.

"Mostly boiled beef jerky." He nodded and drank some more. Then the words the woman had spoken registered.

"Mostly?"

Her big head moved up and down.

"What else?"

Her smile did not remind him of his mother's. "I gots lucky while that lawdog was up a-scoutin'. Catched us a right fair-sized prairie dog."

Kip felt the broth rising up in his throat.

"Drink it all down, Luke."

He sighed. "Kip. My name's Kip. Kip Jansen."

The woman's face stilled. "Oh." She fished a flask from her pocket and unscrewed the cap, bringing the container to her mouth. "I . . ." She made herself smile. "Slip of me tongue." Her eyes found the flask she held and Kip watched her as she refastened the cap and then pitched the flask to another bedroll, one that was rolled up next to a saddle with a big rifle leaning against the cantle.

Kip thought he had seen that rifle before, and then he remembered something he thought he had dreamed.

"Hold it right there, pardner." The speaker is aiming this cannon of a long gun right at Kip's belly.

But that's all he can recall.

Then Kip looked at the lawman, who was walking back, past the rifle, and over to him and the rough woman. He squatted again on the other side of Kip and sniffed. Momentarily his eyes locked on the cup Kip held, then shifted over toward the woman.

"What did you put in my coffee cup?"

"Broth."

The lawman looked back at Kip.

"Beef jerky," Kip whispered. "And prairie dog."

"Good eatin'," the woman told him and nodded. "It'll fix you right up, fer shore."

The man named Colter stared at both and then took the cup, sniffed it, and brought it to his lips. To Kip's surprise, he actually drank some. He wasn't pretending. He drank a healthy dose, and while he made a face that Kip seemed to picture like when Mama made him drink some castor oil, he nodded at the woman and returned the cup to Kip.

"I'll say it'll fix you up," the lawman said and coughed.

"Drink it down, Lu—" She stared at her feet for a long while, then rubbed sand or something out of the corners of her eyes with her massive fists and focused on Kip again. "Drink it down, Kip. I know how to fix folks up. You need something in your belly more than grit."

Kip drank. Then he slept again.

When he woke he felt better, until he looked down at his left ankle. The lawman came back over, saw that he was awake, and squatted beside him.

"I had to reset it," he said. "I don't know how you managed to walk a hundred yards with that foot, even with that coupstick. And I followed your trail—"

Kip knew it showed bad manners on his part—his grandmother would have tanned his hide had he done such a thing before her back in Decatur—but he had to ask the question. "Coupstick?"

The lawman didn't seem insulted or outraged. He simply stopped speaking and searched with his eyes. Then he reached over and behind Kip's head and came back with the fancy stick that had gotten him all the way from Lige Kerns.

"Coupstick," he said. He read Kip's eyes and put it in the boy's hands. "Northern Cheyenne," the lawman continued, "by the looks of it."

Kip tested the words. "Coup . . . stick."

Tim Colter nodded. "You ever heard of an Indian counting coup?"

"No sir," Kip answered, shaking his head.

"It's an act of bravery for most of the Plains tribes. Cheyenne, Sioux, Arapaho." His thumb hooked in the direction behind him. "Comanche and Kiowa farther south." He sat down and stretched out his legs. "To an Indian brave, if he can touch one of his enemy while he's still alive, it's a great honor. They call it 'counting coup.'" He shifted his position. "Anyway, they will use a stick to touch their enemy. Coupstick." The deputy nodded at the coupstick in Kip's hands.

"From the looks of that one, it came from a real powerful Cheyenne. He wouldn't just give it up without a fight."

Kip looked away from the stick and into Tim Colter's eyes. "I found it," he said. "Well, I thought I found it."

He told the lawman about finding the stick, but then seeing the horse tracks. He hadn't known what it was, but he knew he needed it and could use it as a crutch. Nothing else nearby would help. Then he backed up his story and told him about walking and stepping into the hole—prairie dog hole—and he looked at the cup that had held the awful stew.

Smiling, then laughing, he spoke in the excited voice of that boy who had been Kip Jansen back in Morgan County. "Maybe I just got even with that prairie dog who busted my leg. Maybe I got revenge."

Colter, to Kip's surprise, laughed, too. "Maybe," he said, nodding in agreement.

But then Kip told him about the return of the Indians. How he thought he was about to be dead, but the other Indian, the young leader, had intervened. And finally they had made a trade. A sack of mostly pecans for the coupstick.

"Pecans?" The deputy shook his head.

"Yes sir."

Tim Colter smiled again. "Well, that's a good trade." He looked off toward the south. "I can't tell you the last time I ate a pecan."

"Ma . . ." Kip stopped and looked at the dirt. How long he wasn't sure, but it probably was no more than five or ten seconds, and when he saw the lawman again he swallowed. "My mother made really good pecan pies."

"My mother was partial to peach pies."

Kip grinned. "Ma also made a fine peach pound cake."

Colter smiled. "Sounds tasty. Never had that before."

He fiddled with the coupstick in his hands before he looked up at the lawman. "I was wondering. Do you reckon that Indian—the one who traded with me for the coupstick." He paused to think about the word and what a strange trade for a young warrior to make with a boy who had no business being in Wyoming Territory. "Do you think he might have left that stick for me to find? Just to see if I'd have sense enough to use it. And maybe that's why when he came back he was willing to make a real poor trade on his part."

The lawman thought that over for a couple of minutes and finally shrugged.

"That's a solid premise, Kip. I can't say I know what's in the head of a young Northern Cheyenne, but . . ." He considered the idea again. "Maybe so. When we get back to Cheyenne I'll introduce you to a pard of mine. Jed Reno. He's old and ornery, but he knows more about Indians and this part of the country than anyone living. He'd be quite willing to tell you his thoughts. I have to say I had not considered that, but it's a right solid theory. You sure proved your worth to that young Indian."

Kip looked at his foot, then back up at the deputy. "Are you taking me back to Cheyenne?"

"Well . . ." The lawman shrugged. "Why don't you tell me how you wound up here . . . in this big patch of big country, where there are hardly any white men around—any white men who aren't outlaws?"

Kip frowned.

"Let me tell you what I know. Just from sign. You were heading north in a small wagon that was carrying a lot of weight. The other signs I read told me that one mule was pulling that wagon. And from the human prints I could find one belonged to a little man." He nodded at Kip. "That would be you."

Kip straightened. *Little man.* Not little *boy.* He tried not to let his face reveal the pride.

"The other belonged to a woman."

Kip nodded. "That would have been my mother." He could not stop the tears. "She . . . she . . . she was sick before we left Morgan County. It was Lige Kerns's doings. He talked her into heading west. Said it was wide-open territory and that there was gold for the taking up in the Montana country."

The marshal unloosened his bandanna and handed it to Kip when the tears stopped, and Kip thanked him as he wiped his face and held the silk cloth back toward the deputy.

"Keep it," Colter told him. "I have another in my saddlebag." He leaned a bit forward. "Lige Kerns."

"Yes sir. My ma . . . she . . . married him."

"He's not your father?"

"Not by a . . ." The voice fell to a whisper. "No sir. My daddy . . . he died fighting for the Union."

The lawman's eyes widened. "Union?"

Kip nodded. "Yes sir," he said with pride. "Morgan County, Alabama, was pretty much all for the blue."

"Really."

"I ain't fooling, Marshal Colter. Ask anyone. The South wasn't all Rebels and slaveholders. There were . . . well . . . not many . . . but there were more than a few Union soldiers from Alabama and other Confederate states."

Colter seemed to accept this. "So, your father died during the war. Your mother remarried. Your stepdaddy decided to move you all to Montana."

Kip nodded. "That's about the size of it. I wish we never left. I wish . . ."

But wishing wouldn't do him any good.

Chapter 30

Tim Colter let a few long seconds tick past. And he waited till the boy looked back up at him.

"Did you fight in the rebellion?" Kip Jansen asked.

Rebellion. Yes, Colter thought, this boy was union blue, just like his dad. Most Alabamans called those savage four years "The War for Southern Independence."

"I don't know if I'd call it fighting, son," Colter answered in all honesty. "But I was a lieutenant, duly elected, in Company D in the First Oregon Volunteer Cavalry and spent most of the war drilling and drilling at Fort Walla Walla."

The boy must have liked that as he nodded his approval. "How'd you become a marshal?"

"Deputy," Colter corrected. "I got hired to keep the peace in a town called Elkton in Umpqua County." He paused and grinned. "Don't ask me how to spell it or what it means. It's Oregon." He remembered his wife then, and their babies, but knew he had to talk his way through this to get some information from the boy.

"That was before the war," Colter told him. "Anyway, after Lee's surrender and the other Rebels gave up, I learned that my wife and children had died of diphtheria." He paused, wondering if he could continue. "Two sons, one daughter. The youngest, Claude, would probably be a year or two younger than you are now."

"I'm fourteen," Kip told him.

Colter thought and nodded. "Yep. Claude would be turning twelve on August 10."

"I'm sorry, Marshal Colter."

"And I'm sorry for your losses, too. I bet I would have enjoyed sharing a meal with your pa. I bet he would have made a mighty fine deputy marshal, too."

Kip grinned. "He was a good shot. Won three turkey shoots in a row."

"I never was much of a hand with a long gun." That wasn't exactly the truth, but he knew he was better with the LeMat. "Anyway . . ." He had to move on. "I was hired as a deputy marshal in Oregon. And then, because of my familiarity with this country . . ." Colter waved his arms to indicate Wyoming. "It was Dakota Territory at the time—I was asked to come to a town—doesn't even exist today—and help bring peace to the settlement. I took the offer." He looked the boy in the eye. "With my family gone, Oregon had nothing to keep me."

The boy's head nodded in solemn understanding. "I don't think I'd want to go back to Alabama now," he whispered.

"So I stayed," Colter continued. "Eventually got hired as a deputy federal marshal."

Kip's eyes brightened. "And that's when you met Miss Palmer."

That wasn't what either Colter—or, from the look on her face, Patsy Palmer—expected. But Palmer recovered first.

"You might could say that, son." She nodded her head as the final punctuation on the statement.

And that, Colter decided, meant it was time to get the information he needed.

"This . . ." Colter waved his arms, indicating the big, vast, foreboding yet awesome and beautiful country. "This isn't the trail emigrants take to the Montana goldfields."

The boy's face remained blank.

"This trail is used mostly by Indians . . ." Colter smiled. "As well you know." But now he had to get serious. "And . . . outlaws."

The boy stared at Colter for a long while, then dropped his gaze to his ankle. "He weren't no good. Never. I . . ." He paused to wipe away the tears and somehow managed to dam the rest of them from trickling down his dirty face. "Well . . . I just don't know what Mama ever saw in him. There was lots of good men in Morgan County. I mean, lots of good men who fought for Alabama—I mean, the Confederacy—and they didn't hold no grudge against my pa because he wore the blue. They figured the war was over and they might as well get on with their lives."

Colter nodded in understanding.

"But your stepfather, this Lige Kerns . . . he wasn't like most of the men back in your hometown."

The boy's head shook adamantly.

"How did you get from Alabama to this part of the country?" Colter asked.

The river travels from Tennessee to St. Louis didn't interest Colter much, but he paid attention and nodded, listening. Patsy Palmer finally came over and squatted on Colter's right and handed the boy another cup.

"This is just tea," she said. "Not strong but weak tea." She grinned. "No prairie dog."

The boy took the cup and drank a few sips, then went on with his story. From St. Louis the family had taken a roundabout trip to Omaha, Nebraska. They spent more than a week there, and Colter did not press the boy on how this family could have afforded to live in a city of that size. Tim Colter had been through Omaha twice and the prices of everything from a bath to a hotel room had shocked him. He kept listening, but the boy was talking about his mother working and Kip's jobs, too, with a few dishonest enterprises like stealing apples from a merchant or going through the trash bins behind a restaurant for food.

Kip's eyes turned pleading when he stopped, wet his lips, and asked, "You ain't gonna arrest me for stealing, are you?"

"No," he answered with a quick smile. "My jurisdiction is federal. Just be careful what you do in Wyoming Territory." He reached over and patted the boy's right leg. "You're a good kid. You were just doing what you had to do to help your mother. I bet the grocer saw you take those apples and whatnot and knew you were just doing what you had to do."

That seemed to take a massive weight off the teen's shoulders and Colter decided to steer the conversation in another direction.

"So all this while you're helping keep your mother and you in food and such, what was this stepfather of yours doing?"

"He just loafed around."

Colter prodded. "Saloons?"

"Maybe." The boy shrugged. "We moved into a tent outside this place called Camp Sherman. Sherman Barracks is what most folks called it. I didn't know what Lige Kerns thought he could do there. I mean, those were the bluecoats he was always calling ugly names." The boy frowned. "That's when I really hated him. Him calling those soldiers foul things. And my daddy had died fighting in that uniform."

"I understand." He let the boy finish the tea and return the cup to Palmer. "Was he gambling? Stealing?"

"I don't know. I just helped Mama do whatever I could. And it wasn't long before Lige Kerns said he had gotten a good job. And we were finally going west to find our fortune in the gold camps of Montana Territory."

Colter knew to keep quiet now, to let the boy tell the story in his own words.

"Lige Kerns . . . he had this big crate. He said it was mining equipment—well, at first he called it a reaper for farming, but he was drunk then. He was always drunk, or so it sure seemed to me. He had to pay some big, burly railroad hands to load it onto the boxcar. And he was able to pay those big, burly men in greenbacks for their help. I'd never seen Lige Kerns with more than a dollar or two to his name. Usually he was having to borrow a dime or ten dollars from my ma. And Lige Kerns, even after that he still had money to buy us tickets on the westbound train all the way to Laramie City."

The boy stopped to finish the tea. Colter had some questions, but he did not want to ask the boy now. He wanted Kip to tell the story straight through.

"I mean, he didn't spend a whole lot of money for us on the train ride. But it was fun. I'd never ridden on a train before. Ma and I'd read about Pullman sleepers, but Lige Kerns didn't spend any money for that kind of stuff. He even made Ma buy some food we could eat on the train. I guess . . ." He fell silent and stared at his bad ankle. "I guess . . . I wished maybe Lige Kerns was gonna be all right. Start treating my ma better. Maybe treat me better, too. But that was a foolish notion. He gambled some with a man on the train and lost some of his money but not all. That wasn't like him. Not Lige Kerns. And when we finally got to Laramie City he had enough money to buy two mules and a rickety ol' wagon. He hired a couple of mule skinners loafin' at the station to load his big crate of mining equipment onto the wagon and we rode out that evening.

"But he didn't provision us with enough food." He paused and smiled. "Provision. I learned that word on our trip. Never heard it used that way . . . you know . . . as a . . . verb."

Colter nodded.

"Lige had a map somebody had drawn for him and that's the trail we followed. But it didn't take us but one or two days till we learned that this country wasn't nothing like Alabama. One mule died. Just up and died. Ma wanted us to turn back, but Lige Kerns kept promising her he was taking us to the promised land. Well, this wasn't nothing like the country we'd seen whilst we were crossin' Nebraska and even into the eastern parts of Wyoming neither. Wouldn't call it promised. This country was just . . . well, Ma called it 'forebodin'.'"

"It's big." Colter nodded. "Sometimes frightening."

Palmer reached over and patted the boy's shoulder. "And it can be promising. And beautiful. And the wonderfullest country you've ever seen."

Colter nodded. "She's right."

For a long while Kip kept quiet, wiping his eyes, staring at the dirt and rocks, and at length looked up and stared over at Patsy Palmer.

"Ma got sicker. And sicker. And we was just about out of food and water. The map that Lige Kerns had had drawn for him said there was water here. But we couldn't find it. I guess you knew where to look?"

Colter nodded. Patsy Palmer answered, "It's deep down." She pointed to the high rock wall. "You have to know where it is. Mostly Indians know about it. Come a good rain, the water flows down that rock face. But mostly it's all underground. About four feet when it's been a wet winter. Two feet, sometimes one during the driest times. Yer mapmaker should've been more specific. You got to drop your canteen or cup or pot or whatever down and then haul it up. Like you was workin' a well."

The boy's head went up and down.

"Sure glad y'all was here before I got here. I don't reckon I would ever have found it either."

Palmer rose and handed him a canteen. "Ya been gabbin' a lot. Why don't you wet your whistle." It wasn't a question, and Kip drank and returned the container to the big woman. He wiped his mouth with the back of his right hand and looked Colter in the eye.

"Anything I just told you helpful?"

"Very much," Colter said. "How big was that crate?"

Kip measured with his hands as far as the height and said that lengthwise it was about four feet longer than Kip was tall. He knew that for a fact because when he slept in the wagon he was usually right up against it.

"Was there any writing on it?"

"Most of the letters were all painted over in black paint. But there was hand-written in that same black paint to the side, 'Mining Tools and Equipmint.' I noticed that right off because 'equipment' was spelled wrong. I figured either Lige Kerns wrote that himself or the person who sold it to him was just as ignorant as he was."

"And I know it was heavy," Colter said, "because of the depths of the wheel tracks I found."

"Yes sir." Kip's head bobbed. "Lige Kerns and I couldn't lift it ourselves. And we didn't want to." He focused on Colter for a brief moment. "I'm not even sure you and I could have hauled it down. It musta weighed nigh a ton."

Patsy Palmer snorted and spat in the dirt. "I coulda lifted it. With one hand."

The boy grinned but then cocked his head as though remembering. Colter waited.

"There was . . ." Kip paused, closed his eyes, trying to picture something he had seen.

When the boy's eyes opened he stared at the lawman briefly and finally whispered, "I remember something that wasn't blacked out by that sloppy paintbrush. I only got a glimpse of it when they were lifting it onto the wagon at the Omaha depot. It was on the bottom. I was sitting down and they had to do some twisting and turning, and for a moment I could see the bottom of the crate. It read . . . 'Manufactured in . . .'"

He paused and shut his eyes again, then whispered, "'Hartford, C-o-n-n period.'"

The brute of a woman turned immediately toward Colter. "What do that mean?"

"Hartford," Colter answered, "Connecticut."

"Is that important?" Kip asked.

"It's good information. Really good. It might mean a lot." Colter looked up at the sky. "Now I just have to figure out what to do with you two."

"But what's in Hartford, Co—Con . . . ?" Palmer gave up. "What's in that town?"

"Lots of things," Colter said. He knew of several gun manufacturers in that area. Colter's LeMat might have been dreamed up in New Orleans, but it had been manufactured in Philadelphia, and the second models of the big handgun were made in Paris and imported to America by way of Birmingham, England. And while Samuel Colt, the big man of American firearms, might have started his business in Paterson, New Jersey, he had moved the factory operations to Eli Whitney's armory in some town in Connecticut and later set up Colt's Patent Fire-Arms Manufacturing Company in Hartford five years or thereabouts before the Civil War broke out. Winchester and Sharps, whose rifles were found everywhere in the western territories, were now based in Hartford, but Colter was thinking about another. And that one made sense. Now he turned and stared hard at Patsy Palmer, who would not turn to face him.

"Forty-five caliber ammunition was stolen from the armory at Fort Fetterman," he said. "Remember? And now a heavy crate from a manufacturer in Hartford, Connecticut. That mean anything to you?"

"I don't know . . . nothin' 'bout nothin'," she said.

But Tim Colter did. It was just as he had expected all along. Richard Gatling had started off in Indianapolis, Indiana, but he had moved his operations east, where most of the country's leaders in firearms were headquartered.

"Your pal Jake Dugan has got himself a Gatling gun. Doesn't he?"

Chapter 31

Jed Reno did not feel like himself. A drunken Denver Pacific conductor had dropped a nickel onto the boardwalk as he staggered out of a saloon and, not noticing it, crossed the street and never even looked back. The coin had spun around and finally toppled and rattled and stopped right in front of Jed's left moccasin, but he didn't stop to pick it up.

He felt listless. No, he just felt lost. Tim Colter was off with a woman who fought like a man, with the law chasing him, though Reno figured no one in Laramie City had enough savvy or courage to get too close to Colter. Here in Cheyenne all the cooks were busy burning their noontime chuck in the hotels and eateries across town, or mothers and wives were sweating over a skillet to put some food on plates for families. But Reno wasn't in the mood to eat.

By golly, he didn't even want to pull a cork and get rip roaring roostered.

A jehu pulled his mud wagon to a sliding stop, and

the messenger lifted his fanny off the bench and called Reno every foul word he could muster up.

"Watch where you're goin'!" he yelled. "You want to get run over by a six-up?"

Reno didn't even look over at the coach or the men and paid no attention to the dust and sand that peppered him as he kept walking to the boardwalk. At some point he did stop and scooped handfuls of water from the trough in front of Jubal's Café to slake his thirst. He brought up more water and splashed it across his face, and a dun gelding snorted and stamped a forefoot to let him know that this water was spoken for.

"Ya gots plenty, pardner," Reno told the horse and looked across the street. He spotted the American flag lying limp high up across the government building, for this was maybe the one minute of the year that the wind wasn't blowing.

Reno removed his cap, scratched his head, and walked to the end of the hitching rail. This time he looked in both directions before he crossed the street, stepped onto the creaking wood, and stopped at the posters that had been tacked onto the board to the left of the big door.

While he couldn't read the words except for the "US" that spelled "United States," he could see the likeness the artist had manufactured, and while it wasn't the spitting image of Tim Colter, a man who knew the deputy would recognize him. The rest of the poster meant nothing to him.

WANTED
TIM COLTER

FOR SUSPICION OF
ORGANIZING
THE VIOLENT BREAKOUT
OF TERRITORIAL PRISONERS
INCLUDING MAD BEN GORE,
THE MURDEROUS SCOUNDREL
$250 REWARD
INQUIRE UNITED STATES MARSHAL'S OFFICE
CHEYENNE, WYOMING
COLTER HAS BEEN EMPLOYED AS A DEPUTY MARSHAL IN
THE WYOMING TERRITORIAL'S FEDERAL DISTRICT. HE IS
AN EXCELLENT SHOT WITH REVOLVER OR RIFLE AND
KNOWS HOW TO FIGHT LIKE ANY WELL-TRAINED PUGILIST.
HE SHOULD BE APPROACHED WITH THE UTMOST CAUTION
AND CONSIDERED TO BE ARMED AND DANGEROUS.

Reno looked up and down the boardwalk. Most folks must have been eating or, as Reno had heard a few of Cheyenne's best wags say in some of Cheyenne's cheapest saloons, "Nobody works past dinnertime in the federal district."

Because the wind had picked up again, Reno jerked the paper from the nail, wadded it up, and tossed it into the street. He watched the wind take Tim Colter's likeness and all those letters off down the street, where it finally blew itself into an opening in the boardwalk across from the courthouse.

Satisfied with his accomplishment, Reno latched onto the door handle and stepped out of the wind and into the office of the district marshal.

The chief man of the office, Clyde Tobin, stopped talking as soon as Reno came inside. He did not seem happy to see Reno here at this moment, but that was not unusual. Deputies Jack Collins and Frank Smith— Reno still didn't think that was the man's true name— sat at the table opposite Tobin, but there was a stranger sitting at that table, too, a little feller with black hair and Dundreary whiskers. Didn't look like a US marshal to Jed Reno. Looked like a sidewinder of an attorney or a skinflinting store clerk. Might have been a secretary because he had two big, thick notebooks in front of him and pencils all over the place, including over his left ear and one in his tiny right hand.

"Reno." The head lawman scraped the legs of his chair on the floor as he pushed it back and rose. "We are having an interview here that is of no concern of yours. And what in heaven's name are you doing? I thought for certain you'd be riding hard to help your traitorous pal Colter."

Young Jack Collins lowered his gaze and shook his head. "So you could have a couple of Arapaho scouts and Frank here follow him."

Swearing savagely, Tobin turned his wrath from Reno to the young deputy. "Your attitude is beginning to annoy me, Jack. So if you want to keep your job, you might ought to keep your lips tight and your opinions to yourself."

"Yes sir," the youngster whispered.

Tobin pointed to Reno. "Out," he said. "When we need a tracker we will let you know."

But the stranger cleared his throat and pushing the pencil he held over his pencil-less ear, slowly rose and removed his thick eyeglasses.

"I say, I say, but did I hear you right?" The accent

was foreign but from where Reno could not say. "But did you call this man Reno?"

Smith grunted. "That's what he calls himself."

"As in Jed Reno?"

Now everyone was staring at the gray-headed man with the wide scar on his left cheek.

"I'm Jed Reno." He stepped a few paces toward the table and tried to place the runt.

Nope. That fellow was a stranger, but apparently the foreigner knew Reno quite well—or at least had heard of him.

"*The* Jed Reno?" The man gasped as if he were talking to George Washington.

"Well, I'm the only Jed Reno I know."

Everyone stared at the runt, who rose suddenly, knocking the chair to the floor, and rushed around the table, charging right toward Reno, who stood there downright bewildered.

The man stopped, bowed, saluted, and held out his right hand. Reno's hand swallowed his, but it was this little foreigner who shook it so long and hard while he talked that Reno wondered if he'd be able to lift a jug in the coming hours.

"Mr. Reno, my name is Horatio John Paul Jones Irving and I am a contributor for the *New-York Tribune*, the greatest newspaper in the world, founded and run by—till his untimely death—the outstanding Whig-turned-Liberal Republican leader Horace Greeley, who rose from poverty to become a shaper of opinions of world leaders as journalist, editor, writer, traveler, Congressman from 1848 to 1849, patriot, and, yes, presidential candidate against General Ulysses S. Grant, but a loyal American who loved his country, his newspaper, and heroes such as the mountain man of our time, Jed Reno."

Finally the man's introduction stopped and he stepped aside, lifting his right arm high so he could reach close to Reno's shoulder blades and begin escorting the mountain man to the table.

"Please, sir," the tiny gent whispered to Frank Smith, and it pleased Jed Reno to no end when the bullying deputy had to come out of his chair and pull out the one next to him to allow Reno to sit down.

Then this Horatio John Paul Jones Irving rounded the table and returned to his chair, which he settled into.

"Now, sir, mayhap you can tell me what you know about—"

The head marshal cleared his throat and the little fellow turned to look at Tobin.

"Sir, I don't want to tell you how to go about reporting, but this fellow here is known for what we call in this part of our country big windies."

The man tilted his head slightly and peered over the rims of his glasses. "Perhaps, but even in lies we journalists can find truth."

Reno had never seen Tobin's face turn so red in such a short amount of time.

"Did you know, Mr. Reno, that President Grant is considering a trip here, to the finest city of the high plains?"

Reno looked at Jack Collins, hoping his only real friend in this group might answer for him, but the deputy was biting his lower lip.

"Well . . ."

"He is bound for Denver as we speak—President Grant, I mean—and his visit will do wonders for the Colorado Territory. And if he comes north by way of the Denver Pacific, he will bring glory to Cheyenne and the territory of Wyoming. You must remember, my late editor, Horace Greeley, was a champion of the American West. 'Go west,' he said, 'and grow up with the country.'"

Reno waited for the man to say more, but all he heard were a few filthy words whispered by Frank Smith and Clyde Tobin, the latter tapping the knuckles of his right hand hard on the tabletop.

Jack Collins cleared his throat. "We don't even know, sir, if the president will travel to Cheyenne." He turned quickly to his boss. "Isn't that right, Marshal?"

Now everyone looked at Tobin, who stopped beating a tattoo on the table and looked into each man's eye.

"I have received no official announcement from Washington or even Denver." He sighed. "I don't know how he would even travel—"

The newspaperman cut him off. "He will come north from Denver on the Denver Pacific. Then he will return east by way of the Union Pacific. And he took the Kansas Pacific to Denver." The man tilted back his head and laughed and, when finished, spoke to the chief marshal. "Sir, unlike these champions of justice, your deputies Smith and Collins, and unlike this heroic figure who rivals Boone and Crockett and John Paul Jones, my namesake, you are a political appointee. You know all about politics. You know the games that must be played, the votes that must be bought."

Tobin appeared to have stopped breathing and his face got even redder. When he remembered how to work his lungs he quickly resumed his tapping on the table, which steadily grew into a vicious beating.

The *New-York Tribune* gent hardly noticed the marshal's reaction and went right on talking. "Riding the Kansas Pacific and the Union Pacific and the Denver Pacific will lock up President Grant with the railroads for donations and the votes of their myriad workers. Visiting Cheyenne and Denver will give him the support he needs during his second term as president. *Of course President Grant will be visiting Cheyenne!*" He stopped talking long enough to reach into a coat pocket and pull out one of those flimsy yellow telegram papers. "The president will arrive in Cheyenne at the DP depot on Thursday the first of next month."

The marshal leaped to his feet. "I am the federal marshal for this district and I have had no word—nothing—that says the president will be here on . . ." He turned quickly to stare at the big calendar on the wall. "My God . . . Thursday!"

Everyone looked at the newspaperman.

"How do you know this, sir?" The marshal pointed a thick finger at the little man's face. "How do you know this, sir, when I, the United States marshal for this district, do not?"

The meek man shrugged, stuck his pencil over his left ear, and closed his notebook. "Because, sir, and I mean this without any intended offense," he said softly but not with an ounce of timidity, "I do not work for the United States Government. I work for the *New-York Tribune*."

Chapter 32

"You know what Lige Kerns had in that box, don't you?" Kip Jansen asked.

Colter looked him in the eye. His head moved slowly, but it was a confirmation. "I have an idea," the deputy whispered.

"It wasn't no sluice box," Kip said with a sigh. "I figured out that much. Wasn't farming equipment neither. Either, I mean. Lige Kerns didn't have any idea how to plant a potato and the only gold he knew how to get came from stealing, robbing, maybe even killing. He never worked a lick in his life. Never will."

"I don't know Lige Kerns, son." The lawman rose. "But I have a strong notion that you're right. You knew him better than any of us."

"He's up to no good," Kip said.

The marshal did not respond to that but kicked out the fire. The big woman, however, snorted and said, "All menfolk is up to no good. There never was one worth more than used snuff. There . . ."

She stopped, frowning, and stared at Kip for a long while before her head fell.

"No. That ain't the truth." For a long while she said nothing. Then, still staring at the big shoes on her big feet, she whispered, "I knowed a good boy. Woulda been a good man. No, he was a good man. Growed up too soon is all, and God didn't give him long enough to prove to ever'body just how good he coulda been. Name was Luke. A good boy. A real good boy." Her eyes found Kip's and she smiled. "Just like you, Kip."

Dropping her gaze, she whispered, "And his pa was a good man. Real good one. But he didn't get to live out his life the way . . . the way . . . the way I wisht he coulda." She sighed and rose.

"He woulda liked your pa, Lu—Kip. Woulda enjoyed talkin' to him 'bout farmin' and soldierin' and all that. Woulda traded tobacco with him. Davey Canutt said that's what Yankee and Southern soldiers done sometimes. They'd sneak over the lines and swap stuff, maybe a newspaper for them that could read and maybe chawin' baccer for an apple or coffee beans or maybe somethin' different. But you and my Luke, y'all woulda been good friends. Like my man and your pa."

She started packing up the cooking stuff and other things into the saddlebags, while the lawman tightened the cinch on his gray horse. Then, when the marshal pulled out his carbine, she swore and shook her head.

"That's just like you, ain't it, you miserable cur of a lawdog. You's a gonna do ever'thin' you can to catch 'em cur dogs. Even get a boy not fifteen years old kilt. And fer what? To save a Yankee gen'ral who slaughtered as many of his own men as he done Southern boys? To save a big drunk who somehow got hisself elected to become leader of yer country?"

Tim Colter tugged on the horn till he was satisfied the cinch was tight.

"We're going back to Laramie City," he told her and the bag slipped out of Patsy Palmer's hand and clattered on the ground.

The lawman glanced at Kip. "You'll have to ride double with me, Kip," he said. "That Indian pony can't carry more than Missus Palmer." His eyes turned toward the woman. "But don't think I won't stop you and/or that pinto if you do anything stupid."

"Yer . . . gonna go back . . . after all the trouble you stirred up?" She shook her head, then stooped to pick up the sack. "I don't believe it fer one second."

"I don't care what you believe. But I can't risk the life of a fourteen-year-old. I'll have to think of another way to bust up this gang—and save President Grant's life. That's what they're planning. I've known that much. That's why they busted Mad Ben Gore out of the pen."

"President Grant . . ." Kip whispered, unbelieving. "President Grant is coming to Laramie City?"

The deputy shrugged. "Cheyenne. Maybe. We'll see. But I've got to warn you." He pointed south. "We'll be riding through rough country. And there are likely going to be remains of horses and dead men. Maybe picked clean by buzzards by now." He let that sink in. "Those men were killed, I suspect, by the party of Cheyenne Indians led by that young leader who gave you his coupstick."

The lawman stopped, breathed in, and exhaled. "Don't think less of your Indian pard. He did me a favor. He did us all a favor, he and his fellow warriors. He might even have done President Grant a favor. But it's not going to be pretty to see."

Patsy Palmer walked over to Kip and put a big arm over his shoulders. "Jes look the other way. And hold your nose. Try not to breathe. You've growed up a lot. And I guess you'll have to grow up some more."

She pulled him closer, then let him go and walked to her pinto but stopped when she came close to Tim Colter.

"I still ain't figgered you out, buster. We runs into any posse and they'll be apt to shoot you down on sight— and me, too—or at least beat you to within an inch of yer life afore they throw you in that dungeon like they done me."

"We'll see," Colter said. "If we can make it to the cutoff to Cheyenne, with the good Lord's blessings, we might avoid posses. But I think they turned back after they saw . . ." He nodded south.

"They'll still lock you up in Cheyenne, pardner."

Deputy Colter didn't seem concerned. "Most likely. But I can tell Marshal Tobin what I know. And that ought to be enough to save President Grant."

She snorted. "Boy, you ain't as smart as—"

Kip heard the noise, then, and was turning before even the lawman or Miss Palmer heard it.

"Horses!" Kip exclaimed and saw Marshal Colter jerk the Winchester from the scabbard and rush to the rocky corner. He peered for just a second, then sprinted back.

"Mount up!" Patsy cried and pushed Kip toward the gray horse, but Colter countered that.

"No." He tossed the rifle to Miss Palmer. "We'd get cut down if we ran. I've got one notion."

He barely stopped but grabbed his saddlebags and a canteen and darted toward the hidden spring.

"Show yourself, Patsy!" Colter shouted. "Let them see you good and clear! Keep the boy behind you!"

"Where in the Sam Hill is you—" But she stopped and whispered a name.

It was a name Kip Jansen had heard whispered from Lige Kerns's lips.

Jake Dugan.

And then . . . the horses and men appeared.

Patsy Palmer immediately stepped in front of Kip, who glanced over his shoulder but found no sign of Tim Colter.

Horses whinnied, stomped their feet, and men cursed. Above that, Kip heard a rifle being cocked.

Then Patsy Palmer yelled out a string of curses and howled like a wolf.

"Does I look like the law to you, you dumb fools? Don't you recognize yer old pard, the fairest maiden in the land?"

One of the riders let out one of those Johnny Reb war cries, but that died quickly when another man told him to shut up or die.

"Palmer? Is that you?" The accent sounded Southern.

"Ain't nobody else been blessed with the good looks and figger the Lord given unto me," Palmer answered.

Another Rebel yell sang out, and again the leader cursed them.

"We don't know where the law is, you fools. And

we've seen enough Injun sign, I'd warrant, fer you gallant soldiers of the South to know to keep yer traps closed."

Hoofbeats moved toward Kip and the big woman. A saber rattled, the horse snorted, and then the saddle leather squeaked.

"Who you got hidin' behind ya, Patsy?" the voice asked.

Kip's shoulder was released and she stepped away to let Kip see these men closely for the first time.

The leader was big and burly but firm in his build, and tougher than a cob in his countenance. He wore no uniform, though his boots were stamped *CSA* on the tall tops that protected his knees, and he carried at least four revolvers, one on each hip, one underneath each shoulder, and a bandolier across his chest gleaming with brass cartridges.

His hat, like his beard, was black, though caked with dust.

"You have the honor, boy, to be addressing Brevet Major General Jake Dugan, leader of the last army of the Confederate States of America. And who. . . ." He bowed slightly. "Do I have the honor of addressin'?"

"He ain't got no honor." Kip paled when he heard the voice and stepped closer to Patsy Palmer.

"He's a snot-nosed, lazy no-'count whose pappy was a traitor to the sovereign state of Alabama." Lige Kerns drew a massive knife from a scabbard. "And I'm a-gonna gut him like I'd do a catfish afore my supper."

When Patsy Palmer took a menacing step toward Kip's stepfather, the man hissed, "I'll carve you up, too, Madam Ugliness."

"Before you two tangle," the man who called himself a general said, "I'd like Palmer to answer a question." He stared intently at the hard rock of a woman. "I sent some of my best men to break Mad Ben Gore out of prison. And all I see is you."

"She prob'ly murdered Gore in his sleep," Kerns roared. "So I'll kill her fer ya, Gen'ral." The evil man made a quick move.

A shot roared behind them and the knife spun out of Lige Kerns's hand and he dropped to his knees, screaming and cursing. Patsy Palmer spun around, spinning Kip, who fell to his knees, and saw the lawman, Tim Colter, walking toward them with a smoking pistol in his hand. Only . . .

Palmer screamed at the men not to shoot.

Only . . . maybe it wasn't the deputy marshal. Because he was wearing the ugly striped uniform that Lige Kerns said every convict at the territorial prison in Laramie City had to wear.

And Patsy Palmer yelled at Major General Jake Dugan's men and Dugan himself: "Boys, don't y'all recognize our ol' pard, Mad Ben Gore?"

Chapter 33

Tim Colter had no faith in this plan he had concocted, but he had five bullets left in the .45-caliber Colt he had pulled out of the saddlebag. The LeMat would have been a dead giveaway. In all his years in Wyoming Territory the only LeMat revolver he had seen was the one he carried—and that one Colter had, with great reluctance, dropped into the hidden spring. If someone found the LeMat, he wouldn't be alive long. On the other hand he might wind up dead anyway. But he would take as many of Jake Dugan's bunch with him as he could—including Dugan.

He had to pray that Patsy Palmer was right, that he did bear a resemblance to the insane man-killer Colter had bested in that canyon scrape. He walked slowly but steadily toward the gang of cold-blooded assassins, men bent on assassinating President Grant—and how many other innocent people heading to Cheyenne on a Denver Pacific train.

"Of course that's Mad Ben Gore, fellers," Patsy Palmer was pleading.

That was what really surprised Colter. The rough woman was speaking up for him when by all rights he would have sworn he would have to shoot her first to keep her quiet and he would have hated to do that. For one thing, the young boy Kip Jansen seemed to like her, and she certainly had been like a mother to the wounded kid. And then there was the fact that Colter probably would be feeding ravens, buzzards and coyotes if it weren't for Patsy Palmer. Now, instead of thinking how he would have to kill her and what reason he would have to tell Jake Dugan to justify her death, he was silently praying for her.

Praying for the kid, too, and yes, he had to concede, praying a bit for his own life.

Well, he thought, *no one has killed me yet.*

Colter spoke too soon. No sooner had the thought come to him when one of the bushwhackers let out a loud curse, put the reins into his mouth, and drew a pair of revolvers—one Remington, one Smith & Wesson—and spurred his horse into a lope.

The first shot went far to Colter's left, whining off a rock.

Patsy Palmer pushed the boy to the ground. She yelled at the rider, calling him Boise, to stop. But Boise's second shot tugged at the collar of the prison shirt Colter had taken off the real Mad Ben Gore's body.

The rest of the men, controlling their battle-hardened mounts with ease, watched. A few likely made bets on the outcome. Jake Dugan turned his head sideways and a bemused grin appeared between his mustache and beard.

The raider, Boise, let loose with a rebel yell and pulled both triggers at the same time, but his horse stumbled a bit, and both rounds did not come close to Colter.

Colter's Colt—the revolver he always packed in his saddlebags—roared, and Boise somersaulted off the back of his horse and landed face down in the rocks. The horse veered off to Colter's right and slowed to a trot. Colter's gray stamped its hooves, whinnied, and reared, but the hobbles kept it from running off. The Indian pinto that Palmer was riding merely snorted because the Cheyenne had trained it well. So had the bushwhackers with their mounts. Gunshots meant nothing to them anymore. Like killing meant little to the beasts who rode those animals.

Not even slowing his walk, Colter continued, cocking the revolver again as he passed the dead man. He looked straight ahead and told himself that he was Mad Ben Gore now and had to act like Mad Ben Gore. He lowered the Colt and pulled the trigger, putting a round right between the corpse's open eyes. The face Colter did not recognize, but the name, Boise, sounded familiar. Colter had arrested an arsonist who used that handle three years ago. That was before the territorial prison was built, so the man had been sent to Kansas but had escaped. Colter figured he was Kansas's problem, but now he knew that Boise had returned to Wyoming. He had to pray he had not arrested any of the other members of the gang.

Still walking, he holstered the pistol and did not

look at Palmer or the boy. He focused on Jake Dugan, whose likeness he recognized from wanted dodgers and stopped when he was about ten feet from the horse and rider. Then he slowly saluted.

Dugan did not return the salute but folded his arms over his chest and looked past Colter at the dead bushwhacker.

"Boise was a good man," the killer said.

"Not to me." Remembering the die he had found in Gore's pants pocket, Colter turned his voice into a dry whisper. "He recalled I'd cheated him when we was rollin' dice before I got caught. He was right. Mine was loaded."

That at least got a chuckle from Dugan.

"What'd he say?" one of the raiders called out.

Dugan answered and the group of men laughed. But Dugan's grin was gone and he eased his horse forward till he was next to the lawman. He stared down and Colter looked up.

"Where's that mustache you was so fond of, Capt'n?" the gang's leader asked.

"They shaved it off in that stink hole," Colter whispered dryly.

"Lariat!" Dugan called out without looking behind him. "Did they shave your mustache and beard when you was locked in that pen when it first opened?"

"Nah," a man called from somewhere far back. "They didn't care how ya looked as long as they could work ya half to death."

Nodding, Dugan kept his stare locked on Colter.

"Well?" the killer asked.

"Lariat," Dugan whispered, "ain't Ben Gore."

That finally cracked the so-called major general's façade. "What happened to your neck?"

"Cheyenne," he said and hooked his thumb south. "They kilt the rest of the boys." He pulled down the wrapping so that everyone could get a good look at the bullet scar. "Woulda lifted my hair, too, if not for that ugly wench." He made a slight motion toward Palmer but did not look at her.

"When I sent the boys to bust you out of prison I said to fetch you. Didn't say nothin' 'bout her."

"They didn't bust her out." At least Colter could speak the truth now. "That Cheyenne lawdog done it."

"What lawdog?" Dugan asked.

"Colter," and Colter described himself in the profanest of terms.

"The federal deputy?" Dugan pushed back his hat. "You mean he got her paroled?"

"I mean he busted her out. Not the way the boys got me out. He took her out. Figgered she'd lead him to you." He looked at Palmer and chuckled. "And she done better'n that. She led him to me."

"Marshal Colter's dead?" one of the raiders asked excitedly.

"Deader'n dirt." He nodded at Palmer. "But I didn't get the pleasure. That was all that big mama's doin's."

Now was the moment of truth. Looking up at the bogus general again, Colter rubbed his throat, which was actually sore now from talking so much, and talking like a red-handed butcher. "Now my throat hurts. I ain't got nothin' else to say. You say what you want . . . Gen'ral."

About fifty years passed in the next ten seconds.

"At ease, boys," Dugan finally told his men. "Fill yer canteens at the spring. And welcome Capt'n Gore back into our fold."

That, Colter figured, was a test. As the men dismounted and walked past him or rode past him toward the spring, they looked at him. And Colter made no attempt to hide his face. He nodded, or saluted, or spat at them, or shook his head. A few of them he cursed. Some he snorted at. And two he put his hand on his Colt. Because he was a madman, he told himself. And he had to give a convincing performance.

Not one face did he recognize. And when they had passed he made himself show absolutely no reaction. He looked back up at Dugan.

"And the boy?" Dugan asked.

Turning, Colter looked at the kid, whose face was masked in confusion. No, Colter wasn't out of this pickle yet. But this time Colter answered truthfully. He couldn't lie too much. The boy's stepdad was here, likely with the Gatling gun but probably with a better wagon and team now that Jake Dugan's marauders were in charge.

"He limped in here this morn," Colter said. The truth stopped with that. "I was all for cuttin' his throat, but the big wench took a likin' to him."

"He's a good, sweet boy," Patsy Palmer cried out and stepped behind the boy, putting her big hands on his small shoulders.

"We have no use for good, sweet boys," Dugan said in an icy tone and started to draw one of his revolvers.

"Kill the miserable cur," Lige Kerns called out. "He ain't good fer nothin'."

Colter waited till the LeMat came out. A LeMat. Colter couldn't believe it, but then he remembered just how popular that brand of revolver was with Confederate generals. He kept his eyes on Dugan but heard the big woman gasp as she must have stepped in front of young Kip to protect him from Dugan.

"He might be good for somethin'," Colter said when Dugan cocked the big handgun.

"Shoot 'em, Jake!" Lige Kerns sang out. "Shoot 'em both. They's worthless. She's a fat wench and he's a puny boy. Shoot 'em both. Good fer nothin' they is. Good fer nothin'."

But the revolver did not fire and Colter breathed out in relief because he was about to shoot Jake Dugan out of the saddle and then take as many of the Rebel swine as he could. Without Dugan the plan to kill President Grant would probably collapse. But Colter, Palmer, and—most importantly—young Kip Jansen would be dead. Jansen at least deserved a chance to grow into a man. He was almost there already.

"What," Dugan asked without looking away from his first target, big Patsy Palmer, "might he be good fer?"

"Shoot 'em. Kill 'em or let me kill 'em both!" Kerns bellowed.

"If you don't shut yer trap," Dugan said, "I will kill

you . . . Injun style. Stake you out and cut you up and leave you for the buzzards and ants to finish."

But he kept the gun and his focus on Palmer and the boy behind her.

Kerns went rigid and quiet.

"Well?" Dugan asked Colter.

"From what I re—" Colter caught himself. He was about to say "read," but then he wondered if Mad Ben Gore could read. If he couldn't, the gun Dugan aimed at Palmer would turn to Colter and he'd be dead in an instant. "Recollect," he said. "The laws was arrestin' ever'body after Booth won his glory by killin' that scoundrel Lincoln."

The brutal Confederate chuckled. "Washington's a mite more populated than Wyoming Territory."

"Yeah. But not when a president has gotten bush-whacked. Laws and citizens is more prone to shoot first. But when you gots a kid with a gun to his temple they think twice."

The revolver did not move from its target.

"Use him to barter our way out of a ticklish situa-tion," Colter said. "He don't eat or drink much. As long as he keeps quiet, I'm all for lettin' him live—at least till we don't need him no more." He shrugged. "Now my neck's hurtin' and I don't wants to talk no more. Kill 'em or let'm be. Makes no never mind to me."

The hammer clicked and slowly, safely, returned to its place, and the LeMat was holstered.

"You should speak up more often, Capt'n Gore. Prison has made you smarter than just the mad-dog killer you were before. You never used to say more'n a six words a day."

"Ain't likely to say much more," he said and raised his left hand to the bandage on his throat. "Thanks to this." He looked up at Dugan. "But jus' the same to you, Gen'ral . . ." He turned and walked to his horse. "I prefer killin'. You use yer brains for the rest of us."

When he reached the gray and grabbed the saddle horn, Colter let out a long sigh of relief and offered a silent prayer of thanks to God.

"Mount up, boys," Dugan bellowed. "Kerns, you take that pinto hoss. Palmer, you know how to handle a team, so the wagon's yourn. The boy can help you. But if he gets on my bad side, hostage or not, I cut off his head and put it on a post. And if you protest, your head'll be right next to his'n." He must have screamed in the boy's face. "You understand me, boy?"

If Kip answered his voice was too soft for Colter to hear. Finding a stirrup, Colter swung into the saddle. He was sweating. And now his hands were shaking, so he put one on the Colt that he had shoved into his waistband and the other pressed hard against the saddle horn.

"What about Boise?" one of the bushwhackers asked.

"What about'm?" Dugan bellowed. "Buzzards gotta eat, too."

They thundered out of the campground and rode hard to the south.

Chapter 34

Deputies Collins and Smith had their orders, and the youngster was running off in one direction and the touchy older one was heading to the livery. Even the big man himself, Marshal Tobin, chief of this district, moved fast, making a beeline for the telegraph office.

Jed Reno watched that newspaperman gathering his pencils and papers, but the man seemed to have lost interest in Reno. So had the US Marshal and even young Collins, who practically worshipped the mountain man.

Reno left the *New-York Tribune* dude with his notes and his ego, crossed the room, grabbed his cap, and stepped onto the boardwalk, pulling the door shut behind him. For a long while he stared off to the northwest, toward that lawless country where Dugan's raiders hid out, where Cheyenne and other Indians still ruled, where the country was hard enough and unpredictable enough to kill the best of men who knew and lived in the wilderness. That was where Tim Colter was, and Colter, even as rawhide tough and quick and experienced as he was, would always be the green kid who had survived a wagon train massacre all those years ago.

And now . . . Reno shook his head. He didn't even know what had happened to that Pinkerton gal. For all Reno knew, she might have been caught by those . . . what was that word?

Con-something.

Conspirators. That was it. One of those conspirators might have caught her and cut her throat and dumped her body into some hole where it would never be found. Someone like . . .

He frowned at the thought, but it stayed with him, and he even whispered the name.

Walker Chester.

Chester hadn't fooled Jed Reno. Because Jed Reno had managed to live all these years reading signs. He could follow a beaver from river to pond and back again. He remembered what Jim Bridger had said over at that fort he had put up in the western part of this territory.

"Jed Reno's so good a tracker, he can foller the best Shoshone there is to get to where that Injun was goin' afore that Injun got there hisself."

Chester couldn't be trusted now. And that gunsmith. That battle jack hanging in his storeroom was a dead giveaway. Chester's explanation didn't hold rye whiskey to Reno's way of thinking. Those two men were in on that plot. It was just like that dead man had warned Colter and Reno.

Now Reno didn't have anyone to trust. And he remembered what Chester had said about Tim Colter.

Ever'body can go bad, Reno. That's somethin' you might oughta remember.

Yep, everybody could go bad. Including Walker Chester.

Reno's hearing remained sharp.

That reporter fellow was still inside the marshal's office. Alone.

Slowly Reno turned and looked at the door. The office didn't have much in the way of windows, but what it had was covered with curtains. Sharp as he was, Reno hadn't noticed that before he walked into Tobin's headquarters. He looked up and down the street, but people were still filling their bellies. So he pressed his ear to the door. But mountain men and scouts and hunters and, sometimes, posse members often had one thing that wasn't as sharp now as it had been. Shooting Hawken rifles could ruin a man's hearing before he reached forty years. And Jed Reno passed forty years a long, long time ago.

His hand clutched the knob and he turned it slowly. It wasn't locked. He shot a glance up the boardwalk and, seeing just the calico cat that was fatter than the milliner at the corner who claimed that ugly beast, jerked the door open and leaped inside, pouncing like a mountain lion.

"Aha!" Reno shouted, slamming the door and pointing a thick finger at the scoundrel who was sitting behind Marshal Tobin's desk and looking through his papers. "You're a scoundrel."

"No, Jed." The strange accent was gone, but the reporter did not stop rifling through the papers. "I'm a Pink."

Reno blinked.

"Ginger?" Reno finally asked.

She did not look up but asked, "Is anybody coming?"

"You ain't supposed to be looking through somebody's personal things," he told her.

She did not stop. "Don't tell me, Jedediah, that you never took a peek at something you shouldn't have."

He didn't answer.

"And I should look through these papers." She sighed, put them back in the drawer, closed it, and opened another. "The drawers aren't locked anyway."

"You're a scoundrel," Reno repeated.

"Yes. I am."

"And a snoop."

"Agreed. That's why I was hired."

He didn't realize he was walking toward her, dressed as a him. Giving up, he pulled up a chair and sat across the desk.

"But that's Marshal Tobin's desk. He's the head law hereabouts."

She sighed and closed another drawer. "And he might be part of a plot to assassinate President Grant."

Reno froze at that thought. *Ever'body can go bad.* He watched the pretty woman disguised as a *New-York Tribune* reporter examine the contents of another drawer, then heard her curse slightly, and when the drawer closed she looked up at Reno and sighed.

"Well," Ginger Burricchia whispered, "it was a long shot. But I had to take it. We're running out of time."

Reno tried to remember the last time he had a headache that wasn't caused by Taos Lightning, bad water, or a gun butt to his noggin. One was coming on fast now, and it might be one of those real bad ones. He shook his head. "I just don't know what to think."

Leaning over the desk, she took his big right hand in her two small ones and squeezed hard.

"Jed," she whispered, "do you trust me?"

He sighed, and slowly shook his head. "I wanna, Ginger." Stopping suddenly, he stared at her. "Is you really a woman or . . . ?"

"I'm a woman," she said and, releasing his hand, she straightened and breathed in and held it for a moment. When she exhaled she pointed to her upper chest. "Muslin wrappings so my breasts don't show." She smiled as Reno's face reddened. "Stick a pillow against my stomach to make me look fatter. Wigs, fake facial hair, makeup from a theatrical troupe. The rest is mostly playacting. I was trained with some of the finest Shakespearean troupes. Allan Pinkerton found me on stage in Chicago. Recruited me. Trained me. And that's all you need to know about me. So . . . I trust you." The hand returned and grabbed his fingers and they locked together, though Reno had no idea how that had happened. "Because I have to trust someone and I picked you. Because you're a man of honor. Now . . . do you trust me?"

He sighed and saw the hurt in her face. He didn't think she was that good of an actor person to fake that look.

"I cain't," he explained.

She just stared at him through the eyeglasses that were part of her disguise.

Tim Colter would be madder than a hornet at him, but Reno went right on moving his lips and tongue.

"Tim told me I couldn't trust nobody. And that's what that dying man told both of us when we found him up in that bad country." He nodded in that direction. "'President Grant,' is what he said. "'A-sass . . . A-sass. Assassination.' That's it. Then he said, 'Dugan,' and then he whispered, 'Trust nobody.' And then he died. That's how come Tim and me got into this . . . this . . . this mess."

"Oh. Ohhh. Oh no."

Her voice trailed off, and Reno kept looking at his big hand, which she had been holding earlier. Finally he looked up at her. Even through the makeup she wore he could see that she had paled and tears welled in her eyes, then rolled down her cheeks, spoiling the *New-York Tribune* reporter's face she had concocted.

"Poor Tony. Poor, poor Tony."

"Tony?" Reno whispered.

Her head bobbed. "Anthony Vela." Her eyes raised toward his. "Do you know what *vela* means in Spanish?"

Reno shook his big head.

"Watchman." Her smile lasted only a second. "He was a fine watchman."

Remembering, Reno drew in a sharp breath and let it out. "He said 'Secret Service.'"

The hard face returned. "That's right. He worked for the Secret Service. The Pinkerton National Detective Agency helps out whenever we can. What else did Tony tell you before . . . ?" Her Adam's apple bobbed, but she maintained her composure now.

Shrugging his shoulders, Reno shook his head. "Not much. We—me and Tim—we was surprised he could even still be alive, bad as he was shot up and with as much blood as he'd lost."

"Tony was a fighter. He'd hold on as long as he could to pass on what information he had."

Reno nodded in agreement. "Reckon so." Then another moment from that short time in the canyon came back to him.

"I found . . ." No, that sounded like bragging, and Reno had too much of a reputation as a braggart and a liar. "That Tony, he had them dots and lines drawed on his foot. Spelled out 'P' for 'Palmer.' That's how Tim knowed he had to get that hard rock of a woman outta the pen. That's how come he busted her out. To save Gen'ral Grant somehow."

She smiled. "Then Tony and I were on the right track. That's why I was in that prison with that big witch."

Reno said, "He . . . Tony . . . he did tell Tim—I don't know if he even knowed I was there—he said, 'Stop 'em.'"

Her face changed again and she stood.

"And that's what we're going to do, Jedediah. We're going to stop them."

He followed her to the door, which she opened slowly, then stared down the street. When she stepped onto the boardwalk she held the door open for him and he carried his heavy and tall self out about as sneaky as that big ox some kids had left in Miller's barbershop six or seven months ago.

Ginger Burricchia moved like a mountain lion and Reno was out of breath by the time they were behind the courthouse, and that little gal—who wasn't a gal at that very moment—didn't even slow down then. They kept to the alleyways for what felt like a month of Sundays to Reno; then she slipped through an un-locked door and held it open for Reno. There was a hook and latch on the inside, and she secured the door so that anyone who opened it wouldn't have as easy a time getting in as they had.

"All right," she said, motioning to another door. He took the hint and walked to it, grabbing the handle be-fore his nerves failed him.

"It's all right," she whispered. "Go ahead. I'm right behind you."

That didn't comfort him too much, but he opened the door and stepped into a dark hallway.

He didn't recognize the building, but Cheyenne had plenty of buildings, and many businesses and homes were off-limits to a rough and tumble mountain man.

"Stairs are down the hall and to the right," Ginger whispered.

The wooden planks creaked under Reno's weight, but he moved quickly and followed Ginger's directions to the stairs, which were even louder to his ears. Once he reached the second floor he stopped.

Turning quickly, he whispered to Ginger, "Somebody's snorin'."

She nodded. "I'd like to catch up on some sleep myself. Go on. They won't wake up till evening. My room's the last one on the left."

The first room he passed smelled like lilac and the second one, on the right, smelled like pipe tobacco. He didn't know what the fifth room smelled like and didn't want to take a whiff of it again, and some of the rooms had no smells, just light snoring, though one person must have been having a bad dream.

"It's open," Ginger told him when they reached her room.

She was right. He went into a small room that could barely hold both of them. He spotted two big trunks first, then the wash basin, and Ginger slipped past him and pulled up a shade. That was when he saw lots of things.

Two nickel-plated derringers, a sawed-off shotgun—10 gauge by the look of those barrels—a Spencer carbine, a pair of silver-plated Smith & Wesson .32s with pearl handles, a stiletto and a bowie knife, and men's clothing—boots, shirts, vests, and unmentionables scattered about the room. She was messier than Reno himself.

Ginger sat on the bed and kicked off her men's shoes. "Have a seat," she said.

But there was no place to sit.

He blinked and stared at her and she patted the bed next to where she sat.

Reluctantly he eased onto the flimsy mattress and felt the bed and the floor groan underneath his weight.

"Where are we at?" he whispered.

She told him and he felt his face flush.

"But that's a . . ." His mouth remained open.

"Which is why no one is going to be busy till this evening and nobody's gonna notice a man and a woman leaving here together." She put her hand on his beard and turned his head, then pulled his chin hairs down so he looked into her eyes.

"You spoke of trust, Jed," she whispered, releasing his beard. "So I'm going to show you something." Reaching underneath the mattress—if one would call it a mattress—she pulled out a slip of paper, unfolded it, and held it out to him.

He saw the letters and sighed. "I can't read," he told her.

"Oh. I'm sorry. I knew that. Had forgotten." She gave him the most beautiful smile. "You have a way of . . . well . . . distracting me." Her face changed. "That's dangerous in my line of work." Then she read the words to him.

Jed nodded when she finished, then let out a long sigh and whispered, "Trust nobody. Yep. Reckon that's gospel."

She took his beard again and made him look into her lovely eyes. "We're going to have to trust each other, Jed," she told him. "That's the only way."

"Reckon so," he conceded.

"That also means we have all afternoon, all night, and then three more days and nights to figure out what we need to do to make sure President Grant stays alive when he gets here on Tuesday."

He nodded when she released her hold of his beard, but his brain started working again and he whispered, "But you tol' Marshal Tobin that Gen'ral Grant was gettin' here on Thursday."

She grinned. "Exactly."

Chapter 35

They rode only as far as the next canyon, then made a cold camp and waited for the moon to rise. Figuring that a crazed man-killer like Ben Gore would avoid people, Colter did the same. He rolled out his bedroll near the picket line for the horses, and though he certainly could have used the bacon that was frying on a cast-iron skillet and the coffee boiling on another fire, Colter sat alone, then lay on his bedding and stared at the stars.

He had gotten this far. But the ruse, he figured, wouldn't last. Because someone had to point Jake Dugan to the right place and right time to kill the president. And Colter didn't think that was going to happen in the city of Cheyenne. Even with a Gatling gun, the assassination would be too difficult to set up. No, Dugan would have something else in mind—but the bushwhacker trusted no one, not even Mad Ben Gore, and he would keep everything a secret till the last minute.

None of the gang was going to fret over how they were going to kill a former Union general. They had a Gatling gun and they knew that would do the job.

Colter had never found a fondness for tobacco, but one of the cutthroats tossed him the makings, so he rolled one, found a match, and fired it up. The smoke didn't help the bullet crease in his neck any, but he managed to smoke without coughing.

Footsteps sounded, and Colter glanced at the Colt lying next to his right hand but did not lift it. He could tell the person approaching him was not going to be a threat, though why not? Well, that was another problem Colter faced.

"You got us all in a pickle, lawdog," Patsy Palmer said as she gave a handful of oats to the pinto.

"You had an easy way out of it," Colter told her and flicked ash from the cigarette to the ground.

"Not that easy. They'd murder the boy."

Colter frowned. "They will anyway," he told her. "Eventually."

"They'll try to."

He kept staring at the sky. "They'll kill you, too."

She snorted. "I ain't figgered out why they ain't planted me already. Not like any of 'em rapscallions want to pay a dime to dance with me."

"You were part of the gang."

She made no reply, but he heard her humming sweetly to the pinto and then began brushing his mane with her long, thick, rock-hard fingers.

"How's . . . ?" He almost called the kid Luke, he had heard Palmer using the name so much. "Kip?" he finished.

"Sleepin'. Best hope he don't talk none in his sleep."

To his surprise Colter found himself smiling. "I doubt if he's sleeping. He's too smart for that." Not with Lige Kerns in camp with him. Not with twenty-three of the roughest, meanest cutthroats in all of Wyoming Territory all around him. Kip Jansen had as much chance of falling asleep on this night as . . . well . . . Tim Colter had.

"Marshal?" she whispered.

"You best call me Ben Gore," he cautioned her. "Or we might not live to see the moonrise."

She paused for a minute, then whispered, "At Fort Fetterman. When 'em bullets got stoled. Nobody tol' me nothin' 'bout no plans to kill no president or nothin' like it. I figgered it was to be used for some of Dugan's other schemin'. At first, I mean. I thought maybe Dugan planned to go ridin' up into that Montany country to take us a gold shipment or one of 'em big banks in whatever cities is in that territory."

He stared at her till she looked away. "You found out about the Grant conspiracy, though."

"Yeah."

"And didn't seem to object to the idea for a long, long time," he whispered.

"I'm guilty, yes, I is. But that was afore . . . well . . . you've heard that sayin' that a woman can change her mind, ain't ya?"

Colter said nothing.

"Well, nah," Palmer said after another sigh. "I reckon I's as rotten as all of 'em cutthroats. But that boy . . . he shore looks a lot like my Luke . . . and he's just . . . just as innocent."

"Patsy," he whispered.

"Yeah." He knew she had turned away from the pinto and had taken two steps closer to him.

"To get Kip out of this nest of butchers, you and I are going to have to work together."

"I figgered as much."

"The Gatling gun is the key to whatever plan they have. That's still in the crate for now in the back of that freight wagon, but they'll have to assemble it before the president's train is headed to Cheyenne."

"Uh-huh. But when's that gonna be?"

"I don't know. No one knows. No one will know until likely the night before he leaves Denver."

"Why don't he just not come to Cheyenne?"

"Like you said, he's still a general. And nobody ever called him a coward. And no one ever will." He paused just long enough to let out a long breath. "Worst turns to worst, if I get killed, you'll need to blow up that Gatling gun. All that ammunition in the crates in that wagon. One torch. Some coal oil. Whatever it takes."

She mumbled something.

"If I'm not killed, I'll blow it up myself."

"How you gonna get out of there?"

"That's my problem." He knew he wouldn't get out of that wagon. He'd be pinned down, holding off a charging gang of Rebel bushwhackers till the world ended for Tim Colter and a bunch of insane zealots. "Your job will be to get Kip out of wherever we are alive."

She thought of that. "I'll get 'er done, boss man."

"I know you will," he said. He realized he was smiling. "You're a good woman, Patsy Palmer. Just had some bad luck."

"Let's hope we both get some good luck soon. Best get back to that boy. He's likely missin' his ma."

"Be his mother," Colter said. "He needs a mother's love right now."

Well, Colter had an ally. Maybe. He started thinking. With the wagon, heavy as it was with all that arsenal, it would take them two days or more even if they rode when the moon was up, to get to the Denver Pacific tracks south of Cheyenne. That was where these mad-dog killers would have to attack the train.

But they would also have to know what train to riddle with .45-caliber bullets. And nobody in Cheyenne would know that until the president's schedule was set. Colter could figure out why they had come south now. A gang member could have gotten word at the settlement over near old Fort Caspar and taken it back to camp. That was why Dugan knew to head south. But the train? That was a different story.

Someone working with the Denver Pacific? He couldn't rule that out. An officer at Fort Russell? The odds there were low. Maybe an enlisted man who had served with the Confederacy, but enlisted men, and even junior officers, wouldn't know the details of the president's trip until it was way too late to set up an ambush. So that meant somebody in the federal government. Cheyenne was the territorial capital, so there were a lot of men drawing a salary from the United States of America.

Like US Marshal Clyde Tobin?

He studied on that. But then he started thinking about how the real Mad Ben Gore got out of prison. That breakout was well-planned. And that Warden G. Breck Glenn had sure been in a hurry to get out of the prison when Colter arrived with a breakout of his own in mind.

He sighed. He wasn't a detective. He was a lawman. He didn't solve mysteries. He just brought bad guys to justice. He sat up and looked at the camp. And right now he was in the midst of twenty-three of the hardest rocks this country had ever known.

Chapter 36

If I ain't out of this pigsty come tomorrow morn, Jeb Reno thought, *I'm a-gonna jump through this wall and hope a stagecoach runs over me and puts me out of my misery.*

How many days and nights had he been in Ginger Burricchia's room in this bawdy house? It felt like a month of Sundays, which made him wonder if they were just going to hide in this . . . this . . . this house of wickedness till General Grant got here. *If* the president got here alive! Reno had spent days and nights with nothing to do but stretch out on the cot and think back to the olden days, when he was wintering by himself high up in those gloriously wonderful Rocky Mountains. When all his beaver skins were prime.

Of course it was hard to think when it got full dark outside with all the noise coming from downstairs, not to mention next door. The walls were thinner than a summer undershirt and the floors had cracks so that he could take a peek if he wanted to see a bunch of drunken reprobates pay their dime to dance with a cheap woman and then maybe give her some extra money to see if she might haul him upstairs for more wickedness.

Ginger made him promise not to leave, not to stick his head out of the door, and not to take the latch off unless he recognized her voice. Not that the latch would keep even a woman tinier than Ginger from breaking down the door. Criminy, Reno had to share the chamber pot, and poor, sweet Ginger wouldn't let him take it out. She did it each morning. Well, enough was enough, Reno decided, when that Pinkerton redhead got back up here he was going to lay down the law. He was a grown man old enough to be her grandpappy and he wasn't used to wasting away in a bad house while his pard, the deputy marshal, hadn't been seen or heard from in some time and the only news Jed was getting was what Ginger told him she had learned from her snooping—or just reading the newspapers.

Footsteps sounded down the hallway, so Reno got up and moved to the door. His eyes might not have been as sharp as they once were, though he could still see fine enough near and far. And while Reno had never been in any kind of detective business, he knew it was pretty Ginger from just the slight creaking on the floorboards. He put his thumb on the hook but waited for her to whisper, "It's me."

The hook popped out, the door opened and closed, the latch was back in place in an instant, and Ginger handed him a sack.

"Hungry?" she said with a smile.

"Thirsty," he told her and liked the way she put her

hands on her hips and gave him a cute little pouting look.

"Pinkerton detectives do not imbibe when they are on duty, young man," she told him, but her voice was an exaggeration. "And don't tell me you are not a Pinkerton man because I have practically adopted you."

He found a biscuit filled with a large chunk of ham in the sack and ate it before he thought to ask if the redhead wanted a bite. But he didn't need to because she was sitting on the bed and pulling off her shoes, then fishing something out after removing the heel.

"What do you know about Grayson Breck Glenn?" she asked.

"Ain't never heard of him." Crumbs of biscuit but no ham found their way to the bedcover, but the detective did not notice.

"He's the warden at the territorial prison in Laramie City," she said.

"Oh." He found the canteen on the bedstand and washed down his late dinner and later breakfast. It was pushing nigh suppertime the way Reno's stomach ached. "Him." He shrugged when she looked at him. "Don't know nothin' 'bout 'm. Met'm once, twice, when I got deputized to bring some bad guys to 'm. He seemed to be doin' all right, I reckon, till that bust-out—which I mean to tell you Tim Colter didn't have no hand in."

Her eyes flashed up to his again. "Excepting Patsy Palmer of course."

"Well, yeah, but he had his reasons for that. She was gonna get him . . ." He stopped.

Her eyes never left him and he couldn't make himself look away.

"We trust each other, don't we?" she said.

"Yeah . . ." He sighed. "He figgered to make that big woman take him to Dugan's Den. Somehow he'd stop 'em from killin' Gen'ral Grant."

"That was his plan?" She sounded flabbergasted.

Reno sighed. "Well, he's smarter'n me, but when it comes to plannin' he's more of the fightin' kind."

"Well, he's brave. Like you." She tugged his beard, then reached into a valise she had picked up and pulled out more telegraph papers, which she handed to him. "What do you make of these?"

He took them, glanced at them, and handed them back. "Ginger, you know I can't read a lick."

"I know you can't. The thing is . . . I can't either."

"It some foreign language?"

"It's in a code."

"Like that Morse stuff I've heard'm waggle their tongues about?"

"No. Not dots and dashes. But letters and numbers that make no sense."

He held the top telegram closer as though that would help. "Well, didn't that Pinkerton dude tell you—"

"Those telegrams weren't sent to me, Jed. The warden sent them to Marshal Tobin."

He stared at her dumbly.

"Those aren't the actual telegrams. I bribed the man at the depot to hold them till I could make copies of them."

His head tilted to his left and his good eye tried to focus. "You can do that?"

She shrugged. "I work for the Pinkertons. I can do just about anything with a smile, a bat of the eye, an expense account, and threats since I've seen that clerk on this floor and know he's married with four children." She took the papers from him, but one fell to the floor and Reno bent to pick it up. She sat near the head of the bed and was saying something about a code expert in Chicago, but she had no way or time to get him her copies. She might have said more, but Reno wasn't listening to her. He put his attention on the yellow paper she had dropped.

"It's all right." Reno heard her now. "I'm sorry. But yesterday you said you knew that 'US' spells 'United States.' And you can tell what some things are by the letters and numbers. You know, B-A-N-K spells 'bank' because you've been there to cash the checks you get for scouting. And that Tim Colter taught you to sign your name J-E-D-R-period. I thought maybe something here would make sense to you. I know you never learned your letters. I didn't mean to embarrass you. I . . ." She rose from the bed. "What is it, Jed?"

He held out the paper and pointed. She leaned closer. Why, she had found time to wash her hair and put on something that sure smelled nice.

"What is it?" Ginger asked him, still staring at the paper.

After clearing his throat he pointed to some markings.

"Yes," she said. "That's a slash mark. And that's the letter 'G.' A capital 'G.'"

"No, ma'am," Reno corrected. "I mean, I reckon so, but that's also a brand."

"A brand?" she asked.

He nodded. "Cattle ranch. The—" The floorboards in the hallway were creaking again, but the sound told Reno that the person creeping along was not one of the gals who bunked on this floor. One man. Who was a lot heavier. And was alone. Men didn't come up here alone, though they might leave by themselves. They were always escorted by a soiled dove. And rarely did they come up here until after the frolicking had begun down in the raucous saloon and dance hall.

Ginger heard it, too, and stepped back and grabbed one of the fancy Smith & Wesson revolvers. Reno managed to move to the other side of the door, picking up the Spencer carbine that was leaning in the corner. He brought the .52-caliber to his shoulder and as quietly as possible pulled back the hammer.

The footsteps stopped at the door. Ginger took up the other .32-caliber revolver in her left hand, but she did not cock that one.

Reno listened.

With her left hand Ginger raised one finger and Reno nodded his agreement. Only one person. Who stopped at the door to Ginger's room.

In quick succession, Reno made out two hard knocks and a soft one. A quick moment later and there were two soft knocks, followed by a loud one and a soft one. Then he heard one loud knock, three more loud ones, and two loud ones. A voice softly whispered after the strange knocks: "Chiara? It's me."

Ginger let out a sigh of relief, stuck the .32 she held in her right hand into a deep pocket in her skirt, and

kept the left-hand pistol aimed at the floor. She stepped
to the door, released the latch, and stepped back.

"Come in, Tom," she said, "and close the door right
behind you."

Reno had seen the man around town a few times but
only recently. He wore blue denim trousers and a
checked shirt, good boots, and a slouch hat. A hide-
away gun was sticking out from the top of his left boot,
and there was another gun—a new-model Colt—stuck
between the suspenders in his back.

He spotted Reno when he closed the door but didn't
appear surprised. Instead he turned, leaning against the
door—which he had not latched—and nodded at
Ginger.

"You trust him?" he asked.

"With my life," she said and, turning toward Reno,
grinned. "Jedediah, call this gentleman Tom. That's what
the taps meant. G-I-N for Ginger. T-O-M for Tom."

The two men gave each other brief nods.

Reno slowly lowered the Spencer, pointing the barrel at the floor. Music and loud dancing started downstairs, startling the pretty girl and even Reno, who had
been hearing that racket practically since Ginger sneaked
him up into her room.

"He called you something else." Reno had to yell
above the banjo, tuba, and piano. And now it sounded
like everyone in the dance hall had started singing.

I wish I was in the land of cotton,
Old times they are not forgotten;
Look away! Look away! Look away! Dixie Land.

"It's . . . well . . . another name I use."

"You mean you ain't really named Ginger."

In Dixie Land where I was born,

She shook her head.

Early on one frosty mornin',

"Chiara," she told him. "That's what Tom called me."

Look away! Look away! Look away! Dixie Land.

Chiara. Reno tried not to think much about that. She had used lots of names, had been lots of people, female and male.

Then I wish I was in Dixie, Hooray! Hooray!
In Dixie Land I'll take my stand to live and die
in Dixie!

He wished they would shut up with their infernal racket.

Away, away, away down South in Dixie,
Away, away, away down South in Dixie.

"Did you find out?" she asked Tom.

He shook his head. "It's a code, but I couldn't figure it out." He saw the telegraph paper.

"Well," she told him, "my partner here, Jed Reno, just told me something very interesting."

Downstairs they were singing that same dad-blasted song again, and the band was playing even louder and worse than it had before.

"At least part of it," Ginger, or Chiara, said. She smiled at Reno. "Tell him, Jed. Tom used to work for the Pinkerton National Detective Agency, too, but now he's with the Secret Service. We worked on some cases together. He's been a good friend, too. He's been down here since President Grant began considering a trip to Cheyenne. He was here before I even got put in the Laramie City prison. He's one of the best men in the Secret Service. President Grant practically worships him. Isn't that right, Tom?"

She made him sound like Daniel Boone and Jedediah Smith and Jim Bridger and John Colter—even Tim Colter—rolled into one slick-haired jasper with a boyish face that couldn't grow a beard in a year.

Reno didn't feel much like talking. He just listened to that bad and worse singing and the banging on the floor.

Ginger frowned at Reno, but his mouth still wasn't going to cooperate and she sighed and said, "It's a brand."

He wished they would shut up with their infernal racket.

"A brand?" Tom gave Reno a curious glance.

"The Slash G," Ginger told her partner. "A cattle ranch. Have you heard of it?"

"No." The jasper shook his head.

Reno heard that. But he heard something else. Something over that music and song.

Away, away, away down South in Dixie,
Away, away, away down South in Dixie.
Away, away, away down South in Dixie,
Away, away, away down South in Dixie.

He raised the Sharps, drew a bead on Tom Whatever-his-name-was, and said, "Then you're the only person in Wyoming Ter'tory that ain't heard of it."

Chapter 37

"Jed?" Ginger/Chiara whispered.

Reno kept his eye on Tom, who was keeping his eye on the mountain man.

"I got one eye," Reno said. "But it sees all right. I been in this flea-bitten, stinkin' room so long my smellin' ain't too good no more because ever'thin' in here smells like . . . like you do, Mr. Tom! And I'm gettin' well up in my years so that Methuselah is a young'un to me. But my ears still hear good . . . sometimes. And I hear folks singing a right catchy tune downstairs and dancin' louder than they do on the last Saturday of the month with the Slash G and ever' other workin' cowhand has gotten his month's pay."

He paused to catch his breath but never looked away from Tom the traitor.

Away, away, away down South in Dixie,
Away, away, away down South in Dixie.

Reno spoke to Ginger/Chiara now, but he brought the Spencer to his shoulder, the barrel still aimed at Tom's midsection, and sighted down on the center button of the man's shirt.

"They don't sing at this time of day, Miss Ginger. They don't dance neither. Even at their drunkenness, they don't carry on this loud this early. Unless they's trying to drown out some sounds. Like the sounds of 'em loose boards in the hallway that my ears is pickin' up jus' fine."

Laughing, Tom looked away from Reno and faced the pretty Pinkerton lady.

"He's mad as a hatter," he said, but Ginger started to raise the Smith & Wesson higher, at Tom's heart, but in doing so she brought the nickel-plated pistol closer to the traitor and his left hand slapped like a rattlesnake, grabbing the wrist before she could pull the trigger.

"Six feet from the door!" Tom yelled.

Ginger's shriek was drowned out by a cannonade of gunshots that riddled the wall, sending splinters into Reno's beard and face, but he was falling to the floor.

"Get down!" he screamed at Ginger/Chiara, but he knew she couldn't hear.

Reno couldn't see her. She must have fallen to the floor, but he saw Tom holding Ginger's pistol and snapping a shot that parted Reno's hair. Reno squeezed the Spencer's trigger and white smoke blinded him. He knew he missed, for through the thick smoke he saw Tom at the door, jerking it open while aiming the Smith & Wesson at Reno's midsection.

Then blood exploded from Tom's face as a bullet smashed his jaw and sent teeth and parts of tongue into the hallway. He might have screamed. Reno's ears were ringing now, so he could hardly hear anything. He did turn, and another bullet or two drove him out of the room into the hallway.

But bullets continued to fire through the wall. Too high, though, to hit Ginger/Chiara or Reno, who were on the floor. He rolled over, his back shoving the bed back and, now facing the wall that was peppered with holes, began firing the Spencer as fast as he could.

Ginger was doing the same with her pistol, and when that emptied she must have managed to find the sawed-off Greener because both barrels blasted a hole that Tom could have slipped through if he weren't already bleeding or dead in that hallway.

The Spencer carbine held only seven rounds and Reno didn't have any cartridges or one of those cylinders that fellow named Blakeslee had invented for easier reloads. Ginger/Chiara must have been out of bullets, too, but their counterattack must have driven those two-bit assassins back down the hallway because through the massive holes the shotgun had left in the wall, all Reno saw now was gun smoke.

He rose, left the Spencer on the bed, and rolled across it. Ginger/Chiara was on a knee, reloading the Smith & Wesson. Reno saw the two derringers and picked those up off the dresser. They looked like toothpicks in his massive hands.

His mouth was dry.

Two derringers and a .32 weren't going to hold off that mob.

"You ain't got no way out, Yankees!" someone shouted.

Reno recognized the voice. Then he heard a board

creak and a face appeared in the doorway. It was Gene Harriman, the gun shop owner who had some kind of Rebel flag in his storeroom. He snapped off a shot too quickly, the bullet burning Reno's shoulder but not enough to spoil his aim.

The last round of the Spencer blew the man on top of the traitor Tom.

"Come on out!" another Southern voice called again. "We'll just take you to the US Marshal's office. We're deputies, you see. Take you there and you can be tried fair and square for murdering a Secret Service man sworn to protect the president of your United States."

Ginger/Chiara opened her mouth, but Reno shook his head. She turned to him and then looked through the doorway and saw Tom, deader than he'd ever be. Reno saw that Harriman was dead, too.

"Trust nobody," she whispered.

Reno moved slightly and the floor moaned.

"You trust me?" he asked softly.

She turned to him and then smiled. "With my life, handsome."

"Good." Reno slid the derringers into his pockets and took the loaded Smith & Wesson from the Pinkerton gal's hand. Then he came up onto his knees, still holding the .32 uncocked in his left hand, and stretched out his arms toward her.

"Climb aboard, darlin'," he said. And Reno smiled.

She briefly stared at him with suspicion and then she was in his arms and he pulled her tight and close to his chest. Her arms wrapped around his neck as he rose, the boards creaking underneath their weight.

Turning, Reno faced the door. He looked through

the shotgun holes and then through the smaller holes
made from bullets fired from the inside of the room
and into the room by those dirty-dealing, ex-Johnny
Rebs. He knew many a Johnny Reb who had gone on
living in the United States with no animosity to anyone
who wore the blue. He figured one or two of them
might have even voted for Grant—in both elections.

He drew in a deep breath, exhaled, and looked into
Ginger/Chiara's pretty eyes.

"Ready?"

She shrugged. "Reckon so," she said, trying to match
his accent. It wasn't a bad try either.

Reno sucked in as much air as he could and held it.
Then he stepped onto the bed, somehow keeping his
balance as the legs and the springs groaned underneath
the weight.

"This is your last chance, folks!" the voice down the
hallway cried. "Walk out now or we come in a-shootin'
and a-killin'!"

Reno jumped backward. He struck the flooring with
all his weight and then felt himself falling through the
floor, shards of timber ripping his pants, his arms, his
back. Ginger/Chiara made not one sound.

Until they hit the billiard table on the bawdy house's
first floor.

Ginger/Chiara flew out of Reno's arms. Two dolled-
up, fat wenches turned, screaming, and the Pinkerton
gal crashed against them and disappeared. Jed Reno
heard that more than he saw it because the table split in
half where he hit and he tumbled backward, hitting the
sawdust floor and somersaulting over, knocking over a
spittoon, and upending the roulette wheel.

He came up quickly, at least to his knees, holding onto the spittoon, and saw a mustachioed bartender hurrying toward him, raising a billy club over his head, cursing like a wild man. The spittoon left Reno's hand and busted the man full on the face, dropping him to his knees as one hand dropped the stick and then joined the other hand in trying to stop the blood that kept gushing from his nose.

The second man Reno saw was smarter. He was pulling a Remington from a shoulder holster. He was also standing just a few feet from Ginger/Chiara.

The man was smart, but he wasn't fast. Reno leveled the Smith & Wesson and squeezed the trigger. The gun popped and the man spun around, clutching his left shoulder—Reno had been aiming for the gent's right one—but he wasn't seeing clearly with blood trickling down his forehead over his good eye.

Turning around, Reno snapped off another shot that punched a man in a Johnny Reb cavalry coat in the midsection, and that one discharged his hogleg into the floor before he fell to the floor.

Now dance-hall girls began screaming and Reno heard footsteps on the stairs. He turned and saw the first man wearing buckskin britches step into view. A gun roared to Reno's right and the man slammed against the wall, dropped his revolver, and then tumbled down the stairs into a heap on the floor. Another figure leaped back out of view when Reno's shot splintered the step below.

Reno saw Ginger/Chiara holding the wounded gunman's Remington. She turned and swept her arm right to left, then left to right, the .44 cocked.

"C'mon!" she yelled. For a second Reno thought she was challenging the handful of men and women to make a play, start the ball, get themselves shot full of holes.

But she was heading toward the batwing doors, backing away as fast as she could but keeping that Remington ready to spit out lead and death.

Reno moved with her, out of the small gambling area, away from the dance floor that didn't seem as crowded as it had sounded when those folks were shouting more than singing "Dixie."

Batwing doors pounded as Ginger/Chiara went through and slammed against Reno's hindquarters.

Stopping for an instant, Reno found his voice.

"Anybody wants to die, just foller us."

He came through the door and turned.

Ginger/Chiara was already swinging onto the back of a piebald and Reno found the reins to a big sorrel. The boardwalks were crowded with people, but not one town law, not one soldier boy, not one US marshal—nobody with a gun—was there to challenge them.

Trust nobody? Wasn't that the truth.

Ginger/Chiara kicked her stolen horse into a gallop. She was riding north. Reno sent one bullet through the dance-hall window, fired another over the closest gawker's head, and then kneed the sorrel into a gallop.

He caught up with Ginger/Chiara at the edge of town and they rode hard to Dry Creek, which wasn't dry, and splashed into it and followed the creek west, coming out and loping south till they hit the big draw.

There they let the horses rest. Reno handed his stolen

mount's reins to Ginger/Chiara and hurried up the slope, then studied the back trail for ten minutes.

Finally he came down and shook his head. Ginger/ Chiara was wiping her mouth. She had been smart enough to pick a horse that had a canteen hanging from the saddle horn. She passed that to him and he took a drink, nodding his thanks.

"Ain't nobody follerin' us," he said. "Yet."

"Where's the Slash G?" she asked.

He pointed southwest.

"That's that Laramie warden's spread," he told her.

She nodded. "So Breck Glenn's in on it, too. He likely arranged Ben Gore's breakout." She sighed. "Trust nobody." Her eyes found him. "Except Jed Reno."

"There's more," he assured her. "Tim Colter, for one."

"If he's alive," the Pinkerton gal said.

"He's alive," Jed said and he knew he wasn't just hoping.

"Good." Ginger looked down the creek.

"And there's a lot of Union boys in this ter'tory."

"And far too many traitors," she said and cursed that Tom.

Looking up at Reno, she followed her curse with a sigh. "I let it slip that the president was coming on Thursday."

Reno's head confirmed that. "When he's a-comin' Tuesday."

"Right. That wouldn't give the butchers time to put their plan to use. They would plan to start bringing men in for the ambush on Wednesday. By the time they realized President Grant was talking on Tuesday, he'd be on the Union Pacific heading back East."

"Sounds like a good plan to me," Reno said, though his idea of planning was about two seconds before he did what first came to mind.

"Not if this conspiracy goes higher than we thought," the Pinkerton gal whispered. She paused and shook her head. "Warden Breck has a ranch?"

Reno nodded again.

"Does the Denver Pacific cross near his land?" she asked.

"I ain't sure how much of the land is rightfully his'n," he told her. "He filed a homestead claim on one of the water holes. Had a couple of his cowhands who actually work the place on two other good pastures. But, yeah, 'em trains run near it anyhow."

"Then that's where they'll try to kill President Grant." She slammed a tiny right fist into a small left palm, and swore. "Not Cheyenne. But on the train. In the middle of nowhere. Like those train-robbing gangs back East have been doing—away from towns with lawmen and forts with soldiers. Of course. How could we have not thought of that before? What a lousy detective I am."

Reno had never seen her worked up this way. He wanted to reach over and hug her, tell her it would be all right, but he didn't want that gal, riled as she was, to slap his face.

"What I'd give right now for a map of this country!"

She had to stop to catch her breath and Reno made his move. He stepped up to her and handed her the canteen. Then, after a quick smile, he put his left hand on her shoulder and waited for her to look into his big, bloodied, and blackening eye.

"Li'l lady. You don't need no map. You gots me. And I knows this country. Ever' bit of it."

Chapter 38

When he had applied for this job no one ever told Deputy United States Marshal Jack Collins just how many hours—days—he would spend staring at papers. Some of it was all right, though it took a lot of time. After all the government would pay him for miles ridden, most expenses like paying ferry fees, or a stagecoach ticket. The worst of all had to be writing out arrest reports, but Collins never tired of looking at wanted posters.

Sometimes he would dream about what it would be like if he came across some hard rock of a renegade like that bank- and train-robbing Jesse James, though that wasn't likely because those Missouri boys stayed close to home. But Mad Ben Gore had escaped from the territorial prison. And then there was Jake Dugan, who was probably crazier and maybe even a mite more dangerous than Gore and James combined.

The door to the office opened and in walked Frank

Smith, who returned Collins's nod and walked to the window and pulled down the shade.

"Hot outside," he said and moved over to the table where Collins was shuffling through the latest wanted dodgers.

"Seen any of them bad boys?" Smith chuckled as he dragged a chair from his desk and then sat down about six feet in front of Collins, straddling his long legs toward the young deputy and resting his left arm on the backrest.

"Most of these . . ." Collins stifled a yawn. ". . . their last known whereabouts were way off East. Missouri, Iowa . . ." He turned over another dodger. "Alabama." He paused and looked at that one and quickly turned another one atop it. "Well, New Mexico Territory. That's closer."

"Still a fer piece from this patch of nothin'."

Collins nodded just to give himself something to do. He flipped over another poster. "This one was on his way from El Paso, Texas, across the Rio Grande."

"Well, if he's smart he won't come back."

Collins stopped with the posters and looked up. "I haven't seen Marshal Tobin all day."

Smith responded with a shrug of his shoulders. "It's Sunday. Maybe he went to church."

Collins had. But it was getting late in the day now. And it was Marshal Clyde Tobin who always said that a federal marshal has no days off, though he hardly worked as long and hard or rode as many miles as any of his deputies. Still, he would drop in on a Sunday at some point, usually on his way to worship or on his way back. Collins had liked that about the man.

"Maybe he's helping Marshal Russell."

"Huh?"

Looking back at the lawman in front of him, Collins explained, "Walker Chester said some raiders snuck into his livery stable last night and stole ten horses, including Marshal Russell's prized black stallion."

"That so?" But Collins could tell that Smith did not give a whit about any City of Cheyenne crime. He was a federal lawman.

"He swore it was Jed Reno, but—"

"Wouldn't put it past that fat sack of horse apples."

Frank Smith had never cottoned to that mountain man, but Collins knew better than to argue with him. Then Smith laughed. "I suppose you're right. I haven't seen Russell or any of his deputies all day."

"He should have left at least a couple."

Smith spat toward the nearest cuspidor but missed. Wiping his mouth, he said, "You wouldn't if you owned that black." He glanced at the clock, then drew the revolver, flipped open the chamber gate, and, after pulling the hammer to half-cock, spun the cylinder on his left forearm.

Suddenly explosions roared from somewhere down the street. Visions of Jesse James and Jake Dugan flashed through Collins's mind and he sprang to his feet.

"Sit down," Smith barked.

"But . . ." When he looked back at Frank Smith he saw the revolver was cocked and pointed directly at Collins's chest.

"Sit." Smith grinned coldly.

The gunfire continued, then stopped.

"That would be your pard Jed Reno dying," Smith said.

"Trust nobody," Collins whispered, and he moved back to his chair, sat down, eyes trained on the gun. He began to point at the man holding a gun on him, but he started shaking so badly he brought it underneath the table and shoved it into his coat pocket. His left hand began turning back over the wanted posters and those shook terribly until he laid them on the stack. He reached for another and heard Smith clear his throat.

The man was standing now.

"The town law won't be back for a coupla days," Smith said. "Too bad. He'll miss Grant's visit. Russell's a good egg. He and Tim Colter might could have stopped that red-handed butcher from gettin' kilt in Cheyenne."

"I could've stopped that, too," Collins whispered.

"Nah." Smith tilted his head toward the gun cabinet on the far wall. "Not when you unbuckle your rig and leave it way over yonder, boy."

"Trust nobody," Collins whispered again.

"What's that you—"

Gunfire had erupted in town again and Smith spun to look, but he had drawn the shade and now Collins was standing. Smith grinned as he turned back and the grin turned into a savage curse when he saw the pocket Colt revolver in the young man's hand.

The .36 spat flame and lead, twisting Smith to his side, where another bullet shattered his left arm. He dropped to his knees and turned back only to catch two more slugs that slammed him to the floor, face up. His finger pulled the trigger once on his revolver, but it just tore a long trench across the floor.

He tried to raise the gun again, but it slipped out of his fingers and he moved the hand to cover one of the bloody holes in his body.

Coughing, his breath ragged and painful, Smith swore softly and turned his head to spit bloody phlegm onto the floor. Jack Collins made his way and stood over him for a minute. Smith managed to see that the kid held the smoking little Colt in his right hand and a wanted dodger in his left. The pistol was still cocked, but Collins wasn't the sort to put a man out of his misery.

He sank to his knees and looked at the dying killer.

"I said," Collins whispered, "'trust nobody.' Something Jed Reno said."

And he turned the dodger over so Frank Smith could see his own likeness.

WANTED

BILLY RAY NEWTON

ALSO KNOWN AS WILLIAM RAYBURN NEWTON,

BAD B. R., BLOODY BILLY, AND BILLY THE REB,

WHO,

ON THE 12TH OF DECEMBER 1872,

ATTEMPTED TO ROB THE FEDERAL PAYMASTER

IN MUSCLE SHOALS, ALABAMA,

AND DURING THE FAILED

ROBBERY ATTEMPT

KILLED 2 MILITARY GUARDS

IN COLD BLOOD!

A
$1,500 Reward Will Be
Paid
to Party or Parties
Who Bring this Cold-Blooded Killer & Thief
To Justice
Wire T. M. Silas,
US Marshal
Northern District of Alabama
Huntsville, Alabama

Which, the way Jack Collins figured, was the last thing Billy Ray Newton, alias Frank Smith, ever saw in this world.

Chapter 39

The newspaperman just wouldn't shut up and US Marshal Clyde Tobin was in a hurry on this Monday morning.

"Listen, Ted," Tobin finally told him, "for the thousandth time, I have federal jurisdiction—not local. Unless the local law officer—in this case the town marshal—asks me to step in, I can't do a thing." He shook his head and tried to walk to his office, but the editor kept blocking his path.

"Men were killed yesterday—on a Sunday, for gosh sake—inside that house of ill repute," the editor let him know again. He was beating that dead mule something fierce. "A woman and Jed Reno—"

"Jed Reno?" That was the first time Tobin had heard that name. "Yes, Reno. Well, I guess if Tim Colter can go wrong—though I still have my doubts about that—and become a wanted man, I guess Reno is no exception."

"Is Reno . . . alive?"

"Of course he's alive!" The editor gawked at him, but at least he did not suspect Tobin of being in on this conspiracy. Tobin had to remember to watch what he said. "But there are quite a number found inside that wreck who aren't—thanks to him. Now what is going on here? Is the president still coming to Cheyenne? Will this stop his plans? Ruin our chance for newspaper coverage and glory across the nation, if not the entire world?"

Tobin felt like he could use a generous pour of bourbon right now. But now he saw a way to get everything back under control.

"That depends on you, Ted," he said calmly. "A dance hall has been wrecked. A few—how many men were killed?"

"Five. For the moment. Criminy, even Gene Harriman is dead. But I'm not sure Reno was at fault. The way some witnesses put it, some old Johnny Rebs started the whole shooting match. And we found a Rebel flag hanging in Harriman's storeroom. I don't like the idea of Johnny Rebs in Cheyenne. We're a Union town."

"Indeed." Tobin thought, *We have too many fools involved in this plot. They should have left it all to me.*

"Ted." Tobin put his arm around the editor's shoulders. He dropped his voice to a whisper. "If you want national news. If you want your report to be picked up by newspapers across the nation, then if I were editor of Cheyenne's finest newspaper, I wouldn't print a word about this until, say, a week or two after the president is . . ." He had to stop himself from saying *dead.* ". . . back where he belongs."

"But we publish every day, except Sun—" Ted wasn't the sharpest editor Tobin had dealt with during his long and storied political career, but he got the message. "I see," he sighed, and Tobin squeezed his shoulder and made his way out of the wrecked part of Cheyenne's district of wickedness and made his way to his office.

One crisis averted. Now on to . . .

The door was locked.

Angrily, Tobin banged on it but heard nothing. A federal marshal's office was never locked—even on a Sunday. All businesses in Cheyenne were open today. He banged on the door again, then reached into his pockets until he found the key. Luckily he had one and it fit the lock. He pushed the door open and gasped.

"Marshal."

Quickly Tobin stepped back outside, closing the door, putting in the key, and turning until the click sounded.

"Marshal."

Now, after testing the knob to make sure the door was secured, he turned and pasted on one of his political smiles.

"Colonel." He extended his right hand while his left dropped the key into a deep trousers pocket. "What brings you here on the sabbath?"

The graybeard handed Tobin a folded sheet of paper.

"This came by courier," the bluecoat said. "We knew not to risk sending a telegram."

Frowning, Tobin looked at the paper and let out a sharp curse. His fist wanted to ball up the letter, but he restrained. His eyes went back up to meet the Yankee soldier's.

"From the look of what happened at that dance hall, Marshal, I think I should bring my entire command to Cheyenne. If I had my druthers, I would send a courier to Denver and urge the president to return East."

"No." Again Tobin regained his composure. "That was a drunken spree. If our town marshal wasn't after horse thieves, the culprits would already be locked up in jail. I hear . . . well . . ." He managed to fake a grin. "You know how Jed Reno can get when he's had a snootful."

"Right now, sir, I'd give my left arm for just one Jed Reno. And one Tim Colter."

Tobin frowned.

"You'll have everything ready, Marshal?" The colonel waited.

Tobin studied the letter to the governor, which he had forwarded to Fort Russell again.

President Grant was to arrive on Tuesday at 11:45 in the morning. He would eat dinner, hold a reception at the Railroad House, and depart on the Union Pacific eastbound at two that afternoon.

Returning the letter to the colonel, Tobin said, "Everything will be ready, sir. I promise you. I will see to that myself."

"Be sure you do, Marshal." He looked down the street. "Be sure you do." Then he offered an informal salute, spun on his heel, and walked down the boardwalk toward a gathering of other bluebelly officers.

Tobin had to find two men to get the stinking carcass of Deputy Marshal Frank Smith out of the US Marshal's office. That should be easy enough. Just drop him in an alley and Tobin could figure out a story that would have Smith dying a hero. If everything worked out, maybe he could let it out that Smith had been killed in a valiant but unsuccessful attempt to save President Grant's life.

But then he had to get a horse from Walker Chester's livery—a good one, a ride like he'd never ridden before to Jake Dugan's camp on the Slash G spread. He looked at his watch as he hurried down the boardwalk. There was still enough time. He was glad he had eaten a good breakfast this morning.

"Let's go," Jake Dugan said.

Tim Colter pushed the hat that had been shielding his eyes from the sun off his face and stared up at the red-handed butcher.

"Where?"

Dugan's smile was wicked. "To where history will be made. To where the murderin' Grant meets his maker."

The horse Dugan had dismounted from grazed nearby, the reins dragging on the ground.

Pushing himself to a seated position on his bedroll, Colter pretended he had no interest. He made himself yawn and looked up at the gang leader as though he was bored out of his mind.

"It ain't all that far, pardner," Dugan said. "Two miles thataway." He pointed southwest.

"You mean y'all ain't gonna do all that killin' in Cheyenne?" Patsy Palmer walked over with the boy from the breakfast fire. The kid was bringing a plate for Colter and a cup of coffee.

"With all 'em people? All 'em soldiers from Fort Russell?" He snorted. "Not hardly. I'd like to live to see the chaos I have wrought to an illegitimate government."

The boy started to protest, but Patsy Palmer must have squeezed his shoulder hard because he flinched but did not lose hold of the plate or the cup. He looked up at her and she tilted her head toward Colter. Once she released her grip, Kip Jansen walked over.

He took the plate and the cup but did not thank young Jansen, who walked back toward the big woman. He took a sip of coffee—Jed Reno's was much better and Jed Reno's coffee was horrible—and shoveled a forkful of hominy into his mouth. He hated hominy. And these had no salt or pepper for seasoning.

"You comin'?" Dugan snapped.

Colter looked up and gave him the hardest stare he thought Mad Ben Gore could have given anyone, no matter his rank or reputation, and it worked. The renegade stepped back.

"Well, finish your chuck in a hurry. I want you to test out that Gatlin' gun afore our day of glory."

"Test?" Colter had stopped chewing.

"You know why I busted you out of that prison, boy." Laughing, he turned toward Palmer and the kid. "You shoulda seen him at Butterscotch, Missouri, in February of '65. Glory be, I wish I'd seen it. But we all heard about it. The day Butterscotch become Butterscotch!"

Colter had heard about it, too. He just hadn't remembered the connection.

"Fort Wyman . . ." The butcher could not hide his

enthusiasm for a cold-blooded massacre. "Bluebellies came a-marchin' out to the post cemetery to bury one of their own—and they walked right into Mad Ben Gore, who had ambushed a wagon guarded by four Yankees—earlier that mornin'—and what was them yeller dogs bringin' to that fort? A Gatlin' gun. And what did 'em soldier boys walkin' to a funeral get?" He roared so hard he almost doubled over.

"They got ripped to pieces. Mowed down, and when a handful of others come out to help they got kilt, too. A beautiful day of butchery, it was. The ground turned red that day. Glory be, Ben, I don't know how you done it, but that mighta been the last real good day the Confederacy ever had—till Thursday—when you'll top it."

Colter tried to smile but wasn't sure he succeeded.

Nodding again in the direction he had pointed at, Dugan said, "Vengeance Canyon. The perfect place for the Confederacy to reap her vengeance. The perfect place for Ulysses S. Grant to die. Two miles yonder. If the Gatlin' don't kill him, the fall will."

He roared with laughter.

Colter set the plate aside and rose, making himself drink the coffee, making himself stay calm.

"Fall?" he asked. Then he remembered who he was and said, "You sayin' you don't think I can murder that Yankee tyrant? After what I done that fine mornin' in Missouri?"

"No, hoss, course not. It's—"

Everyone turned to the sound of a horse loping toward them and Colter recognized Lige Kerns, who had been posted as one of the sentries about a mile northeast of the camp. He was smiling, though, which did not make Colter feel any easier.

"Gen'ral," the piece of scum said after reining in the dark horse. "Goodrich's wagon's a-comin' in . . . nice and slow. He's a good ways off. Takin' his time. Real careful."

"Excellent." Dugan rubbed his hands together. "Ride back." He pointed again. "Tell him to come easy. Come easy as he can. There ain't no hurry. We got till Wednesday night to set ever'thin' up for the soon-to-be-dead president."

"You ain't got to tell him to come easy. He knows. And I knows, too, close as I'll be to that cargo."

"Watch for prairie dog holes and rocks," Dugan said, but Kerns was already turning his horse around and trotting off.

"Goodrich?" Colter asked when Dugan had turned back to face his best man-killer.

"You know how I operate, Ben." He hooked a thumb toward Lige Kerns. "I wasn't 'bout to think that idiot had sense enough to get that Gatlin' gun to me. So when we learnt that Grant would be in Denver first, Vengeance Canyon came to mind. The drop would sure kill'm deader'n dirt. Don't you think?"

Patsy Palmer spoke up. "You're gonna blow up that there railroad bridge with dynamite?"

Jake Dugan laughed. "Dynamite? Not hardly. You know what some of 'em miners up in Montana Territory is usin' these days. Nitroglycerine. And Clete . . ." He made a vague gesture toward the main camp. "He read a newspaper sometime last summer when we was up Helena way. Some powder works in San Francisco blowed up. Shook the whole city, the newspaper says—least, that's the way Clete read it to us. The hole that was left where that buildin' had been was twelve foot deep and more than a hundred feet wide." He nodded his appreciation. "I'd say that'll do the job."

"I'll do the job," Colter said.

"I expect you to. But we're still gonna blow up that bridge. On account we'll be ridin' hard south into Colorady and don't want all them soldier boys from Fort Russell comin' after us on a train."

He smiled. "Now c'mon. We're gonna set up next to that deep ol' hole in the ground. Remember what you tol' me. A Gatlin' ain't no different from a Colt's revolver or an Enfield musket. Or whatever a body's shootin'. You got to make sure how it aims. And I wants to hear how that Gatlin' barks before you get to kill yerself a Yankee president."

Dugan turned, picked his reins off the ground, and swung into the saddle. He shot a look at Patsy Palmer and the boy and told Colter, "Bring the kid with you. Him and Patsy. They'll want to see this, too."

Colter watched the crazy killer lope off toward deep and treacherous Vengeance Canyon. Slowly he rose and emptied most of the coffee onto the ground, then pitched the cup into the plate of hominy he had hardly touched. He certainly wasn't hungry now, though he briefly thought about how much he could use a drink. And Tim Colter wasn't much of a drinking man.

"Vengeance Canyon?" Kip Jansen asked.

Colter nodded. "It's a deep cut. Why the railroad crews didn't go around that I don't know. There's a shorter and not as deep a cut two miles east." He spat the bitterness of the coffee and the conversation out of his mouth and wiped his lips with the back of his hand.

Three hundred feet deep. Ninety-six feet wide. A long fall to jagged boulders and bones below. Two crewmen had died while building that trestle. Fourteen more were injured. And now there was a decent chance that an American president would be killed there, too. Along with his wife and traveling secretary—and the train crew and however many military guards were with Grant.

"C'mon!"

Jake Dugan's command carried across the wind-swept plains.

"He surely wants you to test that Gatlin'," Patsy Palmer said. She turned, and Colter followed her gaze. Apparently Dugan wasn't the only person interested in seeing this bit of target practice. Half the camp was following the so-called major general to that deep canyon and the railroad tracks that crossed it.

"Have you ever fired a Gatlin' gun, Colter?" the big woman asked.

Colter's strained chuckle lacked any humor. "Ma'am," he answered, "I've only seen pictures of those guns in illustrated magazines."

Chapter 40

Jed Reno didn't like this one bit, but at this point there was nothing he could do about it but keep his hands over the muzzles of the two horses. Make sure they didn't whinny. If that happened, well, things might turn mighty ugly. He stood in a dry creek bed, one that was deep enough so that the riders crossing this patch of Slash G Cattle Company land wouldn't be able to see the horses or Reno. But they could hear the horses. Sound traveled pretty good in this country and the wind was blowing toward the wagon that was creeping along.

Ginger Burricchia, or Chiara, or whatever in the Sam Hill her name was, had seen them first. She had rushed over to Jed, told him what was coming down the trail, ordered him—with not even a pretty please—to keep the horses quiet and out of sight, and then ran up the creek bed about four hundred yards before scooting up and crawling on the ground to the rocks. Then she climbed up the little rise.

Woman moved fast. Faster than Jed could have. He had to give her that. And she had done it in a way that those boys in that big wagon and the four outriders couldn't have seen her. But when Reno thought he saw her pulling out a spyglass he flinched. Sunlight reflecting off those lenses and, well, there could be a right long gunfight in these parts. And Jed Reno had his hands full. He couldn't even move his arms to grab his Hawken.

All he could do was look up at that ridge and watch the lady Pinkerton detective, listen, and keep these two horses—stolen, well, borrowed, not horses trained by a savvy old mountain man.

He was also powerful dry. Hot as the sun was.

Best he could tell, the wagon and riders were alongside that rise by now. Yep. The woman started to turn slowly, looking ahead now rather than northerly. That wagon wasn't in any race. Reno knew that. It moved like a sloth. But at length Ginger/Chiara began backing away from her viewpoint. She didn't rush her way down though. She was too smart for that. Knew better than to raise up dust or stumble over a rock and take a long, painful, dust-cloud-producing tumble.

Reno's horse started to pull on the reins, but a short, soft grumble told the horse not to fool around. He waited till the pretty girl hit the bottom and began a soft trot to the creek bed, jumping in and keeping her balance when she hit the ground, then hurrying toward Reno but slowing down before she got too close to the horses.

It was safe by then, even as slow as that wagon inched along, so Reno dropped his hands over the noses and mouths of the horses and let them lick some of the salt he had set out for them.

Ginger/Chiara was smart enough to grab a canteen and take two long pulls. Not too much. Just the right amount. She wiped her mouth with a shirtsleeve and held out the canteen to Reno, who accepted. She pointed the spyglass southwest.

"What's that way? More of the Slash G?"

Reno swallowed the water. "Well, depends on who you ask. Like I said, deeds ain't what matters when it comes to ranchin' here these days. It's more . . . guns."

"How about the railroad tracks?"

He nodded. "Yes'm." He traced an imaginary line with his finger in the sky, turning as he moved south and then southeast. "Curves there. Flat mostly. Runs on into Cheyenne."

"And northwest?"

"Lot rougher country. That's where 'em boys spent 'bout half a year or more buildin' that big bridge."

"Bridge?"

"Or whatever you call it. Some folks call it a trestle. It crosses Vengeance Canyon."

"How far away?"

"From here?" He shrugged. "Just a coupla miles."

"Vengeance Canyon." She was testing the name.

"The story is that a buffler herd stampeded through a Cheyenne camp right around here years and years ago. Killed the chief's son, who was just born, five months old, a year old, thirteen years old, nobody knows how old. And the chief got angry and demanded vengeance. And since they didn't know what herd done the thing, caused the boy's death, they stampeded six herds over the edge of that canyon. In vengeance. So Vengeance Canyon got its name."

She must have been imagining all those stampedes and the chief getting justice, so he corrected her thinking.

"But there ain't a lick of truth to that story. That was me and Jim Bridger's doin' after we'd had ourselves a snootful. The tribes back then, that's how they harvested buffalo. Just drove 'em over a cliff. Didn't have a Hawken from some trader or mountain man. Reckon they figgered it was just an easy way to get some meat and skins. Me? I'd rather shoot 'em. Less waste."

She didn't seem interested in the least, so Jed started to tell her another windy, but she stopped him by calling him by his name.

"That wagon was carrying one crate. A small crate. Covered with blankets on the floor, blankets all around it, pillows stuffed inside it—the lid had been pried off—and they wrapped the wheels, even the horses' hooves, with animal skins."

"Well, that ain't gonna hide no trail," Reno told her. "We can foller 'em shore enough."

Her head shook. "Jed. That's not to hide their trail. That's to keep them from being blown to kingdom come."

He stared at her.

"Ever heard of Gold Fever Creek in Montana Territory?"

He shook his head.

"It's a mining camp, run by the Gold Fever Mining Corporation. With its own store. A company town, if you'd call it a town. The country there is hard. Real hard. So they were using nitroglycerine. One evening a fire broke out in the company warehouse. It blew the warehouse and a couple of surrounding buildings into oblivion. Estimates were that the four cases of nitroglycerin blew up from the fire. It's really a finicky explosive."

"I heard of it."

"Well, the only man killed was the night guard. The only thing found of him was his head, which was badly burned. Thing is, there was a bullet in his head."

"Coulda been caused by the fire. Bullets go off, too." He nodded. "I knows that fer a fact."

"Could have been." Her head nodded. "But one of our men said that the hole left would not have been caused by four cases of nitro—just three."

He rubbed his good eye and then above the patch over the gone one. "You got a detective that can figure that out?"

"It's all science and math and detection. How long would it take to get a wagon moving at the speed that wagon was going from southwestern Montana Territory to here?"

"I can't say."

"It doesn't matter. I think that's nitroglycerine they're carrying. Maybe it came from Montana. Maybe not. And I think they are planning to blow up the bridge—the trestle—over Vengeance Canyon to kill President Grant. They're not taking any chances. A Gatling gun. And nitroglycerine."

He took the reins to his horse. "What day is it?"

"Monday," she said. "The president is coming tomorrow."

"But they—them vermin assassins—they still think he's coming on Thursday."

"Unless," she said, "someone has told them otherwise. Either way, we have to figure out a way to stop them."

"I don't see no wagonload of nitro," Tim Colter told Jake Dugan, still speaking in a hoarse whisper, which wasn't so much playacting now. His neck burned from all the dust and dirt and sweat.

The bushwhacker laughed. Behind him, three of his ablest men—two of whom had gone through all the McGuffey Readers and the third whose two stepfathers had been gunsmiths—busied themselves assembling the Gatling gun inside the back of an old covered Conestoga wagon. The cover was to keep any Yankees from seeing what was inside.

The food and coffee here didn't help Colter's wound any either, and he didn't want to drink any of the rotgut they served. He had to keep his wits about him. He saw Patsy Palmer and the boy. Too many lives depended on him.

Including President Grant's, Mrs. Grant's, and the president's secretary, Brevet Brigadier General Orville E. Babcock's. He wondered if Mrs. Babcock was with them. Or their children.

Colter couldn't see what was inside either, but the men must have been getting the hang of it because he heard more clicks and clacks than cuss words.

"And I ain't seen no black smoke risin' 'bout a mile high into that sky. Or heard the most awesomest thunder you ever heard in your life." He peeked through the canvas opening and appeared happy. "So I reckon the boys is bein' mighty cautious to get that stuff here."

Colter nodded. "As long as it's here by Thursday."

"That's right." He yelled over the mechanical noises, "How's it goin', boys?"

"It'd go a right smart faster if you'd pull off this canvas. It's hotter than a sick dog in here, and darker than ten at night."

"The cover stays up. If anyone spies us from afar, they'll think we's just workin' cowboys and that's our chuckwagon."

"Well, why don't Mad Ben come give us—"

Someone must have punched him in the arm or warned him to shut up, that nobody talked to Mad Ben Gore that way.

"I shoot that gun," Colter said hoarsely. "You just put it together right."

No one challenged him, other than a soft curse.

"Train!" someone yelled.

Colter turned south. He could hear the rails rattling and, a moment later, saw the smoke from the engine.

The bloody-handed general had pulled out his watch and said, "I'll say one thing 'bout that Denver Pacific. Their trains run on time."

This one would be the freight, Colter figured, and knew Dugan was right. Northbound DP trains came through twice a day, the express around 11:45 in the morning and the freight about 3:30 in the afternoon. The southbounds run right around 1:15 in the afternoon for the express and 5:45 in the morning for the freight.

"It's comin' alon'," said the closest the bushwhackers had to a gunsmith. "Give us half an hour. We'll have it ready for Mr. Gore to show us how he shoots one of these babies."

"All right, boys," Dugan called. "Just make yourself look like cowboys doin' what 'em jokers do—laze around camp." He then barked at those in the big wagon, "And this, you idiots, is why we keep a tarp over that pretty gun yer a-buildin'!"

The train rolled by over the bridge, which rattled but stood firm, and Colter counted the seconds it took a freight to cross it. The express moved a lot quicker. But no locomotive, no matter how fast it was moving, could outrun nitroglycerine when it went off just below the train.

When the train had vanished except for the smoke and the noise, Dugan barked, "A half hour. See it's done in a half hour. I want to get some target practice in for my sharpshooter."

A half hour. Colter looked to the north. No dust. No wagon. No wagonload of nitro yet. Colter had one idea that might save the president. He figured if he could hit that wagon with the Gatling gun, or get his hands on a Sharps—maybe even a Winchester if the wagon was close enough—he could blow that nitro up before they could put it on the bridge. Blow up half the men, if he was lucky.

All he had to do was get Patsy Palmer and the boy to safety. And he had seen one spot here that might keep them alive. Not that the big woman was sinless, but somebody had to be alive to get young Kip Jansen to

Cheyenne safe and sound. And it was starting to look like Patsy Palmer might have to be that woman.

Because Jake Dugan was keeping Colter mighty close. And Colter wasn't seeing much of an escape route for him to survive this last battle of the Confederacy once the shooting started.

Chapter 41

They were pulling off the tarp, revealing the shining, fresh-out-of-the-crate Gatling gun, its long magazine stretching skyward, loaded with death. To Tim Colter it looked just like those drawings he had seen in periodicals—only more lethal.

Dugan's henchmen had put the two wheels on the gun, but they were smart enough to brake the wheels and brace them. Likely they figured they needed the wheels to lift the gun high enough to fire across Vengeance Canyon and into the presidential train. Colter could have saved them some time by telling them to just mount the gun on the front seat of the big wagon. But he wasn't here to save time. He was here to save a president's life—and maybe keep some other innocent people alive, too.

He counted six barrels and saw the crank at the end. Operating it seemed simple enough. Same as working the Colt he had holstered. Turning the crank was the same as cocking the hammer, only the crank also triggered the bullets, and it would shoot a lot faster and much quicker than a single-action revolver.

One of the assemblers was reading a manual. "Shucks," he said and looked down from the wagon at Jake Dugan. "With these here 'drum feeders' this thing can shoot four hundred rounds a minute." He reached up and patted the greasy barrels. "That'll deal plenty of death to that butcherin' Grant."

"Hey!" another man still in the wagon shouted, pointing northwest. "Looks like the wagon finally made it here."

Turning, Colter frowned. He could see the wagon creeping along, the horsemen keeping what they considered a respectful distance ahead of and behind the load of nitroglycerine—but Colter knew they were still way too close. He looked back at the gun, but the boy, young Kip Jansen, was right here. Colter couldn't make his play now. He'd have to hope for the best.

"Lambert," Dugan called to one of his lieutenants, "ride over to them and tell them to park that load there." He pointed at a big rock east of camp. "Show 'em the way."

Lambert said, "Just a respectful observation, sir, but that's a long way for us to take that volatile stuff to that trestle, General."

"It'll be dark soon," the self-made general said. "And I ain't riskin' this plan and blowing half of us to oblivion this late in the game. 'Sides, we'll have to wait till Thursday mornin' to rig up that bridge to blow. You've seen how 'em trains headin' north and south, freights and passengers, rattle 'em timbers. The Yankee tyrant isn't comin' up here till Thursday." He laughed. "We don't want to blow up the wrong train."

One of the outriders spurred his mount away from the wagon hauling the explosives. A gunman to Colter's left said, "Yeah, I'd want to be as far from that nitro as I can get."

Dugan pointed at the Gatling gun and shot Colter a cold glance.

"Let's see how good you shoot, Gore," he said.

Colter glanced at the gun in the wagon and nodded. Well, he figured, a Gatling was just like any other firearm—just bigger, louder, and deadlier. But it couldn't be much different from shooting a rifle. You just had to put the sites on the target and shoot. Aim low. That was what he had been told and had been doing all his life. Aim low.

He'd figure something out. He had to—if he wanted to stay alive. He stepped toward the back of the wagon.

Peering over the gulley, using the spyglass the Pinkerton gal had given him, Jed Reno frowned and pulled the scope from his good eye. He looked over at Ginger Burricchia—Reno liked that name better than Chiara, which he had trouble saying and didn't sing like Ginger Burricchia—and frowned.

"What's Tim doin' in 'em prison duds?" he asked.

"You sure that's your pal Colter?" Ginger asked.

Frowning, Reno put the glass back to his eye and turned, focusing, finding the big man in the Rebel shell jacket, then seeing Colter.

"Yeah," Reno said. "It's him. I've knowed him since he was a young'un." He shook his head. "Somethin' happened to his neck."

Ginger came up beside him, holding out her left hand, and the big mountain man let her take the glass.

"How tall is your partner?" she asked.

Reno told him.

"And his eyes are . . . ?"

He answered that question, too.

Lowering the small spyglass, she shrugged. "I don't see the resemblance, but I never saw Ben Gore with just stubble on his face. He had that thick mustache and a rough beard. But . . ." She looked toward the camp without the spyglass. "There might be a resemblance."

"And the neck?" Reno asked.

"Knife wound. Bullet. Rope. You know how tough this country can be on a man . . . or woman."

"It ain't just the country," Reno said. "It's the low-down curs that live amongst us."

She smiled. "Well . . ." She nodded toward Colter. "It does even the odds."

Reno had just taken the glass from her hand to give himself another look-see. Holding the spyglass, he gave Ginger a curious look.

Seeing that, she whispered, "It's now thirty or so against . . . three. That's better than just two."

He almost laughed but didn't. He couldn't laugh with his pard stuck among all those riffraff. Reno brought up the spyglass and found the wagon, the Gatling gun, what had to be Jake Dugan and Colter. His lungs pulled in a sharp breath and he exhaled a curse.

"Odds ain't in our favor no more, lady," he told her and handed her the glass.

When Colter turned toward the sound of the loping horse he started for his revolver, but at that moment he spotted Kip Jansen bringing him a cup of coffee. By then it was too late because Colter recognized the rider, saw the revolver coming up right at Colter. The boy, seeing Colter's eyes and hearing the horse, turned around. He was right between Tim Colter and G. Breck Glenn, warden of the Wyoming Territorial Prison and traitor to his country.

"You fool!" Glenn roared at Dugan. "You blithering idiot. That's Tim Colter—deputy United States marshal for the territory."

Every gun in camp, it appeared, was now aimed at Colter, who slowly unbuckled his gun belt, let it drop to the ground, and held out his left hand.

"I'll take that cup of coffee, Kip," he said and felt the heat through the tin. "And you best step away from here."

Glenn kept yelling: "He busted Patsy Palmer out of the pen. Well, sneaked her out through some duplicity." Now the warden spun around and pointed a finger at Dugan. "You idiot. You fool. You—"

The bullet that struck Glenn between the eyes ended his tirade. He spun around, dropped to his knees, and then fell facedown in the dirt.

The big LeMat in Dugan's hand now turned toward Colter's midsection.

"I never liked that hombre. He was useful to us, but not no more." He shot a sideways glance at the nearest gunman. "Go fetch Palmer. Best take three or four good men with you. Kill her—"

"No!" Kip shouted.

"Your usefulness, boy, has limits, too." Dugan finished his command: "Kill her if she gives you any sass. But I'd like to hear her side of the story before I throw her to the bottom of Vengeance Canyon."

Another horse was loping in as six of Dugan's men went looking for the big woman. The bushwhacker leader told a couple of men to carry the dead warden to the edge of the canyon and throw him to the bottom. He'd be buried under the debris when they blew up Grant's train and the trestle after riddling it with the Gatling gun. But then he countered that order when he turned toward the fast-riding horse, and swore.

Colter recognized the rider, too, but Jake Dugan did not seem to be scared of another marshal in the midst.

"Pickett," Dugan whispered, "I reckon you'll get the honors of peppering that Yankee's special car with those .45-caliber bullets. And you boys wait a spell before we dump trash into the canyon."

Clyde Tobin reined in the lathered horse hard and slipped out of the saddle, staggering forward and slowly straightening. The bushwhacker named Pickett had climbed into the wagon and was looking over the Gatling gun.

"Colter," the marshal whispered and stopped when

he recognized his deputy. The politician spun around and faced the bushwhacker. "What's he doing here? Why is he in those prison—"

He stopped, stared at Colter, and must have understood. But instead of yelling or gunning down his deputy, he whipped around to look at Dugan.

"The nitro. Listen. Kill Colter now. Then you've got to get the nitro on the tracks. Grant is comin'- —"

"We got till Thursday morn to do that, lawdog."

"No, you don't!" Tobin roared. "The president is coming to Cheyenne tomorrow morning!"

"What?" Dugan fired back.

"That's right. Tomorrow morning. He'll be in Cheyenne at eleven forty-five in the morning. Now if we're going to blow up the trestle just to make sure Grant is killed and no one can run y'all down by train . . ."

Dugan was nodding, and then he turned toward the men near the Gatling gun. "All right. You heard the lawdog. We need to get that nitro ready. Benson, you and Grits . . ."

"You sure you want to do that?" Colter asked.

Dugan turned. Colter saw that even Tobin was looking at him.

Colter smiled. "You'll blow up the trestle all right," he said easily, "and you blow up the southbound freight about five hours before the president gets here."

"Don't listen to him!" Tobin roared. "We have to get—"

Dugan silenced the marshal with a wave of his hand. "He's right." His scowl stopped any further argument from Tobin. "We let the freight pass. Then we rig that fancy bridge."

After a long moment Tobin nodded his agreement. He sighed. Dugan nodded at Tobin's pretty pocket watch. "Let me see that fancy watch you got."

Reluctantly Tobin handed him the Waltham and Dugan opened it and smiled.

"That train'll pass here around eleven forty-five in the mornin'? Right?"

"Yes. But it ain't ever' day that a president comes to Cheyenne, so some smart Secret Service gents or marshals or soldier boys might take a handcart out this way to make sure ain't nobody like Jake Dugan waitin' 'round here to kill him."

"Possible, but I don't think so," Tobin said. "They think you're up at Dugan's Den. Everyone has forgotten about Lincoln."

"I ain't," Dugan sneered.

Tobin pointed at Colter. "You should kill him now. He's trouble. He has always been trouble."

Laughing, Dugan shook his head. "Naw. You seem to forget, lawdog, that I'm a major general and you're a mealymouthed baby-kisser. But I got a job for you to do. Take that cur over there and drag him to the canyon. And push'm over the edge." He chuckled. "Don't get too close. Don't want you to fall over your ownself. It's a long, hard drop to lotsa hard rocks."

Tobin frowned, swallowed, and paled.

"Do it," Dugan ordered.

The marshal gasped when he recognized that the dead body was the Laramie warden.

"He annoyed me. And he was one conspirator too many. Take him. Then come back here."

When Tobin hesitated Dugan whispered, "Do you

know what we do to soldiers who don't obey my orders?"

Colter watched the lawman drag the dead warden. He was about a hundred yards from the canyon's rim when Dugan looked at Tobin's watch and slid it into a trouser pocket. He whispered, "Pickett, that's a good target for you to try out that fast-shooting weapon there. Don't you think?"

Colter closed his eyes as the Gatling gun roared. He smelled the gunpowder, and above the ringing in his ears, the horses snorting, pounding their hooves, and once the Gatling stopped barking, he heard the whistles and curses and laughs from those murdering cowards.

"All right, Marshal Colter," Dugan said. "Now it's your turn. You're gonna drag 'em two carcasses and heave 'em into the pit." Dugan turned toward his men, astonished at their commander's audacity, though they had ridden him through butchery after massacres all during the Rebellion.

"Too many conspirators. That's why all 'em Lincoln killers got hung. We ain't makin' no mistakes like that, boys. You know Jake Dugan. He protects his men.

"Don't worry, Colter." Dugan smiled when he looked back at the lawman. "We ain't wastin' no more lead. Savin' the rest for Mr. Grant. And, well, 'vengeance is mine,' sayeth Jake Dugan. And we gots a long night of vengeance till mornin'. And that vengeance is gonna be all about you. Then tomorrow . . . we'll have a mornin' of glory when Mr. Grant dies."

Chapter 42

"If they keep this up," Ginger told Reno, "there won't be as many for us to kill."

"That ain't funny," Reno whispered. "That's Tim Colter they got there. And a lit'l kid."

"Sorry," she whispered. "Your pard's still alive. So is that boy. And we're gonna keep it that way."

"How?" he snapped. "You see how many men they got."

"But they're not as brave as you, Jed. And they're not as sneaky as Charlotte Cannon."

"Who in the Sam Hill is Charlotte Cannon?" he snapped.

"Me. At least that's what Ma and Pa wrote down in the Bible." She grinned. "Nobody knows that, pardner, except Mr. Pinkerton."

Reno studied her. He wet his upper lip, sighed, and whispered, "Charlotte Cannon?"

"Yes," she said. "Now come over here. Let's figure out a plan, Jed."

Reno sighed. "Well, I ain't . . ." His head shook. "Ma and Pa didn't name me Jed Reno. Hugh Glass done that. Ma and Pa . . . they called me Zebedee Gillespie Thomasdotter."

She smiled and held out her hand. "Please to know you, Jed Reno."

The smile flattened. "We've got a lot of work to do."

"Help your lawdog pal, boy," Dugan told Kip.

"He doesn't—" One of the crazed Johnny Reb's men silenced the marshal's protest by jamming the stock of his rifle into Colter's back, knocking him to his knees.

"Work's good for a kid," the man said. "I was pickin' cotton when I was in diapers."

Kip limped over to Colter and, leaning on his coupstick, somehow helped Colter to his feet. He sucked in a deep breath and they moved to the first dead man, the one who had worked for that prison. Kip wasn't sure he understood why a prison guard or warden—yes, they called him a warden—would be involved with men who belonged in prison, but that didn't matter.

He looked around and let out a sigh of relief. The men hadn't found Patsy Palmer yet. Maybe she had escaped. But where could she go?

"Just grab his hat, Kip," Colter said. "I'll take the body. And tell me when to stop."

Walking backward, the lawman dragged the first corpse, looking everywhere but at the warden. No, he was taking everything in, Kip realized. Figuring out the locations.

"We're about twenty feet from the edge, sir," Kip whispered.

Colter nodded and let the body fall to the ground. Then they walked back to the other murdered man and, again, Kip picked up the hat and the satchel the man had dropped and walked behind the lawman who dragged that body to the edge of Vengeance Canyon, too.

Kip turned, drew in another breath, and limped to the edge of the canyon. Vengeance Canyon. He'd like to have his own vengeance. It was like the earth just ended. If you weren't paying attention, you could just walk right over and fall. Kip drew in a deep breath and moved closer to the edge. He looked down and gasped.

Patsy Palmer, about twelve feet below, brought a finger to her lips, lowered it, and smiled up at the boy.

When Colter dragged the first body closer to the edge Kip told him to move it farther to the right. Colter eyed him curiously but obeyed, then Kip used the coupstick to walk over. Colter turned and saw the ledge where Patsy Palmer nodded.

They made no motion to her, and Colter turned and rolled the body over. Kip looked away quickly. A few minutes later and the other body had dropped out of sight.

As they walked back, Colter whispered, "That's your hiding place, Kip. Before the ruckus starts, you jump down there with Patsy. Jump down there tonight . . . if you can sneak out."

"What ruckus?" Kip asked.

"The one I'm going to start," the marshal said.

* * *

Dugan's killers drank heartily that night. They gave up looking for Patsy Palmer, for what good could that tub of lard do? They were miles from nowhere and all the horses were still around. They had a Gatling gun and a case of nitroglycerine. And in about twelve hours Ulysses S. Grant would be dead.

But they sure were having fun with Tim Colter. He figured two ribs were cracked and they had rubbed salt into the bullet cut across his neck, then poured whiskey over it to triple the pain before someone told them they were wasting good whiskey on a dead man.

They pounded his face, busted his lips, loosened a few teeth, and gave him a good kicking.

They did everything but kill him.

The general, they let him know, was keeping him alive. The general wanted Colter to see President Grant die, see that fancy train carrying him crash into Vengeance Canyon "with a vengeance," one of the killers chuckled.

At some point the killers either got too bored or too drunk and they left him in the pit, hands and feet tied, and went away except for a guard or two.

"Where's that kid?"

Colter awakened. He had meant to sleep, knowing he would need his rest for what was to come in the morning. Though how he was going to get untied and to a gun . . . well . . . he hadn't figured that out yet.

Curses followed. More shouts. Lifting his head, he spotted some torches going west and east.

"It's a dumb kid," Dugan yelled. "Just double the guards at the Gatlin' gun and the wagon with the nitro. He'll likely step on a sidewinder and die from the bite. But we'll look for him in the morn'."

Colter breathed a little easier. He knew where the boy was. He had dropped into Vengeance Canyon but not to the bottom—just to the ledge where Patsy Palmer was hiding. He had seen the little trough carved by falling water. Big enough to hold Palmer and the boy, keep them hidden from any one of Dugan's men putting nitro on the trestle—if that happened. It was a good place to be and would be a lot safer than up here come a little before noon.

A runt of a Reb squatted beside him. He could just make him out by some cookfire forty yards away. Colter grimaced when the Reb lifted his head and giggled. "I oughts to cut yer throat."

"None o' that," the guard said. "Gen'ral Dugan says he lives till mornin'."

The red-mustached Reb turned and spat juice onto the ground. "Iffen he says so, I reckon it's right." Then the butcher turned back and smiled down at Colter.

The voice changed when it dropped to a whisper. "Name's Chiara Romano . . . to you." This wasn't a man but a woman. And she held a knife and sliced through the bindings around his wrists. He felt the handle of the weapon in his right hand.

"Jed Reno says howdy," she told him, and he felt the butt of a revolver in his left.

"I'm getting you out of here."

"No," he whispered.

"Listen to me. . . ."

She stopped, though, and looked over at the drunken guard. Colter saw that he was having trouble staying awake.

"He'll be out in ten seconds," she told him. "Works like a charm. Then I'll help you to our hiding place. I work for the Pinkerton National Detective Agency."

Colter shook his head. "You get back to Jed. I have to stay here. If I'm not here come dawn they'll be looking all over—and they'll find a boy and a . . . well . . . a person who has saved my hide."

"They're going to kill the president if we don't stop them. At around eleven—"

The guard's snores stopped her. She looked back at Colter with desperation in her eyes.

"That's what they think," Colter told her. "Go on. Wait for my signal." That hurt more than he thought it would. "Then . . ." He smiled weakly. "Duck and cover your ears."

Jed Reno woke to the moon. He reached for the Hawken but felt a boot on his hand.

Then the face appeared as the boot crushed harder.

"Howdy, Jed."

Reno looked into the eyes of Walker Chester.

"Ready to die?"

Walker Chester. Who had never owned a livery stable in Lawrence, Kansas. That was what the pretty Pinkerton gal had told Jed. His limp came from a wound at that massacre, but it came while he was riding with Quantrill's butchers.

"Got any last words, pilgrim?" the traitor asked.

Reno nodded. "Yeah. Not ever'body can go bad, pilgrim. Some of us is honest and good to the end."

Chester smiled, then gasped. The revolver dropped to the dirt and slowly the old livery owner moved backward until Charlotte Cannon laid him on the ground. She looked at Reno as she wiped the stiletto on her trousers.

"But," Reno told the corpse, "ever'body dies."

The southbound freight came by right on time, rattling the trestle, but the horses were used to the noise by now. No one came for Colter.

Snores sounded all over camp. And retching. One of Dugan's lieutenants walked over and cursed.

The guard the Pinkerton woman had drugged was still sleeping and when two of Dugan's best—meaning *worst*—men came by, Colter had managed to make the ropes around his wrist look like they were strong.

Though the day was cloudy, Colter caught enough of the sun to tell that it was around ten in the morning. He was led to Dugan's campfire.

"Remind me to have Ellis shot by firin' squad," Dugan told the two men. Ellis, Colter figured, was the guard the Pinkerton detective had knocked out by drugging his whiskey.

"We're gonna make this simple," Dugan said. "Get four men—sober—at eleven thirty." He withdrew Tobin's watch and checked the time. "They will bring that case of nitro."

"The entire case?" one of the men yelled.

"Yes. And walk it out onto that trestle. Lay it in the middle of the track, then hightail it back."

"Sir, if they slip, they'll blow up that bridge."

"That's why you will be leading them, Andersen. You won't let that happen."

The man looked sick all of a sudden.

"That's just fifteen minutes before the train runs through here," the other lieutenant said.

"It is. But if someone comes by on a handcart . . ." He shrugged. "Well, we don't want to kill any innocent people. Except those on that express."

He glanced at Colter. "You shall have a fine view, sir." He pointed. "The train slows down when it reaches the bridge. That's when Pickett opens fire with the Gatling gun. The engineer orders the fireman to give it all he can. The train races over the bridge, while Pickett peppers it with lead. Either the rattling of the crate on those tracks or maybe a stray bullet, *boom*! No more trestle. No more Grant. And then . . . I kill you."

He motioned to the fire. "Sit down. Have some coffee. I always give men a chance to pray and eat a good breakfast before they die."

The wagon with the nitro started moving. Slowly. Barely at a snail's crawl. Getting the cargo closer to the trestle.

Dugan looked at Tobin's watch, then grinned at Colter. "It's gettin' closer to . . . train time!" He laughed.

* * *

"What signal?" Jed Reno asked for the hundredth time.

Ginger whispered, "He didn't say."

He had fashioned a pair of shooting sticks and rested the heavy barrel of his rifle into the "V," aiming at the box in the wagon that was moving inches at a time.

Then came the rattling.

"What the . . . ?"

He saw the smoke, thick and black and whipping around like one of those twisters he had heard about. It was the train. "What time is it?" he asked.

"The train!" Dugan spat out curses. "It is . . ." He looked at the watch again. "It is not even eleven ten!"

"Get to the wagon!" one of the lieutenants ordered the men and they ran toward the slow-moving wagon with the nitro. Though some of them stopped, those at the rear began running as far away from that wagon as they could.

"Stop!" Dugan fired a round and hit one of the deserters in the back. "Cowards!" He turned and found Colter smiling at him.

"The Denver Pacific Railroad," Colter told him, "runs on Omaha time, General. That's thirty minutes faster than Cheyenne time. Which is what Tobin's watch was set for."

"Pickett!" Dugan was drawing his LeMat. "Open fire with that Gatling."

The train was nearing Vengeance Canyon.

Colter dropped the sliced rope and jerked out the Smith & Wesson. His first two shots hit the general in the chest, dropping him to his knees. Whirling, Colter snapped a shot that rang out against the side of the Gatling gun, knocking Pickett off his feet. Colter came back as Dugan raised his head and he slammed the barrel against the man's face, driving him back.

He dropped to a knee, fired twice more, then grabbed the LeMat as he pitched the silver-plated .32 into the sand. He came up, saw Pickett turning that massive weapon toward him instcad of the train.

Which was exactly what Colter wanted.

It was a Gatling gun against a LeMat.

The LeMat won.

Pickett leaned forward, pushing down the Gatling barrel, and he fell against the crank, turning it enough to send a couple of rounds into the Conestoga's floor.

Out of the corner of his eye, Colter saw the train was across Vengeance Canyon, heading toward Cheyenne.

Colter turned, saw a handful of loyalists running toward him. One bullet tugged at his left shirtsleeve. Another sliced one of the bruises he had gotten in his side.

He had shifted the LeMat and sprayed the charging fools with the smoothbore round and that knocked all of them down. Then Colter started running toward Vengeance Canyon.

"I reckon," Jed Reno told Ginger, "that be the signal."

Reno aimed.

"Where's Tim?" Reno asked the Pinkerton gal.

"He's running straight for the canyon."

"And the train?"

"It's about around that rise."

Reno let out a slow breath and waited.

"Oh my God!" Ginger/Chiara/Charlotte screamed. "Colter just jumped into the canyon!"

"That's my boy," Reno said before he touched the Hawken's trigger.

The superintendent of the Union Pacific had insisted that President Grant take his director's car and so it had been attached to the rear of the Denver Pacific's train to Cheyenne. Grant was thinking how many cigars he would have to send Mr. Sickels as a thank-you when loud explosions startled his wife and caused the president to push himself off the sofa.

General Babcock, Grant's personal secretary, was already at the door and had stepped outside. The president followed him.

It sounded louder than firecrackers, and that smoke was mighty thick.

"What do you make of it, General?" Grant asked.

Babcock shrugged. "Fireworks, sir, in your honor. The Magic City of the Plains welcoming you to Cheyenne, Mr. President?"

"Lot of smoke." One firecracker from the other side of a little hill sounded like a cannon. "And some wild Roman candles. But whoever heard of shooting off fireworks at this time of day?"

Babcock gave another shrug. "Well, sir . . ." His old friend smiled. "You know how these Westerners are. They do things their own way."

That made sense. Julia stepped out to join them, and so did Babcock's wife.

Grant made an executive decision. "Have the train stopped, General."

Babcock looked at his watch. "We'll be late to Cheyenne."

"So we'll be late. If the good people of this territory went to all this trouble to greet me with fireworks, by thunder, we'll watch the show. Even if it's just smoke and a lot of noise."

Chapter 43

Jed Reno shuffled his feet at the Union Pacific depot and handed the heaviest valise to the porter.

Then Ginger Burro Chicka or Chiara Something-another, but mostly Charlotte Cannon, turned toward him and smiled.

"If you ever get to Chicago, Jed, will you look me up? Charlotte Cannon. *Miss* Charlotte Cannon."

He shuffled his feet. "Awww, I dunno. I'm gettin' right up in years now and too stove up to ride all the way to wherever Chicago is in a train. Reckon I could ride a horse there, though. How fer is it?"

"Oh, a bit under a thousand miles, I'd say."

He grinned at her. "Shucks, Gin—Miss Charlotte. I walked that fer durin' my trappin' days. Many a time."

"Well."

Her smile faded when the conductor yelled, "All aboard."

"I can always take a vacation. Cheyenne is right pretty."

"Mostly," he told her. He frowned. "I'm easy to find."

"So am I." She reached up, put her arms around his neck, and put her head up to his face, where her little, pretty, luscious lips found a way through his beard and to his mouth.

"I look forward to the pleasure of a wonderful evening with Zebedee Gillespie Thomasdotter," she whispered. "Till that day."

She kissed him again. Then she dropped down, spun, and hurried past the frowning conductor, who stared at Reno, then shook his head, turned around, and climbed into the coach.

Reno shuffled his feet as the train pulled away, but he saw an arm hanging out the window, waving.

Slowly he raised his right hand and waved back.

"You going to be all right?"

Turning, Reno saw Tim Colter, on crutches, bandaged in all sorts of new places, but smiling—and wearing a new suit, with a badge pinned on a lapel.

"Reckon so." He sniffed. Springtime in Cheyenne brought out all sorts of sniffles to folks, he reminded himself, and then wiped his good eye.

They had to walk slowly down the boardwalk because even though President Grant had only stayed in town for a few hours—and that was a week ago—folks were still abuzz.

Reno and Colter could hardly get five steps in before someone came over and shook their hands, or patted their backs, or offered to buy them dinner, a whiskey or two, a free shave, a free bath, or if they would like to sample this or that.

Eventually, they reached the US Marshal's office and went inside.

The cells were all but empty now. The survivors of the scrape at Vengeance Canyon had either escaped into Wyoming or been captured, like that cur Lige Kerns, and had the good sense to plead guilty and be shipped to the Laramie City prison, which had a new warden, or to the federal facilities in Detroit and Leavenworth.

The boy, Kip Jansen, was sitting on a stool in front of the jail. Behind the bars sat that big woman, Patsy Palmer, the ugliest and meanest woman Jed Reno had ever known—and he had known many a wildcat in his fur-trapping years. Why she hadn't been hauled out of here to some prison—or hanged from the nearest tree—Reno just could not figure out.

They were playing checkers. Checkers! A woman like her ought to be busting rocks.

Colter leaned the crutches on the wall and sat on a desktop near the cell.

"Fetch the keys, Jed," Colter ordered.

Frowning, Jed walked all the way back to the pegs on the wall, grabbed the heavy ring, and brought it back to Colter, who nodded at the lock on Patsy Palmer's cell.

"You ain't lettin' this wild gal out?"

Kip Jansen spun around, his eyes hopeful.

"I'm not." Colter opened his coat and reached inside, pulling out some papers. "But President Grant is."

"Huh?" rang out from Kip, Palmer, and Reno.

"Open the cell, Jed," Colter told him, and with great reluctance, Reno did as he was told and stepped back to get out of reach from Patsy Palmer's long arms and hammering hands.

She wasn't dressed in prison duds. After hearing everything she had done Cheyenne's finest women—even the sheriff's, mayor's, and governor's wives—had pampered her like she was a hero along the lines of, well, Jed Reno or Tim Colter . . . or that Pinkerton gal.

The boy and the big woman stared at Colter, who unfolded the paper and started reading, then stopped when he saw Reno's face.

"Words are too big for him," Reno heard Colter whisper, then saw the wink the lawman gave either the boy or the evil woman or maybe the both of them. "But the president of our United States has granted you, Patsy Palmer, a full pardon, effective on this date, allowing you to resume your life and restoring you all the rights a woman has—and in Wyoming a woman has a lot more than in many states and territories."

Reno grumbled something.

"Really?" Kip Jansen asked. "She's free?"

Colter handed the young'un the paper.

"Golly," the boy said and turned and let Patsy Palmer pull him into a hug.

Colter cleared his throat. "But if you do anything illegal you'll be answering to me."

"You ain't gots to worry 'bout that, Marshal. I'm gonna raise this boy up right."

"Going home?" Colter asked.

The boy smiled. "I think this is home."

"Me too," Palmer said, and the two left their game of checkers unfinished and walked outside.

"You're gonna rue the day you let her out," Reno told him.

"Like I rue the day we met."

They smiled, and Reno slapped his hand too hard on Colter's shoulder, causing a wince and a cry.

"You used to be tougher," Reno said and stopped. His hand moved to the badge and turned it up. His head twisted a bit and then he stared into Colter's eyes.

"This one's differenter than 'em others."

"Not really." Colter took the badge and tilted it for a closer look.

"It ain't the same."

"No, Jed. This one says, 'United States Marshal.' Not 'deputy.'"

Reno swore and shook his head. "Is you that ignorant? You tol' me yerself that you wasn't no marshal. Marshal's got all the headaches. Deputies . . . they's the ones who's gotta work. Risk their hides—our hides—bringin' in scum like that rapscallion Lige Kerns or some dirty dog like that Dugan feller."

"Well, it's only temporary."

"Balderdash." Reno shook his head. "Ain't the president the one who picks the top lawdog?"

"He has a say, but . . ."

"You done sold out on me, pardner."

"I get paid better," he whispered.

Reno stared, then grinned. "How much better?"

Colter reached out his arms and let the big man pull him off the desk.

"You hungry?"

Reno grinned. "Got a thirst, too."

"Let's see how much damage you can do." Reno was already heading for the door. "But I warn you. If you get out of line, I'll have to lock you up."

"Don't you worry 'bout me. But after we gets our whistles wet and our bellies filled . . ." He turned and tugged on his beard.

"You happen to know how much it'd cost a feller like me to ride a train to Chicago?"

"I can find out. After we celebrate. And maybe you can tell me about . . . what was the name . . . ? Some gent named Zebedee Gillespie Thomasdotter."

**JOHNSTONE COUNTRY. HOMESTYLE JUS-
TICE WITH A SIDE OF SLAUGHTER.**

**In this explosive new series, Western legend Luke
Jensen teams up with chuckwagon cook Dewey
"Mac" McKenzie to dish out a steaming plate of hot-
blooded justice. But in a corrupt town like
Hangman's Hill, revenge is a dish best served cold . . .**

**BEANS, BOURBON, AND BLOOD: A RECIPE
FOR DISASTER**

The sight of a rotting corpse hanging from a noose is
enough to stop any man in his tracks—and Luke
Jensen is no exception. Sure, he could just keep riding
through. He's got a prisoner to deliver, after all. But
when a group of men show up with another prisoner
for another hanging, Luke can't turn his back—especially when the condemned man keeps swearing he's
innocent. Right up to the moment he's hung by the
neck till he's dead . . .

Welcome to Hannigan's Hill, Wyoming. Better known
as Hangman's Hill.

Luke's pretty shaken up by what he's seen and decides
to stay the night, get some rest and grab some grub.
The town marshal agrees to lock up Luke's prisoner
while Luke heads to a local saloon and restaurant

called Mac's Place. The pub's owner—a former chuckwagon cook named Dewey "Mac" McKensie— serves up a bellyful of chow and an earful of gossip. According to Mac, the whole stinking town is run by corrupt cattle baron Ezra Hannigan. Ezra owns practically everything. Including the town marshal. And anyone who gets in his way ends up swinging from a rope . . .

Mac might be just an excellent cook. But he's got a ferocious appetite for justice—and a fearsome new friend in Luke Jensen. Together, they could end Hannigan's reign of terror. But when Hannigan calls in his hired guns, it'll be their necks on the line . . . or dancing from the end of a rope.

National Bestselling Authors
William W. Johnstone
and J.A. Johnstone

BEANS, BOURBON, AND BLOOD
A Luke Jensen-Dewey McKenzie Western

On sale now, wherever Pinnacle Books are sold.

Live Free. Read Hard.
www.williamjohnstone.net
Visit us at www.kensingtonbooks.com

Chapter 1

Luke Jensen reined his horse to a halt and looked up at the hanged man. The corpse swung back and forth in the cold wind sweeping across the Wyoming plains.

From behind Luke, Ethan Stallings said, "I don't like the looks of that. No sir, I don't like it one bit."

"Shut up, Stallings," Luke said without taking his gaze off the dead man dangling from a hangrope attached to the crossbar of a sturdy-looking gallows. "In case you haven't figured it out already, I don't care what you like."

Luke rested both hands on his saddle horn and leaned forward to ease muscles made weary by the long ride to the town of Hannigan's Hill. He had never been here before, but he'd heard that the place was sometimes called Hangman's Hill. He could see why. Not every settlement had a gallows on a hill overlooking it, just outside of town.

And not every gallows had a corpse hanging from it

that looked to have been there for at least a week, based on the amount of damage buzzards had done to it. This poor varmint's eyes were gone, and not much remained of his nose and lips and ears, either. Buzzards went for the easiest bits first.

Luke was a middle-aged man who still had an air of vitality about him despite his years and the rough life he had led. His face was too craggy to be called handsome, but the features held a rugged appeal. The thick, dark hair under his black hat was threaded with gray, as was the mustache under his prominent nose. His boots, trousers, and shirt were black to match his hat. He wore a sheepskin jacket to ward off the chill of the gray autumn day.

He rode a rangy black horse, as unlovely but strong as its rider. A rope stretched back from the saddle to the bridle of the other horse, a chestnut gelding, so that it had to follow. The hands of the man riding that horse were tied to the saddle horn.

He sat with his narrow shoulders hunched against the cold. The brown tweed suit he wore wasn't heavy enough to keep him warm. His face under the brim of a bowler hat was thin, foxlike. Thick, reddish-brown side-whiskers crept down to the angular line of his jaw.

"I'm not sure we should stay here," he said. "Doesn't appear to be a very welcoming place."

"It has a jail and a telegraph office," Luke said. "That'll serve our purposes."

"Your purposes," Stallings said. "Not mine."

"Yours don't matter anymore. Haven't since you became my prisoner."

Stallings sighed. A great deal of dejection was packed into the sound.

Luke frowned as he studied the hanged man more closely. The man wore town clothes: wool trousers, a white shirt, a simple vest. His hands were tied behind his back. As bad a shape as the corpse was in, it was hard for Luke to make an accurate guess about his age, other than the fact that he hadn't been old. His hair was a little thin, but still sandy brown, with no sign of gray or white.

Luke had witnessed quite a few hangings. Most fellows who wound up dancing on air were sent to eternity with black hoods over their heads. Usually, the hoods were left in place until after the corpse had been cut down and carted off to the undertaker. Most people enjoyed the spectacle of a hanging, but they didn't necessarily want to see the end result.

The fact that this man no longer wore a hood—if, in fact, he ever had—and was still here on the gallows a week later could mean only one thing.

Whoever had strung him up wanted folks to be able to see him. Wanted to send a message with that grisly sight.

Stallings couldn't keep from talking for very long. He had been that way ever since Luke had captured him. He said, "This is sure making me nervous."

"No reason for it to. You're just a con artist, Stallings. You're not a killer or a rustler or a horse thief. The chances of you winding up on a gallows are pretty slim. You'll just spend the next few years behind bars, that's all."

Stallings muttered something Luke couldn't make out, then said in a louder, more excited voice, "Look! Somebody's coming."

The town of Hannigan's Hill was about half a mile away, a decent-sized settlement with a main street three blocks long lined by businesses and close to a hundred houses total on the side streets. The railroad hadn't come through here, but as Luke had mentioned, there was a telegraph line. East, south, and north—the direction he and Stallings had come from—lay rangeland. Some low but rugged mountains bulked to the west. The town owed its existence mostly to the ranches that surrounded it on three sides, but Luke knew there was some mining in the mountains, too.

A group of riders had just left the settlement and were heading toward the hill. Bunched up the way they were, Luke couldn't tell exactly how many. Six or eight, he estimated. They moved at a brisk pace as if they didn't want to waste any time.

On a raw, bleak day like today, nobody could blame them for feeling that way.

Something about one of them struck Luke as odd, and as they came closer, he figured out what it was. Two men rode slightly ahead of the others, and one of them had his arms pulled behind him. His hands had to be tied together behind his back. His head hung forward as he rode as if he lacked the strength or the spirit to lift it.

Stallings had seen the same thing. "Oh, hell," the confidence man said. His voice held a hollow note. "They're bringing somebody else up here to hang him."

That certainly appeared to be the case. Luke spotted a badge pinned to the shirt of the other man in the lead, under his open coat. More than likely, that was the local sheriff or marshal.

"Whatever they're doing, it's none of our business," Luke said.

"They shouldn't have left that other fella dangling there like that. It . . . it's inhumane!"

Luke couldn't argue with that sentiment, but again, it was none of his affair how they handled their law-breakers here in Hannigan's Hill.

"You don't have to worry about that," he told Stallings again. "All I'm going to do is lock you up and send a wire to Senator Creed to find out what he wants me to do with you. I expect he'll tell me to take you on to Laramie or Cheyenne and turn you over to the law there. Eventually you'll wind up on a train back to Ohio to stand trial for swindling the senator and you'll go to jail. It's not the end of the world."

"For you, it's not."

The riders were a couple of hundred yards away now. The lawman in the lead made a curt motion with his hand. Two of the other men spurred their horses ahead, swung around the lawman and the prisoner, and headed toward Luke and Stallings at a faster pace.

"They've seen us," Stallings said.

"Take it easy. We haven't done anything wrong. Well, I haven't, anyway. You're the one who decided it would be a good idea to swindle a United States senator out of ten thousand dollars."

The two riders pounded up the slope and reined in

about twenty feet away. They looked hard at Luke and Stallings, and one of them asked in a harsh voice, "What's your business here?"

Luke had been a bounty hunter for a lot of years. He recognized hard cases when he saw them. But these two men wore deputy badges. That wasn't all that unusual. This was the frontier. Plenty of lawmen had ridden the owlhoot trail at one time or another in their lives. The reverse was true, too.

Luke turned his head and gestured toward Stallings with his chin. "Got a prisoner back there, and I'm looking for a place to lock him up, probably for no more than a day or two. That's my only business here, friend."

"I don't see no badge. You a bounty hunter?"

"That's right. Name's Jensen."

The name didn't appear to mean anything to the men. If Luke had said that his brother was Smoke Jensen, the famous gunfighter who was now a successful rancher down in Colorado, that would have drawn more notice. Most folks west of the Mississippi had heard of Smoke. Plenty east of the big river had, too. But Luke never traded on family connections. In fact, for a lot of years, for a variety of reasons, he had called himself Luke Smith, instead of using the Jensen name.

The two deputies still seemed suspicious. "You don't know that hombre Marshal Bowen is bringin' up here?"

"I don't even know Marshal Bowen," Luke answered honestly. "I never set eyes on any of you boys until today."

"The marshal told us to make sure you wasn't plannin' on interferin'. This here is a legal hangin' we're fixin' to carry out."

Luke gave a little wave of his left hand. "Go right ahead. I always cooperate with the law."

That wasn't strictly true—he'd been known to bend the law from time to time when he thought it was the right thing to do—but these deputies didn't need to know that.

The other deputy spoke up for the first time. "Who's your prisoner?"

"Name's Ethan Stallings. Strictly small-time. Nobody who'd interest you fellas."

"That's right," Stallings muttered. "I'm nobody."

The rest of the group was close now. The marshal raised his left hand in a signal for them to stop. As they reined in, Luke looked the men over and judged them to be cut from the same cloth as the first two deputies. They wore law badges, but they were no better than they had to be.

The prisoner was young, maybe twenty-five, a stocky redhead who wore range clothes. He didn't look like a forty-a-month-and-found puncher. Maybe a little better than that. He might own a small spread of his own, a greasy sack outfit he worked with little or no help.

When he finally raised his head, he looked absolutely terrified, too. He looked straight at Luke and said, "For God's sake, mister, you've got to help me. They're gonna hang me, and I didn't do anything wrong. I swear it!"

Chapter 2

The marshal turned in his saddle, leaned over, and swung a backhanded blow that cracked viciously across the prisoner's face. The man might have toppled off his horse if one of the other deputies hadn't ridden up beside him and grasped his arm to steady him.

"Shut up, Crawford," the lawman said. "Nobody wants to listen to your lies. Take what you've got coming and leave these strangers out of it."

The prisoner's face flamed red where the marshal had struck it. He started to cry, letting out wrenching sobs full of terror and desperation.

Even without knowing the facts of the case, Luke felt a pang of sympathy for the young man. He didn't particularly want to, but he felt it, anyway.

"I'm Verne Bowen. Marshal of Hannigan's Hill. We're about to carry out a legally rendered sentence on this man. You have any objection?"

Luke shook his head. "Like I told your deputies, Marshal, this is none of my business, and I don't have the faintest idea what's going on here. So I'm not going to interfere."

Bowen jerked his head in a nod and said, "Good."

He was about the same age as Luke, a thick-bodied man with graying fair hair under a pushed-back brown hat. He had a drooping mustache and a close-cropped beard. He wore a brown suit over a fancy vest and a butternut shirt with no cravat. A pair of walnut-butted revolvers rode in holsters on his hips. He looked plenty tough and probably was.

Bowen waved a hand at the deputies and ordered, "Get on with it."

Two of them dismounted and moved in on either side of the prisoner, Crawford. He continued to sob as they pulled him off his horse and marched him toward the gallows steps, one on either side of him.

"Just out of curiosity," Luke asked, "what did this hombre do?"

Bowen glared at him. "You said that was none of your business."

"And it's not. Just curious, that's all."

"It doesn't pay to be too curious around here, Mr. . . . ?"

"Jensen. Luke Jensen."

Bowen nodded toward Stallings. "I see you have a prisoner, too. You a bounty hunter?"

"That's right. I was hoping you'd allow me to stash him in your jail for a day or two."

"Badman, is he?"

"A foolish man," Luke said, "who made some bad choices. But he didn't do anything around here." Luke allowed his voice to harden slightly. "Not in your juris-diction."

Bowen looked levelly at him for a couple of seconds, then nodded. "Fair enough."

By now, the deputies were forcing Crawford up the steps. He twisted and jerked and writhed, but their grips were too strong for him to pull free. It wouldn't have done him any good if he had. He would have just fallen down the steps and they would have picked him up again.

Bowen said, "I don't suppose it'll hurt anything to satisfy your curiosity, Jensen. Just don't get in the habit of poking your nose in where it's not wanted. Crawford there is a murderer. He got drunk and killed a soiled dove."

"That's not true!" Crawford cried. "I never hurt that girl. Somebody slipped me something that knocked me out. I never even laid eyes on the girl until I came to in her room and she was . . . was layin' there with her eyes bugged out and her tongue sticking out and those terrible bruises on her throat—"

"Choked her to death, the little weasel did," Bowen interrupted. "Claims he doesn't remember it, but he's a lying, no-account killer."

The deputies and the prisoner had reached the top of the steps. The deputies wrestled Crawford out onto the platform. Another star packer trotted up the steps after them, moving with a jaunty bounce, and pulled a knife from a sheath at his waist. He reached out, grasped the dead man's belt, and pulled the corpse close enough that he could reach up and cut the rope. When he let go, the body fell through the open trap and landed with a soggy thud on the ground below. Even from where Luke was, he could smell the stench that rose from it.

He didn't envy whoever got the job of burying the man.

"How about him? What did he do?"

"A thief," Bowen said. "Embezzled some money from the man he worked for, one of our leading citizens."

Luke frowned. "You hang a man for embezzlement around here?"

"When he was caught, he went loco and tried to shoot his way out of it," Bowen replied with a shrug. "He could have killed somebody. That's attempted murder. The judge decided to make an example of him. I don't hand down the sentences, Jensen. I just carry 'em out."

"I suppose leaving him up here to rot was part of making an example."

Bowen leaned forward, glared, and said, "For somebody who keeps claiming this is none of his business, you are taking an almighty keen interest in all of this, mister. You might want to take your prisoner and ride on down to town. Ask anybody, they can tell you where my office and the jail are. I'll be down directly and we can lock that fella up." The marshal paused, then added, "Got a good bounty on him, does he?"

"Good enough," Luke said. He was beginning to get the impression that instead of waiting, he ought to ride on with Stallings and not stop over in Hannigan's Hill at all. Bowen and those hardcase deputies might have their eyes on the reward Senator Jonas Creed had offered for Stallings's capture.

But their horses were just about played out and really needed a night's rest. They were low on provisions, too.

It would be difficult to push on to Laramie without replenishing their supplies here.

As soon as he had Stallings locked up, he would send a wire to Senator Creed. Once he'd established that he was the one who had captured the fugitive, Bowen wouldn't be able to claim the reward for himself. Luke figured he could stay alive long enough to do that.

He sure as blazes wasn't going to let his guard down while he was in these parts, though.

He reached back to tug on the lead rope attached to Stallings's horse. "Come on."

The deputies had closed the trapdoor on the gallows and positioned Crawford on it. One of them tossed a new hangrope over the crossbar. Another deputy caught it and closed in to fit the noose over the prisoner's head.

"Reckon we ought to tie his feet together?" one of the men asked.

"Naw," another answered with a grin. "If it so happens that his neck don't break right off, it'll be a heap more entertainin' if he can kick good while he's chokin' to death."

'Please, mister, please!" Crawford cried. "Don't just ride off and let them do this to me! I never killed that whore. They did it and framed me for it! They're only doing this because Ezra Hannigan wants my ranch!"

That claim made Luke pause. Bowen must have noticed Luke's reaction because he snapped at the deputies, "Shut him up. I'm not gonna stand by and let him spew those filthy lies about Mr. Hannigan."

"Please—" Crawford started to shriek, but then one of the deputies stepped behind him and slammed a gun butt against the back of his head. Crawford sagged forward, only half-conscious as the other deputies held him up by the arms.

Luke glanced at the four deputies who were still mounted nearby. Each rested a hand on the butt of a holstered revolver. Luke knew gun-wolves like that wouldn't hesitate to yank their hoglegs out and start blasting. He had faced long odds plenty of times in his life and wasn't afraid, but he didn't feel like getting shot to doll rags today, either, and likely that was what would happen if he tried to interfere.

With a sour taste in his mouth, he lifted his reins, nudged the black horse into motion, and turned the horse to ride around the group of lawmen toward the settlement. He heard the prisoner groan from the gallows, but Crawford had been knocked too senseless to protest coherently anymore.

A moment later, with an unmistakable sound, the trapdoor dropped and so did the prisoner. In the thin, cold air, Luke distinctly heard the crack of Crawford's neck breaking.

He wasn't looking back, but Stallings must have been. The confidence man cursed and then said, "They didn't even put a hood over his head before they hung him! That's just indecent, Jensen."

"I'm not arguing with you."

"And you know good and well he was innocent. He was telling the truth about them framing him for that dove's murder."

"You don't have any way of knowing that," Luke pointed out. "We don't know anything about these people."

"Who's Ezra Hannigan?"

Luke took a deep breath. "Well, considering that the town's called Hannigan's Hill, I expect he's an important man around here. Probably owns some of the businesses. Maybe most of them. Maybe a big ranch outside of town. I think I've heard the name before, but I can't recall for sure."

"The fella who was hanging there when we rode up, the one they cut down, that marshal said he stole money from one of the leading citizens. You want to bet it was Ezra Hannigan he stole from?"

"I don't want to bet with you about anything, Stallings. I just want to get you where you're going and collect my money. Whatever's going on in this town, I don't want any part of it."

Stallings was silent for a moment, then said, "I suppose there wouldn't be anything you could do, anyway. Not against a marshal and that many deputies, and all of them looking like they know how to handle a gun. Funny that a town this size would need that many deputies, though . . . unless their actual job isn't keeping the peace, but doing whatever Ezra Hannigan wants done. Like hanging the owner of a spread Hannigan's got his eye on."

"You've flapped that jaw enough," Luke told him. "I don't want to hear any more out of you."

"Whether you hear it or not won't change the truth of the matter."

Stallings couldn't see it, but Luke grimaced. He

knew that Stallings was likely right about what was happening around here. Luke had seen it more than once: There was some rich man ruling a town, and the surrounding area, with an iron fist, bringing in hired guns, running roughshod over anybody who dared to stand up to him. It was a common story on the frontier.

But it wasn't his job to set things right in Hannigan's Hill, even assuming that Stallings was right about Ezra Hannigan. Smoke might not stand for such things, but Smoke had a reckless streak in him sometimes. Luke's hard life had made him more practical. He would have wound up dead if he had tried to interfere with that hanging. Bowen would have been more than happy to seize the excuse to kill him and claim his prisoner and the reward.

Luke knew all that, knew it good and well, but as he and Stallings reached the edge of town, something made him turn his head and look back, anyway. Some unwanted force drew his gaze like a magnet to the top of the nearby hill. Bowen and the deputies had started riding back toward the settlement, leaving the young man called Crawford dangling limp and lifeless from that hangrope. Leaving him there to rot . . .

"Well," a female voice broke sharply into Luke's thoughts, "I hope you're proud of yourself."

Visit our website at
KensingtonBooks.com
to sign up for our newsletters, read
more from your favorite authors, see
books by series, view reading group
guides, and more!

BOOK **CLUB**
BETWEEN THE **CHAPTERS**

Become a Part of Our
Between the Chapters Book Club
Community and Join the Conversation

Betweenthechapters.net